# The Boyfriend

D E McCluskey

D E McCluskey

The Boyfriend
Copyright © 2023 by D E McCluskey Ltd.

ISBN 978-1-914381-13-3

Dammaged Productions
www.dammaged.com

**This book is dedicated to anyone who has been, or is currently, a victim of abuse.**
Be it physical, mental, sexual, bullying, or intimidation.
Do not suffer in silence, there are people out there who can help.
More importantly, there are people out there who *want* to help.
#reachout

## Prologue

'PLEASE … PLEASE, NO. Don't!' the man sobbed. As he pleaded for his life, spittle, thick and white, gathered in the corners of his mouth. Some shot from between his dry lips, sticking in the coarse hairs of the beard growing around his open mouth. His eyes were wide, petrified, but focused. They were staring at the masked figure looming over him, the one wielding the long knife, the same knife that was dripping with his wife's blood. As his eyes moved from the figure, they scanned across the room, settling on the dark puddle at the foot of the bed. He assumed by the amount of blood present, the hopes of his wife still being alive were slim.

This thought crippled him, shook him to his core, while he sat quivering in the corner of his room, his warm urine turning the light grey of his underpants dark, pleading for his life.

The figure with the knife hadn't spoken. Not even once.

Fifteen minutes earlier, he'd been lying in bed. Safe, secure, and warm. Then the bedroom light had snapped on, waking him instantly. With sleep disorientation, it had taken him a few precious, important moments to comprehend what was happening. By then, it was too late. The shadow had crossed the room and taken his wife by her long hair. The gloved hand had pressed over her mouth, instantly waking her into their shared nightmare. She struggled briefly before something was produced that made him curl into a useless ball, his back pushed against the headboard of the bed. The sight of it had made him lose control of his bodily functions, not to mention his faculties.

Without hesitation or explanation, the figure used the knife he was sporting and sliced, slowly, across the throat of the woman he loved. He watched her struggle. The fight in her was brief as the blade cut deep.

The gurgle of fresh blood bubbling, gushing from the laceration would be a sound he would take with him to the grave, whenever that might be!

The figure released her. Her head dropped lifeless onto the soaking duvet.

She died on their marital bed as blood pumped in slowing arcs from her deep wound.

Instinctively, he reeled from the unbelievable yet oh so real horror. He fell off the side of the bed with a heavy thump, narrowly missing the bedside table. His eyes were wide, his flesh covered in goosebumps, as he became hyper-aware of the situation. He watched with a rapture he couldn't understand as the tide of crimson, his wife's lifeblood, spilled over the side of the bed and onto the carpet below.

He knew that stain would never be removed, not completely. There would always be a ghost of this night etched into the fibres of that carpet. *It'll have to go,* he thought, surprising himself with the absurd clarity.

The figure loomed over him again. He guessed he was next for the knife. All thoughts of the ruined carpet disappeared as he remembered his daughter and his son, asleep in their own rooms across the landing.

'Get out of my house,' he whispered. He'd wanted to shout, to sound authoritative, but there hadn't been enough wind in him to force out the words. 'Get out before I call the police …'

The androgynous figure was in no rush.

The shouting, or the lack of it, hadn't fazed him. He assumed this *was* a man, although he couldn't be sure.

The man reached into a pocket of the dark jacket he was wearing and produced a shock of hair. It was the same colour as his daughter's.

The hair was matted with blood.

The gift brought the tears. 'Wh-why?' he sobbed. 'Why us?' His voice was little more than a croak, a hoarse cackle made almost illegible by the tears and the mucus streaming into his mouth. There was no answer. The figure just threw the hair at him. The moisture acted as an adhesive, and the gift stuck to his face and semi-naked torso.

He grabbed it and looked at it. His body, heaving with the force of his sobs, was making it difficult to see what it was he was grasping.

The figure stayed silent, although he did shuffle a little closer.

Movement in the background caught his eye. He knew he had more to worry about, but his eyes were drawn to it. It was another figure, another man.

The intruder wasn't alone.

This newcomer was male. He wasn't wearing a mask. *Why is he not wearing a mask?* He had an inkling why, but he didn't want to voice that thought, not yet.

He stepped into the room. 'She's dead,' he said, his voice deep but with a lack of any real emotion in it. These were the only words uttered in the madness of this scene.

They were the only words needed.

There was something about the newcomer's voice, something he recognised. He looked at him, really looked. His eyes narrowed, and his tears stopped. The newcomer was only a boy. His mouth attempted a smile, one that held no humour. 'You,' he sobbed, recognition, or optimism, filling the words; he was hoping for the latter. 'It's you ...'

The boy looked at him. His face was a blank card.

The first figure, the man in the ski-mask, the one holding the knife with his wife's blood on it, looked at the boy before turning back to him. He shook his head, then slipped the blade into his neck.

At first, there was no pain, just a strange, cold sensation.

He tried to swallow, but every time he did, large lumps of what he thought could be phlegm stuck in his throat. It felt like he had a cold and needed to bring mucus up off his chest. Only phlegm didn't usually have such a horrible coppery taste.

Another cold feeling surprised him; this one was in his stomach, and this one brought pain. It also brought another feeling that, in his deranged mind, he likened to a balloon deflating. As he moved to see what was happening, the wound in his neck screamed. He lifted a surprisingly heavy arm, grasping at it, and was shocked to feel a slick, oily fluid covering his fingers. The agony in his stomach intensified, and he began to slip sideways onto the already ruined carpet. His eyesight blurred, but he could see the figure, the original murderer, remove his ski mask.

*You,* he thought, as the room dimmed. *But why?*

1.

<u>One month earlier</u>

The breeze running through the night air was welcome and cool. It carried with it a number of scents—pine from the trees of the nearby park, and a mixture of perfumes from the award-winning flowers that were planted and maintained by the locals. The evening sky was darkening into a fine dusk. The pink clouds on the horizon promised another warm, sunny day tomorrow. There were few streetlights in this part of town. Because of this, the heavens could usually be relied on to perform a spectacular nightly extravaganza.

Tonight was no different; it was as beautiful and as clear as it could be.

Car tyres broke the silence of the suburb as they crunched the gravel of the driveway leading up to a large, well-maintained, house; one of many on this street. As it came to a stop, the driver pressed the button for the handbrake but left the engine idling with the headlights still on. Rock music was playing inside the car. It wasn't blaring like some of the local kids liked it but set to an acceptable level, one that offered a background ambience to any conversation that was happening inside—or indeed act as a security blanket in case the conversation dried up, causing an awkward silence.

'Well,' the driver said, turning to look at the beautiful girl in the passenger seat. 'Here we are, as promised. Back home, safe and sound.' He looked at his watch and grinned. 'And well within the allotted time.'

Smiling, she looked out of the window. Her long dark hair had been curled especially for this date, and it bounced and bobbed around her shoulders as she turned. Sheepishly, she looked back at the driver, her dark brown eyes were large, filled with all the excitement and adventure a first date could muster. The rest of her body, however, was stiff and awkward. 'Yup, it looks like we're here all right.' Her voice was breathless, almost raspy. She was shocked she'd managed to get any words out at all, as her heart was racing so fast. She could almost feel her throat closing over.

The driver, a young man, tall, handsome, with a roguish smile and dangerously blue eyes, continued to grin. She hoped there was a little blush on his cheeks but thought she might be imagining it.

'Did you have a good time?' he asked as his hands fiddled within the holes of the steering wheel he was leaning on.

She loved the way his eyes twinkled when he smiled. *I could stare into them all night,* she thought before instantly admonishing herself for such cheesiness. His piercing eyes *had* dazzled her when she'd first seen him, and she thought she might have drowned in them tonight, her first ever date.

She felt her stomach flip, releasing the butterflies that had been itching to be set free all night. She knew what was about to happen. It was something she'd wanted to happen. She'd had an inkling that Sean was almost as shy as she was and wouldn't make his move until they'd parked outside her home.

She shook her head at his question and flashed a smile. 'Oh yeah, it's been, erm, lovely. Thanks for dinner, and the movie was great.'

Sean smiled again in a playfully patronising way. He ruffled his brow and nose. 'Well, I wouldn't go that far. I'm not really into movies about bridesmaids with hearts of gold,' he laughed.

Lisa bowed her head, raising her hands to stifle the girly giggle that was brewing. 'I'm sorry I put you through that, but I'm not a real horror fan, you know,' she said with a laugh.

Nodding, he moved his hand towards her, brushing away a few strands of hair that had fallen over her face. 'It's OK. I wasn't there for the movie anyway,' he whispered, looking deep into her eyes.

She thought her heart might melt right there and then. *He's going to do it*, she thought. *This is it, my first kiss, and it's with Sean Knight.* She noticed that he didn't have his seatbelt on anymore and wondered when he'd removed it. He'd definitely had it on when they were driving. Nervously, she dragged her eyes away from his beauty and back up the driveway, towards her house. There were a few lights on inside. She knew her mother would still be up. She would be doing things that she normally *wouldn't* do, like reading a book in the living room or on her laptop playing a game, pretending she wasn't waiting for her little girl to come home from her first date.

She watched the sprinkler that had been left on, keeping the front lawn quenched. It was getting warmer recently, and her mother would have wanted to keep the grass moist but also obey the watering restrictions. She noticed it was missing most of the grass and flowerbeds and mostly just wetting the paving stones and the walkway. She didn't know why she'd made this observation, especially with the handsome young man sitting next to her, but she did.

'Hey.' Sean snapped her out of her little dream by touching her cheek lightly with his fingers. She turned towards him and was rewarded with his charming smile. 'Penny for them?' he asked.

Her cheeks flushed; she could feel the heat rising within them as she played with the hair around her ear. She didn't want to tell him that she was thinking about a lawn sprinkler at a moment like this. 'Oh, it's nothing,' she smiled coyly. 'I was just thinking about what a great night I've had. Thank you so much, Sean.'

His eyes told her everything she needed to know. 'I've had a great night too.'

He moved towards her. It didn't matter that it was more than a little bit awkward, or that her heart continued to pound, making her lose her breath. All that mattered was what was about to happen.

'I was thinking that I don't want it to end so soon,' he whispered.

Her skin broke out with a rash of goosebumps as she squirmed in reaction to him being so close. 'Well, I ... erm,' she stammered. 'I have to get in. My mom, she'll be up, waiting for me.'

Sean laughed, and she began to feel a little silly. He shook his head. 'No, I didn't mean for us to *go* anywhere. For one thing, you've got a curfew. I do too. No, I just meant ...'

He put his hand to her face and caressed her cheek with his fingers again. Her skin tingled where he touched, and she felt the goosebumps rise again. 'Ah shit,' he whispered into her ear. 'I'm just going to have to do this. If I think about it anymore, I'll be far too nervous.'

His face was inches from hers. The proximity felt wonderful. His smell brought feelings of danger and adventure through her head. It was a heady mixture of mint, cologne, and nervous energy. Suddenly, she felt like she had taken a dip in the lake. Her skin was wet and clammy from her head to her toes.

All of this because she was about to kiss Sean Knight.

Before she had a chance to overthink what was happening, he made his move. He slipped his hand behind her head and gently guided her face towards his.

She went willingly.

The sensation was electric.

The feel of his lips touching hers sent tingles all over her body, sparking life into parts where she didn't even know she had nerve endings. She couldn't believe she'd waited almost seventeen years for this to happen.

The kiss continued. There was an awkward moment when he opened his mouth, and she felt his tongue probe into hers. She didn't know how to respond. Her first instinct was to pull away, but luckily, her second instinct kicked in, and she responded in kind. She not only allowed his tongue in but sent her own on a fact-finding mission and wasn't disappointed with its findings. The tingles continued through her body. Her nipples hardened, and there was a strange but very pleasant aching below.

*All of this from one kiss?* she thought, wondering why she hadn't done it before.

She slipped her hand around the back of his head and ran her fingers through his hair, enjoying the closeness. She surprised herself somewhat, that what she was doing came so naturally.

Finally, after a short while, which, to her, could have been a thousand years, she felt him pull away. She didn't want him to; she wanted him to keep doing what he was doing for another thousand years. She resisted his retreat by following his head with hers, not wanting to allow his delicious lips to escape. Then a voice whispered in her head, making her stop what she was doing almost immediately. *You're being too forward, Lisa*, the voice of reason and sanity, which sounded suspiciously like her mother, admonished her. She felt a rush

11

of heat as the already ruddy skin of her face flushed even deeper. Eventually, she allowed him to retreat.

He sat back and looked at her, his eyes half closed and dreamy and complementing his goofy smile perfectly. Lisa noticed, with a little alarm, that he was squirming in the seat, looking more than a little uncomfortable. She didn't know why she did it, but she was compelled to look towards the crotch in his jeans. There, she saw the source of his squirming. She giggled but couldn't take her eyes off the bulge he was fighting to conceal.

*I did that to him!*

She smiled her own secret smile at the delicious but inappropriate thoughts that were passing through her head.

'Erm, I-I really need to go in,' she mumbled. 'My mom will be waiting just inside the door.'

He sat back in his seat with his hands in the air. Lisa took another moment to spy at the bulge that was still attempting to burst through his jeans with all the might that eighteen-year-old boys' erections can muster.

'Hey, yeah. I-I totally get that,' he answered, smiling. 'Listen, thanks. I really mean it. I've have had a fantastic night tonight.'

He looked at her with the same intense stare he'd given her just before they'd kissed. Another sensation overwhelmed her; it felt like her insides were melting.

'Can … I, erm, I mean, should we, you know, kind of … do this again?' he fumbled.

The emotion that washed over her as he squirmed and bumbled his way through this question made her feel dizzy. The awkwardness of him just asking a question made her skin tingle, along with the rest of her insides, or what was left of them after the melting. Right there and then, she felt herself falling for him. He had caught her, hook, line, and sinker. Trying her very best to sound nonchalant but having to take a few breaths before attempting to speak, she croaked, 'Oh yeah! Absolutely. You've got my number there, don't you?'

He picked his cell phone up from the dashboard, pressed the button, and illuminated his face in the twilight of the car. He searched for a moment before finding what he was looking for. He held it out to her. 'Yup,' he replied with a grin.

'Then call me,' she said, opening the door.

# The Boyfriend

Before she got out, she stopped for a moment and leant back in over the seat and gave him another lingering kiss. 'Call me tonight, if you want,' she whispered, pulling away from the caress. Smiling from ear to ear, she exited the car.

It was Sean's turn to blush as he offered an excited smile back. 'OK,' was all he managed to say.

She closed the door behind her. 'I'll talk to you later then.'

'You will.'

'Goodnight, Sean, and thanks again for everything.'

She lingered for a few moments before drumming her hands on the open window frame. Then she turned away and walked up the path towards the front door of her house.

~~~~

He watched as she made her way up the path, enjoying the view of her strutting slowly up the driveway, towards her front door. 'Man, that is some serious ass,' he whispered. He nodded, enjoying the way her body moved in the tight jeans and white top. She knew what she was doing. She was showing off her hard body. A body that was kept tight by pilates, yoga, and afterschool fitness classes. Even though she'd kept everything covered, he appreciated that she'd had the foresight to selects clothes that would show off her curves as much as modesty would allow.

He was nodding as he pressed the button to wind the window up.

~~~~

She was floating on air, straddling a fluffy cloud, smiling a goofy, dreamy grin, she turned back towards the car and waved.

He waved back, then she heard the engine gunning as the black car pulled out on her street. With her back leaning against the closed door, she sighed, relishing the calm and tranquillity of the night. Taking more than a few moments to reflect on *that* kiss, she closed her eyes and sighed.

'Mom ... I'm home,' she shouted as she entered the house.

## 2.

AS SEAN DROVE off, offering a goodbye wave to Lisa, a wolf-like grin spread across his lips, and his eyes narrowed into humourless slits. He plucked the cell phone from one of the recesses in the dash and slipped it into the empty dock. Allowing a few moments for the Bluetooth to connect, he pressed a button on the car's built-in display screen, and an electronic female voice came through the speakers. '*SELECT THE CONTACT YOU WANT TO DIAL,*' the voice instructed him.

'Call Jay,' he said, clearly and slowly.

'*CALLING JAY,*' the voice responded.

The sound of the phone ringing played through the speaker system. It was answered on the third ring.

'Sean. Did everything go as planned?' the voice on the other end of the line asked.

'Yup.' The P popped in his mouth. 'All's good. She's putty in my hands.'

'You think she's up for it?'

'Yeah,' he spat, with a dry laugh. 'She's up for it. I can't wait to put this in motion. I'm so ready to really stick it to this pig.'

'Good, we should talk later then,' the voice replied.

He pressed the button on the display to disconnect the call. He flicked the radio on and turned it up extra loud, then pressed his foot on the accelerator as far as it would go. The car responded by breaking the speed limit as he ran a red light. He laughed as he sang along to the rock song blaring through the speakers.

## 3.

'WE'RE IN THE kitchen, honey,' the woman's voice called from deep inside the house after the front door closed behind her. Lisa almost floated through the large, airy hallway, past the grand staircase that was the main feature of the hall, and into the kitchen towards the rear. She'd known her mother would still be up, waiting for her but pretending otherwise.

Both her parents were at the island in the centre of the kitchen. They were both in their early fifties, both beaming with the health and happiness that affluence can bring. It was apparent that Lisa had taken most of her good looks from her mother's side of the family. Mrs Quinn was tall and athletic. Her long black hair hung below her shoulders, and even though she would openly admit to dying it to stave off the greys, it still had the lustre of youth. She also had the same large, dark brown eyes as Lisa.

Mr Quinn was not a tall man, but there was no way that he could be described as short. He was well muscled and looked his age, a healthy fifty-four. His receding hairline was tailored to his head, and his deep, dark eyes looked like they never missed a beat.

They both looked up from what they were pretending to do as she drifted into the room. 'Well, by the looks of that face, the date went well,' her mother noted as she stood to pour herself another glass of white wine from the bottle in the cooler. She offered the bottle to her husband, who shook his head, placing his hand over his glass.

'Daddy,' Lisa shouted, rushing to give him a hug. 'When did you get home?'

'About an hour ago,' he replied, returning his daughter's hug and kissing her on the forehead.

'Erm, don't think you can dodge that question just because your father's back after a few days,' her mother admonished with a laugh.

Lisa unwrapped herself from her father's embrace and looked at her mother. 'Oh, Mom, it was fantastic. We went to that new burger place over by the dock. Sean ordered and paid for it, then we drove to the movies. He was a real gentleman.'

Her mother raised her eyebrows as she took a small sip of her drink.

'You know, I really wish I'd had the chance to meet him,' her father said, looking at his daughter.

'Oh, Daddy, you'll get to meet him. I think we'll be going out again. He really is a nice guy. I think you two will get along just fine.'

Her father exhaled slowly, cocking his head jauntily. 'I don't know about that. I'm not sure anyone's good enough for my little pumpkin.' He grinned, letting her know he was joking.

Lisa pulled her own grimace, the humour in it obvious. 'Anyway, I've got loads of stuff to do. So, if you two will excuse me, I'm off to bed.'

Her mother stood and gave her daughter a kiss on the top of her head. She flashed her a secret smile and a wink. 'I'm glad it went well,' she whispered conspiratorially.

'Thanks, Mom,' she mouthed back. 'Goodnight, Daddy. I love you. I've missed you,' she said as she wrapped her arms tight around him, giving him a hug.

'Goodnight, baby.' He kissed her on her cheek. 'I've missed you too.'

With that, she made her way out of the room.

~~~~

Her father watched her go, shaking his head with a sad smile on his face. 'Jesus, Flo. Wasn't it just last year I taught her how to ride a bike?'

His wife eyed him over her drink. 'For you, it was,' she replied. 'For her, that was a lifetime ago.'

'My little girl's all grown up.' A melancholic smile spread across his face as the words left his mouth. He absently took another sip of his wine and looked at his wife. 'Did you meet him?'

She took another sip of wine and leaned into the high-backed stool she was sitting on, regarding her husband. 'I did. He was nice. Very good looking, and polite too. He brought me flowers, over there, look.' She pointed to the corner, towards a bunch of lilies in a vase.

'Smooth bastard,' he quipped.

Flo laughed. 'I seem to remember a certain young man bringing my father some fish he'd caught that day at the lake on our first date. And I also seem to remember that young man stinking the rest of the night.'

Tony chuckled and shook his head. 'Shit, yeah. I remember that.' He took another sip of his drink and looked wistfully towards the door where Lisa had exited. 'Talk about another lifetime ago.'

Flo raised her eyebrows again as she got up from the island and rinsed her glass in the sink. 'So, how about cutting the boy some slack and letting Lisa make her own decisions? I think we've brought her up well enough to do that. Don't you?'

Tony joined her. 'I do. But you know it's never going to stop me from worrying. She'll always be my little girl.'

Flo looked at him as she put her glass onto the rack. 'Tony,' she offered him a stern face. 'Stay out of this. OK?'

He pouted as he thought about it. Eventually, he sighed. 'OK, but if anything, and I mean anything happens, then it's on you.'

He put his glass onto the rack alongside hers.

She shook her head. 'How did I ever fall in love with someone as paranoid as you?'

'Because of my pulsating personality, not to mention my sizzling good looks,' he offered as he grabbed her, holding her close before kissing her.

'Yeah, that and the stink of fish ...'

4.

SEAN ARRIVED HOME about thirty minutes after dropping Lisa off. As he turned onto his street, he saw several cars and motorcycles parked outside his house. He gripped the steering wheel, closed his eyes, and sighed. 'Not again!' The pulsating sound of the speaker system his father installed in the backyard was belting out rock songs that could be heard all over the street.

He parked the car and got out. The moment his feet touched the ground, he was accosted by an elderly couple wearing matching robes. 'Excuse me, son …' the old man called to him.

Ignoring the pleas, Sean carried on walking, far too invested in what was happening in his house to be bothered by the old-timers.

'I said *excuse* me, son,' the old man shouted, grabbing his arm.

Sean turned, offering the man a fierce glare. The man stepped back, obviously cautious to the potential danger.

'First of all, I'm not your son,' Sean hissed. 'And second of all, stop touching me, you *homo*.'

The man reeled as if he'd been slapped. Sean turned and walked towards the house, dreading what he was walking into more with every step.

'Well, boy,' the man called out after him. 'You tell your so-called parents in there to turn that music off, or I'll be calling the cops.'

Sean turned and flipped the old man and his wife his middle finger. The gesture was met with gasps. The woman pulled on her husband, muttering for him to leave it alone.

# The Boyfriend

Sean continued towards the house, kicking an empty beer can on the front lawn. As he pushed open the side door, he realised that the music *was* too loud, even to his standards, and he was eighteen.

He walked into the living room, bumping into a middle-aged couple making out on one of the couches. He almost missed them because the room was so thick with cigarette fog. He only just missed stepping on another couple who were on the floor, and as his eyes adjusted to the darkness and the smog, he saw more couples leaning against the walls of the room. There were numerous red plastic cups, beer cans, and empty, or almost empty, bottles of various boozes strewn all over the room. A couple of women by the door acknowledged him with a nod.

He ignored them.

With a scowl etched onto his face, he peered into the kitchen, dreading what he would witness in there. He felt his eyes sting and his stomach churn as he saw his mother, semi-naked, being slobbered over by some guy he'd never seen before. He clenched his fists and closed his eyes. He wanted to get that image out of his head, but he had a feeling that whenever he closed his eyes for the foreseeable future, that would be the sight he would see.

He shook his head, more in dismay than anger, before backing out, leaving his slut of a mother to do whatever, or whoever, she wanted.

He made his way upstairs, climbing over another, older, couple. He didn't know if they were just making out or if they were actually fucking. He didn't care. He longed for the sanctuary of his bedroom and to close himself off from the loud insanity.

The couple on the stairs didn't even notice him stepping over them.

He did a double take at the long-haired man with the leather vest. There were some of the ugliest tattoos he'd ever seen in his life inked on the man's arms. They looked like they were supposed to be demons but were badly drawn and sketchy.

He recognised the tats.

It was his father!

He was almost certain that the woman he was with lived a few doors down. Sean thought he'd gone to school with her kids.

Biting the inside of his cheek, he continued his climb.

He needed to go to the bathroom but didn't know if he could dare. He didn't know what other layer of Hell he might witness inside. *Who the fuck lives like this?* he thought, opening the door. The two guys inside, both snorting cocaine from the cistern, turned and scowled at him, their moustaches almost white from the copious amounts of powder they were sniffing.

He decided he'd come back later.

He backed out of the bathroom and slammed his fist into his bedroom door, pushing it open. He was tired. He'd had a good night, and he knew there were going to be better, much better, ones ahead, but all he wanted to do now was sleep. As he flicked the switch for the lights, a muffled scream came from the direction of his bed.

He stopped as his bedsheets shot into the air.

Two naked women and one large, tattooed man, looked out from beneath the sheets.

'Hey, you little shit. This ain't no fucking peep show. Turn that light off and get the fuck out of here, now,' the man growled. The two women were giggling. They were either drunk, drugged, or both. They smiled at him with dazed expressions. Sean wondered if they even knew where they were.

'This is my fucking bedroom,' he protested.

The man growled and got up off the bed. He was twice the size of Sean, twice his age, and naked. In another scenario, that would have been the worst part of this confrontation, but the man was sporting an erection that was swinging from left to right. Sean thought it was pointing at him, accusing him of something.

'You're going to want to get the fuck out of here while you still can, boy!' the man threatened, his voice low but the malice within it palpable.

Sean swallowed hard. His eyes roamed from the man's angry face, down to his thick, dangerous looking cock, and then back to the two giggling women. He slunk out of the room, turning the light off as he went. Relief washed over him as the door closed, shutting out the sight of the angry man and his angry dick.

*I suppose it's the garage for me then*, he thought as he made his way back downstairs, careful not to step on his father, who was now openly fucking their neighbour. He managed to make it through the kitchen unmolested, trying his best to ignore his naked mother, who was bent over the dining table while a complete stranger, with his trousers around his ankles, pulled her hair and called her a bitch.

Refuge was in sight as he made it to the side door that led to the garage. He walked out of the house and back to the car. As he parked the car inside, he closed the automatic door and breathed a sigh of relief. The garage was blissfully empty, and the noise from the speaker system was muffled, as the party was now behind two sets of doors. He sighed as he climbed into the back seat. He located the blanket he'd stashed there for this kind of emergency and pulled it around him. He rested his head on the cold leather and closed his eyes.

It wasn't the first time he'd slept in the car.

5.

'SO, COME ON, spill it.'

Lisa felt the blush rising. Her skin had become hot and itchy, so she knew it was a deep one. 'What do you want to know?' she asked. The kind of smile that said *I don't want to tell you anything, but on the other hand, I* REALLY *do* spread over her face.

'You *know* what we want. All the gory details,' the tallest of the four girls huddled around the lockers in the hallway replied. The other three were giggling nervously.

'Did you get to first base? Did *HE* get to first base?' another girl asked in a high-pitched, shrill voice.

'Janice, you're such a dirty-minded bitch. Did you know that?' Lisa laughed as she playfully hit out at her.

'If the shoe fits, girlfriend,' Janice retorted, dodging the playful strike.

'You're so crude,' Nichola laughed as she linked Lisa's arm and pulled her away, down the corridor, towards their next class. 'Come on, tell me what it was *really* like.' It wasn't only Nichola's brown skin and high afro haircut that made her stand out within the group, it was also her lavish and colourful clothes. Lisa rolled her eyes and began to laugh just as Janice appeared on her other side and linked her too.

'Like I said before,' Kate, the tall girl, added from behind them. 'All the *gory* details.'

Lisa, never one to court the limelight, was loving this attention. 'Well, he picked me up in his car, which is totally cool, by the way. He had a load of old rock bands playing over Bluetooth.'

'Woah!' Paula, the fourth girl, ran in front and stopped them in their tracks. 'Rock bands? That's lame. How did he get past your dad? Did he grill him for at least an hour before you got out?'

Lisa smiled, raised her eyebrows, and shook her head. 'Nope. Dad's been away on business for a few days. He was home last night when I got back, but I knew he wouldn't be there when he came to pick me up.'

'Wicked girl,' Nichola chided as she tugged on Lisa's arm, starting the chain moving again.

'We went for a burger at the new shake place, then we went to the movies, then he drove me home.'

Janice's face fell. 'What? In all that time there was no titty action?' she asked, grabbing one of Lisa's boobs and pinching it playfully.

Lisa pushed her away, laughing. 'No, not at all.' She unlinked the arms of her friends, put her head in the air and walked ahead of them. 'He's a real gentleman.'

'That's not what I've heard,' Kate said as she trailed the girls along the corridor. 'I heard there was a skank a grade above who blew him under the bleachers during a football game.'

All the girls looked at her.

Kate threw her hands in the air. 'Hey, don't shoot the messenger. It's what I heard, that's all.'

Lisa shook her head. 'No, that's a lie. He was as nervous as I was. I'm telling you. I don't think he'd do anything like that.'

'So, just fucking tell us then. Put us out of our misery,' Nichola continued, trying her best to change the subject. She shot a glare at Kate, warning her to shut her mouth. Kate shrugged and looked at her as if *she* was the victim.

Lisa laughed again. 'I told you. We went to the movies, and he drove me home. We kissed a little and then arranged to meet up again sometime soon. That's it. That's all that happened.' She walked ahead again, a playful smile on her lips. 'Well, all I'm telling *you* anyway.'

'Dirty bitch.' Janice laughed as she followed Lisa into the classroom. 'I fucking knew it,' she finished.

6.

SEAN WAS STARING at his phone. It had just vibrated in his pocket, informing him he'd received a text. As he took it out, he saw that it was from Jay. The class he was currently in was both hot and deathly boring. He was glad of the distraction; it stopped him from falling asleep.

'WEN R U GONNA DO THE BITCH?' it read.

Sean smiled. It was a question he'd been asking himself since they'd had their first date, three days earlier. Since then, they'd had a few conversations over the phone. They were usually a little hushed and out of normal hours. It seemed that she didn't want daddy knowing anything about him.

'GONNA MEET 2NIGHT. GETTING FEET UNDER THE TABLE' he sent.

'NICE,' came the rapid reply. 'KEEP ME IN4MED.'

'Sean Knight, what are you doing there?' the teacher shouted over the classroom.

'Me? Nothing,' came his quick-fire reply as he stuffed the phone into his pocket.

'Precisely, Mr Knight, nothing. Unfortunately, that's all I've come to expect from you. Nothing. Nothing in class, nothing in life, nothing at all.'

The older man in the tweed jacket walked up to him and held out his hand. The rest of the class turned to watch the drama unfold. Inwardly, Sean smiled as he regarded them. *Literally anything is better than history for these jackals,* he thought.

'Hand over the phone, Mr Nothing!'

The Boyfriend

Sean looked around the room. He was embarrassed and was trying his best to get the class on his side. 'I don't know what you're talking about, sir,' he stammered.

'Stand up, boy,' the older man ordered while standing back, allowing the rest of the class to witness his humiliation.

He could feel his face turning red. He hated everyone looking at him. This tale would continue through the rest of the class and right through recess. He would be the main topic of conversation, probably through to tomorrow at this rate. Once again, he'd be the laughingstock of the school. He eyed the smug teacher. Hatred and scorn filled his head as he fished about in his pocket to produce the cell phone.

The teacher took it from him, holding it between his finger and thumb as if it was something dirty. 'You obviously have other ideas about your future, don't you, Mr Knight? I hope it was a future employer you were texting.'

The scorn in the old man's voice as it mingled with the sniggers of the rest of the class felt like a towel wrapping around his head. His skin flushed hotter than he could remember it flushing before. But the teacher wasn't finished with him, not yet. He was enjoying abusing the control he had over him.

'I taught your father, you know,' he said as he dropped the cell phone onto his desk. Sean noted that it was from a height, and he winced at the cracking sound as it hit the hard surface. 'He was a lazy, arrogant, no-good, redneck. Tell me, Mr Knight,' he said as he sat on the corner of the desk, looking at his embarrassed student. 'How did he get on in life?'

Sean was done with this ridicule. He glared at the teacher as he stood up, shoving his desk away from him. He pushed past the teacher, snatching the cell phone from the desk, and exited the classroom. The chorus of laughter was still ringing in his ears as he hit the corridor.

'Yeah, I didn't think so,' the teacher continued from within the classroom. 'Now, does anyone else want to have a cell phone conversation during this class? No? Good. Shall we continue?'

Sean bumped into two pupils as he exited the classroom. They both wore badges reading *Hall Monitor,* and both turned on him at the same time.

'Excuse me?' the girl asked. 'Can you tell me why—'

Sean didn't allow her to finish her question. He lashed out with his fist, catching her square on the jaw. Blood flew from her mouth as she fell backwards from the force of the punch, her eyes registering the shock of the assault as well as the shock of her banging her head against the lockers that lined the walls.

As she fell, her male colleague tried to help her. He glared at Sean. Disgust filled his narrow eyes and ruffled brow. 'What the fuck are you doing?' he shouted as he knelt to tend to his friend.

Without thinking, Sean kicked out at him, catching him in the side of his head, knocking him over, on top of his stricken colleague. Sean then looked both ways before running towards the large exit sign at the end of the corridor.

Once outside, he was free.

He only stopped running when he approached the end of the football field. Breathless from his exertions, he turned to look at the old building that had served as his prison for the last few years. He had no feelings about it whatsoever. The only thing he was sure of was that he was never, ever going back there again. Summer was beckoning, and he knew it was going to be a summer filled with opportunity.

7.

'I WAS THINKING tomorrow.' Sean was lying in the back of his father's Chevy with his feet up on the driver's side chair. His phone was lying next to him, the speaker activated.

'Well, we could, but I don't think you're going to be able to dodge my father forever, you know. He's wanting to meet you,' the female replied over the speaker.

'Well, if it means I get to see you again, then it's probably a fair price to pay. I could come around about seven. Will he be home then?'

'Yeah. He mostly works from home anyway. Should I ask Mom to cook us something for dinner?'

Sean smiled as he absently played with the rubber lining of the car window. 'That would be great.' He listened to the loud rock music coming from the house and shook his head. *At least I won't have to fend for myself*, he thought.

'OK then, seven it is. Mom will be thrilled. She's been dying to have you over. You seriously impressed her with the flowers."

Sean smiled at this. *Thank you, Jay*, he thought.

'Even though my dad can be a bit overprotective, I've told him nothing but good things about you. So, it won't be that bad, I promise.'

The delight that he could hear in her voice cheered him up. 'OK then, I'd better get a shower and clean myself up, especially if I'm about the meet the folks. I'll ask my dad if I can borrow one of his ties.'

She laughed. 'See you tomorrow then?'

'Tomorrow at seven,' he reiterated before pressing the button, terminating the call.

Balancing the device in the palm of his hands, he looked out of the window towards his father's empty tool wall. He pressed the button to access his messages and selected the New Message option. Scrolling down his short list of contacts, he paused when he came to the name Jay. He began to type.

'ITS ON 2MOROW NITE. MEETING MOM AND POP, HAVING DINNER. NICE AND COZY'

After he pressed send, he looked at his watch. It was nearly five. He stretched out and put his hands behind his head, closing his eyes. A satisfied, smug expression filled his face.

8.

LISA AND HER friends were in the same milk bar where Sean had taken her on their first date. The decor was bright, flashy, and very modern. The owners turned it into a milk bar to give the local kids somewhere to hang out.

The end of semester was in sight for them all, the exams they had all been cramming for were over, and a summer filled with bikinis, sunbathing, and boys was spread out before them.

They were sitting in a booth underneath a large window, giving them a full view of the park opposite in its full twilight beauty.

'I can't believe you're going to allow him to meet your dad,' Nichola said in between sips of her thick peanut butter milkshake.

'I can't believe you got bacon bits in your shake,' Paula said, looking at Nichola with a disapproving expression.

'Oh, babe, you need to try it; it's fantastic. It's the full sweet and salty vibe.'

Janice ruffled her brow pointing to the straw that was protruding from her large, white cup towards Lisa. 'Well, I know someone else who's going to get a little something that's sweet and salty very soon.' She leaned into her friend and tickled her ribs.

Lisa blushed while pushing her off. 'Stop it; I'm not like that. Besides, if you get that shake on my top, I swear ...' She giggled. All the girls were laughing loudly as Lisa tried to hide behind her large cup. 'Plus ...' She flicked her eyes around at her friends, her smile coy, maybe a bit *too* coy. 'My dad would kill me,' she finished.

The others roared, laughing.

'So, seriously, you're actually going to introduce him to your control freak of a father? Jesus, the man vetted us for months before he'd allow you to hang with us,' Paula said after being momentarily distracted by a group of young men walking into the bar.

'I talked to my mom, and she said she was going to have a word with him. He'd already promised he'd stay out of it. He's going to leave it up to me to decide.'

Janice leaned into the table and drew everyone in with her. 'Did you hear what I heard about him?' she whispered.

'About who?' Nichola asked. 'Lisa's dad?'

Lisa rolled her eyes and sat back. She knew what was coming next. 'Janice, we all heard about it,' she retorted.

'Heard about what?' Paula asked, suddenly more interested in the gossip than the boys in the far booth. 'I'm confused. Are we still talking about Lisa's dad?'

'No, you dummy. Keep up. We're talking about Sean,' Lisa said, ready to defend her boyfriend. 'Apparently, he managed to get himself thrown out of a class in school. I heard he called the teacher a dick or something because he was bullying him. It's nothing huge.'

Janice sat back again, smiling, but it was one more of concern than humour. 'Tell your dad that,' she said, picking up her cup and taking a sip through the straw.

'What was it about?' Paula asked.

'Something to do with his dad. Apparently, the teacher used to teach him, and they didn't get along. He was taking out his frustrations on him. It's no biggie,' Lisa explained, shrugging and taking another sip of her drink.

Nichola raised her eyebrows and sat back, joining in the sipping.

'It really is nothing,' Lisa stated, flustering. A sheen of sweat was bobbling on her forehead. 'Can we change the subject now? Please.'

They raised their eyebrows at each other as they fell silent.

Paula looked towards Nichola and smiled. She began to dance in her seat, swinging her shoulders back and forth. Nichola picked up on what she was doing and began to copy her moves.

'Bad, bad, bad, bad boys …' Paula began to sing.

'They make me feel so good,' Nichola continued, laughing and clicking her fingers.

This cracked the others up, and the whole table began singing along, everyone except Lisa, who was pretending, unsuccessfully, to be angry.

'I want you, bad, bad, bad, bad boys ...' they all continued.

Lisa did see the funny side of it and, in the end, succumbed to the peer pressure and joined in with the dancing and singing.

It caught the attention of the boys in the far booth. One of them made his way over. He was tall, good looking. He was wearing shorts that went over his knees and a red hooded top. There was an NYC baseball cap perched on the top of his head. 'You girls like the bad boys, do you?' he asked. There was a swagger in his movements, like he was overcompensating for something. 'Well then, may I introduce myself and my crew over here?'

The singing and dancing stopped almost instantly and was replaced by sniggers and giggles.

Janice looked up at him from her seat. She offered him a flirtatious smile and fluttered her eyelashes, just a little. 'What's your name?' she asked with more than a hint of innocence in her voice.

'I'm Ryan. Pleased to meet you.' He held out his hand with a pout and a nod.

Janice looked at the outstretched hand and then up to the grinning Ryan. 'Well, pleased to meet you, Ryan. Now why don't you and your crew go and fuck off back to whatever hick town you crawled out of. This is a private conversation, dickhead.'

The boy looked like he'd been sucker-punched. He gawped at her; his expression lost. It was obvious he didn't have a contingency for a scenario like this. His gaze shifted from face to face of the other girls. They looked almost as shocked as he did.

Only Janice's face remained the same.

'I ... erm,' he stammered, still with his hand held out towards her.

Janice shrugged, her eyes faking confusion as she shook her head, slowly from side to side. 'Why are you still here?' she asked.

Ryan's face was almost purple as he turned away. Once he caught the attention of his friends over the other side of the room, his bravado came back, and he gestured something rude about the girls as he walked away from them. They all began to jeer and boo.

'What the fuck was that, Janice?' Nichola asked when Ryan was out of ear shot.

'Yeah, those guys are cute,' Paula said, leaning into the table.

'Didn't you see them leering at us when they walked in?' she defended herself, picking up her milkshake and taking a sip as if nothing had happened.

Paula pulled a face. 'Erm, yeah! That's what teenage boys are supposed to do.'

'Well, I didn't like it. That or the way they were high fiving each other and stuff while looking over at us. Besides, there's four of them.'

'There's four of us, or can't you count?' Nichola hissed as she leaned into the table, getting closer to Janice.

She pointed at Lisa. 'Three, you mean. Lisa's spoken for,' she said, talking about her friend as if she wasn't at the table.

'Girl, you're crazy,' Nichola said standing up and crumpling the empty paper cup that had once held her drink.

'Am I? Look at them,' Janice replied, standing and collecting the other two empty cups. The girls looked towards the booth where the boys were laughing and joking again, slapping palms and shouting. 'Are they the kind of guys you want to be hanging out with?'

'Yeah,' Paula said, making her way towards the exit. As she did, she caught the eye of Ryan. He gave her a little nod and a small smile.

She replied in kind.

'Well, I don't know about you guys, but I've got to be getting home now anyway,' Lisa said, standing up with her hands in the air, stretching.

The boys in the booth were watching. It was obvious they were enjoying the way her shorts and small top stretched tight across her body, clinging to her curves.

Janice shook her head. 'Look at them; there's only one thing on their mind,' she snapped.

'What the hell is wrong with you, woman?' Nichola asked. 'It's the only thing I've got on *my* mind too.'

Paula laughed and high-fived her friend, mimicking the way the boys had been doing it earlier. The four girls, including Janice, were laughing as they exited the bar.

'All right, girlies, I'm going to make my way home before it gets fully dark. I'll see you in school tomorrow.' Lisa waved as she walked away from the others, heading towards the park that was the shortcut to her house.

Janice looked at the other two. She could see they were still a little pissed with her for her actions inside. 'I'm going too,' she announced. 'Listen, I'm sorry for that just then.'

Nichola and Paula shook their heads. 'So are we,' Paula said, but she gave Janice a hug anyway, as did Nichola, though reluctantly.

'I'll walk back with Lisa, make sure she gets home OK. See you guys in school tomorrow.'

The two girls waved her off.

'Have you got any money on you?' Paula asked Nichola.

Nichola returned the crafty grin. 'Enough to go back in there and order another milkshake,' she said, raising her eyebrows.

They looked in the window, making sure Ryan and his friends were still there.

They were.

'Well come on then,' Paula said, laughing as she held the door open and dragged her friend, semi-reluctantly, inside.

As they entered, the boys stopped what they were doing and watched them walk to the counter.

'Where's your friend?' Ryan asked as he walked up behind Paula.

She turned, a little surprised to find him directly behind her. She eyed him, flashing her best, most flirtatious smile. 'She had to go home.'

'Well, that's a shame, because there's four of us here, and my friend Kevin, well, he really likes one of the others. The *other* one who's not here.'

Nichola looked at the boys. There was a tall, muscular boy who caught her attention. He was looking back at her. 'Well, Kevin would have been mightily disappointed since Lisa's spoken for. But we're not,' she announced, twirling her hair around one of her fingers.

Another boy at the table stood up. This one was muscular too, built like a football player but without the fat. 'So, who's she with?' he asked.

'What's it to you?' Nichola asked, her eyes coveting his body through his tight t-shirt.

'I'm Kevin.'

'Oh, well. As I said, you'd have missed out anyway. She's already hooked up with someone.'

Kevin didn't seem to want to give up too easy. He stepped out of the booth and walked over. 'I just want to know who it is. Do we know him?'

Paula shrugged. 'I don't know if you know him. It's a guy named Sean Knight.'

The boys shot each other a look.

Kevin shrugged and turned away, sitting back at the booth. Ryan kind of cooled his interest in Paula too. He backed away nodding his head. 'OK, well, that's cool. We're just finishing up in here now anyway, so … what's your names?'

'I'm Nichola, and this is Paula.'

One of the other boys flashed a smile. 'Well, Paula and Nichola, are you guys on the Network?'

'Yeah, Paula James and Nichola Longstaff, look us up.'

'I will.' He grinned.

All four boys got up and left, each giving the girls second looks, small smiles, and curt nods.

Nichola turned to Paula and shrugged. 'What the hell was all that about?'

'I've no idea. We mentioned Sean and they cooled off real quick.'

'Oh well.' Paula looked at her watch. 'Maye it's time we went home anyway.'

Nichola curled her lip and reluctantly agreed.

## 9.

'DO YOU THINK it's serious then?' Janice asked as they walked through the park arm in arm.

It was almost full dark, and the shadows from the bushes and trees around them were beginning to look like sinister traps. Lisa was glad Janice had come with her.

She shrugged and offered a pout. 'I don't know. I've only been out with him once, although we do talk on the phone all the time.'

'Yeah, but he's taking you out again tomorrow, isn't he? That's a big thing. You must have done something right.'

Lisa smiled. 'Yeah ...' she replied. 'I must have.'

'So, do you think he's, you know, the one?' Janice asked, pulling her friend closer and raising her eyebrows.

Lisa was thankful for the dark for the first time since they started this route. It hid her face as it flushed again. 'I don't know. Jesus, Janice, I'm not even seventeen yet, there's plenty of time for that.'

Her friend's face went blank, and she raised her eyebrows, just for a moment, and looked away from her, back towards the direction they were walking.

Lisa looked at her, and her face fell into amused shock.

'Oh my God! You haven't! Have you?'

Janice unbuckled their arms and walked a little ahead. Her head was held high, and there was an amused look on her face.

Lisa's eyes grew wide as she hurried to catch her up. 'You have, haven't you? Oh wow! Janice you ... slut,' she laughed. 'Who was it?'

Janice didn't say anything, she just continued to walk towards the entrance of the park.

'Janice Bowen, you tell me right now,' she demanded.

~~~~

A silhouette emerged from the darkness of the bushes. It watched the two girls as they laughed and giggled along the path.

Sean reached into his pocket and produced a packet of cigarettes. He lit one and took a long drag. As he released the smoke between his clenched teeth, the girls exited onto the street beyond, both of them now only a block or two away from their homes. He stayed there for another few moments, watching them disappear from view while he pulled on his cigarette.

Before long, he stubbed it out on the trunk of a nearby tree and walked off in the direction the girls had come from.

10.

LISA ARRIVED HOME just after dark. As she expected, her mother and father were still up watching TV. 'I'm home,' she shouted, closing the front door and shrugging off her coat.

'We're in the living room, honey,' her father shouted. 'Do me a favour would you? Put the kettle on, I'm dying for a cup of tea.'

'On it.' She made her way into the kitchen, filled the kettle, and flicked the switch. As she waited for it to boil, she pondered on Janice's confession. It was still buzzing around her head as she prepared the cups.

*I can't believe she never told me.*

Then a horrible, jealous thought crossed her mind.

*Was it Sean?*

The kettle clicked off behind her.

*No. There's no way it could have been Sean. He'd never go with someone like Janice.*

Her brow ruffled.

*How do I know if he'd go with someone like Janice? I hardly know him at all. I don't know anything about him. Am I making a mistake here? I mean, he did get thrown out of class yesterday. Dad would kill me if he knew I was going out with a trouble-maker.*

Her brow ruffled further, and she crossed her arms as she leant back on the tabletop, thinking.

*No, not Sean. Not the one who took me out the other night and who's been nothing but nice ever since. Come on, Lisa, you're acting stupid. He's a nice boy, and it's not like you're planning on actually having sex with him. Are you?*

'Lisa,' her father shouted from the lounge. 'Have you gone to China for that tea?'

She was thankful for the voice, for it snapping her out of her spiralling thoughts. 'Sorry, Dad. It's coming now.'

As she re-boiled the water and poured it into the waiting cups, a secret smile broke on her lips. *If it's good enough for Janice ...* she thought, then shook her head, hoping it would rid her of the deviousness racing through her. *Or maybe not!*

She carried three cups into the living room, where her mother and father were sat on a long couch, or at least her father was sat, her mother was lying with her head in his lap. They both looked up as she walked in. Her mother eased herself up and helped her with the cups.

'Did you have a good night, honey?' her father asked, accepting the steaming cup.

'Yeah, we just hit that new milkshake spot across the park.'

'You didn't walk home on your own, did you?' her mother asked, offering a stern look.

'No, Mom,' she sang. 'I was with Janice. I think the others were interested in a few of the boys who were in there.'

'There were *boys* in there?' her father asked in a mocking tone. 'Mark my words, young lady, you are *not* to go back there. Do you understand me?'

Lisa laughed as she sat down on a large chair opposite the TV and held her own steaming cup on her lap.

'Lisa, we've got something to tell you. I hope you're going to be OK with it,' her father said with a rather serious expression.

She noticed her mother was looking at her with the same expression.

'Please don't tell me you guys are having a baby. I don't think I could handle the competition.' She feigned a small faint into the chair, spilling a little of her tea as she did. She giggled, wiping it off her jeans.

Her mother laughed. 'No, it's not that. But it's important, and we have to talk to you about it.'

Lisa sat up and put her cup on the table in front of her. She then looked at her mother. A chill ran through her as she noticed her face had lost most of the humour it had only moments ago.

'Your father and I are going on vacation. We'll be gone for ten days.'

'We're going to Europe,' her father added, his face as serious as her mother's. 'Just the two of us.' He grinned a humourless grin, showing off his expensive dentistry.

Lisa's face beamed. 'Really? You're going to leave me here, all by myself, for ten days?'

Her father looked at her, and then at her mother. 'See, I told you she'd be fine with it. She's outgrown us, Flo.'

Lisa laughed.

Her mother was smiling, but Lisa could see a tinge of sadness in it. 'I think she *has* outgrown us,' she said, nodding.

'When are you going?' Lisa asked, trying her best not to sound *too* happy at the thought of the house to herself for ten days.

'Well, we fly out a week from Friday. We're going to Paris for a few days, then off to Spain for a few days of sunshine. Just flying visits really, but it's something we've been thinking about for a while,' her father explained.

'But we wanted to give you the option of coming with us, as a gift for maintaining your grades,' Flo offered, eyeing Tony. 'It's summer vacation as of next week, and we think you deserve a break before the intensity of next year. What do you think?'

Lisa sat in her chair and looked at them both. Her half smile told them both exactly what they needed to know. For the first time in their lives, a vacation would just be the two of them this year, and probably every year after.

Her father grinned. 'Listen, I know you're not the type to have any wild parties or anything. We can trust you, can't we?'

'Of course you can, Daddy.' She gave him the sweetest, most innocent smile she had in her arsenal.

'Oh, look how all of a sudden I'm Daddy again.' He grinned.

Lisa jumped out of her seat and flung her arms around him. 'You'll always be Daddy to me. You know that, right?'

11.

'THEY'VE JUST TOLD me they'll be away for ten days.'

'Where are they going?' Janice asked. Lisa could tell that she was excited, even over the phone.

'Europe.'

'Wow, this is awesome! Will we be able to stay over?'

'Well, yeah. That goes without saying, but we won't be able to have any parties or anything. You know what my dad's like. He'd find out somehow.'

Janice laughed. 'Yeah, mister eyes in the back of his head. Have you told Sean yet?'

'Sean? Why would I tell him?'

There were a few moments of silence on the other end. Lisa envisioned Janice shaking her head and rolling her eyes. 'Because he's your boyfriend, stupid.'

'What? One date does not a boyfriend make.'

'Yeah? Well, you need to tell that to your face. It lights up every time anyone mentions him.'

Lisa felt her face heat up as what felt like all the blood in her body rushed to it. 'No I don't ... Do I?'

The sound of Janice laughing on the other end of the line was all the answer she needed. 'Listen, Lisa, I've got to go. My mom is calling me. Make sure you tell the others about our good fortune, OK? I'll see you tomorrow.'

Janice hung up, and Lisa was about to call Nichola when a message popped up on her screen. It was from Nichola.

'OMG ... Janice just told me. So cool. Call me!'

# The Boyfriend

Lisa shook her head and narrowed her eyes at the phone. *She must have been texting and talking at the same time*, she thought.

Another message, this time from Paula. 'Party time in Lisa Central. We've got just the boys to bring too.'

'Shit. News really does travel fast, doesn't it?' she whispered, reading the message.

Then, almost as if on cue, her phone rang.

It was Sean.

As she saw his name on the screen, her heart began to beat faster, and the butterflies in her stomach began their merry dance. A modicum of doubt ran through her head. *Did she message him too?* She dismissed the idea as stupid. Janice didn't have Sean's number. 'Hey, you,' she purred as she answered the phone. 'I was just thinking about you.' She cringed at her overtly flirtatious tone. *Slow down, girl,* she thought.

'Good things, I hope.'

She sat back on her bed and began to curl her hair behind her ear nervously. 'Always. Anyway, what's happening tomorrow night? Where are we going?'

'Well, I thought I'd get to your house about seven and meet your folks. I'll charm them for a good fifteen, maybe twenty minutes while I force myself to eat your mom's food. Then we can go to our regular haunt, get a shake, and then …'

He left the sentence hanging, while he raised his eyebrows.

'And then?' Lisa asked impatiently.

'And then, I was thinking we could park someplace. Somewhere dark and secluded.'

A flash of worry ran through her. She'd never parked before, not with anyone, and was not entirely sure of what she would be expected to do. 'Erm, yeah. That's sounds great.' She could hear the doubt in her own voice.

Sean picked up on it too. 'Listen, you don't have to if you don't want to, you know,' he reassured her.

'No,' she giggled, a little too shrilly for her liking. 'It's not that I don't *want* to …'

She heard him laugh on the other end of the line, and she blushed. *He knows that I'm worried about it,* she thought.

'It's because you've never parked with a boy before, isn't it?'

At this, even though there was no one there to witness her embarrassment, her face flushed like a beetroot. 'Well … yeah,' she eventually answered.

'Listen. There won't be any pressure on my behalf. To tell you the truth, I've never parked with a girl before. I'll be as nervous as you.'

Lisa hoped beyond hope he was telling the truth. 'Really?' she asked, hoping she didn't sound too desperate.

'Honest. I've never been with a girl. I've been kind of saving myself, to be honest. When I do it, I want it to be with someone I really care about.'

This was music to her ears, and she thought she could feel her heart melting in her chest. 'Well, I've got some news,' she continued, instantly cringing. She hadn't wanted to tell him about her parents going away, and she really couldn't believe she was about to. 'My mom and dad are going to Europe for a while next Friday.' After what he had just told her, she didn't want him to think she was throwing herself at him. *Maybe I'm the one he'll care about*, she thought, smiling. *If it's good enough for Janice …*

'Are you having a party?' he asked.

'Oh no. Nothing like that. My dad would kill me if I did. I'd be grounded for life. No, it's just going to be a few close friends. I think they might have some boys they'll want to bring over.'

'Oh, OK. Do you know the boys?' he asked. She hoped she could hear an edge of jealousy in his voice.

'I don't know. I think they only just met them tonight.'

'Do you want me to come over and make sure everything's OK?'

'Well,' Lisa replied, wrapping her hair around her fingers again. *It's going to end up looking like I've had rollers in soon,* she thought. 'I was kind of hoping you'd be coming over anyway.'

His laugh on the other end of the line reassured her. 'Oh, you did, did you?'

She mused on if it was possible for a person to blush so much that they would lose precious blood to other important parts of their body and die. She thanked God she wasn't using a video messenger right then. 'Yeah, as my date,' she replied a little tartly.

Sean laughed again.

# The Boyfriend

She thought she had already fallen in love with that sound. *What the hell is happening here?* she chastised herself.

'OK, I'm going to have to go and do some studying,' he said out of the blue, once again snapping her back into the real world.

'OK.'

There was a moment of silence before Lisa, her heart in her mouth, dared to ask the question burning on her lips. 'Sean?'

'Yeah?'

'I heard you got thrown out of school the other day. Is it true?'

His laugh was coming down the other end of the phone again. It was filled with mirth, and it lightened her mood somewhat. 'No, it was nothing. I mean, yeah, I did get removed from class, but it was a misunderstanding with a teacher who hated my dad back in the day. He thought I had my phone on in class. Ridiculous old fucker, probably wouldn't even know a cell phone if he saw one.'

Lisa laughed, relieved.

'So, he threw me out of the class. I went to see the principal, and I was right back in. I don't know why I bothered; school's out next week. But I did get an apology from the old bastard.'

She relaxed on her bed, her hand on her chest as her heartbeat began to slow back to something approaching normal. 'Thank God for that. My dad would never allow us to see each other if you weren't at school, or working, or something.'

'Well, there's no danger of that. I'm straight A's all the way. Well, except for math. I just don't seem to be able to get my head around that trigonometry shit.'

Lisa chuffed; it was a horrible sound, and she wished that she hadn't done it. 'Yeah, me neither,' she lied, trying to hide the noise she had just made. 'Well, don't let me get between you and your studies. I'll see you tomorrow night, yeah?'

'Seven o'clock. I'm looking forward to it already.'

'So am I,' she said before hanging up.

When the phone line was dead, she lay back on her bed with the device clutched to her chest. Her smile ran almost from ear to ear as she stared up at the ceiling.

Her thoughts were mixed and unfocused.

12.

'WHAT THE FUCK are you doing in here?'

As Sean clicked off his phone, he looked through the window of the Chevy to see the hulking, tattooed, angry figure of his father staring down at him.

'I'm making a phone call,' he replied. 'I needed somewhere quiet.'

'Get the fuck out of there, you little shit. I need you to run an errand,' the big man growled. 'We're having people over tonight. I need you to score me some good shit. You know what I need. Weed, coke, and some of that green meth you got last time.'

His father opened the door to the car and threw a wad of cash at him.

Seething, Sean got up from the back seat and retrieved the dollar bills that were scattered at his feet. The notes were old and well used. As he picked them up, a strong hand grabbed the back of his t-shirt, pulling him up.

There were equal amounts of anger, fear, and shame in his expression.

'I want the change too, you little prick. Don't even think about screwing me over with any of that weak shit you got last time. That was a fucking embarrassment.'

Sean scowled at his loathsome parent as he was let go to fall back into the seat.

'And be back in an hour. They'll be here by then. You understand me, boy?'

Sean grunted as he climbed out of the car and slid past his father. He reached for his jacket from the empty tool bench as he went. He could feel the big man's eyes on him as he exited the garage door.

'And don't be taking any of the shit yourself. You're too young. I'm a responsible fucking parent, you know.'

Sean heard him laugh at his own joke as he made his way down the path, putting welcome distance between him and the house.

13.

'ITS ON 4 2MORROW 7 @ HER PLACE. MEETNG FOLKS THEN PARKING... ITS ON'

Sean was typing this into his phone as he made his way along the street, heading to the part of town where he knew he could score the drugs his father wanted for his party.

Within a minute, his phone vibrated with a reply. It was from Jay.

'XCELNT... REMBR STICK IT 2 THE PIG'

*You don't need to tell me twice.* He grinned. *I'm going to ruin that innocent pussy.*

With this pleasant thought running through his head, he began to walk faster down the run-down road. Things were looking up for him, and there was almost a skip in his stride.

The area he was in was neglected, the buildings becoming shabbier the deeper into the area he went. They were mostly empty factories and warehouses with broken windows. Burnt out or abandoned vehicles were the order down here. Dark shadows resided in the empty hallways inside the open, vacant doors. He tried not to look too far into these gaping chasms. He was old enough to know better than to believe in boogiemen and monsters, but he'd seen enough movies to know that if they did exist, they would live in this part of town.

He was suddenly aware of the large wad of cash in his pocket, and he slid his hand inside his trouser pocket, gripping the handle of the switchblade he always carried.

He reached his destination, thankfully, unmolested. It was an old, abandoned building, just another derelict warehouse on a road full of them. Back in its glory days, the building might have been something special, majestic even, but now it was another den of iniquity. He smiled to himself, proud of the thought he'd just had. *Lisa would like that,* he thought. *Iniquity, that's a word!* He put the phrase to the back of his mind, happy it was there.

Gripping the handle of his knife for reassurance, he crept down the dark alleyway to the side of the building and removed an old wooden board disguising the entrance. As he entered, he looked behind him. There were two young kids, probably not twelve years old yet, sitting on bikes, watching him from the other side of the street. One of the kids grabbed at the shoulder of the red woollen sweater he was wearing and appeared to speak into it.

Sean knew the drill.

He continued down the alleyway, careful to replace the wooden board into the same position he'd found it.

Two tall and skinny youths appeared out of the darkness before him. Their stealth made him jump. One was Black, the other was White. Both were wearing vests and baggy jeans, but most importantly, they were holding guns and were pointing them at him.

'Whoa, man, relax,' Sean said, fixing the wooden board. 'What's with the guns?'

The White youth relaxed a little as he recognised him. He clicked the safety on his gun and put it into the back of his pants. 'Can't be too careful, man. Those spic assholes on the east side have been putting the pressure on.'

'Well, fuck, man, you knew it was me. Charlie out there told you already,' Sean said, wiping white plaster dust from his hands.

'Come on, this way,' the Black kid said, putting his gun away and turning into the darkness behind him. 'Watch your step on the shit, we ain't got no insurance.' He laughed as he disappeared down the alley.

Sean followed. Even though he knew they were only maybe two years older than him, their experience on the street made them seem a lot older. He had no doubt they'd killed people during the course of their 'business careers.'

'You after the same order?' the Black youth asked.

'Is it for your dad?' the other asked.

Sean nodded his reply to both questions, removing the wad of cash from his pocket. The Black youth produced a radio and spoke into it, something that Sean couldn't decipher. A door opened ahead of them, and another White youth, again about the same age, made his way down the alley.

'Sean,' he said with a curt nod of his head.

'Sharpie.' Sean nodded his acknowledgement back at him.

Sharpie rubbed his fingers together, and Sean handed over the wedge. Sharpie counted it, nodding his approval.

'Your old man's wanting a lot of product these days.'

'He's having another party. I was hoping to get a little for myself, on the side, you know, for bringing the business and all.'

Sharpie stared at him. His young face was betrayed by his aged eyes; they were the eyes of an older, world-weary man. They looked older than his soul.

Eventually, Sharpie smiled, although there was very little humour in it. He had a face that didn't look used to smiling, and Sean could see why. What few teeth he had left were rotten and on the verge of giving up the lost cause like the others had already done. 'You looking to party yourself, dude?'

'Something like that,' Sean replied.

Sharpie winked and put the money in his back pocket. 'Because you're a friend, you get the good stuff. Your piece of shit old man? Him and his cronies are gonna be sniffing thirty percent plaster and talc. Serves the old fuckers right, yeah?'

Sean nodded. 'It needs to be half decent, otherwise he'll serve me my ass.'

'Don't worry about that, man. They'll think they're sniffing pure China White,' Sharpie replied, disappearing back through the door he'd appeared from, leaving Sean with the other two boys.

'You using now?' the Black kid asked him.

Sean scowled. 'What's that got to do with you?'

The boy shrugged and pulled his mouth down in a leer. 'Not my shit, man. I just think you're better than that. Just saying.'

Sharpie appeared again a few minutes later and handed him two bags and a cheap looking plastic cell phone. 'The bigger bag is for your dad, the smaller one for you. The phone is a burner. Charlie and Roy will escort you home. One in front, one behind. If there's any heat, they'll message you to take a different route. You get home, you smash the phone to pieces, and you snap the SIM. You hear me?'

Sean nodded as he accepted the stash. 'Loud and clear, man.' He made his way out of the alleyway, through the wooden board, and back the way he came. He only saw the kids on the bikes twice in the whole journey, and he made it back to his street without incident.

As he got home, he received one text message on the burner phone, from an unknown number. 'ALL CLEAR,' it read. Absently, he put the phone back into his pocket and continued to his house. As he got closer, he could see his father waiting at the door.

'Where the fuck have you been?' he demanded, grabbing the boy by the back of his head. 'You got what I asked for?'

'Fuck yeah, I got it. Let go of me and I'll give it to you,' he snarled as he tried to wriggle free of his father's grip. He produced the bigger of the two bags. His father snatched it, let go of Sean's hair, and hastily opened it. He licked an oil covered finger and poked it into one of the individual bags inside, then rubbed the finger onto his gums.

He nodded his approval.

Sean shook his head. *Stupid fuck wouldn't know good shit if he was rolling around in it,* he thought.

'Is everything in here?'

'Yeah, coke, weed, and meth. Everything you need for a good night fucking Mrs Wazloszki.'

'Watch your fucking mouth, kid,' his father warned and smacked him hard across the back of the head. 'Now fuck off up to your room and leave me and your mother alone.'

Sean trudged back into the garage. There'd be no point going to his room as he'd only be kicked out of it again at some point during the night. He didn't mind too much, though; he'd soon be as far away from the huge fuck-up that was his homelife as he could get.

He climbed into the back of the car and lay down. He put his hands behind his head and smiled. Then he took out the other, smaller bag and looked at it, 'Ah, Lisa ...' he whispered. 'You're not going to know what's hit you.' He put the bag back into his pocket, and as he did, the burner phone fell out and hit the floor.

He didn't notice it.

14.

LISA PACED HER bedroom for what felt like the five-hundredth time. She looked at the clock on her wall, frustrated to see that it wasn't even seven o'clock yet. The whole day in school, she'd been a bag of nerves, unable to concentrate on any of her classes. Janice had been protective of her and sensitive to her feelings, but the others had been oblivious to her turmoil, gabbling on about the boys they'd met the other night in the milk bar.

'Jesus Christ, it was six thirty-five hours ago,' she muttered, looking out her window again. She scanned up and down what she could see of the street, searching for Sean's Chevy.

A few cars passed by, but none of them were his.

Her mind was working overtime. She was envisioning a million different scenarios that might stop him from turning up tonight. A crash, a natural disaster, World War Three!

As she was musing, a car pulled up outside, and she pulled her drapes aside to look.

Her heart almost missed a beat.

It was him.

She watched as it pulled up and he got out. He looked sharper than he had the last time they'd met. *Has he had a haircut?* He was carrying a bouquet of flowers, a box of chocolates, and what looked like a bottle of wine. She smiled as her heart leaped. *He's not taking any prisoners tonight, is he?* she thought.

She burst from her room and ran along the landing to the stairs. Taking at least three steps at a time, she traversed the whole flight in seconds in her attempt to get to the door before it rang.

Which she didn't quite manage to do.

'I'll get it,' she shouted into the kitchen, where her parents were keeping themselves busy, and opened the door seconds later. Her heart was all aflutter.

He was standing in the doorway wearing what must have been his nicest clothes, which were much the same as his normal clothes but looked a little newer. His face was obstructed by the flowers he was holding, and as she opened the door, he looked comically around the side of them.

'Delivery for a Miss Lisa Quinn,' he announced in an exaggerated English accent.

She giggled and covered her mouth. 'Come in, you fool, before someone sees you.' She stepped back from the doorjamb, inviting him inside, and he walked past her, tipping her a wink.

'Mom, Dad, Sean's here,' she shouted into the house.

'Well, don't leave him standing in the hallway, honey, bring him in,' her father replied.

Lisa sighed and shook her head. 'OK then, here goes,' she muttered under her breath as she ushered him through the hallway and into the spacious kitchen.

Lisa's mother's face dropped as she saw the bouquet he was holding. She clapped her hands together, looking more than a little flustered. 'That's a, err, nice bouquet you have there,' she cooed.

'Oh, they are for you, Mrs Quinn, the chocolates too.' He handed them to her with a charming smile.

'Why, thank you, Sean. These are lovely. You shouldn't have,' she gushed, sniffing the offered flowers. 'I'm not sure about the chocolates, though. I have to look after my figure at my age.'

Sean smiled. 'I wouldn't say that, Mrs Quinn. I can certainly see where Lisa gets her good looks from.'

Flo blushed a little, as did Lisa. *First impressions are going well*, Lisa thought. *Dad's turn now, though.* This thought caused her anxiety.

'Are you trying to say I don't have good looks, young man?' Tony stood up, offering his hand.

Sean swallowed and took the gesture.

Lisa noted that her dad didn't do his usual 'power' handshake that he did when meeting new people he wanted to make an impression on. The one where he pulled the unsuspecting person towards him, making them lose their balance a little and putting them at an instant disadvantage. This time, her father just offered a normal, everyday handshake.

Lisa loved him a little bit more for that.

The man and boy were roughly the same height, but Tony was rounder and had considerably less hair.

'Err, no, not at all, Mr Quinn, I was just commenting—'

'Tony, stop teasing the boy,' Flo said putting her hand on her husband's shoulder.

Tony's face broke into a smile, and as it did, Lisa's heart began to slow down to what she considered a manageable pace.

'I'm sorry, Sean. I'm just kidding. I'm very pleased to meet you. I've been hearing a lot about you.'

Sean accepted the handshake and extended the bottle of red wine he was holding. 'This is for you, Mr Quinn. It's Argentinian. A 1997 vintage, which I'm told was a very good year.'

He handed the bottle to Tony, who took it with a look of surprise. He turned it over in his hands to read the label, to confirm that it was indeed an El Diablo 1997. 'Sean, this must have cost a pretty penny.'

He shrugged and bobbled his head a little. 'I wanted to make a good impression. I hope you like it,' he said, turning towards Lisa, widening his eyes.

Lisa replied with an approving nod.

Tony looked back at the boy. His eyes couldn't hide the sudden suspicion within them. 'This must have cost you upwards of ninety dollars. Can I ask you, son, what do you do for a job?'

Sean smiled. 'My dad owns a motorcycle shop. I mostly do errands and chores. I don't really go out much, so I've got a little bit of savings.'

'Well, I'm impressed. Thank you very much. Would you like to sit down? Flo has made some chicken in basil infused rice; we were just about to eat.'

'We're going to go to the milk bar for a shake after this,' Lisa said, hoping to expediate their exit from this horrible situation. 'We don't want to ruin our appetites, do we Sean?' she asked glaring at him.

Sean cocked his head and smiled. 'There's no rush, Lisa. If your mom's gone to all the trouble, it'd be rude not to eat her food.'

Lisa's shoulders sagged as she sat down on one of the high-backed seats at the island. 'Fine, but just a small bowl, then we're out of here, though. OK?'

Tony fished a corkscrew out of one of the drawers and opened the bottle. He sniffed the wet end of the cork and looked impressed. 'It has an excellent bouquet. I'd offer you a glass, but you're only eighteen and also driving my daughter out tonight.' He smiled. 'So ...'

Sean laughed and held his hand out as if to refuse the offer. 'Thanks, Mr Quinn, but I would have refused anyway. I don't drink. It just doesn't appeal to me.'

Tony smiled as he poured the wine into an expensive looking glass. 'Good man. I'd keep it like that, if I were you. The amount of time alcohol has gotten me into trouble ...'

'Enough with your drink fuelled stories. I'm sure Sean doesn't want to hear about your military days,' Flo interjected.

'No, I know he doesn't,' Lisa agreed, glaring at her father.

They ate the chicken, and Sean and Lisa drank a cloudy lemonade each, and the half-hour they spent in the kitchen passed pleasantly. Eventually, Lisa pushed her plate away from her and stood up. 'OK, Sean, I really think we should be going. The others will be wondering what's happened to us.'

Sean looked at her questioningly before figuring it out and taking her lead. 'Oh, yeah. I'd forgotten about Nichola and Paula. Well, thank you for a lovely evening, Mr Quinn, and I hope you enjoy the rest of that bottle. Mrs Quinn, thank you for the delicious meal and the lemonade.'

'Well, you're quite welcome, Sean. It's been a pleasure to have you,' she replied.

Tony stood and offered his hand to Sean again. He took it and was offered a strong, pumping handshake. 'You drive safe now, son. Remember, you have my most prized possession in your ward tonight.'

'Yes, sir,' Sean replied as he and Lisa made their way out of the kitchen.

As they got to the front door, Lisa heard her father shout from the kitchen. 'Be in before eleven, OK?'

'We will,' Lisa replied. 'See you later.'

Then the front door closed.

~~~~

Flo was opening the box of chocolates as Tony poured another glass of wine. 'I told you he was nice, didn't I?' she stated more than questioned.

Tony was looking at the front door, chewing on his own cheek. 'Hmmm,' he replied.

Flo glared a warning. 'Tony, you promised you'd keep out of it.'

'I know, I know, and I will, but still,' he mused, sniffing the dark liquid in his glass.

15.

'YOUR FOLKS ARE swell,' Sean said, opening the door of the Chevy for her.

Lisa laughed. 'Did you just really say that?' she chided. 'Where are we? In a seventies comedy show?'

Sean laughed as he closed the door behind her. Her window was already down as there was a nice warm breeze in the air. He shrugged. 'Maybe so!'

'You think that?'

'Yeah. Much nicer than mine anyway.'

'Well, you don't have to live with them.'

He smiled as he walked around the front of the car and got into the driver's side. He looked at her as he buckled his seatbelt. 'So, what does your dad do for a living? That's a nice house.'

'I don't really know,' she laughed. 'He doesn't really talk about it. He's some kind of computer analyst or something. He works freelance. He has to go away quite a bit, usually for a few days at a time.'

'Did your mom say he was in the military? He's got some handshake on him for a computer analyst.'

'Yeah. It was before they met. I think that's one of the reasons he left. Anyway'—she wanted to change the subject—'do you want to skip the milk bar and go straight to the parking?' she asked with a shy but excited smile.

She watched as a roguish smile broke on his face. 'You're fucking right, I do,' he laughed, putting the car in drive and pulling out onto the street.

16.

THE EVENING WAS beautiful. Sean parked the car in a quiet lane that overlooked the park by her house, and they sat and talked. They talked about her parents, his parents, school, future ambitions, what colleges they wanted to go to.

But most of all, they laughed.

At some point, a policeman pulled up behind them from out of nowhere and tapped on the windshield. Lisa jumped, terrified at the man suddenly in the window. But Sean, cool as anything, just wound his window down and spoke to the looming figure.

'Can I help you, Officer?' he asked in a polite tone.

'I was wondering what you kids were up to out here in the park,' he replied.

'We're just talking, Officer, nothing else. I promise you.'

The officer shone his torch beam inside the car. He lit up Lisa's, embarrassed face, then he illuminated the back seat. Finally, he shone it back at Lisa. She smiled and gave him a timid wave, instantly feeling stupid for doing it. Then the officer looked away.

'Well, I'm going to have to ask you to move on anyway. There are always bad sorts up this way. You don't want your lovely girlfriend to be in any kind of danger now, do you?'

Lisa giggled a little at the word 'girlfriend.'

'No, you're right, Officer. I was going to take her home soon anyway. It's late.'

'OK, drive safely, son,' he said and walked off.

Lisa felt a little disappointed. 'Are we really going home?' she asked.

# The Boyfriend

Sean winked as he gunned the engine. 'Nope. I know a little place where no one will find us.'

She was grinning as they pulled out of the car park.

They drove in silence for about five minutes before he indicated to turn right onto a small one-lane road. It was covered on both sides by thick, lush foliage. In the twilight of the night, it looked dark and ominous.

'Are you sure were allowed in here? Is it even a road?'

'Yeah, don't worry about it. I used to come down here with my dad riding motorbikes all the time. It opens up out about a mile further on. We'll be well secluded, don't you worry,' he reassured her.

Lisa wasn't so sure. She sat back and fidgeted nervously at her seatbelt.

Five minutes later, the road did open out a bit. However, it was still surrounded by thick trees, and she felt a little *too* isolated. Sean turned into a small outlet in the track and parked the car. As he turned off the engine, he looked at her with a smile. Something about that smile reminded her of a shark looking at its prey in the water.

Suddenly, she wasn't very comfortable.

'Are you OK?' he asked, undoing his seatbelt.

'Yeah. I'm fine,' she replied, the stumble in her voice giving life to the lie.

He put his hands in the air and looked at her. There was a reassuring look on his face. 'Listen, if you want to go home, it's not a problem, you know. I just thought you might have wanted to be totally alone with me at some point tonight.'

He went to put his seatbelt back on, but she stopped him.

Then she unbuckled hers.

'No, it's nothing, I'm just ...'

'Nervous?'

'Yeah, nervous. I've never done anything like this before.'

Sean laughed; it wasn't a harsh noise. To Lisa, it sounded sympathetic and nice. 'You're a virgin?'

Her heart dropped into the pit of her stomach, and she lowered her head, ready to turn back and re-buckle her seat belt.

'Don't sweat it,' he reassured her. 'I'm a virgin too. Look, I know that you don't want to do anything to change that, and I'm cool with it. I mean, I would like to kiss you again. I really did enjoy that the other night.'

She looked up at him. A coy smile on her lips. 'You did?'

'Fuck yeah, I did. You're a dynamite kisser. I mean, I'm a virgin, but I've kissed a few girls. You're the best out of that small list.'

She laughed and turned away, looking at herself in the reflection of the window.

'Come here,' he said softly, putting his arm around her.

His touch sent shivers through her. Nice ones. She allowed herself to be pulled towards him. His hands moved up to her face, and he held her. Where his fingers touched her cheeks, she imagined electric arcs lighting up. She even thought she could feel the tingle of the electricity. There were callouses on the tips of his fingers. *Must be from where he helps his father repair the motorbikes*, she thought, enjoying the rough touch. But right now, all she was really interested in were his deep blue eyes and full lips.

Slowly, he pulled her closer, and their lips met again.

Once more, she sensed the imagery of the electric sparks arching from him to her, with the familiar tingle coursing through her body like a hot flush.

They kissed like that for about half an hour.

At one point, Sean reached up to touch her neck and accidently cupped her breast. Even through the bra and the sweater she was wearing, she felt her nipples stiffen at his touch. Involuntarily, she drew in a deep breath and bit lightly down on his tongue, which was currently exploring her mouth. She wanted to let him but didn't think it would be appropriate to get to second base on their second date. She allowed his hand to linger; it felt nice; it felt right. Ultimately, the decision was taken away from her as his hand, after prolonging its stay maybe a little longer than it should have, continued its way up to her neck.

'I really think we should be getting home now,' she breathed between caresses. Inwardly, she cursed herself for sounding so square, but she knew if this continued … they needed to adhere to her father's wishes and be home before eleven o'clock.

'I know,' he replied in the same fashion. 'I just don't want to.'

# The Boyfriend

She grabbed him by the face and continued to kiss him. 'Neither do I. But I have to.' She pushed him away lightly, hating the void between them when their lips parted.

With a sideways glance and a cheeky grin, she watched him squirm as he tried to hide the erection pushing within the folds of his jeans. Inside, she was proud that she'd managed to do that to him again. Feeling brave, she pointed to it. 'You best not let that policeman see that,' she giggled. 'He might think it's a dangerous weapon.'

As he fumbled, trying to hide it, he smiled an embarrassed grin.

Once he'd sorted himself out, he put his seatbelt back on, started the car, put it into reverse, and slowly pulled onto the track.

Within a few minutes, they were on the open tarmac heading towards Lisa's street.

They were outside her house with ten minutes to spare to her curfew. He killed the engine and looked at her. 'Did you enjoy tonight?' he asked with a wolfish grin.

As she returned his stare, her face gave only a hint of the exhilaration she was feeling. 'Yeah, I did. I was nervous, especially in those trees. But I'm glad we went.'

He smiled again, looking away, pulling his best James Dean. Lisa thought he played that part so well.

'So, when can I see you again?' he asked, still looking out the window.

She shrugged. 'I don't know. Sometime this week, maybe? I do have quite a bit going on, what with the end of the quarter and all, but I'm sure I can fit you in now that you've charmed my parents.'

'Yeah, I did kind of win them over, didn't I?' The wolfish grin resurfaced. Lisa liked it.

Reluctantly, she opened the car door and shot him a look. 'Yeah, you did. I've never seen my dad take to someone so fast. You and him, you could be best buddies.' She climbed out of the car and leaned back in the open window. 'I'm serious, you got along really well. I'll ask if you can come over to study one night next week or something.'

Sean was leaning over too; he was looking up at her. 'That sounds really good, but …'

She felt her stomach drop at the sound of the 'but'. 'But what?' she asked, her face complementing her stomach.

He grinned at her. 'The only end of quarter I've got pending is biology. If you know what I mean?' The wolfish grin was back, enforced by the wink he gave her.

Lisa blushed and shook her head. 'You're incorrigible,' she said, moving away from the window. 'Call me tonight when you get home,' she shouted as she made her way up to the walkway to her house.

~~~~

Sean sat in the car watching her walk away. 'You don't know how right you are,' he whispered. When he turned to face the road, his wolfish grin was gone, his eyes were vacant, and his jaw was fixed. As he pulled away from the house, he tapped his phone and called Jay.

'Sean,' the excited voice on the other end of the phone almost shouted. 'Tell me you did it. Tell me you stuck it to that little shit.'

'Whoa, calm down. Calm the fuck down, will you.'

There was silence on the line, broken only by excited breathing on the other end.

'You didn't, did you?' the disappointed voice spat. There was not only anger and malice in the voice, there was disappointment too.

'No, I didn't. But I did something way better.'

There was another pause, only for a few seconds. 'What? What did you do?'

'I got my feet totally under the table. Her fucking saps of parents loved me. Her old man's a pussy, and her mom is kind of hot. I wouldn't mind taking a bite out of that apple too, once this is over.'

'Why is that better? I need it done soon, man.'

'Chill the fuck out, Jay. Her parents are away next week. Until then, I'll be the model boyfriend. I'll lead the little piglet on, then I'll stick the fuck out of her.' He laughed. There was no humour in it, only malice and hate.

Jay was laughing too. 'Give me an update tomorrow, OK?'

'No worries,' he laughed before hanging up his phone.

17.

THREE DAYS LATER and Lisa was in the locker room after PE. She had just removed her sweaty top after a gruelling session in the gym and was struggling to remove her sports bra so she could shower.

'Come here,' Janice offered as she walked around to help her friend.

Lisa turned, allowing her access to her sweaty back. She sighed as she did.

Janice shook her head as she started to work. 'It feels like I haven't seen anyone for ages. My dad's got a list of chores for me to do every day and wants me reading the fucking classics for English Lit through the summer,' she said.

Lisa knew she wasn't lying. Her father was a notorious task master. A couple of years earlier, James, Janice's brother, had a mental breakdown. It was widely thought that his father had pushed and pushed him, in the end, taking it too far, and it all became too much for him. He had been sent to a psychiatric hospital last Lisa heard. It had hit Janice hard, and there had been concern over her mental health for a while too, but she'd proved everyone wrong by bouncing back.

Everyone except her parents, that was.

And Lisa's dad.

'Can you slide your fingers underneath? I just need this thing off me, it's getting itchy now,' Lisa said as she struggled to lift the bra over her chest.

'So, how did it go with Sean the other night? I haven't had time to ask,' Janice asked.

'Yeah, it was great. We just parked all night and talked.'

Janice slid her fingers underneath the tight, moist elastic and tried to pull it up. The material stretched but just not enough. 'Jesus, Lisa, I hope you didn't have a bra on like this when you were parking.' She laughed.

Lisa turned her head to look at her friend. 'I'll have you know he was a complete gentleman. We went to first base, with just a slight detour to second. I'm not ready to put it all out there, *like someone else we know.*' Her emphasis on the last part of the sentence was meant in jest, and Janice saw it that way.

'Shh, don't tell everyone. You're the only one who knows,' she reprimanded Lisa.

'Ow! Fuck, Janice,' Lisa shouted as they finally managed to pull the bra up over her head. However, the material was now stuck in the scrunchie keeping her hair back in a ponytail.

'Oh shit, sorry,' Janice said, reaching down to pick up her towel before handing it to her.

Lisa, almost bent double, caught the towel and covered herself with it.

'I think you're going to lose either the bra or the scrunchie,' Janice said.

'I don't care either, just get this fucking thing off me,' she half laughed.

Janice pulled at both until something gave. Surprisingly, it was the bra. The elastic snapped back, and Lisa yelped.

She stood, and both girls looked at the side of her breast. A small red line where the elastic had snapped back was forming, just to the side of her nipple.

Janice looked at it, a grimace forming over her mouth. She reached out, as if attempting to sooth it. 'Shit, it's a good thing that missed your nip. That would have stung like a son-of-a-bitch.'

Lisa wrapped the towel around herself, covering her whole body, and shimmied out of her panties from underneath. She then made her way towards the showers.

'So, he was a gentleman? That must have been frustrating for you,' Janice shouted as she got herself undressed.

'Yup, he met my folks and totally won them over. Can you believe that?'

# The Boyfriend

'Your mom, yeah. Your dad ... not so much.'

'He totally did. He came waltzing in with flowers and chocolates and a really expensive bottle of wine,' Lisa explained as she made her way out of the shower, the towel around her. 'It was almost like he knew the chocolates and wine could win them over.'

'Lisa, chocolates and wine will win almost *anyone* over.' Janice looked at her friend before she got into the shower. She took in a sharp breath and pointed at the reddening welt on the side of Lisa's boob. 'Well, I wouldn't let your mom see that. She'll think Sean did it. Let's see how fast his feet are kicked out from under that table then, you know?' she quipped.

Lisa looked down; the red line was already starting to bruise.

Janice entered the shower cubicle. Just before she immersed herself underneath the water, she popped her head around the door. 'Let's meet up tonight. I haven't seen the girls for ages. They're a little too busy now with Ryan and Andrew for little old me. And now that you've got Sean ...'

Lisa was dry now and was clasping a fresh bra on her front prior to twisting it around her back. 'What about the guy you—you know, did it with? Why not go out with him?'

Janice pulled an exaggerated, exasperated face. 'Yeah right, like I want anything to do with that loser.'

'It was just a thought,' she said, looking in the mirror and examining the darkening bruise on her breast.

18.

THE MILK BAR was busy. Every night since it had opened just a few weeks earlier, it had attracted interest from high school kids from all over the area, eager to make it their regular hang out. With the summer vacation looming and the warm nights hanging in the park ahead, they would need somewhere to water themselves for the upcoming onslaught of parading and preening as they vied to attract the opposite sex. Lisa, Janice, Nichola, and Paula had gotten there early to secure a table. They were glad they did.

'I can't believe tomorrow is the last day of school for ten weeks,' Paula said, throwing her head back and laughing. All the others were laughing too. The last day of school was always a time to look forward to. Endless opportunities, hot days, warm nights.

Just bliss.

'Next Friday is on then?' Nichola asked, looking at Lisa. 'Ryan and Andrew asked if they could come over too.'

Lisa pulled a face. 'Nichola, my mom and dad will go ballistic if they know I'm having boys over.'

Paula looked at Lisa, her eyebrows peaked in surprise. 'But it'll be OK to have Sean over, I suppose?'

'No, it won't, actually. I've promised them the only people coming over will be you guys,' she replied, hoping they believed her.

'Why don't I believe you?' Paula asked, pulling her thick drink through the paper straw. 'It's my bet that no sooner they're in the car, before they even hit the freeway, lover boy will be there like a shot.'

'No, he won't, and he's not my lover boy.'

'Don't give me that,' Nichola replied in a high-pitched tone. 'It's been all over school that you two went parking down Glover's Farm Lane.'

Lisa looked at them, shocked. It was her turn to hit the high-pitched notes. 'What?'

'You and Sean, down the Farm Lane. Getting it on, apparently.'

'Who told you that? It's a lie,' she protested, feeling the nerves in her arms beginning to twitch. A blanket of dread descended over her. *Why are people talking about me?*

'You heard it too, didn't you, Janice?' Paula asked, putting the spotlight on Janice.

Janice looked down at the table, anywhere other than looking Lisa in the eye. She nodded, a rather reluctant nod. 'Yeah, I heard it. Yesterday in the lunchroom. Some of the seniors were talking about it.'

Lisa glared, devastation covering her features. 'Why didn't you tell me? You were with me this morning in the showers, you could have said something then.'

'I did ask you about it.'

'Yeah, but you didn't say anything about people talking.' Lisa folded her arms onto the table and dropped her head. 'Oh, shit. If my dad finds out about this, not only am I not going to be able to see Sean again, he'll kill me. They might even cancel their trip.'

All four girls were silent at the table as Lisa sank into depression.

'I'm going to have to call it off with him. I can't have people spreading lies about me over the school. Talking about me as if I'm a tramp.'

Janice leaned over and put her hand on the back of Lisa's head, gently stroking her hair. 'You don't need to do anything like that. We'll put the word out that nothing happened. Everyone will know you're not a slut. Won't we, girls? Anyway, vacation as of tomorrow. By the time we'll get back, one of two things will have happened.'

'What?' Lisa asked.

'Well,' Janice continued with a grin. 'You'll either be yesterday's news, or you'll be knocked up, dropping out, and living over a pizza shop with Sean.'

She glanced around at the others, hoping for a laugh.

Nicola glared at her. 'Listen, of course we'll take care of it. We can't have love's true story going awry because of loose lips, can we?' she said to the table.

'Come on, Lisa,' Paula offered, nudging her friend, who still had her head on the table. 'It's all just bullshit anyway. Tomorrow they'll be talking about … I don't know, maybe about Janice being a lesbian!'

Janice looked up, her face a picture of surprise. 'Yeah? You wish I was a lezbo, bitch,' she quipped, laughing.

Lisa giggled at this. It was only a small sound, but it spoke volumes. Nichola and Paula looked pleased that they'd lifted Lisa's spirits somewhat.

'Come on, the next round of shakes is on me,' Janice offered. 'The tits on the girl behind the counter are totally doing it for me.'

This got everyone laughing as she walked off to the bar.

'I'm sorry about that, Lisa, I didn't mean to accuse you of anything,' Nichola apologised. As Lisa looked at her, she could see the pain on her friend's face; it told her she'd meant what she'd said.

'Well,' Lisa said, picking herself up off the table and wiping her eyes. She didn't want to be the one who brought the evening down. 'I'll tell you something for free. I'm really sorry we didn't do anything now. I mean, if I'm getting called a slut anyway, it's disappointing that I'm accused of doing something I didn't. He did get a little bit of tit action, though; that's about as far as it went.' Lisa began to laugh, eliciting strange looks from her friends. 'The funny thing is … he even apologised for it.'

'Well, there you go,' Paula laughed, breaking the tension around the table. 'You really are a dirty bitch.'

'Listen, you can bring those guys over on Friday if you want,' Lisa said. She was feeling more light-hearted now.

Nichola and Paula looked at each other, raising their eyebrows; when they looked back to Lisa, there were smiles on all their faces.

'Nah,' Paula offered, shaking her head. 'Let's make it a girls' night. Just the five of us, if Kate can make it. Popcorn, movies, makeup, just like old times. What do you say?'

# The Boyfriend

'I say I'm behind that idea, girlfriend. Who needs boys anyway?' Nichola replied, snapping her fingers in a lame attempt to be sassy.

Janice had heard the conversation from over by the counter. 'Amen to that, sisters,' she shouted, sticking her tongue between her two fingers, and flicking it back and forth.

This grossed them all out, and they fell about laughing.

'You are one weird sister,' Nichola shouted over to her.

'You better believe it. I wouldn't have trusted me not to put a little something in your drink, girlfriend,' Janice laughed as she handed the cups over the table.

Lisa was laughing too, but there was an inner dialogue going on, a real conversation with herself. *I think I do! I think I need boys in my life, or maybe just one in particular.* Regardless of these thoughts, she continued to laugh and joke until the night was over and the bar was closing.

~~~

'Do you think it's safe to cut through the park?' Janice asked, looking at the dark expanse before them. Nichola and Paula had gone off the other way, towards their homes, leaving Janice and Lisa faced with either cutting through the park and getting home on time or walking around it and getting home at least ten minutes late.

They decided to cut through.

'What's the worst that could happen?' Lisa asked, offering her arm to her friend.

'Well, we could get accosted, kidnapped, raped, and mutilated. We could even get eaten by a British werewolf,' Janice offered.

Lisa thought about it, nodded, and grinned. 'I'd go with the werewolf.'

'Every day of the week.' Janice took the offered arm, and the pair made their way into the scary darkness.

'Do you think your mom and dad are going to go away more often if you're good for this week?' Janice asked.

Lisa thought it was more like a question to pass the time and distance of their walk than one with any real meaning to it. She gazed into the darkness before her; the trees were impenetrable black holes, and her imagination conjured all sorts of horrors lurking within their shadows. The noise of the wind rustling through them only added to the spooky ambience. She'd passed through this park a million times before and had been OK every single time; she had no reason to believe this time would be any different. *I wish I hadn't mentioned the werewolf, though,* she thought nervously.

'I think that once they see I can be trusted, then—' she began, but her words were cut off mid-sentence as a sudden noise, a loud snap from the blackness of a copse of trees behind them, made them jump. Lisa squealed a little.

Janice clung to Lisa's arm, seemingly for dear life. 'What was that?' she whispered.

Lisa was suddenly aware of how alone they were. She looked behind her, towards the dim lights of the milk bar where they had been safe not ten minutes earlier. Mentally, she calculated how long it would take them to run back that way, or if it would be safer to head into the park in the hope of getting to the gate on the other side, the same side as their homes. Her heart was pounding ten to the dozen, and she could feel the hated sensation of blood throbbing in her ears. 'It was probably nothing. Come on, let's not hang around to find out, though. Let's just get out of here.'

The snapping noise came again.

The sound wasn't particularly loud, but in the quiet of the night, and to Lisa's heightened sensitivity, it sounded like thunder rumbling in the heavens. This time, it was accompanied by the rustling of leaves. She looked in the direction the sound was coming from, but there was nothing to see. Nothing out of the ordinary except for the impenetrable obsidian of the trees, the vast expanse of the field, and the surrounding dark foliage.

Panic was rising in her stomach, making her feel sick. 'Someone's in the bushes,' she whispered to Janice, who was still holding on to her as if her existence depended on the attachment. 'We should run.'

'I think you're right,' Janice replied in a similar whisper. Her voice was stuttering as if she was cold. Lisa knew she couldn't be, as the night was still warm.

The snapping came again. It sounded nearer this time.

'Go!' Lisa shouted, and both girls readied themselves to sprint across the park towards the faraway exit.

'Woah! What's the rush?' A male voice shouted from out of the trees. Both girls turned to see where it had come from, *who* it had come from.

Sean Knight stepped out of the darkness; his hands were raised.

'Sean,' Lisa gasped in relief.

Janice looked at him, a scowl etched on her face.

'Sorry for scaring you girls.' He smiled as he made his way out of the bushes. He was buttoning the fly on his trousers as he did. 'I was trying to catch up, but I needed to take a leak.'

'This is Sean?' Janice asked, hitching her thumb towards him but looking at Lisa.

Lisa nodded. She was finding it difficult to speak in between deep breaths. She hadn't realised she'd been so scared. Without thinking, she flung herself at him and wrapped her arms around his shoulders. 'Oh, thank God it's you,' was all she managed.

Sean was laughing as he pried her off him. He looked at her through squinted eyes. 'Are you OK?' he asked Lisa, but his eyes brought Janice into the question too.

'Yeah, we just thought ... well, you know, you hear stories,' Janice replied, looking into the dark environment around them.

'I saw you come out of the milk bar and was trying to catch up. You shouldn't cross the park on your own, not in the dark. You never know who could be lurking.'

Lisa looked at him, her eyes glassy with tears, but she was smiling. 'Yeah, there could be weirdos peeing in the bushes,' she said, giving him a little punch.

He laughed, rubbing his arm theatrically. 'Yeah, there's some real perverts out there, you know. Come on, let me walk you home.' He turned to Janice and offered her his hand. 'Hey,' he said with a smile. 'Lisa is obviously not going to do it, so I'll introduce myself. I'm Sean, Lisa's ... erm, friend.'

Janice flung her arms around him then. Once she peeled herself off, she accepted his hand and pumped it, laughing nervously. 'From what I've heard, you two are a little more than friends,' she laughed.

Lisa continued to walk. 'Janice, you're embarrassing me,' she said in a sing song voice.

'Oh? Well, excuse me.'

The trio made their way across the park, laughing and joking as they went. Mostly poking fun at Sean for taking a leak in the park, on his own, in the middle of the night.

They walked Janice to her front door. 'Well, thank you, you pair of lovebirds. I'll leave you to get in trouble from your dad for getting home late on your own.' She opened the door and turned to face them. 'Sean, it was nice meeting you. Lisa, you two are adorable.' She laughed.

Lisa felt herself turn crimson, while Sean just laughed. 'Nice meeting you too, Janice. Maybe we can double date sometime?'

Lisa looked at her, cocking her head to one side and raising her eyebrows.

Janice rolled her eyes. 'Yeah, well, maybe once I find someone who's worth dating, I'll take you up on that offer,' she said, giving Lisa a wink.

Lisa nodded. 'OK, I've got to go. My dad'll have the search helicopters out looking for me if I'm not back soon. Goodnight.'

'See you in school tomorrow,' she said getting ready to close the door. 'Sean, it was lovely to meet you. I feel like I know you already with the way she talks about you ... all the time.'

Before Lisa had a chance to reply, Janice closed the door, leaving her and Sean on the stoop, alone in the moonlight.

It was only a three block walk back to her house. They looked at each other, and Lisa turned away, playing with the hair behind her ear. Sean took her hand, and they walked on.

'I've just thought of something. Where's your car?' she asked.

'Outside the milk bar. I'll go back and get it after I've dropped you off,' he said, shrugging off the question.

'I'll get my dad to drop you off. I can't have my knight in shining armour going back through the park on his own.'

'I like what you did there. You know, knight in shining armour, Sean Knight ... Shining Knight?'

'I have no idea what you're talking about,' she replied, grinning.

'Well, I don't need a lift to get back though the park. I'm a big boy, you know,' he stated, smiling at her.

Lisa felt her heart pound in her chest and her throat. She couldn't believe she was actually going to do the thing she wanted to do. She turned towards him and cupped her hand between his legs. 'Are you now?' she asked, a wicked smile across her face.

Sean's face registered the shock. His eyes went wide, and his mouth hung open. For once, for the first time since she'd met him, he seemed completely lost for words.

Happy that she'd done it, she turned away and continued walking ahead.

'*What the fuck?*' he gasped from behind her. A smile stretched itself across her face.

The rest of the three-block walk was spent kissing and fooling around.

'Well, this is me,' she said reluctantly as they reached the gate of the nice house on the nice street.

Sean looked at it, running his fingers through his hair. 'So, it is.' He pulled her close. She allowed herself to be pulled. He looked at her for a moment and then kissed her.

'Sean,' she whispered.

'What?' he replied.

'Next week, when my mom and dad go away, are you going to come over?'

He pulled away and held her at arm's length. As he gazed at her, she thought she might drown in the deep blue of his eyes.

'Do you think it's wise?' he asked. 'I mean, I do want to, but … your dad!'

She smiled and looked at the ground. After a moment or two, she looked back up at him. 'You really are different, aren't you?'

'What do you mean?' he asked.

'Well, I'm guessing any other guy would have jumped at that invitation. You thought about my reputation and my relationship with my father. Not just about yourself.'

He held her hand, put it up to his mouth, and kissed it. 'When you've got something special …' He paused, his eyes keeping hers within their hold. 'It's sometimes worth the wait.'

She looked at him, a tear about to fall. He reached in and lightly brushed it away with his thumb.

'I have to go in now,' she said shyly.

'I know.' His wink melted her heart.

They kissed again, and gently, she pulled away, walking backwards towards her house. She kept hold of his hand for as long as she could. 'Be safe through the park.'

He gave her a smile and nodded. 'I will. I'll call you when I get to the car.'

'Make sure you do.'

'I will. Goodnight, Lisa.'

'Goodnight, Sean.'

As he made his way back along the street, he looked back, just once and waved.

Floating as if on a cloud, Lisa made her way up the path. She opened the door and slipped silently inside.

19.

AS SEAN RE-ENTERED the park, he allowed the darkness to envelop him. He welcomed it. It made him feel safe. He checked behind to see if there was anyone about. There wasn't, so he stopped in the centre of the field, lifted his head up towards the moon, and howled.

He began to jump around in excitement, enjoying the anonymity of the dark. When he was done, he fished in his trouser pocket and retrieved his phone. He laughed as he put the device to his ear. If there had been anyone passing, they would have thought him mad.

'I fucking NAILED it tonight,' he shouted down the phone. 'She invited me over next week when her parents are away. The stupid little bitch actually *trusts* me.'

'Excellent news,' Jay replied on the other end of the line. 'You're going to be big news after this.'

Sean let out an excited laugh. It made him sound like one of those stupid hillbilly caricatures on TV he hated, but right now he didn't care. The scene had been set. 'The stupid bitch really *likes* me. She even thinks I like her back.'

'Oh, you'll like her well enough when you're sliding it deep inside the little cunt, when she's screaming for you to stop.'

Sean was almost crying with laughter. 'You won't let me down, will you? This'll get me in, won't it?'

'Are you kidding me? You'll be a fucking legend after this. Taking a rich snob like her and making her want it, in her own home? This is an instant in.'

Sean looked at the star filled sky and howled again.

'There's no time for patting yourself on the back just yet. You need to get the job done. The sooner that little fuck gets what's coming to her, the better.'

Sean hung up his phone and made his way out of the park and towards the milk bar, where his father's Chevy was parked in the empty lot.

There was a little more than a spring in his step.

## 20.

The school year ended, and the long days of summer began with a stretch and a yawn, a lazy start to what she was hoping would be a summer of love and kisses. The days passed with telephone flirting and evenings hanging in the milk bar.

Soon enough, it was time for Lisa's parents to embark on their adventure, leaving her to embark on her own.

'ARE YOU SURE we've got everything? Passports? Insurance? Tickets?' Tony Quinn was fussing around the house like a whirlwind. In and out of every room looking and searching for things that might have been forgotten. Flo was at the island in the kitchen, propping her head on her hand and rolling her eyes. Lisa was sat opposite her, eating a bowl of cereal.

'You know I packed everything last night, don't you?' Flo sighed.

Lisa nodded with a mouth full of cornflakes.

'I don't know why I bother. It's the same every time we go on vacation. I never learn.'

'Honey, have you seen my sunglasses, you know, my vacation ones?' he shouted down the stairs.

'They're in your travel bag,' Flo replied, sounding bored.

'Are you sure? You know, the dark ones, not my driving ones.'

'Yes, Tony, I'm sure. I put them in there last night.'

'What about the currency calculator?'

'Oh, for fucks sake,' Flo shouted, standing up. 'That's an app on your phone,' she snapped.

The surprise of her mother swearing caused Lisa to laugh and spit cornflakes out of her mouth, over the countertop.

Flo moved away from the island, and Lisa watched her go to the bottom of the stairs. 'Tony, the taxi will be here in a few minutes. I packed *everything* last night while you were working. Now come down and enjoy breakfast with your little girl and your wife, because if you carry on like this while we're on vacation, it might well be your last.'

Lisa was enjoying the performance between mouthfuls.

Eventually, her father made his way downstairs. He looked flustered, agitated as he walked into the kitchen. 'Hey, babyface,' he greeted his daughter, absently kissing her on the top of her head. 'Is there any coffee?'

Flo walked in behind him. She stopped and put her hands on her hips. 'I don't think coffee is a good idea. You've got enough stress already.'

'Come on, Daddy, have something to eat and drink some OJ with me. I'm not going to see you now for almost two weeks.'

Tony ran his hands through what was left of his hair and breathed a resigned sigh. 'So, you've packed everything?' he asked Flo again.

'*Everything*!' she shouted.

He heaved another sigh, then sat at the island.

'Daddy, stop stressing; you're only away for a few days.'

'I know, I know, but sometimes I just can't … let go. You know that,' he replied, rubbing his hands together.

Lisa got him a bowl and filled it half-full with muesli, then got the carton of milk out of the refrigerator and poured some into the bowl. She gave him a kiss on the cheek and then kissed and hugged her mom. 'While you two stress birds fight it out, this little chick has to go to school. So, I'll see you guys in ten days. Have a boat load of fun, OK?' She grabbed her bag from the back of the chair. 'And send me loads of pics, OK?' As she made her way out of the door, she turned back to them. They were both looking back at her.

'I love you guys,' she said.

'We love you too, honey,' they replied, almost in unison.

With that, she left the house.

The next time she saw them, she was a completely different person.

## 21.

AT LUNCH TIME, as her mother and father were stepping onto the plane, Lisa sat alone outside the milk bar. It was a beautiful day, and she was enjoying the feeling of the sun on her face. Her peace was not long lived, as she was joined by three excited and babbling witches; Nichola, Paula, and Janice.

'Sooooo, today's the day then, huh?' Nichola asked, bubbling with excitement.

Lisa looked up from her lunch, groaning inwardly.

'Have they gone? Are we free to roam your house for a full week?' Paula added.

Knowing her peaceful lunch was well and truly over, she smiled at the excited gaggle before her. 'Yes, my parents have gone.' She looked at her watch. 'Right now, they'll be boarding a plane to Spain. So, in answer to your question, yes, you are more than welcome to come and roam around my house for the full length of their vacation.'

'Can we ask the guys over?' Paula asked a little tentatively.

Lisa pulled a wide, humourless face. She clicked her tongue behind her teeth. 'Paula, I don't know if I'm comfortable having a bunch of guys at my house. I mean, I don't even know them.'

Paula raised her hands as if to stop her and turned away, looking a little annoyed. 'All right, all right. I was just asking.'

'I was thinking about a pyjama party tonight, like we talked about before. A little make up, a little booze. What do you think?'

Paula perked up instantly. 'What time were you thinking?' she asked, a smile threatening to crack her sullen face.

'About seven-thirty. Bring your own booze. I don't think I'll get served at the store ...' she began to twirl her hair, '... because I look so young and innocent.'

The others laughed.

'Maybe that would be a good reason to invite the guys,' Janice interrupted. 'You know, so they can get the booze.'

Lisa sighed. 'Let me think about it. I've got loads of stuff to do in the house. I'll call you all later.' She stood up, tossed her trash into the trashcan, and headed off towards the gates of the park and home.

'We're so asking the boys tonight,' Nichola said as their friend walked off. 'I bet Sean will be there.'

'Totally,' Paula said in agreement.

They all stood up and headed inside the bar.

## 22.

LISA BUSIED HERSELF cleaning the house once she got home. Even though her mother always kept it immaculate, she still wanted to give it a once over before her friends arrived. The vacuum cleaner and her loud music drowned out all the other noises, and she missed her phone ringing three times. When she was done, she looked at the screen; it informed her of the missed calls and one voicemail message. The missed calls were from Sean, Nichola, and Sean, in that order. She selected the button for VOICEMAIL and listened.

It was from Nichola.

'Lisa, we totally got carded at the Seven Eleven. So, Ryan and Andrew are going to get us some vodka and bring it over later on if that's cool. They won't be staying; apparently, there's some sports thing happening tonight that they don't want to miss. Hope this is OK with you. See you at seven-thirty.'

Lisa clicked her phone off and rolled her eyes. It really wasn't OK. She knew Nichola and Paula would start to make excuses for the guys to come in, then they'd want them to stay for just a little bit, just for one drink. She was fuming to herself as she put the vacuum cleaner away. 'Why the hell did I trust them *not* to ask the guys?' she mumbled, making her way out of the living room and towards the kitchen. She toyed with the idea of asking Sean now that the others would be coming, then thought that Janice would be on her own if she did that, and she wasn't about to let her best friend spend the night as the spare part.

Still fuming, but at least a little calmer, she called Sean. He answered on the third ring.

'Hey, are you lonely already?' he joked.

Lisa smiled as she held the phone to her ear. 'Kind of,' she replied.

'I could be there in half an hour, you know.'

'I know, and I kind of wish you were.'

'Well, all I'm doing tonight is a whole lot of nothing. So, if you want me, just holler.'

'I will. I was thinking we could do something tomorrow. You know, take advantage of my parent's vacation, and go and drive somewhere?'

He was silent on the other end of the line for a few moments. Lisa's heart began to pound again, thinking she'd pushed it too far. 'That's a great idea,' he replied eventually.

Her heart leaped again, then, in anticipation of what she was going to say next, it continued its rampage. 'Maybe we could find somewhere to ...' she paused; the words caught in her throat. 'Stay the night,' she finished, her mouth totally dry. She could hardly believe she was saying these things.

'Really?' Sean sounded shocked.

The words nearly caught in her throat as she said them. 'Yeah, really.'

'Well, OK then. I'll take a look online for somewhere and sort it all out. I'll see you tomorrow.'

As she hung up, she really couldn't believe what she'd just done.

With sweaty palms, she called Janice.

The line was busy. She put her phone back in her pocket and continued to put away the vacuum cleaner.

A few moments later, her phone rang again. It was Janice. 'Hey, honey, just getting ready to party at your house. What can I do for you, sweetie?'

'You'll never guess what's just happened,' she gasped.

'Whoa, slowdown, girlfriend. What has just happened?'

'Me and Sean are going to drive somewhere tomorrow. We're going to stay over.'

Janice fell silent on the other end. 'What?' she finally asked, sounding as excited as Lisa felt.

'Yeah. Do you want to know the worst thing? It was all my idea.'

'Your idea?' Janice almost spat down the phone.

'Yeah, mine. Am I a slut, or what?' she laughed.

'Well, it sounds like you're about to join the club,' Janice laughed.

'What club?'

Janice tutted. 'Duh! *The done it* club.'

'Oh, yeah,' Lisa laughed again. 'Listen, don't tell the girls tonight, though. I don't want anyone else to know, at least until ...'

'Until they've done it themselves?'

'Something like that.'

'The way those two are going with those guys, I don't think they'll be too far behind,' Janice said. Lisa could hear the humour in her voice. 'OK, your secret's safe with me. If they ask where you are tomorrow, I'll tell them that you've gone to your aunt's house or something.'

'Thanks, Janice, I knew I could count on you. You really are my best friend.'

'I know, sweetie. Now, fuck off with your neediness and let me get ready, OK?'

23.

NICHOLA AND JANICE arrived at Lisa's house together. Kate had called and cancelled at the last moment, but that was nothing new with her; they had been seeing less of her as the year wore on. Paula had called ahead; she was running a bit late. There was a problem with the guys getting the alcohol, and she was meeting them somewhere before bringing it back to the house.

The three of them were sporting their pyjamas and sitting in the living room, doing each other's makeup. Lisa was cross-legged on the floor, while Nichola put some finishing touches on her face as Janice brushed her hair. 'We've got to make you look beautiful for tomorrow night now, don't we?' Janice said, with a wicked smile.

Lisa turned and glared at her. *If looks could kill,* she thought, *I'd obliterate you right now.*

'Watch it, I nearly took your eye out then,' Nichola shouted, putting the mascara on the floor. She looked at the two girls and cocked her head to the side. 'Why? What's happening tomorrow night?' she asked.

'Janice, you promised,' Lisa protested.

'I'm sorry.' She smirked with a playfully deviant grin. 'It just kind of popped out.'

'What's happening tomorrow night?' Nichola asked again.

Lisa sighed and shook her head. 'Sean's taking me away for a night in a hotel.'

Nichola's face fell in surprise. 'WHAT?' she shouted. 'Just you and him?'

# The Boyfriend

She jumped up and began dancing about the room, laughing. 'Oh my God, you're gonna do it ... You're gonna do it ... Lisa's gonna do it ... She's going to pop her cherry!'

Lisa felt her face flush while Janice continued brushing her hair.

'It's no big deal. It's nothing like you think it is. We're just going to see how we get along together for a day or two.'

Nichola shook her head and sat back down. 'Girl, you'll be getting along all right. You'll be getting *it on* all night long. Shit, if this is the case, then we need to make you extra beautiful. This is going to take a lot of hard work.' She picked up her cell phone.

'Who are you calling?' Lisa asked.

'Paula. I need to find out where she is. We're going to need a lot more booze to get that filthy mouth of yours loose.'

She walked away with the phone to her ear, and Lisa turned to Janice. 'I thought you weren't going to say anything,' she snapped, the annoyance evident in the hiss of her voice.

'I couldn't help myself. Lisa, this is huge. It's not every day you lose your virginity to a hottie. I thought it should be something the girls were in on.'

'Well, they're certainly in on it now.'

Nichola came back, swiping her phone off as she did. 'She'll be here in about ten minutes. Ryan is giving her a lift.'

Lisa's shoulders slumped a little. 'Ryan's coming?' she asked.

'Relax, he's just dropping her off with the liquor, and then they're all off to watch a game or something.'

'All?' Lisa asked.

'Yeah, Ryan, Andrew, and the others.'

Lisa looked away, a long breath escaping through her nostrils. She knew the girls were going to want the guys to come in. It would be for ten minutes tops, then half an hour, then before Lisa knew it, they would have been there all night. She could feel the evening getting away from her already, and it hadn't even begun.

Ten minutes of intense hair and makeup later, the front doorbell rang.

'That'll be Paula,' Nichola shouted and ran to open the door. Lisa and Janice followed closely behind.

As the door was opened, Lisa's fear was realised. Paula was there with four grinning boys leering in behind her. She had an apologetic look on her face. 'Lisa, the guys just wanted to know if they could use your bathroom before they leave.'

She closed her eyes and fumed a little more.

'Hey, just a quick leak and we're out of your hair, is that OK?' the first boy, who was wearing a baseball cap, back to front, asked, grinning. She recognised him as Ryan from the milk bar the other night.

'Yeah, OK. Listen, I'm not being rude or anything, but you'll have to go after that. If my dad finds out ...'

'Great, thanks' Ryan, said as he and the three other boys barged into the house carrying plastic bags filled with bottles and cans.

'Where should I put these?' another boy, Andrew, asked, holding the bags up.

'In the kitchen if you would,' Lisa replied, pointing behind her.

Another boy strutted in, looking all around him. 'Wow, this is a nice house,' he marvelled, taking in the grandeur of the hallway that led to the living room and kitchen.

'Thanks, my dad works a lot to afford it,' Lisa replied, not really knowing what to say.

She heard the boy in the kitchen putting the bottles on one of the marble counters, and then she heard the unmistakable hiss of four bottles being opened. She wrinkled her brow as she looked around.

Andrew was coming out of the kitchen with four opened beers.

'I thought you guys were just going to the bathroom and then leaving,' she said, her eyes flicking from the open bottles to Paula.

'Oh, Lisa, come on, relax a little. The guys have just driven me all the way over here. Can't they just have one little beer before they leave?' she asked, looking pleadingly towards her host.

Lisa looked away before she said something she might regret. She was angry with Paula, but then she saw Nichola taking one of the beers from the other boy and giving him a kiss on the cheek.

'Come on, Lisa. They'll be here for an hour, and then they'll leave. Anyway, with the news that you just gave us, aren't *we* allowed to have a little fun?'

# The Boyfriend

Lisa turned to look at Janice, who was standing on the stairs behind her. She shrugged and pulled a 'I don't mind' face.

'OK,' she relented. 'But only for one hour. Do me a favour, though, please don't break anything. My dad will kill me if anything's broken.'

Ryan smiled at her and turned to the open front door. He thrust his head outside and shouted. 'It's cool, guys, come on in.'

Lisa' stomach flipped. 'I ... no,' she stammered.

Ryan brought his head back inside; he was laughing. 'Relax, I'm joking. There's only us here.'

She closed her eyes and sighed before managing to force a small laugh herself.

He grinned. 'See, relaxing already.' He pushed past her and entered the living room, where the guys, Paula, and Nichola had all congregated.

'Janice, what are we going to do if they don't leave?'

Janice was looking past her at one of the other boys, who was sitting perched on the arm of the couch. She was shaking her head. 'I don't know, but the ass on that one there is F-I-N-E fine.' She made her way down the stairs and into the living room with the others.

Lisa shook her head and entered the kitchen. She looked at the beer and vodka bottles on the counter, and all the bottles of cola too. She decided that her best course of action would be to pour herself a large drink. 'If you can't beat them ...' she said to herself. 'I might as well get in the mood,' she finished, clinking ice into a tall glass.

24.

THE NIGHT WASN'T going *that* bad. It had been well over two hours since the boys had turned up and stayed; and now there was a nice alcohol buzz happening around the revellers. Lisa had started to lighten up after her third vodka and coke, which in turn allowed the other girls to let their hair down, and now everyone was enjoying themselves.

Paula and Ryan were sat next to each other on the couch; they were laughing and holding hands. Lisa had noted they hadn't been able to take their hands off each other all night. Nichola and Andrew were sat on the floor, equally as flirtatious

Janice had been talking to one of the other boys, Clinton, and it was obvious they had some sort of connection. That just left the last boy, one she had never met before, Peter. They were having a good time, but she had been careful to keep a decent distance from him. They were currently sat at the island in the kitchen.

'You do know that you're gorgeous, don't you?' Peter smiled at her. There was a mischievous look on his face, and he raised his eyebrows, nodding towards her. 'Even with all that shit on your face,' he laughed.

Lisa remembered that she still had a face that was half-finished with make-up. 'Oh,' she laughed, attempting to rub it off. 'I forgot about that.'

'Whoa, stop. You're going to make yourself look like KISS.'

Lisa couldn't help but laugh at this comment, imagining herself with black stars around her eyes or looking like the legendary bass player.

'So, are you, like, with anyone?' he asked as he looked around, watching everyone else getting it on.

She smiled and nodded.

He pulled a face and rolled his eyes. 'Figures. A beautiful girl like you, you're not going to stay single for long. Is it serious?'

'It's kind of new, but kind of serious too,' she replied, taking another sip of her drink.

He sat back in his chair and sighed. 'Story of my life,' he said as he reached over the counter to grab his half-finished bottle of beer. He knocked it over accidently, and the frothy liquid spilled everywhere, dripping off the table and onto the floor.

'Oh, shit. I'm so sorry,' he said, jumping up.

Everyone in the living room turned to see what the fuss was in the kitchen.

'Shit, Pete, what have you done?' Ryan asked, looking a little angry.

Pete shrugged as he looked into the living room with an embarrassed smile.

'It's OK,' Lisa shouted as she got up from her high-backed chair. 'It was an accident. I'll clean it up.'

As she stood up, her head began to whirl a little, and she felt unsteady on her feet. She took a moment to compose herself, laughing. *No more vodka for me,* she thought, bending down to open the cleaning cupboard.

She turned around and was shocked to see Peter leaning over her with a strange look on his face. 'It was my accident, Lisa. Give me the stuff and I'll clean it up.' He held out his hand to accept the cleaning materials.

'No, it's fine,' she replied, turning back to the cupboard, hoping the boy would go away. 'I'll do it. It's no problem.'

She manoeuvred herself past him. As she did, he reached out and grabbed her. He lunged forward in a clumsy attempt to kiss her.

She turned and, without thinking too much about what she was doing, slapped him hard across the face. 'What do you think you're doing?' Anger was welling inside her.

Peter smiled as his hand came away from his face, he looked at it as if he was expecting to see blood. 'Come on, Lisa, you've been giving me the come-on all night. I only wanted a little kiss, nothing more. What do you say, huh?'

He lunged at her again. She slapped out one more time and connected a heavy-handed smack. It struck him across his face and the bridge of his nose. Once again, he brought his hand up to his face to see if he was bleeding.

Although his eyes were watering heavily, there was no blood.

Lisa backed away until she hit the side of the island. Her arms reached around and grabbed it, more for a connection to something solid than for support. Her eyes were wide, and her mouth was hanging open. She had never hit anyone before. The adrenaline in her body was peaking. 'I think you should leave,' she breathed. It was an effort to form the words, as she could feel herself hyperventilating. 'You and your friends have to go.'

Without warning Peter lashed out at her and smacked her across the face. He put his whole weight behind the swing, and the force of the impact almost knocked her off her feet. It would have if she hadn't been leaning against the island.

There was a scream from somewhere in the living room. All Lisa could make of it was that it was female. Which one of the girls had issued it? She couldn't tell, and right at that moment, she didn't care. It was the first time she had ever been hit in her life. The sting was unmerciful. When her vision restored itself from the blur it had become, she looked up and around the room. She could feel the heat of the welt where Peter's hand had made contact. If she had been looking in a mirror, would she have been able to make out the unmistakable pattern of a man's hand?

There was a line of drool hanging from Peter's mouth as he gaped, angered and shocked at what he had just done.

'Pete, what the fuck are you doing, man?' Clinton, the boy who Janice had been speaking with, appeared in the kitchen doorway. His face gave away the fact that he was struggling with what required his attention first.

'This little bitch likes to tease,' Peter seethed through his teeth.

'Come on, man, leave it.' Clinton grabbed his friend by the hands and pulled him away from Lisa, back towards the sink.

'Fuck that! She came at me first, man. The uppity little bitch needs a lesson.' As he hissed the words, thick, white spittle flew from his mouth.

'Yeah, well, it looks like you've delivered that lesson. Now it's time to get the fuck out of here.' Clinton disappeared into the living room. He returned a few moments later with everyone else in tow.

The girls' faces were ashen and pale. They looked at Lisa, who was defiantly refusing to cry as she nursed the dirty red welt on her face.

'What happened here?' Paula asked, running over to her friend, lifting her face to inspect the red mark. She gasped, putting her hand over her mouth. The shock that registered on her face finally pushed Lisa over the edge, and she began to sob.

Nichola turned to Peter. 'Get the fuck out of this house,' she spat.

'Whoa, hang on just a minute,' Ryan started. 'We don't know what happened here. For all we know, she attacked him. Look at his face, it's red as fuck.'

'I don't care,' Paula began. 'Look at her.'

Janice had made her way into the kitchen and was putting her arms around Lisa. 'You guys should definitely go,' she said without looking at any of them.

'We're not going anywhere,' Andrew snarled. The aggression in his voice was shocking. 'We came here to party, and this little incident isn't going to change that.'

Nichola was raging; her face was flushed, and she was baring her teeth. 'Paula,' she hissed. 'Tell your boyfriend that the night's over. Tell him and his goons to get the fuck out of here, right now.'

Andrew looked at Paula with a wrinkle in his brow. 'Paula, you said—'

'I don't care what I said, Andrew. My fight's not with you. It's with your thug of a friend who likes to hit girls.'

'Well, if we're going, we're taking the liquor with us,' Ryan snapped, as he began to collect the bottles together, putting them into the plastic bags they had brought them in.

The other boys looked at him.

'We're leaving? Just like that?' Peter asked. 'After what that bitch did to me?'

Ryan nodded. 'We've outstayed our welcome, and we should just go,' he said, picking up one of the bags.

'Please, just leave,' Lisa pleaded. Her voice was wavering, but there was relief in it.

The guys collected their things and left. Ryan gave Paula a little kiss as he passed her. Andrew gave Nichola one too, though she turned her head so he had to kiss her cheek.

Clinton was holding Janice's hand as he, too, walked out.

'You fucking skank,' Peter hissed through clenched teeth as he moved out of the kitchen towards the door on the other side of the hallway.

Lisa recoiled as if she'd been slapped again.

The slamming of the front door heralded the boys' exit from her house. As Lisa gazed around at her friends, the sense of relief that had descended over her was short lived.

All she received from them were hostile looks.

'What the hell was all that about?' Nichola snapped, her words stinging Lisa almost as much as the slap from Peter had.

Paula looked down her nose at Lisa. 'Way to ruin a fun evening, Lisa,' she said, brushing past her and heading towards the living room. She picked up her bag that contained her clothes, opened it, and began to take things out.

'What are you doing?' Lisa asked.

Paula looked at her and hissed. 'I'm going somewhere fun.'

Nichola was doing the same; trying her best to not make eye contact with Lisa.

'You too?' Lisa asked, her lips beginning to tremble.

Both girls had put clothes on over their pyjamas and looked in a hurry to leave. Lisa turned to Janice for solace. Her face was filled with pain, and tears were already falling down her still reddening cheeks.

Janice looked back at her; her face was a true dichotomy. 'Lisa, I …' she began.

'I know what you're going to say. Just go. I *want* you to go. I want to be on my own. Go on, go with them.'

Janice put her head down as she walked past. She dressed in complete silence.

When they were done, they filed past Lisa, heading for the door. She refused to let them see her sobbing, even though it was all she wanted to do. She opened the front door, and they trudged out, one by one, heads down and silent.

'If you want to go with those assholes and bail on one of your friends, then be my guest,' she whispered. 'It shows me just how much you've all changed.'

Paula looked at her; Lisa could see tears in her eyes too. 'Ever since you got with Sean, you've changed, Lisa.'

'Yeah? Well maybe it's for the better, because I wouldn't just up and leave for a guy with asshole friends.' She shook her head and sniffed. 'Just get out. All of you,' she demanded.

Nichola looked at her as she left the house. 'I'll call you, OK?'

'Don't bother,' she spat and slammed the door behind them, leaving them stranded on the path.

As the door clicked into place, her heart broke. She leaned back against the heavy wood and slid down, crouching on the floor, holding her knees to her chest. Sobs wracked her body as she cried. Questions regarding how her friends could have deserted her—that she'd been the one who had been attacked, in her own home, and none of them were on her side—played a merry dance in her head

'Fuck them,' she stuttered between sobs. 'Fuck them all,' she whispered, banging the back of her head against the door.

25.

A SHORT WHILE later, she had no way of telling how long she'd been crying, Lisa gained control of her emotions. She wiped away the tears from her cheeks and eyes and, wincing at the pain of where she had been hit, got up from the floor. A shudder ran through her as the chill of the house and the memory of what had happened hit her. Her exposed flesh was suddenly covered in goosebumps. Wrapping her arms around herself, she moved into the living room and began to tidy up the mess that had been abandoned when everyone had unceremoniously left.

There was a strong smell of beer in the room, and it prompted her to remember what she went into the cupboard for in the first place. There was beer drying on the counter and on the floor. She went over and tested it with her foot; it had turned sticky. She shook her head.

'How did it all go so wrong, so fast?' she asked herself, making her way back towards the cupboard to get to the cleaning things.

The shrill noise of her cell phone ringing made her jump.

*Yeah right, like I'm going to answer that,* she thought, snarling her lip. 'Fucking skank! That piece of shit called me a fucking skank.' The anger was building up inside again. 'I'm no fucking skank,' she shouted, banging her hands on the counter of the island.

The phone rang again. This time she wanted to answer it; she wanted to give her *so called friends* a piece of her mind. She searched everywhere for the device but couldn't locate where the noise was coming from.

Then it rang off.

This annoyed her, so she began to throw the cushions of the couch all around the room. Finally, she found what she was looking for and looked at the screen. She wasn't quite ready for what it said.

'SEAN, 2 MISSED CALLS.'

She began to cry again.

~~~

'Hey, what's the matter?' Sean's electronic tinged voice asked from the other end of the line. He sounded concerned.

'Oh, it's nothing,' she lied. 'It's just we were supposed to be having a girls' night tonight, and the guys turned up and ruined everything.'

'Guys? What guys?'

'Nichola and Paula have new boyfriends, Ryan and Andrew. They brought two friends around too, uninvited, by the way, and then one of them, kind of, tried to make a move on me.'

'Tried to make a move on you?' he asked. She could hear the urgency and the anger in his voice. She kind of liked his protectiveness. 'Who was it? What's his name?'

'Peter. I have no idea what his last name is.'

'Should I come over? I could be there in about twenty minutes if I drive fast.'

'No, not tonight. I'm too upset about fighting with my friends. I've had a couple of drinks, and I just want to go to bed, to tell you the truth. Will you come over tomorrow? Nice and early, and we can get away like we said we would?'

'No problem. You're sure you don't want me to come tonight?'

'No,' she lied again. She wanted nothing more than to have him come over tonight. She needed someone to hug her, to tell her everything was all right. 'I think I'll be good. I'm just going to go to bed and put it all behind me.'

'OK then, well, goodnight. I'll call you early. Get you out of bed, yeah?'

'Yeah, that'd be nice. Goodnight, Sean.'

'Goodnight, Lisa. I'll talk to you in the morning, baby.'

She hung the phone up, cleaned up the mess in the kitchen, checked all the doors were locked, as her father had taught her from an early age, and turned the lights off. She then set the house alarm and made her way upstairs to bed.

She was tired beyond belief.

She washed her face, careful not to put any pressure on the red welt that was turning dark. *I'll have to cover that up in the morning,* she thought with a tinge of melancholy. She changed into clean night clothes and climbed into bed.

As she turned off the light, she pulled the covers over her head and released a long, tired sigh. A smile broke on her lips as she drifted off.

'Baby, huh?' she whispered into the darkness.

It wasn't long later that sleep took her.

The last sleep of the innocent!

26.

A NOISE SNATCHED her from the clutches of a restless sleep.

It was only a small noise, insignificant in between the normal noises of the night, but something about it woke her with a start. As she sat upright in the bed, her mouth was instantly dry. It took a few moments for her eyes to register the objects in the dark room; the only illumination was from the dim light radiating from her alarm clock at the side of the bed. She looked at it and was shocked to see that it wasn't even half-past twelve yet. Sleep had taken her for less than an hour.

She held her breath and listened, as if the sound of her breathing might give away her location to whoever, or whatever, was in her house wanting to kill and eat her, or whisk her away into slavery, or any other horrific scenario a petrified brain will conjure.

She couldn't remember if it was a noise that had spooked her or just a feeling, but something was different, something was wrong.

*The alarm! Did I set the alarm?* She cast her mind back to going to bed. She remembered typing in the code, but she couldn't remember pressing the ARM button. Her pyjamas were suddenly clinging to her moist skin, and all she wanted to do was crawl underneath the covers, go back to sleep, and wake up in the morning, laughing about this with her friends.

*What friends?*

A creak from somewhere in the house broke her train of thought.

This time, she knew it was a definite noise.

Was it inside or outside?

She prayed for the latter.

Relief washed over her as she realised where the noise had come from. It *was* outside.

Then it happened again.

A panic was on her in the wink of an eye. Her heart was banging in her chest and marching through her head, beating its drum to its very own thrash metal song.

Was it Peter, coming back for vengeance? She hoped not.

The noise came again. This time there was no doubt it was coming from outside and it was made by a person. There was a cough and a mutter, followed by some light banging. Thanking her father for being a security nut and for having such a robust security system that was almost impenetrable, she remembered the CCTV. When they had moved in, her father insisted on covering the whole house with cameras for when the alarm system switched on.

She crept out of bed and tiptoed, trying her best to be as silent as possible, as if the person loitering outside would be able to hear her sneaking down the stairs towards her father's office. She knew the office would be locked, but she also knew there was a false wall panel to the side of the door that housed an emergency key. She retrieved it and let herself inside her father's ultra-neat sanctuary.

Any other time, she would never have been allowed access to his computer system, but before he had gone away, he'd shown her how to use the network of CCTV equipment. She powered his computer on and sat looking at the two monitors that housed four video feeds each. The feeds were in high-definition colour, giving the viewer a panoramic view around the house.

She was looking for movement.

It was a while before anything revealed itself. She was just about to give up when somebody, standing in the darkness of the bushes by the back gate, moved. Whoever it was stepped forwards, only slightly; it looked as if he was about to attempt to scale the gate. She pressed a button and the camera zoomed in.

It was Peter.

She allowed herself to fall back onto the leather chair behind the desk, and it rolled back a little on its wheels. She swallowed hard as she leaned forward, dragging herself back towards the desk. She wanted to get a better look at whoever it was, just to make sure. She wiped sweat from her face and looked closer.

It was him.

This knowledge scared her more than not knowing who it might be. She knew what he was capable of. The way he'd looked at her when he called her a 'fucking skank'. There had been hatred, even malice in his eyes.

She watched as he drunkenly attempted to climb the gate. He hadn't realised that there was vandal grease, razor wire, and nails along the top, designed to stop this kind of thing. He climbed halfway up before he slipped and fell, clutching his hands as he did. He'd obviously cut himself in the failed attempt, but it didn't deter him from having another go.

For the next few minutes, she followed him around the house as he jumped from camera to camera, making attempt after attempt to penetrate the perimeter.

She didn't know what to do. If she called the police, her father would find out she'd had boys around, and he wouldn't trust her on her own again for a long time.

She decided to call Sean.

~~~~

'I'm on my way. You stay inside. I'll take care of this scumbag. I'll be there in twenty minutes, no longer.'

He sounded angry, and she wondered if she'd done the right thing. The last thing she needed was for Sean to beat this guy up and end up getting arrested.

'OK. Should I try to speak to him or anything?'

'No,' Sean shouted down the phone, scaring her a little. Then he seemed to calm down. 'No, just make sure the CCTV is recording him, but make sure it's turned off before I get there. I'll text you and let you know when to turn it off.'

'OK.'

The connection broke, leaving Lisa alone in her father's office, staring at the screens before her. Trembling hands covered her mouth as she searched for signs of Peter on the monitors. It turned out he was around the back of the property again, still trying, unsuccessfully, to scale the walls, hurting himself rather badly each time.

She looked at the clock on the wall, willing the twenty minutes between her talking to Sean and him turning up to pass. Dismay filled her as she saw it had been less than five.

The monitor was now showing Peter sitting at the bottom of the large tree that was on the perimeter of the fence. He stood up and looked around, searching for a different route into the property.

That was when he looked up at the tree.

Lisa remembered when she was younger, she would use the branches of that tree to get over the fence without her father's knowledge. She'd never told him about it, as she thought she might need it one day.

Today, she wished she had told him.

'Why don't you just go home, you fucking jerk,' she hissed into the empty room. Her words sounded funny, spooky somehow.

Peter looked up at the branches of the tree, and she watched as he traced the overhang of them into the garden. He wiped his hands on the back of his trousers and proceeded to climb.

Her eyes were flicking nervously back at the clock. It had only been seven minutes since her conversation with Sean.

Peter got a little way up the trunk and stopped. She remembered he was drunk, and as he reached out for the next branch, he missed and fell. Despite her fear and her nerves, she couldn't help but laugh, as it was a comical scene.

He dusted himself off and attempted it again.

'He really wants to get in here,' she mumbled, and the fear inside gripped her again.

Twelve minutes.

Her heart was thumping against her ribs as she watched Peter's persistence play out on the screen.

She was of two minds to call the police anyway when her phone beeped. She looked at the clock and saw it had been seventeen minutes since her phone call. *He must have broken every speed limit in the county,* she thought with a small sense of swelling pride.

She grabbed the phone, and relief surged through her as she saw it was Sean's name on the screen

'TURN CCTV OFF' it read.

She watched as Peter, still halfway up the tree, looked at something, or someone, off screen. He then climbed down the tree trunk and walked off the screen, looking threatening.

She reached over to the machine and pressed the pause button. The small red circle in the corner of the screen changed into two parallel white lines. Closing her eyes, she prayed to whatever God would be listening at this late hour that Sean would be OK.

After a few long and agonising moments, her phone eventually beeped again.

'OPEN THE GATE AND THE FRONT DOOR. HE'S GONE.'

Lisa sighed and turned off the alarm system and opened the main gate remotely.

With a smile on her face as big as a whale's, she ran to the door, turning the lights on as she went. She didn't want it to be dark when her hero made his entrance. She undid the lock on the front door and flung it open.

27.

SEAN WALKED UP the path slowly. Lisa saw that he was either strutting or she was imagining it, but he was looking at her and grinning.

'Is he gone?'

He nodded. 'Yeah, he is. I don't think there'll be any more trouble from him.'

She beamed, looking at his hands to see if there was any blood on them. There wasn't. It was the happiest she'd felt for a few hours. 'You really are my hero,' she said, laughing as he got nearer. 'Do you want to come in? I'll make us some coffee.'

'Now that sounds like a plan to me,' he said with a wolfish grin.

*That's the sexy smile I fell in love with*, she thought. As he brushed passed her into the house, she caught a whiff of his aftershave. She couldn't place it, but she knew that it was already her favourite.

She closed the door behind him and locked it.

~~~~

Her vision doubled right before her world turned black. There was a strange, tingling pain shooting from the top of her head, down through her nose, and into her neck.

Confused, her face banged into something solid as her legs gave way beneath her.

28.

THE WORLD SWAM before her eyes. It was a haze of greens, blues, and reds. Nothing would focus. It confused and scared her in equal measure, but most of all, it nauseated her. Every time she moved, there was a build-up of saliva in her mouth, the ugly precursor to vomiting.

However, the vomit never came.

As she moved her head to the side, to allow for the flow of the puke that was currently churning in her stomach, pain kicked in. Closing her eyes was the only way she could make the nausea caused by the dizziness abate.

The back of her head and her neck were aching, as was the inside of her head. Her nose was in agony also, and she could feel her lips were swelling. With her eyes still closed, she moved her arm and felt around the floor. Beneath her was a cold, hard surface. She surmised she was lying in the hallway, on the wood floor.

Her fuzzy mind raced, trying to remember how she'd found herself in this predicament. *Peter must have gotten in somehow*, she thought with a panic. *If that's so, where's Sean? If Peter's done this to me, what's he done to him?*

She wanted to move, to push herself up from her prone position. Tentatively, she opened her eyes. The last thing she needed was for the colours and the nausea to come flooding back, but she had to assess her predicament. The agony in her limbs hampered all movements, but the world began to swim back into something resembling focus.

She could see a dark figure. It was looming over her, looking at her. She couldn't make out who it was, but she could tell roughly by his shape, it was male.

Her first thought was that it was Death himself come for her. The Grim Reaper, complete with his bloody sickle, ready to reap her soul and carry her off into whatever came after this world.

'Peter?' she asked with a lisp as the word flapped from her swelling lip. 'Why are you doing this? What have you done to Sean?'

There was a sharp laugh before a hand grabbed her chin, forcing her to face him. Her eyes attempted to focus again. There was something about the figure she recognised, but it wasn't from what little she could see.

It was his smell.

Her world crashed around her. Everything she knew was wrong. Up felt like it was down, black had become white.

It was the aftershave.

She had smelt it only moments ago.

'It's not Peter. It's me!'

She didn't want to hear Sean's voice.

Her brain tried to reprocess the information it was receiving, but it couldn't. *It's the bang on my head,* she thought. *My senses are playing with me ... messing with me.*

She blinked, attempting to clear her vision. Even this small movement caused another bloom of pain to explode in her head. Oddly, this pain helped her focus, just a little but enough to know that her ears and her nose had not deceived her.

The figure looming over her was Sean.

'Sean, what happened?' she mumbled, surprised and scared by how weak her voice sounded. 'Did I ... Did I slip? Am I OK?' she asked. Her voice was frail, and her words sounded fluffy to her, like she was speaking through a mouthful of cotton wool.

She watched her boyfriend shake his head slowly as the grip he had on her chin tightened. 'No, Lisa! You're far from OK,' he whispered. 'You're about as far from OK as you can get, you fucking *pig!*'

He growled the last word, and she watched, fascinated, as a line of drool dripped from his clenched mouth. She flinched. Surely, she'd fallen down a rabbit hole and this was a strange new world, one that looked like her world but was polar opposite to it. He let go of her chin, pushing her head painfully to one side before standing up.

'Sean?' she croaked. 'What's happening?'

'Get up,' he spat.

'What? Sean, no, I think I might have—' She didn't get to the word *concussion* before a strong hand grabbed a handful of her hair. Agony surged through her body as she was dragged up from the floor. She felt clumps pull out of her scalp from the roots. She whimpered, 'Stop, you're hurting me.'

'You're going to know the meaning of the word *hurt* by the time I'm finished with you, little piggy,' he snarled, bringing his face up close to hers.

She tried to see the handsome boy she'd trusted, fallen in love with, but all she could see was a rictus of hate. She didn't recognise the person before her.

He grinned.

It was humourless.

He hocked up in his throat and spat a thick, foul-smelling glob of phlegm into her face. He laughed and pushed her back against something solid. In her dazed state, she could only guess it was the front door. As she hit it, fresh pain exploded in her head, and she slid back down to the floor.

'Sean ...'

She was crying now. A dribble of warm, salty mucus dripped into her mouth; her lips stung where the salt sunk into her lacerated and swollen flesh. 'Why?'

He squatted in front of her and slapped her across the face.

This brought more stars.

It was harder than the one she had received earlier from Peter, or maybe it just felt that way because of the betrayal.

'Because me and my friend Jay want to. Is that OK with you, *pig*?' Again, he spat the last word, and she cowered, raising her arms, scared he might hit her again.

'Who's Jay?' she whispered.

He sat on the floor, resting his back against the wall, effectively barring any escape route for her. 'Now, let me get this straight. Your parents are away for ten days. Your friends think you're away with me for at least two days, and if what you told me about tonight is true, I don't think they're going to be calling you for a few days anyway.' He looked deep into her face. His blue eyes were piercing, almost glowing. There was no smile, no love, no warmth, in them at all.

They were devoid of emotion.

Except for maybe pure, unadulterated hate.

'So, that leaves me and you with plenty of time for us to get … shall we say, acquainted?'

Lisa was sobbing again; her eyes were closed, and her breathing was deep and laborious. 'Who's Jay?' she whispered again.

'Shut up now, piggy. Daddy's thinking about what he needs to do to you for the next forty-eight hours.'

'*Who is Jay*?' she asked for a third time. Although it was hardly a shout, there was an audible amount of venom in her voice.

He looked at her and smiled. His beautiful smile was back. For one moment, he was the same Sean who'd picked her up and taken her to the cinema, the same Sean who bought her a burger, the one who kissed her so sweetly. Her mind began to spin. *Maybe it's a dream,* she thought. *Maybe I'm still in bed, asleep, having a nightmare.*

Then he hit her again.

She watched the back of the cell phone get closer before it hit her.

She was right about the nightmare, but not about the being asleep.

Her world went black again.

## 29.

SHE COULD FEEL momentum. The ground was moving beneath her, and with the movement came more pain, more dizziness, more nausea.

As she became more aware of what was happening, the realisation that she was being pulled along the floor by her hair did nothing for her fragile state. Her face throbbed. Her nose, her lips, and her temples were all screaming in agony. She moved her head, trying to get her bearings, to see what was happening, where she was being dragged to, but it was too difficult. All she could make out was Sean's back as he dragged her. The effort of moving was too much, and she found herself floating in and out of blackness.

A tune was stuck in her head, one that had floated in from some childhood memory. *Where the fuck did that come from?* It was a few dazed and confused moments before she realised it was coming from Sean. He was whistling it as he dragged her along.

*Hi Hooooo ... Hi Hooooo!*

The floor changed beneath her from wood to black marble tile. It marked her passing from the hallway into the kitchen. 'Please, Sean ... don't do this,' she managed to plead, hoping her captor could hear her and understand her through her new unattractive lisp. 'You don't need to do this. I'll do anything you want; I promise, I will.'

Ignoring her, he continued dragging her for another few yards before dumping her unceremoniously onto the floor.

'Let me go, please.' She hadn't given much thought to how dry her throat had become until her words came out as a dry rasp rather than the shout she'd intended.

He looked at her. His mouth pulled down in a grimace. He regarded her as if she were something disgusting, vile, shit on the floor that needed cleaning up. Without warning, his top lip curled, and he lashed out his foot, connecting with her stomach, hard.

'Don't … fucking … talk … to me … *pig*,' he said, emphasising each word before walking around the other side of the island.

The kick to her stomach robbed her of the last of her wind. The pain was something she had never experienced before. For the first time since she'd let him into the house, she began to fear for her life.

Looking down at her hands and feet, she was surprised to see them wrapped in tight silver tape. How she hadn't noticed this before she didn't understand, as it was wrapped so tight it was almost impossible to wriggle her extremities, but it didn't stop her from trying. The agony pulsating from her stomach was, thankfully, subsiding, but it left a dull ache. Her face was stinging as tears ran down her cheeks.

Sean was somewhere behind the island. He was rummaging around the cupboards, obviously looking for something. The noise as the things in the cupboard rattled and the sounds of pans falling onto the tiles hurt her ears.

'Yes! Here we go,' she heard him celebrate. Her heart dropped to her stomach in fear of what he'd found.

His shoes were the first thing she saw as he reappeared. Before she knew anything else, his rough hands were around her, dragging her up off the floor and onto a stool. Through teary eyes, she couldn't believe what he was holding.

It was a knife.

One of her father's chef knives. The ones he kept in the cupboard, hidden away because they were so sharp.

He lowered his head but kept his eyes on her. He looked like a cartoon villain, one who thought he was going to get away with whatever dastardly deed he was about to do right before the hero would burst in and stop him.

He pointed the knife at her and grinned.

She wished for that hero, someone to protect her from … her boyfriend. Alas, no one was coming to rescue her. No one would even suspect anything for the next two days at least. The irony that this bastard had actually *been* her hero was not lost on her.

'Now, my little piggy. You need to know that you're allowed to scream as much as you want.' He laughed, indicating the kitchen around him. 'It's not like anyone is going to hear you. The wall around this property will give us all the privacy we need to play our little games.' As his face drew close, there was a faint taint of alcohol on his breath and, of course, the aftershave she had liked so much.

In another life.

She would never be able to smell it again, not without remembering this night.

It went from her favourite smell in the world to something to be feared in the same night.

'Do you want to play games?' he hissed. A maniacal smile had taken over his features.

She didn't reply; she just hung her head. She didn't know why this was happening; the world was just pure confusion. A small yelp escaped her as he pushed her body into the island top, grabbed her by the back of her head, pulling it back, exposing her neck.

'You know I've got the power right now to *end* you, don't you?'

She couldn't respond. There wasn't enough air getting through her throat to allow her to form words, or even breathe.

'Don't you?' he asked, anger rising in his voice.

Her response was small. It was nothing more than a guttural noise squeezing from her constricted throat, but it *was* a response, and he seemed happy with it.

'Good, then you already know that you belong to me now. You're my plaything, and I like to play with piggies.'

She shivered as the tip of the knife traced its way down her cheek. It was only light, but the threat was palpable. She closed her eyes as the tip of the knife traced its way down her back, leaving a stinging sensation in its wake. Her pyjama top fell from her shoulders. The knife was so sharp it had easily cut through the fabric, and her top opened with very little effort. The tingle of the air-conditioned kitchen pinched at her exposed flesh, causing goosebumps to rise, covering her flesh.

She was helpless to prevent the top falling away, and she felt exposed and ashamed. She turned her head, trying to look at him. Her face was throbbing from the beating she had taken and where, she assumed, it had hit the floor. She attempted to look at him with dignity, hoping to get him to see her as the girl who was on the verge of falling in love with him and as a human with feelings and emotions. It was difficult to achieve as she was pushed over the island-top. 'Why are you doing this?' she snivelled. 'I thought we had a … a connection. I thought we had something special.'

He began to laugh. 'I don't have feelings for pigs, Lisa. I'm so far out of your league you should be thanking me, praising me for taking any interest in you whatsoever. The only kind of interest something like you is worthy of would be from the fucking *Peters* of this world.' He indicated towards the kitchen window with the knife.

Her gaze followed it.

She now wished she'd let Peter in. If she had, she wouldn't be in this mess now. *Don't kid yourself, girlfriend,* a voice not dissimilar to Nichola's spoke in her head. *You were all set to go away with this monster, this creep, tomorrow.*

The voice wasn't helping as he grabbed her and turned her around to face him. She screamed and squirmed trying to cover her breasts from his gaze.

This only seemed to excite him more. He looked at her with wide, hungry eyes. 'You know, for a pig, you have great tits.' he snarled.

His hands pulled her arms away from covering herself, and she felt his rough fingers, fingers that had once held her hand so gently, grab and pinch at her. Her chest heaved as a sob escaped her. A sick boiling sensation was growing in her stomach as his fingers snapped at her sensitive nipples.

'See, you're enjoying that. I can tell,' he laughed as he used his finger and thumb to flick her already stinging nipple.

It hurt like Hell!

'Yeah, look at those bad boys. You're so into this. Are you enjoying this, little piggy?'

She ignored the question. She refused to warrant it with an answer; she was far too scared to encourage him.

'Lisa,' he whispered. She felt his sour breath on her face as he leaned in closer. She opened her eyes and looked into the face of pure evil. Handsome, smiling, but with cold, dead eyes. 'I asked you a fucking question.' As he hissed the last word, his finger and thumb gained purchase on her nipple. He gripped it and twisted it with a great deal of force.

Agony surged through her. Somehow, it was worse than the kick in the stomach he'd administered earlier. It was localised and in a very sensitive area. She didn't want to give him the satisfaction of showing him a reaction, but the searing torment was too much, and a cry was forced from her lips.

This excited him!

It was the exact reaction she had wanted to avoid.

He looked at her breasts and licked his lips. His other hand reached towards her other breast and found the nipple with ease. His finger and thumb twisted that one too, with equal force and malice.

This time it was more than a cry that escaped her. Despite her dry throat, she shouted, 'Fuck, you sadistic motherfucker!'

He let go of the nipples and offered her a lop-sided grin. Then, without any warning, he slapped her across the face, hard. It surprised her more than hurt her. Her face was still smarting from bashing it against the floor, so this attack caused stars to flash in her vision. She panicked for a moment as she thought she was going to pass out, but thankfully, the wooziness passed. A gossamer strand of bloody spit dribbled from her swollen bottom, lip. It landed between her breasts.

He reached out and rubbed it into her skin.

'Watch your mouth, piggy. Little pigs shouldn't use language like that.' He was laughing as he leaned back and leered at her. He shook his head as his eyes focused on her throbbing nipples. 'I need to take a photo. This is fucking gold. Jay'll love it.' He laughed again. It was a moronic sound, almost like a donkey brey. It was a million miles from the cool laugh he'd had on their dates. He took his cell phone from his jeans pocket and pointed it at her. She tried to shy away, but he pushed her back against the island, pinning her again while snapping photos of her breasts with her own blood rubbed into them.

'Hey, look,' he said, pointing at the mobile screen. 'Your nipples are already turning purple. You must have really sensitive skin.' He was nodding as he turned the phone towards her for her to see his handiwork.

She turned away, determined not to look.

He reached in and pinched the skin on her breast. This time, he missed the nipple and pinched just above it.

She took in a sharp intake of breath as her skin rubbed between his finger and thumb again. It hurt more than the nipple. He pinched again and then pulled before letting go. She looked and could see the spreading red welts, knowing that soon they would begin to turn into ugly purple patches.

He nodded his approval as he looked at her, suitably impressed with her changes of colour.

He did it again, and then again. Leaving red marks everywhere, all over her stomach and chest.

Each mark shamed her more than the last.

Eventually, he stopped and stepped back again to admire his art. She took this moment to gulp in some much-needed air. Nodding, he raised his phone again and took another series of photographs. This time, she could tell he made sure her face was in them. Happy with his photoshoot, he made his way towards the gas stove on the other side of the room.

She was relieved at the space between them. Her skin ached from his torment, but she wasn't naïve enough to think he'd finished with her yet. Dread overcame her as he lit one of the burners. That dread turned to relief as he bent over and lit a cigarette. He took a long draw and breathed it out towards the ceiling. The blue smoke streamed from his mouth and nose before dissipating.

The noxious air made Lisa cough.

He laughed at the sound. 'What's the matter, piggy? I though you would have liked the smell of smoke. A little bit of smoked bacon never hurt anyone.'

'Stop calling me that,' she croaked. 'Why do you keep calling me that?'

'I'm calling you it because it's what you are. A stuck-up, fat little fuck pig.' He made his way towards her, a disturbed, menacing look chiselled onto his face.

She turned away from him.

'Don't you like it, *pig*? Doesn't the posh little fuck pig like her pet name from her brave, heroic boyfriend?'

She tried to move away, hoping to keep as much space between them as possible. It was a futile gesture. He was back, leaning even closer into her than before, breathing out thick smoke into her face.

She coughed and recoiled.

'I hate you, you little cunt!' He said this as if it was nothing special, just a matter of fact, a mere snippet of information. 'Did you know that?'

She closed her eyes and shook her head. She was too scared to even look at him.

'Well, I do. I hate you and your shitty friends. I hate that little prick of a father of yours. I even hate your hot mom, although I don't mind telling you that I've jerked off a few times thinking about fucking her, about hurting her.' He smiled, raised his eyebrows, and pointed his cigarette at her as if this disgusting piece of information might have been something she had wanted, or even needed, to know. 'But most of all, I hate *you*.' His face twisted as he spat the last word. He stabbed at her with his half-smoked cigarette. The orange tip brushed one of her bruising nipples.

She screamed.

The pain was immeasurable. It eclipsed the kick *and* the pinches, all of them, combined.

He grinned. His eyes widened in amusement as he saw how much he'd hurt her. He looked at the glowing tip and grinned. 'You didn't like that, did you?' There was building excitement in his voice.

She sat back, trying to cover herself with her arms. There was no way she could hide the tears that were now streaming down her cheeks.

He grabbed her hair, pulling her head back again. He dragged her off the chair and pushed her back into the island top, forcing her tied hands over her head, stretching both her breasts. There were welts all over her skin that were already turning an ugly purple. Her left nipple was dark from the pinching, and her right one was red. The tip of it glistening, wet, looking like it was about to blister.

He leaned forward, his mouth less than an inch away from her sore flesh. She could feel his hot breath on her.

He opened his mouth and licked her.

The feel of his tongue on her wounded nipple made it sting, and she cried out.

'Oh yeah,' he breathed. 'Oh, fucking yeah, bitch! You want me to do that again?' he asked, his voice excited and maniacal. 'Well, OK. But only if you insist.'

He licked her again, only this time he bit down with his front teeth.

She screamed.

The feel of his incisors cutting into the inflamed, sensitive skin made her head swim. He bit so hard that she was almost sure he'd bitten the nipple clean off.

He lifted his head and released her hair. She looked up at him and saw there was indeed blood around his mouth. Panic set in again as she tried to look down to see if her breast was still intact, but her neck was too sore from the dragging she'd endured, so she couldn't see.

The pain told its own story.

He was laughing again as he grabbed her by the chin and pushed her head against the marble of the island. Her senses swam again as the sick, dull ache of her headwound, where he had initially hit her, once again took the full force of the blow.

He was still laughing as she felt the heat from the glowing tip of his cigarette getting closer to her skin.

'*Please no,*' she tried to plead, but his hands tightening around her jaw prevented her from talking. Her pleas were redundant, as the searing heat of the cigarette brushed over her other nipple. She couldn't even scream to vent the agonising searing of her flesh as the red-hot poker of torture pierced her very being.

The heat subsided, but it brought no relief from the continued white-hot agony it left.

Then the heat was burning into her again, a little lower this time.

Sean's mouth was as wide as his eyes were. His tongue was licking his bottom lip as he watched the glowing tip of the cigarette cook her skin. 'I can smell the pig's flesh burning,' he sang. 'It's like bacon. It's making me hungry, you little fucking whore.'

The line of drool hanging from his mouth finally got too heavy to sustain itself, and it dripped onto her exposed stomach. Thankfully, it landed on one of the burn marks, temporarily extinguishing the ugly sensation.

Despite the pain, fear, anger, and downright terror she was experiencing, her mind still took time to register how bad his breath smelt. It was a heady mixture of cigarettes, garlic, and alcohol.

He banged her head onto the marble countertop again so that her back arched. Once again, he held her bound arms over her head. She had no choice but to comply, but she wouldn't do it without a fight.

'Stop wriggling,' he growled.

She ignored him and continued to thrash.

'I said STOP IT!' he shouted, pushing the cigarette into her belly button.

Every last bit of fight she had left in her drained at that moment. She screamed in torment. The release of her neck allowed the scream to fully form, and she let it fly with everything she had.

He leaned in close and looked at her, his stinking breath bathing her face. 'Squeal, you fucking pig,' he spat. Spittle flew from his mouth onto her face. 'Scream this fucking house down. There's not a soul who can hear you. Your daddy made sure of that with all the security in this place.'

The spittle had turned into drool now, and it once again dribbled from his mouth as he hissed, dripping onto her swollen, bruised face. There was nothing she could do about it.

'Do you know *why* I hate you so much?' he asked.

Lisa's swollen eyes were as wide as she could get them. She needed to know why the boy who had pursued her, asked her out, and treated her so nice hated her. Unadulterated terror surged through her as she realised that this boy, this once beautiful boy, was a textbook sociopath, hiding his emotional black hole, masking it with faked human empathy. But deep down, deep in his psyche, he was a vacuum. There was nothing except his own sick, depraved morality.

'Because you're you. You're so fucking pretty, and you're so fucking popular, but really, deep down, you're just a nasty little cunt like the rest of them. You've got no time for the likes of me.'

'That's not true,' she whispered. 'I … I was in love with you,' she managed.

He pulled his face closer and growled. The full weight of his body pinned her to the island. She couldn't move an inch even if she tried hard enough.

'If you took the time to find out who I am and not who you think I am, who you want me to be, then you'd have nothing, *not one single thing* to do with me. You don't know me, *pig*, but I fucking know you.'

His hand, the one that had been holding the cigarette, moved slowly up the leg of her pyjama bottoms. It wasn't long before it had made its way to the top. She cringed as she felt his fingers force their way inwards, towards her crotch. She tried to fight it, trying her best to kick her legs, to clench them closed, to deny him any access to any part of her, but it was all in vain. He had her in too tight a hold for her to offer any real resistance.

Fresh tears welled in her puffy eyes as his fingers gained purchase of the elasticated waistband of her pyjama bottoms and forced them down.

The material tore.

'The irony to all of this is …' He breathed heavily into her face as his hands entered into her pyjama bottoms. '…is that you were going to allow me to do all of this tomorrow night anyway. Weren't you? Well, with me being the impatient type, I decided to bring the party forward just a little.'

He jerked at the material, tearing it away from her, and rubbed himself against her. Revulsion, shock, and deep horror filled her as his erection rubbed against her leg. Even through his jeans, she could feel the strength of it.

She had a flashback to the car, to him fumbling with it, trying to hide it from her. Her heart broke as she remembered the sweet comedy of that situation. The same sweet comedy that was roughly one million miles away from what was happening to her right now.

Frantically, he began to unbuckle his belt.

Then his phone beeped.

He stopped to acknowledge it, and Lisa breathed a small sigh of relief.

He grabbed the phone from his pocket and looked at it. A smile stretched across his face. He raised his eyebrows as he looked at her. 'That's Jay. Replying to my photography.'

He eased his body off her, and all of a sudden, she could breathe again.

'Jay,' he laughed. 'Did you get it?' His voice had gone up in pitch as the excitement of what he was doing relayed in the conversation.

Lisa took the momentary relief to ease herself up from the island and use her bound hands to pull her pyjama bottoms back up and to try to cover her exposed, ruined breasts. As her arms brushed against her wounded nipples, she took in another sharp intake of breath.

'Yeah, nice tits, huh? I knew you'd like them.'

Through her fear, pain, and discomfort, she was listening to every word, trying to glean something, anything from the one-sided conversation that she might be able to use to get herself out of this situation.

What she heard chilled her to the bone.

'Plenty more where they came from, I'm telling you … Yeah, well, I've got two full days, after all. Her parents are away, none of her friends are going to be calling any time soon. She's off popping her cherry … Oh, fuck yeah, that cherry is so going to be mine … Yeah, of course, the dirty little pig. I'll record every minute and send it to you …'

She closed her eyes. The sting of the burns on her skin and the blistering on her areolas stole her every thought, but she needed clarity. She needed a safe place to retreat to.

'Well, back to it. No rest for the wicked. I'll give you updates when I have them.' He was laughing as he ended the call. He looked back at her; she had removed herself from the island top and was now sitting on one of the stools.

She had tried to cover herself but hadn't been too successful. Her semi-nakedness displayed the deep welts on her skin. Her face was bruised, swollen, and bloody.

She looked sad and defeated.

He smiled and moved in close.

30.

PAULA WAS IN bed. She was wide awake; for some reason, sleep was elusive. There was something niggling at her, in the back of her mind. Whatever it was, it was keeping her mind active and sleep at bay. She lay in the dark, looking up at the ceiling. Finally, just as her eyes began to droop and she began to wilt, her phone beeped, and the screen lit up her room.

Instantly, she was awake again. Cursing, she leaned over to look at the bright screen on the bedside table.

It read 'JANICE'.

*What the hell could she want at this time?* She looked at the clock, it had just gone twenty past two.

It was a text message. She sighed and opened it up.

'P… IM WORRIED ABOUT LISA! DO U THNK WE SHUD HAV LEFT HER LIKE THAT???'

She read the message, then lay back on her bed with another sigh. She looked at her phone again, then closed her eyes. Moments later, she shook her head, tutted, and clicked on the REPLY button.

'WAS THINKING SAME THING… LETS LEAVE IT 4 NOW, SHES AWAY 2MORROW WITH SEAN. TALK WEN SHES BCK.'

She clicked the SEND button and turned over in bed. She put the covers over her head and tried to re-enter the zone she was just rudely snatched from.

31.

TONY AND FLO were sitting outside a small café on the Champs-Elysees in Paris. The weather was fantastic, and they were enjoying a well-deserved beer. 'I'll tell you what,' Tony said, looking up the street towards the magnificent Arc de Triomphe. 'I could get used to this.'

His wife was sitting back in her chair, sipping her beer with her eyes closed and her head held high towards the sky. 'Get you away from all those computers and cell phones, and you're a totally different man.'

He put his drink back on the table and grinned. He rubbed his foot up her leg. 'Get me back to the hotel room, and I'll show you how much of a different man I am. I'm feeling all … European!' He raised his eyebrows towards her and continued his grin.

'Don't be coming over all French on me now,' she chided. 'We haven't even been here a day.'

He laughed and picked his drink back up. 'What time is it back home?'

Flo looked at her watch, she'd left it on EST time so they could co-ordinate their phone calls home. 'It's just half past two. She'll be asleep by now.'

Tony raised his eyebrows as he took a sip of his drink. 'Either that or in the midst of a wild drugs and sex party,' he mused. Flo noticed there wasn't much humour in the statement.

'Leave her be,' she warned. 'She's a big girl, and she's not stupid. We've raised her better than that.'

'I know, but I just worry.'

Flo chuffed. 'That's because you're trained to worry. It's because you don't have any control over the situation. You need to let go. She'll thank you for it in the long run.'

'I know, but ...' He shook his head and sipped his beer. 'I know, I know ... forget it, Tony.' He took a long swig from the frosted glass, draining the amber liquid inside. He then looked at Flo and grinned. 'So, what were you saying about coming over all French?' he asked with a pout.

Flo was laughing as she finished her own drink.

32.

LISA WAS BENT over, face down on the island in the kitchen. The marble countertop was steaming up with every laboured breath that escaped her swollen nose. The fog would recede again as she breathed back in before steaming again on her next breath. This was all she could focus on right now as Sean's hand pressed the back of her head, pushing her face into the cold, hard surface.

She was trying to resist, but it was futile. He was just too strong, and she was far too sore, physically and mentally. His free hand was underneath her, and she could feel him fumbling around, trying to remove her pyjama bottoms. She closed her eyes, desperate to find a happy place, somewhere she could retreat to in her head, but alas, this, too, was a futile gesture.

'Give it up, you fucking pig,' he snarled, grabbing her hair, pulling her head up off the marble top.

She had no intention of making anything easy for him, even though she knew the inevitable was going to happen. As according to her initial plan, albeit in a twisted, horrific manner, she was going to lose her virginity to Sean after all.

He tugged her head back with such ferocity that she issued an involuntary squeal, and another clump of hair tore out by the roots. She was on her feet again. The sway of her head, due to the sudden rush of altitude, made her body reel. Her knees were buckling, but Sean compensated for this by pushing her midriff closer to the island for support. His rough hands continued tugging at her pyjama bottoms, and she felt her last defence against this violation fall. Her bottoms and her underwear dropped uselessly around her feet.

Humiliated and petrified, she complied to his physical exertions and allowed herself to be pushed back onto the counter. Her bound hands were held over her head, her sore, swollen breasts squashed roughly against the cold tabletop. Dark bruises had already developed up the side of her body where he had beaten her, and the red welts on her breasts and stomach looked dangerous, vibrant, and purple.

Sean was behind her. His hand was on her bare lower back, pushing her against the island, while his other hand pulled at the front of his jeans, attempting to release the demon that was fighting against the buttons.

She laid her head on the table. The cold of the marble offered her aching face light relief from this ordeal. Her tears formed pools beneath her face, yet she refused to look at or acknowledge the filthy animal behind her. She refused to beg him to stop; she would not be giving him that satisfaction.

'You're fucking gorgeous, do you know that?' he whispered breathlessly. 'For a dirty, filthy whore-pig, that is.' As he laughed, the sound was almost tender.

She still refused to acknowledge him.

'Did you hear what I just said?' he asked. The tenderness in his voice was gone, replaced with a dark, ominous threat of violence in the deep monotone words.

Again, she ignored him.

He grabbed her chin and turned her head to look at him. She heard rather than felt her neck crunch as it was forcefully twisted. She closed her puffed up eyes, determined not to look at him, not to give him any satisfaction.

'Don't fucking ignore me, you cunt,' he spat. The anger in him was boiling. 'I will *not* be ignored. OPEN YOUR FUCKING EYES.'

She refused.

The slap that snapped her head back was so surprising and so painful, that her eyes opened involuntary. Her vision doubled, just for a moment, before snapping back into focus as his hand grabbed her chin again.

Breathing heavily through her engorged and bloody nose, she closed her eyes again.

'Fucking bitch!' This time he did spit on her. She felt the warmth of the saliva on her face before she could smell the staleness as it dripped from her nose. Then the rough hands were back. One was on the back of her neck while the other pushed her forward again over the cold island. As her breasts were forced against it, the stinging from her burnt nipples rippled through her body. But something much worse was happening behind her.

She felt him squirm and reposition himself. She heard his jeans fall to the floor.

The noise of him spitting up in the back of his mouth knocked her sick. She closed her eyes again and readied herself for the inevitable. She wasn't stupid or naïve, she knew what was about to happen, but what scared her was that she had nothing to measure against what it would feel like. A disgusting warmth spread over the exposed skin of her buttocks, and she felt the ugly sensation of rough hands rubbing thick, warm saliva into her dry vagina.

She gasped.

A pathetic whimper escaped her as two fingers entered her, stretching her.

'You asked me if I was a big boy not so long ago. Well, little piggy, it looks like you're about to find out.'

She cried silently as Sean Knight slowly and painfully took away her innocence on the kitchen island, in the sanctity of her own home, against her will.

33.

AS A YOUNG girl, she had idolised and followed a teen boyband called Family Tree. There were four of them in the vocal band. Three of them where white, with perfect teeth and perfect hair, the other was brown skinned, with perfect teeth and perfect hair. They were the epitome of nice boys, the kind she would have had no problems bringing home to meet her parents, and she knew they would have been nice as pie to all of her friends.

Their songs were all about innocence. About the growing pains of liking girls in school but not having the courage to approach them to ask them out.

They were clean cut too, always on TV talking about the dangers of drugs and emphasising that school life and respecting your parents were the key to a happy, productive, and successful upbringing.

They were the ultimate manufactured pop band.

Lisa's favourite member was George. He was British and spoke with the Queen's English accent. His hair was a dusky blonde, and never once was he seen with it out of place. He wore it just a little too long for her individual taste, but she was confident she'd be able to talk sense to him, to persuade him to cut it for their huge celebrity-filled wedding.

But really, it wasn't a deal breaker.

The wedding would be in Switzerland, in a big hotel overlooking Lake Geneva. There would be a huge guest list, and every member of her family and all her friends would be in attendance. The ceremony would take place on the shores of the lake. It would be a beautiful summer morning, and the wedding breakfast would be in the grounds of the hotel. There would be a party, a party that would last long into the night.

At some point in the proceedings, George would whisk her off, out of the hall, sweeping her off her feet. He would carry her to their penthouse suite in his strong arms. There, she would find a chilling bottle of expensive sparkling wine. There would be rose petals adorning the bed sheets and dim romantic lighting. He would take her in his arms, look her in her eyes, and whisper to her that he loved her and would continue to love her forever.

They would kiss, and he would slowly undress her, revealing the underwear she had bought especially for him. They would fall back onto the huge four poster bed, where they would make slow, tender, but passionate love for the first time.

Afterwards, she would relax into his arms, and they would drink the wine, basking in the glow of their love and adoration for each other.

Then they would make their way back down to the main hall and engage with their guests, all the while keeping their liaison a special secret, just between them two.

That was what her first time was going to be like. That was how she planned on losing her virginity.

34.

SHE WAS FINDING it difficult to catch her breath. Each time she tried to inhale, even a shallow one, Sean pulled her head further back and thrust himself deeper inside her. She could only manage a few harsh and involuntary gasps through her tight wind pipe. The thought occurred to her that if she didn't die from the pain of his forced entry into her, she might suffocate from restricted breathing.

The only thing that kept bringing her breath back was the dull pain from the punches to the back of her head, delivered at random intervals.

The first punch shocked her, but it allowed her to pull in a deep gulp of much needed air before he snapped her head back again, so violently she was convinced he might have snapped her neck.

His sickening rhythm was gaining momentum. Although the only reference she had to gage what was happening was from movies and from reading books, she guessed he was nearing climax. She closed her eyes, trying to ignore the horrible intrusion and hoping upon all hope that he would just cum and bring this whole ordeal to an end.

His breathing became rapid, and he pulled her hair tighter. Suddenly, he let go of her. Her head, not expecting the instant freedom, fell forwards, and she banged her temple on the tabletop.

Stars flashed in her vison again.

Both his hands grabbed her around the hips, his fingers digging into her flesh. He made one more deep thrust inside before crying out.

She felt him pull out of her and then felt his hot release spray over her aching buttocks and back.

The feel of it sickened her. She suddenly felt every inch the filthy pig he'd been calling her. She felt used, dirty, violated, and worthless.

She felt like a whore.

Despite the dizziness from the bang on her head, a single tear welled in her eye before dripping onto the tabletop, merging with all the other tears she'd spilt tonight.

She thought she could still feel him inside her. A moan of despair escaped her before she was roughly pushed away. She fell from the tabletop and a strange sensation of falling enveloped her. In her fragile state, it felt like she was falling from a great height, from a cliff or maybe out of a plane. The slow-motion feeling of freedom was nice, invigorating even. It was her mind telling her she would soon be free from this ordeal.

Then reality hit her as she crumpled to the floor, once more crunching her temple, bringing the dreaded stars back. She was no longer free; she was on the kitchen floor, naked, cold, wet, and hurting.

She clenched her fists and opened one eye. She had never seen the kitchen from this perspective, and it was a few moments before she recognised the feet of the bar stools on which she had sat laughing so many times before, eating breakfast or evening meals with her parents, with her friends.

Happy times!

She found her happy retreat ... only for it to be ripped away from her moments later as her ears began to ring with mental, silent screams.

'You enjoyed that, didn't you, piggy?' Sean hissed, buttoning up his trousers. 'Oh yes, you fucking did. I could tell by your moans and yells.'

Physically, she was exhausted; mentally, she felt ruined. She tried to talk, wanting to shout, to order him out of her house, out of her life ... maybe even off this fucking planet.

But the words wouldn't come.

She had nothing left to offer, just a deep, shivering moan.

The sound of him shrieking above her made her feel sick again. 'I fucking knew you'd liked it; you really are a slut.' Something else dripped onto her back, mingling with the now cold semen. It took her a moment to realise that he had spat on her again.

His rough hands were once again in her hair, pulling her into a standing position. Her broken face was mere inches from his laughing one.

She wanted to spit on him. She longed to see his reaction as her thick, probably bloody, saliva dripped down his smug, ugly face, but her bloated lips wouldn't work, and her mouth was so dry that she didn't think there would be enough moisture in her body to go through with it.

'Can you feel that?' he whispered. 'Can you still feel my cock in your dirty, wet cunt? Can you? That's me. The *big boy!* The same me you were going to let do it to you anyway.'

She could feel the horrible wetness of his saliva and his thick cum dripping down her back and her sides. She could trace it sliding its vile way between her sore buttocks. She heard something splat on the tiles of the kitchen floor.

She could smell it.

It was the worst stench in the whole world. She never wanted to smell anything like it again.

More tears welled in her eyes. She closed them, feeling the itch of the moisture dripping down her face. When she opened them, Sean had his cell phone in his hand. Before she knew what was happening, he was snapping photos of her. She was bruised, battered, naked, and covered in semen and spit.

He leered cheerfully at her and nodded his head. 'Jay is going to *love* these.'

'Who's Jay?' she croaked.

As the words formed, bloody spit flew from her mouth; it sprayed onto Sean's black t-shirt. He looked at her and then down at the offending spittle. His face registered his disgust. 'Jay is someone who has your, shall we say, best interests at heart?' he said, wiping at the blood on his top.

Then he punched her in the stomach.

The shock, surprise, and pain caused her to double over in agony, gasping for breath. As she fell, he grabbed her by the hair again and ground her face into the floor.

# The Boyfriend

He held her there, her cheek pushed into the cold floor tile. She did her best to breathe, pulling in some of the stinking grey and pink liquid that had dripped from her.

Sean's semen mixed with her virginal blood.

It was her innocence.

It was her shame!

'You need to be more careful who you let into your life, piggy,' he hissed. As he did, another streak of drool dripped from his mouth, wetting the other side of her face.

It trickled over her skin before mingling with the bloody cum on the floor.

35.

SHE SURMISED SHE must have blacked out, or something like it, as she woke in her own bed with no knowledge of how she got there. As she opened her eyes and saw her familiar surroundings, a silent prayer ran through her head, and she thanked whatever God there was for allowing it all to have been a dream, a horrendous, vivid dream, but a dream nonetheless.

Then pain hit her, and then reality, like a double slap in the face. The vile, disgusting, degrading reality crashed all around her. With this reality came shame, like an uninvited guest to the worst party imaginable. She wanted to curl into a ball and either cry or die. Both options had their appeal. She tried to move her arms but found she couldn't. Slowly, she moved her head, ignoring her screaming joints, needing to know why she couldn't move before the panic that was rising within her boiled over the top like hot milk in a pan.

She was tied to the four posts of her bed.

Her whole body was wracked in torment.

Suddenly, she was cold, freezing cold. She managed to raise her head enough to look down her body. She was naked. There was a wet, itchy patch underneath her, on the bed sheets. She guessed that she must have wet herself at some point during the night.

There was an agonising dull ache between her legs.

Lifting her head again, straining to look down her body, she saw there was blood, not a lot of it, probably not enough to say she had been mortally wounded, but more than enough to scare her. The flesh of her stomach and chest was covered with burns and bruises. Raw, wet wounds had formed where the cigarette had been put out on her. Her burnt, crusted, and scabbed nipples were throbbing, keeping perfect rhythm with the pulsing between her legs.

Lifting her head had hurt like hell, but she needed to see the rest of her room. She needed to know if she was alone.

She was.

She turned to see what she had been tied to the posts with, dreading to see plastic cable ties that she knew her father kept all over the place. She was relieved to see that Sean must have been in a hurry, as all he had used was black pantyhose, She knew the knots weren't very tight as she could still feel her fingers. So, she began a concentrated effort to escape her bonds.

It kept her mind off the pain tearing through her body.

Her wrists were hurting from her bonds, and her arms and chest were hurting from the bruises and the burns, but she ignored all of that. She needed to be free.

As she tugged, bolts of pain—no, torture—shot down her arms, into her chest. She was convinced she was going to give herself a heart attack; the agony was too intense, and she had to rest.

As she did, she consciously relaxed her body, and her heart began to slow. She tried again, tugging at her binds, and this time she felt them give.

It spurred her on.

With more tugs, a lot of tears, and what felt like a bucket full of sweat, not to mention pure, gritty determination, she found herself free.

~~~~

'Did you get the photos? You did? Excellent. What did you think? Did you see anything you liked?' Sean was laughing down the phone as the person on the other end said something funny. He was relaxing on the couch in the living room. His feet were up on the arm, and the remains of a sandwich were on a plate next to him.

'Yeah, I know! The last thing you wanted to see was my boner, but, you know, needs must and all that. You told me to make sure she got it good and hard … Well, she did.'

A bang from somewhere upstairs distracted his laugh, and he looked up at the ceiling. 'Hang on, Jay. I think our little piggy might have just broken her pen.'

There was a protest from the other end of the phone.

'OK, OK! I'm sorry, I won't call her a piggy anymore.' *Well at least not to you,* he continued in his head. 'I have to go. I need to see what's going on upstairs. I'll call you back later.'

He ended the call and slipped his phone into his trouser pocket. He walked out of the living room and up the stairs, shaking his head. 'Piggy, you better not be doing anything you shouldn't be up here. I'm warning you,' he shouted, gripping the handle to her bedroom door.

Before he opened it, he hesitated, listening for any movement inside. Happy that he couldn't hear anything out of the ordinary, he opened the door.

Something hit him. Hard.

Lights spun around his head as he reeled in surprise, holding his head.

More blows rained down on him.

He staggered back but kept hold of the door handle to stop himself from falling. He raised his other arm, protecting his face as another barrage of blows came. These mostly missed his head as his protective arm took the lion's share of the beating. It gave him precious seconds, all he needed to clear his head from the initial surprise of the attack. He used them to clear his thoughts and grasp what was happening.

He opened an eye and saw something standing inside the doorway. It looked like a cheap, low budget horror special effect. It was naked; its face resembled the boxer from the movies after he had been twelve rounds with the huge Russian guy.

It was Lisa.

She had taken a stance as if she were ready to bat in a baseball game, but instead of a bat, she was holding a long, smooth piece of wood. It looked like the bottom half of a pool cue.

Regardless of what it was, she was ready to take another strike.

It came, only this time he was ready for it.

She screamed as she lunged at him.

It was a mistake.

All the scream did was give him notice of the attack, and he easily countered it. He reached out and grabbed the weapon.

The force of the blow stung his hands but fell way short of making contact with his head. He watched with amusement as the shock of his fighting back registered on her face. He tasted blood in his mouth from where she'd hit him; it tasted good, spurring him on.

With a twist of his arm, he wrenched the makeshift weapon away from her, and with his other hand, he pushed her back into the bedroom she had almost escaped from. The surprise of the counterattack made her an easy target, and she fell with ease. He grinned as she clattered into the closet doors.

Then he was on her just as fast as she'd been on him.

He pinned her to the floor with one knee and leaned over her, his face a mixture of amusement and disgust. Blood was pouring from a wound on his forehead and was dripping onto her face.

Her eyes were wide, and she was trembling beneath him. He could see his reflection in her wide eyes, and it made him laugh.

'I'm going to let that one go, piggy,' he whispered. More blood and spit dripped down onto her. 'I like my bacon with a bit of fight in it. Although, right now, I'm tired of it. I want you to just lie back like a good little piggy and take what's coming to you.'

He picked up the pool cue and looked at it. He nodded, appreciating it for the effective weapon it was. He then turned his attentions back to her. The humour, no matter how sick and twisted it had been, was gone now. 'If you fight me again, I swear to whatever God there may be on this planet, or on others, I'll use this on you. I'll use it in ways it was never, *ever* supposed to be used.'

Lisa blinked. It was only a small gesture, but it was all he needed to know that the fight had left her. She had succumbed to his will. She was now his, a plaything to be used and ultimately discarded at whatever whim compelled him.

'If you resist me, if you do anything to even try to fight back and stop me, then this cue goes to work. Do you understand?'

Her wide eyes flicked briefly to look at the cue before flicking back to him. She nodded slowly.

'I'm sure Jay would be *very* interested in the pictures of what I would be doing with it, but I'm not a hundred percent sure you'd survive it.'

131

He leaned over and placed the cue above her head, tantalisingly close to her reach. He grinned, looking from the cue back to her, daring her to grab for it.

He moved his knee further up her body so he was straddling her chest and began to undo his trousers. As the metal buckle fell, it hit her on the chin, making her gasp a little.

'Have you ever heard of a stuck pig?' he asked, whispering now. 'No? Well, I'm going to skewer me a little piggy.'

With his trousers undone, he stood up. He slid them down before pulling them off, one leg at a time. He was naked beneath, and his erection was proudly pointing upwards, ready for business, whatever that business was. He wrapped his hand around his shaft and began to massage it up and down, all the while looking at her. Her complete and utter submission excited him. He knelt back down and rubbed his cock on her face.

She sealed her lips to his advancement. Undeterred, even amused by this, he rubbed his balls and then his engorged head on her lips. He watched as his pre-cum left a wet trail over her puffed, ruined face. 'Open wide, piggy,' he whispered. There was a slight judder in his voice, as if he was enjoying this a little too much.

She turned her head away, a pathetic whimper escaping her. As she did, he grabbed the pool cue. He showed it to her, grinning what might have been a good-natured smile if they had been in a different situation.

Her eyes focused on it.

He then leaned backwards and hit her with it between her legs.

It was a heavy whack, and the instant she opened her mouth to scream, he slipped his cock inside it.

She gagged.

He laughed. The knowledge of knowing she really hadn't been expecting him to do that made him happy.

For a short while only.

She bit down. Her teeth cut into the sensitive skin around the head of his shaft, and it was his turn to cry.

'Fuck,' he yelled. 'You fucking cunt!'

He punched her in the side of her head and felt her jaw slacken enough to allow him to pull himself back out. He looked down at her terrified face and then at his bitten penis.

Apart from some red teeth marks, which he could live with, there was no real damage. He dropped his weight on top of her, pinning her tighter to the ground. He took hold of the cue again. His face was filled with mirth.

'Piggies aren't supposed to bite,' he whispered as he hit her again between the legs.

~~~~

The feel and the smell of his penis as it moved over her lips turned her stomach. The wet, slimy trace it left in its wake sickened her. She was determined not to allow the foul thing into her mouth, knowing that if it did get inside, she would surely vomit.

'Open wide, piggy!' she heard him whisper.

She let out a sickened whimper as she turned her head away.

He picked up her father's pool cue and showed it to her. He then leaned back and swung. The pain that blossomed between her legs was, up to now, the worst thing that had happened to her this night. She was already sore from the pounding she had taken earlier. As the polished solid wood of the cue connected at a high speed with the delicate flesh of her vulva and her pubic bone, red blooms of pain blossomed in her eyes. Her breath was instantly gone, and she opened her mouth to scream.

As she tried to inhale, taking in precious fuel for the scream, her mouth was suddenly filled. She felt the vile thing that had been rubbing against her lips push into her, choking her. Instinctively, she bit down onto the thick, fleshy appendage, and she heard her aggressor scream in surprise and pain, almost as if he were in another room.

He shouted something unintelligible before punching her in the side of the head.

The ferocity of the punch slackened her jaw, and the disgusting thing slid out of her mouth. Her relief was only short lived. She looked up at his wounded penis and genuinely became scared for her life. The fear intensified when, after realising there was nothing wrong with it, he pinned her to the floor with his whole-body weight. The pressure of him took her breath away. She looked up and saw the pool cue again.

*What's he going to do with that now?* she asked herself. Blind panic set in as her brain imagined the horrors, the inflictions he could administer with it. It was an awful thing to think that getting hit in the head with the heavy pool cue would be the lesser of evils he could perform. It would be a blessing compared to what he had threatened to do to her with it.

He surprised her by laughing. He held the cue in the air, allowing her, wanting her, to see it before leaning in and whispering. 'Piggies aren't supposed to bite!'

More excruciating pain wracked through her. It issued, once again, from between her legs as the cue whacked her for a second time. She buckled as unimaginable torture coursed through every nerve-ending in her body. She very nearly bucked him off in her throes.

Then he hit her again. 'Piggies aren't supposed to bite,' he reiterated. Then a third time. 'Piggies aren't supposed … to bite.'

She lost count.

All she knew was he continued to hit her again and again and again. Her vision blurred. There were two Seans kneeling on her. *One's bad enough,* she thought as her body began to tingle before going numb.

Everything was going numb.

This was fine with her.

Nothing mattered anymore. The repeated blows with the cue, the foul-tasting cock, her aching and stinging nipples. None of it. Everything was distant, far away. *Is this what death feels like?* If it was, she welcomed it. She relaxed as the world swam away from her.

*I hope you fucking die soon, you sick bastard!* This was her last thought before something thick, warm, and bitter squirted into her mouth. There was a brief moment where she smelt detergent. She gagged, dribbling whatever it was over her chin.

Then everything went dark, and she fell into the welcome, warm embrace of nothingness.

## 36.

HE WAS IN a frenzy now, and he couldn't stop himself from hitting her. Laughing, he forced his cock into her mouth every time she opened it to scream. He looked down at her. She was helpless, dazed, broken. The rush of ultimate dominion over her, over another human being, was bringing him close to orgasm.

He wondered if he could kill a person by forcing his dick too far into her mouth.

He hit her again. He lost count of how many times he did it. *Not enough,* he thought with a grin.

Her eyes flickered towards the back of her head, and something akin to a smile spread across her face. That was too much for him. He felt his orgasm rising in the tingling of his feet and the buckling of his knees. Seconds later, he cried out as his seed exploded from the tip of his head, filling the inside of her mouth. The ejaculation was so strong that it shot over her hair and even over the carpet around her face.

The feeling was so intense that the very world around him seemed dimmed slightly in his ecstasy. His head swam, just a little, and every stress, every horrible thing that had happened to him in his miserable little life meant nothing.

Just for a few blessed seconds.

He dropped the cue next to her lifeless body and fell forward onto his hands.

He was spent in more ways than one.

His heart was thudding. It must have been pumping at least ten times faster than it should be. His arms and legs were aching from the physical workout he had given them. His nose was swollen, and he would have two bruises around his eyes tomorrow. The tip of his dick was tender from her bite, but all in all, he thought what he'd managed to do tonight was worth the effort spent.

He looked at her as she lay on the floor in her bedroom. Her face was covered in his semen. It was in her hair; it was coating her chin as it dribbled from her mouth; it was everywhere.

He felt a sense of pride in how much he had managed to produce. Her once beautiful face was now a mixture of grey, pink, and purple.

A horrible thought occurred to him, and he leaned in to check her pulse. He panicked when she didn't appear to be moving. After a few, frantic moments, he found a slow rhythm beneath his finger. He reached into the inside pocket of his jacket. He removed his cell phone and began to snap photographs of her ruined face and body.

He stood, stepped back a little, and looked at her. He was concerned that the wounds he'd caused were a bit too deep and wouldn't heal quickly. Then he remembered her parents were away for at least another eight days. 'Plenty of time to heal,' he mumbled.

He looked at her again, marvelling at his art.

He thought something was missing. Just a little something to finish off, to compile her indignity, to add to the humiliation he had forced upon her. He giggled to himself as he stepped over the twitching body of his former girlfriend and squatted. He emptied his bowels over her wounded chest, sniggering to himself as he did. He wiped himself on her bedsheets, put his trousers back on, and regarded his handiwork.

He took his phone out again and looked at her through the screen. She was perfectly pathetic. His defecation was dripping from her chest onto the floor, soaking into the carpet. His hands were shaking as he took another series of pictures.

He selected the contact JAY in his phone, and after highlighting the pictures he had just taken, he pressed SEND.

He then released a hot, thick flow of urine all over her. It washed the pinkish cum/blood mix from her face and mingled with the red of her blood and the beige of his faeces. He chuckled, wincing a little as he shook his stinging appendage, allowing the last of the flow to trickle out over her. Before he put himself away, he examined the bite marks on the head. *That's going to hurt tomorrow,* he thought. He then grinned as he looked around the room. *Nothing too untidy*. He buckled up his belt and picked up the bloody pool cue lying next to her body, then made his way down the stairs, unlocked the front door, and let himself out of the house.

~~~~~

It was early morning. His cell phone told him that it was not even six yet. The neighbourhood would still be asleep at this early hour. He made his way along the street towards the park at the end of the block, still carrying the cue. He found an open storm drain and forced it down before continuing towards his car. As he walked, he whistled a jaunty little tune to himself, one that he remembered from an old cartoon about some little people going to work.

He loved this time of the day.

37.

PAIN …

There was nothing else in her world.

Pain was the beginning, the middle, and, as she felt it, the ending.

There was only pain.

It was pure. As if it were all she had ever known. Like nothing else had ever existed in her world other than pain.

The top of her head, her hair, her eyes, cheeks, nose, mouth, teeth, jaw. She felt sick as wave after wave of agonised nausea washed over her, drenching her, pulling her under its unrelenting tides. Drowning her in its undulating relentlessness.

Her neck!

*Have I broken my neck?* Searing agony flowed from her head, through her shoulders, and into her chest. *Have I fallen? Am I dead?* She honestly had no recollection of how she got to where she was.

She knew she was on the floor. She knew this because she could feel the warm fuzz of carpet beneath her screaming, pain-wracked back.

She wanted to move, but her arms screamed at her. They stabbed her with millions of pins and needles. It was a feeling she used to enjoy, but not today, probably never again. With pure determination, she shifted her arm from beneath her; her shoulders shrieked, ordering her to stop. She opened her mouth to vocalise the shriek but found her jaw wouldn't work either. This discovery intensified her horror at the situation she had awoken to.

She opened her eyes.

Or at least she tried to.

# The Boyfriend

Her eyelids wouldn't work. Hell, her eye *sockets* wouldn't work. Panic rose in her, and sweet adrenaline coursed through her torso. She wanted, needed, to move, to get up, but her arms were too weak to hold her weight.

However, it wasn't the only reason why she couldn't get up.

Her legs throbbed, and tear-inducing agony ebbed from her crotch.

Yet again, this wasn't the sole reason she couldn't get up from the floor.

Her head swam as she moved it. It was just another part of her body letting her down. Her neck was too weak and too filled with pain to support its weight.

The main reason she couldn't get up was because of the vomit she could feel sitting in her stomach. It was there, ready to spill at the first given opportunity. It was ready to add itself to the vomit that her dizziness had already expelled, to mix with the stink of blood, semen, and what she assumed must have been her own ablutions, until she felt the cold slime on her chest. She forced herself to raise her hand, to investigate what it was.

She didn't like the findings.

The stink caused the vomit to make its threatening appearance. The warm, thick fluid stung as it raced from her stomach to pour from her mouth and nose.

The sheer effort of retching made her weakened body shudder as her arms and legs shook uncontrollably. Her battered and bruised body broke into a cold sweat that seemed to sting every single pore in her flesh. She turned her head slowly, and the cooling vomit that her stomach had just released tickled her cheek.

Then there was nothing again.

Only pain and darkness. The stink of what she was lying in was her only external sensation.

Internally was a different matter entirely. She felt something inside. It was only for a moment or two, but her mind was rational enough to register it before she blanked out entirely.

It was shame!

38.

'SO HOW DID it go with Ryan last night?' Nichola was lying on her back in her bedroom, talking on her cell phone via the speaker function. She was talking to Paula, brimming with excitement as she had something she wanted to tell her friend about her and Andrew, but she was determined Nichola would spill her news first.

'Shhh, hang on, I'm in the same room as my mom,' Paula whispered down the line. 'I'll call you back from my room.'

Nichola hung up the phone and laughed. 'Oh, you dirty bitch,' she giggled as she lay back on her bed, willing her phone to ring. A few agonisingly long moments later, the phone rang, and she pressed the button on the first ring, making sure it wasn't on speakerphone this time. 'So? Speak to me, girlfriend.'

'So, after we left Lisa's, I couldn't go home; I'd told my mom we were sleeping over.'

'And ...'

'After we finally manged to ditch that prick Peter, me and Ryan walked back through the park. Holding hands in the moonlight.'

'Ooooh, get you,' Nichola gushed. 'All romantic and shit.'

Paula was laughing but still trying to keep quiet at the same time. 'Then, one thing led to another, and we were making out big time on the grass.'

'Eeew ... you slut,' Nichola squealed playfully. 'In England, they call that dogging.'

'What?'

'Having sex in a public place while people watch. It's called dogging.'

# The Boyfriend

Paula was silent for a short while. Nichola thought she'd hung up. 'Are you still there?' she asked, concerned.

'Do you think there were people watching?' Paula asked, all the humour dropped from her voice.

'Totally. I would have. Plus, I'd have had my mobile with me. Sister, you'd be all over the internet by now.'

Paula was totally silent.

Nichola shook her head in amusement. 'Don't worry. I've been on all the sites this morning, and there's nothing about you,' she said, rolling her eyes at her friend's naivety.

Paula breathed a sigh of relief.

'Yet,' Nichola concluded with a laugh.

Paula was laughing now too. 'Anyway, have you heard from Lisa?'

'Nothing. I can't believe she'd ruin the night like that,' Nichola said with a pout, thinking back on the blow out, just when it was getting interesting. 'But then, didn't she say something about Sean taking her away for a few days?'

'Oh yeah, her cherry popping getaway. That's today, isn't it?'

'I don't even think the bitch would tell us anything about it anyway. She's so stuck up these days. Sean this, and Sean that. I'm fucking bored with Sean.'

Nichola was laughing. 'Don't be mean. She's just excited, that's all. Wouldn't you be if a big, handsome guy was that into you?'

'Well, I suppose so, but … I don't know. I just think there's something kind of off about him. That picture she showed us, did you see his eyes? They looked cold as fuck to me.'

Nichola didn't answer for a few moments, as if considering what her friend had just said. 'Yeah. I saw them. I kind of liked them. I mean, I wouldn't mind them looking up at me from between my legs, if you know what I mean.'

Paula screamed down the phone. 'Nichola, you are one dirty *be-atch!* But I totally get what you mean.'

'So, do you want to hear my news?' Nichola asked, ready to spill the beans on her own love life.

'Totally,' was Paula's enthusiastic reply.

39.

LISA WAS IN the shower cubical. She had been in there almost constantly for the last three days. If she wasn't trying, unsuccessfully, to sleep, then she could be found in there with an endless stream of hot water sluicing over her ruined body, washing away the stream of hot, salty tears pouring down her cheeks at the same time. She would scrub and scrub, wanting to wash the blood, the semen, the excrement (*I can't believe he shit on me,* she would sob and sob for hours) from her body.

Every now and then, she would look at her wounds. The more vicious ones, the burns, on her breasts and thighs were still red raw, blistered, and painful. She had used almost a whole tube of antibiotic ointment on them, but her nipples were still far too sore to touch.

They were even worse to look at.

After a few false starts, she managed to pry herself out of the cubicle, knowing it was time to brave a look into the full-length mirror on the bathroom door. With the constant ache in her limbs becoming the norm, she frowned as she wiped the steam from the glass, horrified by what she saw. After another breakdown into frantic tears and gut-wrenching self-loathing passed, she realised that the bruises and scratches on her face, neck, arms, and lower legs looked like they were settling down. The redness had passed, and they were now ugly deep purples and greens.

'Thank heavens for small mercies,' she whispered through lips that were returning to something resembling a normal size. She thought about her parents not being home for a few days yet. *Hopefully, my face will have healed by then, or at least to the point of using makeup.*

It was her hair that concerned her. The bastard had managed to pull clumps out of her scalp, leaving patches of scabbed bare skin. She was going to have to cut her hair short and style it over the patches until they could grow back. She cried again at the constant reminder of what had happened until she could build up the courage to cut it.

Her gaze dared to move down, to look at the burns on her nipples. They were raw and weeping. She tried to trace the cigarette burns up her stomach with a finger but couldn't, they were still too tender to touch. The lines of bruises across her stomach and pubic area where he'd pinched her and hit her with the cue were bruising too. Through her tears and the pain, all she could think about was being thankful she didn't have any broken bones.

Thankful she was still alive.

As she inspected her naked body, a thought occurred to her. It was a horrible thought but one that she needed to process. She would never be the same happy-go-lucky person ever again.

*How could someone do something like this to another person? How could someone who had seemed so nice, be so ...* She couldn't even finish the thought before more tears began to fall.

She winced as she eased herself into the bath she had run earlier, gasping as the cold water caressed every nook of her body. She needed this to ease the pain and the terrible, horrible ache between her legs. It also helped to clean the areas, washing the dirt, the stink, imaginary or not, and the shame away, although she knew it would take more than sitting in a cold bath to erase that.

The house telephone had been ringing almost constantly, as had her mobile, for the last three days, since ... She didn't know what to call it. *Was it an attack? It was certainly rape. Had he wanted to kill me? Why had he let me go?* Thoughts like these had been circling like buzzards in a cheesy western film all during the sleepless nights and the restless days that followed.

Tears began to flow at the thought of her and her father watching those cheesy western films.

'Daddy,' she sobbed in the cold water.

She had been ignoring the telephone. There was no one she wanted to speak to right now, that even included her parents and her friends. She knew her mother and father would be going out of their minds with worry. She had sent them text messages, lying about missing their calls. *I'll talk to them tonight,* she thought between sobs as she attempted to relax into the water, enjoying the numbing sensation between her legs and in her joints. She scoffed angrily at the thought of calling her mom and dad. She would have to pretend to be normal, as if life hadn't just been ripped up and the pieces scattered to the four winds. There was nothing they could do; they were thousands of miles away now and thankfully, tragically, still days away from coming home.

She looked at her disfigured breasts again, and the thought that nothing would ever be normal came back to slap her in the face.

Tears came again. She loathed herself for them. She had always looked down on self-pity, but now, stripped of everything else, including her dignity, it was all she had.

When the tears dried up and her body had taken in too much cold water, she eased herself out of the tub, grimacing as every muscle, every bone protested at her movements. She rested with her feet still in the water, preparing herself for the mammoth task of stepping out of the tub and onto the cold floor of the bathroom. Once back on dry land, she wrapped herself lightly in the warm towel waiting for her on the rail. As the towel came into contact with the raw wounds she used to call nipples, she drew a surprised intake of breath and pulled the fabric away to stop irritating the injuries any more than they already were.

There was a bottle of old painkillers and some water waiting for her in her bedroom. She shook two pills out, popped them into her mouth, and took a swig of the lukewarm drink. Then she looked at the bottle. The neck of the brown plastic container was so inviting. There were enough pills in there to do the job of what she was contemplating if coupled with the whiskey her father kept in his cabinet. She took a deep, shaky breath. In her current mindset, it was plausible, maybe even desirable. She shook the bottle, listening to the pills rattle. She swallowed, closed her eyes, and put the lid back on, making sure to twist it extra tight.

She couldn't do it.

Wouldn't do it.

She wouldn't give that bastard the satisfaction of knowing he broke her. There was no way she would let him win.

# The Boyfriend

Putting the bottle back on her side table, she sat slowly and carefully on the bed and began the nightly routine of tending and dressing her many wounds. When she was finished, she took her cell phone and looked at it. There were twenty-two missed calls and fifty-five text messages. She sighed and began scrolling through them.

Most were from her mother and father, a couple from Nichola and Paula, quite a few from Janice, and there were two from *him*. She couldn't bring herself to even think of his name. Each time she looked at his number, her heart hammered in her chest. *How could that bastard call me after what he's done?* The sight of his name sent the tears flowing again.

After a small while, when she had composed herself enough, she knew it was time to attempt that phone call with her mother.

Everything would be better once she had spoken to her.

'Lisa, where the HELL have you been? We've been out of our minds worrying about you. Your father's downstairs now, trying to get us an early flight home.'

On hearing her mother's voice, Lisa broke down, sobbing.

'Lisa? Lisa, honey, is everything all right? What's the matter, baby?' Her mother's voice changed from angry to scared in a flash. 'Lisa, answer me, child. Is everything all right?'

'Oh, Mom!' was all she could let out before another set of sobs ripped through her.

'Lisa, you're scaring me now. Tell me what's the matter; tell me right now.'

'Oh, Mom, it's nothing,' she lied. 'I've missed you, that's all.'

'Aw, honey,' Flo replied, her voice settling back to normal tones. 'Listen now, Lisa, take a moment to compose yourself. We've both missed you too, especially these last couple of days. How come you haven't answered our calls? We've been thinking the worst!'

She wiped her eyes, giving herself a moment or two to compose herself. She thought about what she should tell her mother, thousands of miles away in Europe with no way of getting home within twenty-four hours. She didn't want them to worry, and she didn't want them to see her looking like she did right now. It was easier to lie about everything. They both worked so hard; they deserved a worry-free break. Besides, they would ask questions, the police would be involved, and she would have to go to the hospital, answer a million questions, and re-live what had happened a million times over. It was the last thing she needed right then. She re-lived it enough each time she closed her eyes, without having to relate the story over and over again to strangers who would probably think it was her own fault anyway, allowing the boy into her house, on her own. *I was asking for it, they'd say.*

'But we've been calling on your mobile too, honey. Your dad has been tearing out what's left of his hair. He can't even log on to the CCTV system.'

She snorted at that; it was an ugly sound. 'Oh, well, I couldn't find the damned thing for a while. I thought one of the girls was playing a joke on me until I found it. It had fallen down the side of my bed,' she lied again, taking a deep, shaky breath. She was getting so good at it. 'And it was set to silent, so I missed them all. I did text you when I found it. I don't know what's wrong with the CCTV, though. Daddy taught me how to use it before he left, but it all went over my head.'

'Well, OK then,' her mother replied. Lisa thought she could hear mistrust in her voice. 'I believe you; millions wouldn't, though. We'll be home in a few days. I hope the place is tidy … and I hope you haven't been having boys around.'

She swallowed, gulped really. *Just the one,* she thought touching her breasts and wincing at the sting. She looked at the gauze pads on the wounds and managed a half-hearted laugh that she hoped would pass as genuine. 'What? Me? No, just me and the girlies, chilling out. I don't have time for boys.'

'So, you haven't seen anything of Sean?'

On hearing his name, she winced, almost as if he were still there, ready to hit her again, to put that ugly, stinking *thing* back into her. It was almost as if mentioning his name might conjure him up like an evil spirit or a demon. She looked around her bedroom, surprised to feel goosebumps rising on her skin.

Every part of her body ached and throbbed uncomfortably.

'Sean? No,' she lied again, hating herself for the deception but not wanting to ruin their vacation. 'I don't think I'll be seeing him again, actually. He turned out to be a bit of a creep, to tell you the truth.'

'Aw, baby, I'm sorry to hear that. He seemed nice.'

*Yeah, he did!*

'Well, I can't say I'm too disappointed. I'm just glad you're OK. We were worried. Your father would have wanted to say hello, but he's still at the main desk.'

'I love you both; you know that don't you?' Lisa said, feeling sad in her heart.

'We love you too, baby, and we'll see you in a few days.'

'OK, Mom. I can't wait. I'll see you when you get back.'

'Bye, baby. Dad'll call a bit later; make sure you answer. Maybe have a look at the damned CCTV system. I swear he's driving me crazy about it. Goodnight, sweetheart.'

As Lisa hung up, she curled herself into a ball on her bed, ignoring the screaming agonies of her body. She ignored the blood and the pus seeping through the dressings on her many wounds, ignored her intimate parts that had done nothing but throb for days. She hugged her arms and legs to her chest and cried.

The tears turned into sobs and, eventually, screams.

The screams surprised her somewhat, as she wasn't expecting it and, at first, didn't even realise it was her own voice causing it.

The screaming carried on for a while, until sleep came and took her away from her suffering. But it opened her up to another form of torment.

She just couldn't get away from what had happened.

This time, her torment was psychological. Her dreams were deep and unpleasant.

40.

*WHY DID IT happen to me? What did I do for him to hate me so much? Who is Jay, and why does* he *hate me so much?* These thoughts were racing through her head on a continual loop, what felt like every minute of every day since it happened.

Lisa was sat in dirty pyjamas in the living room, staring intently at the area next to the island, where the main part of her ordeal had taken place. She had been sitting there for what felt like forever. The whole horrific scene, the beatings, the taking of her virginity, the loss of her innocence, it all happened right there.

The idea of burning the house down, with her inside, had occurred more than once. The suicidal thoughts from the other night had not gone away. She trusted herself and knew she would never succumb to them; she was more determined than that. Sean Knight would *not* break her, she knew this, yet the ugly, dark feelings just would not pass.

She would see him. She would smell him, that aftershave he'd worn that had smelt so sexy in the middle of the night. She would hear him sneaking around the house in the dead of night. He was in the bathroom every single time she wanted to go inside. He was in her head; he was in her dreams–Sean Knight was everywhere.

However, she steadfastly refused to allow him to win.

She toyed with the idea of going to the police, filing an assault and battery and rape charge. She wanted him to be prosecuted and punished to the full extent of the law. In reality, she wanted more than that. It was probably his first offence; he was still only eighteen years of age. He would probably get a lighter sentence, out on probation after a few years. Then he would be free to hunt her down.

That was even *if* it made it to trial. She was a young girl who'd allowed a boy into her home while her parents were away. She'd turned the CCTV system off. They would argue she'd led him on.

They would call Peter as a witness. He would tell them she had led him on the same night.

No, the police were out. Besides, she wanted him to suffer, not only for the shame and the degradation he had put her through but for having the audacity to call her cell phone afterwards, not once but twice.

She wanted to see him hurt.

She wanted revenge. Only, the thing about revenge was that you needed to know how to deliver it.

She had absolutely no idea what she could do.

During the long, lonely hours of sitting, being a prisoner in her own home, licking her wounds, she mulled it over.

She thought long and hard about it.

In time, she thought of little else.

She considered getting a gun. Only she had no idea how to go about obtaining one since she couldn't get one legally, add to that the fact that she didn't think she would have what it took to go through with it anyway. In her mind, she imagined pulling the gun, him quickly disarming her, and then he, psychopathic Sean Knight, would hold the gun on her. Now she knew what he was capable of, having first-hand knowledge of it, she didn't think he would have a problem pulling that trigger and killing her.

*That might be a blessing,* she thought, the dreaded melancholy filling her head again.

She thought about hiring someone to do it for her. It had been done a million times in the movies. *With my luck, the person would get caught and it would all end up on my head anyway,* she thought miserably.

The hours and days rolled on. She spoke to her parents a few more times, convincing them all was well and that she was having a good time, faking that she didn't know what was wrong with the CCTV. She didn't answer the calls from her friends. She didn't want them to see her like this, and if the truth be known, she was still mad at them for leaving her after Peter …

She didn't want to think about Peter right now.

The most persistent caller had been Janice, her best friend. A number of times she had contemplated answering, longing for someone to talk to, someone who could hold this dreadful, despicable secret with her, for when it all got too much … but she was still mad at her too …

It was a tough decision but a much needed one. She made the call to Janice.

~~~~

'LISA, WHERE THE hell have you been? We've all been worried about you. Paula and Nichola have been calling you, Kate too.'

Silence was Lisa's reply.

'Lisa? Lisa, are you there? Come on, girl, you're scaring me now.'

A small, pathetic sob broke from the confinement of her mouth. She didn't want these emotions to see the light. She wanted to be stoic, reserved, but her friend's voice on the other end of the phone caused everything she was trying to hold back to release.

'Are you crying?' Janice asked.

'Janice … can you come over?' Lisa fought hard for every last word in that sentence. Her body hadn't wanted her to speak. Her lips were quivering, and her breath kept threatening to steal the words.

'Of course I can. I'll leave right now. I'll be there in ten. Are you OK?'

'I'll … I'll let you know when you get here. Call me when you're outside. I don't want to answer the door to anyone I don't know.'

'Lisa, I'm freaking out here. What's the—'

She cut her friend off mid-sentence. She didn't want to talk over the phone. Janice would know soon enough what had happened to her. She had decided that Janice would be the crutch she needed to get her through this whole ordeal, whether she wanted to be or not!

41.

'HOLY SHIT! LISA, what happened?'

At the very moment she opened the door, at the precise second she saw her friend's worry and concern, Lisa's wall crashed down around her. She broke down. Without invitation, Janice stormed inside the house, dumped her bag on the floor, and held out her hands to touch her friend's discoloured face.

Lisa flinched from the contact.

This was the first person she had seen in days. She was the first person who had seen her since ... The only person to see her wounds. A lot of the swelling had gone down, and other than the fading purples, the shape of her face was mostly back to normal. But some scars, physical and psychological, would take a lot longer to fade.

'Was this Sean?' Janice asked, watching tears fall from Lisa's panda bear eyes. 'Did he do this to you?'

She couldn't speak. She flinched again as both Janice's hands touched her. Stepping back just out of Janice's reach, she folded her arms over her chest and nodded between sobs.

'That bastard,' Janice gasped. 'Why? What happened?'

Lisa walked into the living room and sat carefully on the sofa, indicating for her friend to sit beside her. Janice did as she was bidden, once again putting her hands out to caress her friend's face, and once again, Lisa pulled back. She put her hands up to stop the touching while shaking her head. It was only a small gesture, but she hoped it would speak to Janice.

She seemed to understand, and Lisa was thankful for it.

With itchy tears streaming down her face, Lisa began to relay everything she could remember from when the girls left. She told her about Peter coming back, making a nuisance of himself, about her ringing *him*, and *him* turning up.

Every last detail she could recall, which, it turned out, was far from the whole story.

Thankfully, Janice sat silently through the whole gruesome tale. Her face fell more and more as the story unfolded. She winced as Lisa explained what happened with the pool cue, and her hand covered her mouth as she explained about him forcing his penis into her mouth.

Thankfully, she didn't ask any questions, she just allowed Lisa to flow. When she had finished, she sat back on the couch and wiped her stinging eyes.

'Oh, Lisa. I feel like I need to give you a hug.' Janice sobbed.

Lisa shook her head. 'I can't, Janice. I just can't.' She thought about it, weighed it up in her head, the pros and the cons of showing Janice just why she couldn't bear a hug from anyone.

She thought it was justified.

'I ... I need to show you something.'

Janice looked at her, her face was full of questions, but Lisa was thankful she sat back and allowed her to outpour in her own way. 'What is it? You're scaring me right now.'

Lisa closed her eyes and slowly began to undo the buttons on the stained pyjama top.

'Oh, fuck, Lisa, what are you doing?'

Lisa didn't say anything, she just continued to undo her buttons.

Janice's eyes narrowed as the front of the pyjama top came loose. She swallowed hard in anticipation of what she was about to be shown. When the top was almost open, she shook her head. 'Lisa, can't you just tell me what it is?' she pleaded. 'I'm not sure I want to ...'

Lisa continued, unperturbed. She needed her friend to see.

When she'd undone the last button, Lisa looked at her. 'What I'm going to show you is the worst part of it. It's the reason why I can't hug you, why I'm scared I won't be able to hug my mom and dad when they get home.'

She opened her top.

Janice gasped.

Her stomach and breasts were littered with green and purple bruises. There were ugly red, mottled burn marks down her stomach. The gauze pads covering her nipples were discoloured with pus that had seeped through.

Janice's wide eyes stopped roaming over Lisa's ruined body and made their way up to her face. 'Bastard,' she hissed, leaning forward, her hand outstretched as if to touch her.

Lisa flinched again, shaking her head.

'You can't touch me, Janice. It's too sore.'

Janice put her hand up to her mouth and sniffed. 'Are your nipples as bad as your stomach?' she whispered.

Lisa nodded. 'Worse,' she managed.

Janice gulped, making an ugly sound. 'Can I see?' she whispered.

Lisa closed her eyes and began to slowly remove the tape from the pads. She was taking rapid, shallow breaths, and her eyes were closed tight. She endured the pain of peeling the sticky pads from her skin. There was a moment when she couldn't hold back the wince, and her whole body shivered, as the pad had stuck to the wound underneath.

Her hand still at her mouth, Janice watched her struggle.

With a last painful tug, the pad came away, and her nipple, or what was left of it, was free.

Janice was shaking her head. Lisa could see the tears welling in her eyes. She looked down and saw the mess of scabbed skin and amber fluid. There were little bits of white fluff from the pad still stuck to it. Her nipple was a swollen, ugly little knot of red flesh.

Janice's whole face was a grimace. 'Lisa, what the fuck? How could that bastard do *this* to you?' she whispered.

'Cigarette burns,' she replied, shocking herself with her stoic answer. 'He did it to both of them, and all down my stomach too.'

This time Janice did hug her. She approached her slowly and wrapped her arms around her, careful not to touch the brutal wounds on her exposed flesh.

Lisa shied away at first, but then, as Janice was showing no signs of giving in, she tentatively welcomed the embrace. It felt nice having human contact from someone who wasn't trying to hurt her, or kill her.

They sat that way for a long time. Both rocking, both crying.

After a while, Janice broke away. She sniffed and wiped her eyes. She looked at Lisa, and her lips began to tremble again.

Lisa could see the sympathy in her friend's face as she struggled to release a sad little smile.

There was warmth in that smile.

Janice's hand reached out, and once again, Lisa backed off. However, remembering how tenderly she had just hugged her, she gave in and allowed the touch.

Janice's hand went up to Lisa's hair. There were bald and scabbed patches where it had been pulled out in clumps. Janice ran her fingers through it. 'We're going to have to do something about this, you know. I think you should go to the police.'

Lisa shook her head. 'I don't know what to do. I feel so …'

'I know. Listen, I'll support you in whatever you decide to do. If you want to go to the police and get this bastard locked up, then I'll go with you. I'll be there for you. However, your folks will be back soon, and I'm guessing that you don't want them to know about what's happened,' Janice said, still delicately running her fingers through Lisa's hair.

Lisa began to put the pad back over her nipple. 'I haven't even thought about what to tell them,' she confessed.

Janice looked at her watch. 'Well, I'll tell you what, let me go to the store before it closes. We'll load up on ointments and sprays. Also, what do you think about me cutting your hair? Hide those patches. Yeah?'

Lisa ran her own hand through her hair, wincing as her fingers brushed against scabs that had formed where Sean had dragged her from room to room, pulling the hair out by the roots. They were still tender, and they stung as her fingers caressed the sensitive skin. She nodded. 'Yeah,' she muttered. She had always loved her long, dark hair. Now it was just another thing that *he* had taken from her.

'OK. I'll be about twenty minutes tops. Do you want me to take a key, so you don't have to let me in?'

Lisa shook her head. 'No, my dad would kill me if he found out. I'll let you in.'

'All right. Are you going to be OK?'

She smiled. It was the first smile she'd managed in days. It felt strange, nice, but strange. 'Yeah, I'll be fine.'

As she turned to leave, Lisa looked up at her from the couch. 'Janice?'

'Yeah?'

'Would you be able to stay over tonight? I think … I just think it would be nice to have some company.'

Janice smiled, closed her eyes, and nodded. 'Of course.'

'Your folks won't mind?'

She laughed a little. 'My folks won't even notice. My brother's home from the hospital, and all of a sudden, everything is about him. Believe me, I won't be missed,' she laughed.

Lisa breathed a sigh of relief as she heard the door close. Although she loved Janice, she was glad she was gone. She would have enough of her tonight.

She got up to go to the kitchen to make herself a cup of tea when a thought occurred to her. *James is home? Is that what she just said? Her brother, James, is home?* Janice's brother had been in a secure facility ever since he had a mental breakdown. *Jay … James … Could he be the Jay that* he *was talking to? Messaging?*

The thought didn't sit well with her, and she returned to the living room, the cup of tea all but forgotten.

42.

SEAN WAS HOME. He'd been laying low ever since his night of fun. His parents had been having their usual sex and drug parties, so he'd now come to think of the garage, and the back of the car, as his permanent bedroom. He was dozing to another rock song blaring from the house when his phone beeping snapped him awake.

He fished around in his pocket, eventually retrieving the device, and looked at the screen. It read 'JAY.'

Intrigued, he opened the text message.

'HAVE U HEARD NYTHING FROM R MUTUAL FRIEND?'

Sean smiled at the message before typing back.

'NO ... DO YOU THINK SHE WENT 2 POLICE?'

'U WOULD HAV HEARD BY NOW. SHAMED HER GUD. GUD WORK MAN!!!'

Sean smiled as he read the reply. He'd been worried about the police, as he'd been thinking that he might have taken it a little bit too far. But it seemed that the little piggy must have enjoyed it after all. He contemplated calling her again like he'd done the day after the deed, but he thought girls with bruises were not attractive.

He'd leave it for a little while.

He leaned up to put the phone back in his pocket when a thought occurred to him. He took his phone and lit it up again. 'DID U TALK 2 THE GUYS? AM I IN?'

He waited for Jay's reply. When no return text was forthcoming, he put the phone back in his pocket, grinning himself to sleep.

43.

'DO YOU KNOW anyone named Jay?' Lisa asked as she sat in one of the high-backed kitchen chairs. She had taken great pains not to sit on the one *he* had forced her into. She was looking into the mirror that Janice had brought down from her bedroom. She couldn't take her eyes off the bruises on her face; even though they had receded quite a bit, they were the evidence of the beating she had taken and the ordeal she'd survived. *I'm never going to be able to forget it,* she thought as Janice stood behind her with scissors and a comb.

'Jay?' Janice asked, shaking her head. 'I don't think I know anyone named Jay. Why do you ask?'

'Doesn't your brother get called Jay sometimes?' She had been thinking about this for a while and had worried about how to bring it up to Janice. She could be sensitive about her family sometimes.

Janice pouted as she thought about the question. 'Not that I know of. What few friends that loser has mostly call him Jamie. Why?'

Lisa didn't even want to say his name, but she'd started the conversation and now had to continue it. 'It's someone who Sean was in contact with when he was … well, you know.'

Janice smiled at her in the mirror. Lisa could see the pity in that smile, and in that moment, she hated Janice. She didn't really hate her, she hated herself for her friend pitying her in the first place. She supposed that if this continued, she'd begin to hate the world.

*Pity!*

She was aware of how pathetic that sounded, even in her head.

'Nope, I can't think of anyone. Do you think it might be someone from his school?'

Lisa shrugged, shaking her head. She didn't want to, but she thought she had to for the sake of her own sanity—she changed the subject. 'How are things with you and ...' Lisa tutted and shook her head. 'Oh, I can't think of his name.'

'Clinton? Oh, I ditched that loser. All he was interested in was getting into ...' she paused, stopping what she was doing with her scissors and looked at Lisa in the mirror. 'Lisa, I'm so sorry. I didn't mean to ...'

Lisa laughed. Once again, the noise sounded funny to her; she'd done so little of it since ... 'Don't worry, I know the world moves on. So, when did your brother get home?'

'About three weeks ago. Ugh, he's such a fucking creep. He makes my skin ...' Janice paused again. Her eyes widened as she looked in the mirror. 'You don't think this Jay could be Jamie, do you?'

Lisa's face flushed.

'You do, don't you?' Janice put the scissors down on the kitchen counter and walked around the stool to look Lisa in the face. 'You totally think my brother is Jay and that he's got something to do with what happened.'

Lisa wanted to backtrack. She could feel her face burning, and as she looked in the mirror, she saw that the flush brought out the green of her bruises. 'No, Janice! I never ...' she began, stuttering to get her words out, afraid of upsetting her one and only friend in the whole world.

'Shhh,' Janice shushed her, shaking her head. She was staring above Lisa's head into nothing. 'What if you're right? Think about it,' Janice said, still looking at the kitchen wall, seemingly in a world of her own. 'He's been away due to a much-publicised mental breakdown. He comes back, and within a week, this happens. You could be right.'

Lisa was relieved she hadn't offended her friend.

Janice shivered theatrically as she picked the scissors up, getting back to work on Lisa's hair. 'It all fits. But why would he hate you? Not to mention hating you enough to get someone to do this to you?'

# The Boyfriend

Lisa couldn't answer that one. She'd never had anything to do with James, Janice's brother.

With a few more snips, her hair was finished. 'Ta dah!' Janice exclaimed, putting the scissors back onto the table. 'It's done. It's a little, erm, radical, and your mom and dad are definitely going to notice, but I think it looks gorgeous.'

Lisa sat back and admired the drastic cut. It was now short up the back with length at the sides. The lengths were combed over in a way that covered her exposed scabbed patches of scalp. There wasn't much of a smile from her as she teased it back and forth.

'I know it's not fantastic,' Janice offered. 'But it's the best I could do. It'll totally cover you up until it all grows back again.'

'No, it's not the cut, it's just why I've had to have it done in the first place.' She shook her head. 'Ignore me, I'm just depressed.' She reached out her hand and took hold of Janice's and squeezed it. The small smile that she had been hiding showed itself, just a little.

It was enough to make Janice smile too.

44.

JANICE BECAME LISA'S crutch. She stayed over, and Lisa revelled in the comfort of having her best friend and a confidant with her at all times. The next day, they ventured out to the local store and purchased some steaks, as they had both looked up online that a juicy steak can draw out a bruise from human flesh, and Lisa was willing to do anything to resemble normal when her mother and father returned from their vacation.

With a small touch of good luck, her father called to tell her their flight had been cancelled due to storms in Germany, so they would be a day late coming home. Lisa had been relieved, as it would give her wounds just that little bit more time to heal.

The steak worked wonders. After applying it for a few hours, her face was only showing a trace of the bruising. It turned her stomach having the raw meat touch her face, not to mention the stink of it after a while, but it was a small price to pay. Janice had been able to conceal the worst of it with clever makeup.

Despite her spirits lifting, sleep was still hard to come by.

She woke in the middle of the night screaming, trying to fight off unseen attackers hellbent on raping and killing her. Other times, she was convinced someone was in the house, someone who, unsurprisingly, wanted to rape and kill her.

Each time, Janice soothed her. She walked her around the house, explaining to her that the doors were locked and that her father's security system was in place; they were safe and secure inside the house. There were no bad guys trying to get her.

They sat and talked about what had happened. They conversed and theorised about who Jay could be and why *he who won't be named* had been so vicious towards her. Lisa told her all the nice things that *he'd* done for her in the few times they had been out, but then she countered all of that by telling her about the horrible, sick, perverted things he did to her here in the house.

Janice rubbed antibiotic cream into Lisa's wounds, taking special care with the cigarette burns on her nipples. They had purchased vitamin E gel that was supposedly good for burns and scars. If the label was to be believed, it would make them all but disappear. Up until now, it seemed to be doing a decent job.

Nichola, Paula, and Kate had all been in touch to see where she had been and how she was. Lisa knew that they had wanted the insight into how the little holiday had gone with *him*. She didn't want to talk to them, remembering how it had all been left on that fateful night, but Janice persuaded her to give them titbits of information. She urged her not to tell them anything about what had really happened; they couldn't be trusted to keep their mouths closed. 'You don't want the whole school knowing, do you?' Janice asked.

Lisa saw the logic and decided to tell them that her and *him* hadn't been compatible and that she'd come home the very next morning. She said she hadn't been in touch because she knew they would have been with their new boyfriends and she would have only been jealous.

The ploy worked. After a few messages back and forth about how it was going with their boyfriends, they changed the subject to other, more trivial matters.

They were back as close friends.

Lisa knew they would be there for her if and when she needed them, but right now, she had Janice to reassure her there was nothing to worry about her parents getting back home, and that was ample.

Janice had become the sister she'd never had!

~~~~

It was also Janice who had decided that they should follow up on her brother's possible involvement, just to see if there was any link between him and *him*.

'What happened with him anyway?' Lisa asked as they sat on the couch, watching some boring TV.

Janice sighed deeply.

From her friend's expression, Lisa wished she hadn't asked.

'He was getting bullied in school,' Janice offered. 'It was big time too. Like, they would beat him up even after he surrendered his lunch money. Then one day, he just flipped. He beat the main bully, a kid named Chapman. I can't remember his first name, but he was known as someone not to be messed with. He was one of those kind of kids, top grades, football team, he was totally good looking too, but deep down, he was a real creep.'

*Just like someone else I know,* Lisa thought.

'Jamie was in the park, hanging with his friends, when this Chapman kid tried to steal his bike. It was the day after his birthday, and the bike had been his only present from Dad. You know, money has always been tight growing up. This Chapman guy tried to take it; all Jamie could think about was the beating he'd get if he turned up back at home without it.'

'Your dad does have a bit of a temper on him,' Lisa stated.

Janice nodded. She let out another sigh before continuing. 'Jamie flipped on him. Some people say the Chapman kid pulled a knife; that's why Jamie broke his arm and all his fingers. He pummelled the kid. The guy had to have reconstructive surgery on his face; that was how intense the beating was.'

Lisa touched her own face when Janice mentioned the reconstructive surgery. *How close was I to needing that?*

The story seemed to be taking its toll on her friend, but to her credit, she continued. 'He ran off, leaving the bike and all his stunned friends behind him. He was gone for three days. Three days that my mom and dad spent drinking on the porch while the town looked for him. They couldn't care less where he was, pretty much like they probably don't even know that I'm still here and haven't been home for two days.'

'What happened then? Where did they find him?' Lisa asked.

Janice snorted a small, gruff laugh. 'They found him naked, up a tree in the park. He was starving, thirsty, and on the edge of hypothermia. Apparently, he thought he was a bird, a cuckoo in fact, and that he'd moved into another bird's nest.' Janice paused; she looked like she was thinking. She then turned back to Lisa, a big beaming smile on her face. 'If only, huh?' she laughed. 'So …

enough about my fucked-up family. We need to talk about yours. Your mom and security-conscious dad are going to be home tomorrow. We need to have a story ready for them. Why you're not with Sean, sorry, I mean *him*. Why you've had your hair cut, and why you're spending all your time with your friend with the fucked-up family.'

Lisa turned back to the TV. She sighed and took another swig of her drink. 'I can't wait to see them, I really can't, but there's something inside me telling me I really don't want them to see me. When they went away, I was their sweet, innocent little girl … Now I'm used goods. Sullied, soiled, dirty!' She couldn't help herself; she'd set off down a particular path, and tears were now inevitable.

'Lisa, stop it,' Janice snapped. The harsh tone of her voice snapped Lisa from her downward spiral. Janice took her in her arms and hugged her carefully.

Even though Janice held her tighter than she had done over the last few days, she still winced at the contact and her heart began beating faster. Her body might have been healing, but she knew it was going to take some time before her mind caught up.

If it ever did.

'I'm going to go home now,' Janice whispered, letting Lisa go. 'I want to check up on Jamie. I'm going to steal his phone and see if there's anything on there that might link him to *him*, and if there is, I'll find out why *he* would have done this. Will you be OK?'

Lisa wiped her eyes and laughed. 'Yeah,' she lied; she didn't know if, or more probably when, she was going to lapse back into freefall tears. 'I'll be fine. You go and see if your brother had anything to do with this, and I'll get the house and myself ready for Mom and Dad coming home.'

Janice leaned in and gave her another hug and kissed the top of her head. Lisa looked at her. 'Thank you, Janice. I mean that, from the bottom of my heart. I don't know what I'd have done if you hadn't been here for me.'

'Hey, stop it. You don't need to thank me. I'm your friend; it's what friends do.'

Lisa nodded and surprised herself by instigating the final hug herself. They lingered for a few more seconds, just looking at each other.

Lisa broke the awkward silence. 'OK then.' She smiled. 'You go and get things taken care of, and I'll get myself ready to face Mom and Dad. I'll call you tonight, OK?'

'OK. You're sure you're going to be all right?'

'Yes, now get going before I throw you out myself.'

Janice was laughing as Lisa showed her to the door.

## 45.

'OH MY GOD! I've missed you both so much. I'm so glad you're home!'

'Really, you missed us?' her father asked, putting the bags down in the hallway.

'More than you can believe,' Lisa shouted, running down the stairs, barely keeping her tears in check. 'How was Europe?'

'Honey, Europe is Europe. It hasn't changed in centuries. Tell me, how did you do alone?' her father asked, wrapping his arms around his little girl.

She winced as the pain of the hug sent slivers of agony through her body, but she thought she had hidden it well.

Lisa's attentions turned to her mother next. Another painful hug ensued, and she thought she was doing well hiding the revulsion she felt in the physical contact.

'Come on, young lady,' Flo chided. 'Spill the beans on what you've been up to.'

'Aw, you know me, Mom. I'm real boring. The girls came over a few times, but mostly I read. Big year next year, you know that.'

'We do, honey, but you know, you need to have some fun now and then too,' her father continued. There was a mischievous glint in his eye. 'You should have had Sean over some nights. He'd have looked after you. He'd have stopped you from being lonely. I'm sure he would have shown you how to smoke cigarettes, drink booze, and then maybe he'd have taken your virginity and your innocence.'

'Not forgetting my self-esteem and self-worth,' Lisa laughed, wearing a smile that made her face feel like a mask. A very bad and very dangerous mask.

Her father broke into a laugh, and Lisa reached out and touched his face. When she felt he was real, that he and her mother were really back for her, something happened to both of their faces. They began to crumble, and the façade they had been presenting fell away. As it did, Sean's grin burst out from both of them.

Her mother was laughing as her lips curled into a vicious snarl.

With a growl and a snap of his jaw, Sean, wearing her father's clothes, reached out for the hand that was still touching his face and bit it …

46.

LISA JUMPED IN her sleep. As she did, she fell off the couch onto the thick pile carpet of the living room. Her body shrieked as she hit the floor, igniting old and almost healed wounds. She looked around the well-lit room, relieved she was alone. Her heart rate began to slow as she used all of her strength to drag herself up to a sitting position with her back propped up against the couch.

She released a long, shaky breath and held her knees to her chest, ignoring the almost passive-aggressive aching from her crotch, stomach, and breasts.

A noise, just a small click from the hallway, alerted her. Instantly, the hairs on the back of her neck and arms were on edge as goosebumps covered her skin. She grabbed her cell phone, which was languishing on the couch behind her, and unlocked it.

She had one unread message, but she ignored it and went straight to the contacts list. In her heightened state of fear, her sweat-lined fingers wouldn't make the correct contact on the glass of the device, and she had to dry them on her already damp pyjamas. Pyjamas that covered her entire body from neck to feet.

Janice's number was on speed-dial, and she clicked on her friend's name. With her heart beating in her throat, her thumb hovered over the CALL button, ready to call, ready to get her over here and rescue her from *him* and whoever Jay might be.

'Hello … Hello, Lisa? Are you still up, honey?'

The sound of her mom's voice coming through the hallway instantly put to bed all the fears she had rushing through her head. The sound of the familiar, safe, and much loved and missed voice made her want to cry. It made her want to jump up and rush towards it, to hug and kiss her mother. It made her want to sit and cry and tell both her parents everything that had happened.

Instead, she attempted to fix her hair behind her ear, forgetting there was no long hair there to fix there anymore. Slowly, she got up off the floor and stood in the living room, awaiting the arrival of the two people she loved the most in the whole world.

'In here, Mom,' she called, trying to hide the shake in her voice. 'In the living room.'

She heard her father fussing with the bags and her mother tutting at him. This small thing, this small *normal* thing made her smile, the smile made her sad, and before she knew it, tears were streaming down her cheeks and deep sobs were racking through her body.

'Oh my word,' her mother whispered as she made it into the living room. 'What's the matter with you, baby?'

With her handbag dumped on the floor and her coat still on, Flo rushed to her daughter, wrapping her arms around her tightly. 'Shh, baby. It's OK. We're here now. We're here.'

Even though the hug was too tight for her body to bear, Lisa buried her damp face into her mother's neck. The smell of her perfume and the feel of her warmth brought back happy memories. This made her sadness even deeper. 'Oh, Mom. I've missed you so much. Both of you. Promise me, promise me you'll never leave me alone again.'

Tony hurried into the room and saw the two embracing women. 'Hey, honey, Daddy's home,' he shouted, holding his arms out towards her.

Flo swung herself around to face him; her concerned look was one he recognised as not to be messed with. 'Not now, Tony,' Flo whispered, indicating towards their daughter with a creased brow.

Tony's face changed from happy to concerned in the wink of an eye. He made his way over to the two women and wrapped his arms around them both.

'Daddy ...' Lisa sobbed. The cry was one of both pain and happiness to see him, but she did well to conceal the hurt.

'Shhh, Lisa. Come on now,' he whispered.

She then transferred her attentions from her mother to her father. He hugged her tight, happy to see her but worried about this strange welcome.

Lisa felt her body tense slightly under her father's embrace, but it was enough for her to understand that he'd acknowledged it. In response to her reaction, he lessened the intensity of his hug but still held her close.

After a few moments, Lisa broke away from the reunion and stepped into the kitchen, wiping her eyes as she did. Both Flo and Tony looked at each other, attempting to understand the uncharacteristic emotional outburst from their daughter.

'I'm sorry, guys.' Lisa sniffed as she sat at the island in the kitchen. 'I just missed you both so much.'

'Well, we're home now, and we're not going anywhere else for a good while,' her father said, speaking softly as he sat next to her at the island.

Lisa noted with revulsion that her father was sitting in *the* seat where *he* had taken her innocence away.

Her mother followed behind and began to fuss about in the cupboards. 'Does anyone want a cup of tea? I'm a day out of Europe, and already I'm craving tea.'

'Yeah, Mom. That sounds lovely,' Lisa replied, getting herself back together.

'OK. I'll turn the kettle on, then we can all have a nice long chat about what's been going on while we were away! What happened with Sean?'

Lisa sat up; she couldn't believe her own mother had just mentioned *his* name so casually. Then she relaxed, remembering that neither of her parents had any idea what had happened while they were away. 'Why do we need to talk about that? Can't we just talk about what you guys did?' she asked, hoping to change the subject.

Tony's eyes narrowed as he watched Lisa's attempts to calm herself, but he didn't say anything.

'Well, Paris was fantastic. The city is so romantic, well, parts of it are. We went to the Moulin Rouge, of course, you have to when in Paris. But, wow, the street that it's on is so rough at night. It's right in the middle of the red-light district. The number of bars that were trying to pull us both in, to go and see sex shows and the like, it was

169

awful.' Her mother sat back at the island, waiting for the kettle to boil.

'So, after our fifth show, we decided to get a taxi back to the hotel,' Tony said with a grin.

Flo turned and put her hand on top of his, smiling a fun-filled smile. 'Tony,' she warned. 'Tell her the truth!'

Tony nodded as he looked at his daughter. 'I'm sorry, Lisa, it was only three.'

All three of them laughed.

The kettle boiled, and her mother got up to finish the tea. 'So, what's with the hair?' her mother asked, returning to the table with three steaming cups. She reached forward to touch the new hair style.

Instinctively, Lisa recoiled. She looked at her father and saw his reaction. It was only very small, but it was there. She cursed herself before cursing him. *He never misses a trick, does he?*

'Oh, just me and Janice were messing around, putting colours and stuff into my hair, and it all went wrong. It was a mess, to tell you the truth. So, she cut it and styled it for me. What do you think?'

As Flo ran her fingers through it, Lisa felt her father's eyes watching. His scrutiny, his searching for every little flinch, was almost physical. Her eyes flicked his way and then away again, back to her mother. A crocodile smile washed over her face. 'So, do you like it or what?' she asked.

'It'll take a little getting used to, but I can't say I hate it,' her mother stated as she continued to run her fingers through it.

'Well, things look to be pretty much OK here,' Tony said, standing up from the island, picking up his cup. 'I'm going to take the luggage upstairs, I'm going to dump them on the bedroom floor, and then I'm going to flop into my bed and fall asleep for at least sixteen hours.' He leaned in to give Lisa a kiss. Once again, her body tightened at his physical presence, but he pressed on regardless.

Once he'd kissed her lightly, she wrapped her arms around him and kissed him on the cheek. There was a smile on her face, but it felt like it belonged to someone else.

'I'm going to go too,' Flo said. 'We'll catch up properly in the morning.'

'Or afternoon,' her father chirped as he picked up one of the suitcases and attempted the stairs.

Flo laughed. 'He may be right, I'm destroyed. Goodnight, sweetheart,' she said, kissing her daughter.

'Goodnight, Mom. I'm so glad you're home.'

'We're glad too,' her father shouted from the hallway.

Lisa bit the side of her cheek. The ulcers from her beating were still stinging, but she chewed on them, thinking there might have been another meaning to her father's words.

47.

FLO WAS ASLEEP almost as soon as her head touched the pillow. She was snoring lightly as she lay on her side, wearing the aeroplane's complimentary eye mask over her face. Tony watched her sleep as he toyed with reading the book he had started in Germany. It was a great book, but right now, it couldn't hold his attention.

Something about Lisa's body language concerned him. She had never, not once in her whole life, shrunk away from a hug or a kiss. She had always been tactile. Her facial tics had screamed at him to notice them. He was a professional. He was trained to recognise and understand small *tells* the body gave, the ones that show if a person is lying or, at the very least, hiding something.

It had won him a fortune in poker over the years.

He'd heard Lisa creeping up the stairs about half an hour after they'd gone to bed. He guessed she would be asleep by now. She always had been a heavy sleeper.

Sparing a glance at his wife, he removed the covers and slipped out of bed, turning his reading light out as he did. Within a few seconds, he was at the door of their bedroom, silently turning the handle.

He'd promised Flo he would leave Lisa alone to her own devices and not meddle or interfere with her life in any other way than was normal for a parent. But he wasn't a normal parent. The professional inside him was screaming. It was an instinct he couldn't ignore. It wasn't only his professionalism that was calling to him, it was the caring, loving parent within him too. If his baby was hurting, then it was his duty to find out what was hurting her.

# The Boyfriend

*I'm only going to scan through the CCTV footage, that's all,* he thought. *It's only what any self-respecting parent would do anyway.*

He crept noiselessly across the landing, making his way downstairs, towards his office. He took the key from the false panel next to the door and unlocked it.

He noticed that the key had been moved.

It was slightly off. He had put the tiniest of notches in the wood of the panel so he would know if it had been used.

This didn't anger him in any way. He had shown Lisa how to use the CCTV before he went away; he had even shown her how to get into the room. She'd promised him she wouldn't go in there, but since the CCTV system had seemingly crashed, he guessed she'd gone in there to try and fix it. She didn't know how to use his other "toys", as Flo called them.

Tony saw that as a good thing.

His work was secretive and sensitive, after all.

He entered the room and embraced the coolness of the air, a necessity for the servers he ran. He sat in his leather seat and leaned back. Even when he had work that wasn't enjoyable, or nice even, he still revelled in the creak of the old leather as it welcomed his body into its well-worn seat. Tonight, he ignored the sound as he logged in.

He went straight into the logs and looked through the time stamps, beginning from the day they left. It wasn't long before he found the discrepancy. He knew the CCTV had gone down for a day or two; this had bugged him non-stop while away, but they had come back up a few days later. He needed to know why they had gone down.

The logs revealed they had been turned off manually late the same night they left.

*Why would she turn the security off?* he thought as he began checking everything. He logged on to the server and selected the ARCHIVE folder.

There were hundreds of folders within this one, but he knew the folders he wanted would be down at the bottom of the list. He noted that from the day they left until just two days ago, nothing had been archived.

Intrigued, he clicked on the video file that was inside. Instantly, a high-definition picture opened up on one of the multiple monitors.

He watched as Janice and Nichola turned up at the house and were welcomed by Lisa. *Nothing sinister there,* he thought. He began to push forward over the long periods of inactivity, then about an hour or so later, he saw, with some real chagrin, Paula appeared with four boys in tow.

He felt the familiar adrenaline surge through his body as he moved into what he thought of as *work mode.*

He paused the frame and zoomed in on each of the boys' faces. He didn't recognise any of them. He saved the images and imported them into an app he had on his desktop. He drew a square over the first image and right clicked his mouse. A series of dots covered the boy's face, then he clicked SEARCH.

He did the same for the other three.

He then left the room and went to the kitchen to make himself a latte. There wouldn't be much sleep for him tonight.

By the time he'd gotten back to his study, the app had done its work. There were four profiles sitting on his desktop, awaiting his attention. All four showed the young men who had turned up at his door with Paula.

All of them had a resume.

The first boy, the one with his arm around Paula and carrying the bag that Tony assumed contained booze, was Ryan Agatha. He was seventeen years old and currently a senior at Lombard High school, the same school that Sean Knight went to. He still lived at home with his parents, and there was no criminal record.

The second Boy was Clinton Matthews, eighteen years of age and a senior at the same school. He had gotten a track scholarship to UCLA and was set to major in Applied Mathematics. Still living at home with his parents, no criminal convictions.

Third on the list was Peter McMahan. Dropped out of school at sixteen. Currently employed in a fast food restaurant in the next town over. Tony leaned into his screen; this one interested him. There were misdemeanours on his record. Petty theft, minor assault, drunk and disorderly, traffic violations. *Why the hell is Lisa letting this rat into the house?* Tony thought, sitting back in his chair.

174

# The Boyfriend

He was living in a one-room apartment above a laundromat in the centre of town.

Tony dragged that file to one side for consideration later.

The last boy was Andrew Snow. Pretty much the same as the first two. Clean cut, good school attendance, living with parents, no criminal convictions.

Tony's hackles were up. Peter was trouble that had been brought into his house.

He clicked back to the archive stream, then clicked on the triangle icon, and the video kicked into life. Once the boys were inside, he switched onto the internal cameras, the ones no one knew about.

They showed a normal teenage party. Drinking and the coupling up of the boys with the girls. Tony kept a tight eye on Lisa. Even though he'd resigned himself to the fact that his daughter was almost seventeen and that boys were about to become, or already were, a large part of her life, he still hated the idea of her with a boy in the house while he wasn't there to protect her. He was happy the other girls were the ones getting cosy, but it left her and this horrible Peter character excluded from the party.

His hands became moist as he watched them talking in the kitchen. He could see that Peter was flirting with his daughter, but Tony was more than happy to watch her rebuff him again and again.

As he continued to watch, counting the drinks Peter had consumed, his hands began to clench into fists, and his brow became low as a nasty exchange between them occurred right before his eyes in high-contrast footage. His breathing sped up when he watched her slap him across the face, not once but twice.

*Good girl,* he thought.

Then he saw him strike her back!

A rage built up inside him that was greater than anything he'd felt in years.

It consumed him so fast that he scared himself more than a little.

He wanted to pause the film, to rewind it and watch it again. Only he knew that would piss him off even more than he was already. As his hand hovered, shaking, over the rewind button, he watched the other boys run in and grab Peter, pulling him away from her. Then the girls were in there too.

*Good thing too, for him,* Tony thought as his teeth ground together. He took a few deep breaths before watching the rest of the video.

The boys left the house. He shocked himself to find he was growling as he watched them leave. Then he was surprised to see the girls leave too. All of them, including Janice.

He watched as Lisa moped around the house for a while before turning off the lights, checking the doors, and going to bed.

He switched the feedback to the outside cameras and scanned through them.

Nothing happening for a while.

He was almost ready to go click off the archive when something caught his eye. Someone was loitering outside the perimeter of the property. Tony's heart was back in his mouth as he watched the individual try several times to scale the fence. The youth looked drunk. He recognised him.

He paused the feed and zoomed in.

Peter McMahan!

Dreading what he would see, he flipped one of the feeds back to inside the house. He watched as Lisa entered this room. *She's checking the cameras,* he thought. *Clever girl.*

Peter was still trying to climb the fence; he grinned as he watched him cut his hands. Then the boy sat underneath the tree overhanging the fence. *Why haven't I cut that down yet?* he cursed.

Back inside the house, Lisa was on her phone. Fifteen minutes of footage had passed since he first saw the boy, so he guessed that whoever she was talking to already knew the situation.

He then watched as Peter looked like he was talking to someone just off the camera. He saw him stand up and walk off screen, obviously confronting someone.

Then the feed went dead.

He scanned the internal camera footage forwards.

They were dead too.

She had closed the whole system down, not just the cameras.

'Fuck,' he muttered under his breath, wanting to smash his fists down onto the desktop. He didn't do it; he knew if he let the rage out now, he might not be able to stop it—also, he didn't want to wake the girls.

He began to pace the room, his frustration reaching its zenith. He wanted to break something, to smash something to pieces, but the rational, professional side of his brain told him that wouldn't help the situation any. He wanted to burst into Lisa's room and grab her. He wanted to shake her from her sleep and demand to know what happened when the cameras went down.

He sat down again and sipped his coffee. It was difficult at first, as his hands were shaking so badly.

He wasn't a man to overreact in stressful scenarios, but this one was just too close to home. He rewound the recording and paused it on Peter's face. He then brought back his records on the second screen.

His address was right there.

He swallowed, tasting the milky coffee and feeling a chill creep into his fingers. There was an icon on his screen, one he'd used countless times before but never for anything this close, this personal. He hovered the cursor over the bland icon and double clicked it.

He was now logged on to a government virtual private network. Something he had vowed he would never do regarding his family, but right now he couldn't *not* do this. Lisa was a different person since they'd left for Europe. She was doing a good job at trying to hide it, but she was definitely not the same little girl they had left just eleven days ago, and he would do anything to protect his family. He entered the information for the fast-food restaurant where Peter worked. He accessed the personnel files, then accessed the work schedule for the upcoming week.

Peter McMahan was working a shift tomorrow night.

*Good,* he thought.

48.

'I'VE TRAILED HIM everywhere he goes. He's not allowed to go beyond a mile of our house without permission. All he does is walk around the park watching the birds. Part of his parole from the hospital prevents him from having a cell phone. I really don't think Jamie could be Jay.' Janice was sitting on the edge of Lisa's bed, relaying her information.

The room was meticulously clean, with fresh sheets on the bed and not a single dust mote to be seen. After what had happened to her in there, Lisa felt the need to clean it thoroughly every single day, sometimes even twice a day.

She was sat at the top her bed, her back against the headboard. Her hands were wrapped around her hiked up knees. She knew Janice could see her ravaged, bitten fingernails. The edges of them were raw and painful, but it didn't stop her from gnawing at them all day. 'So that's that then? Jamie isn't Jay, so we just give up and let the bastard win?' She snapped her fingers, and her hand went to her mouth, her teeth hungry for fingernails. They only just made it because of the shakes running up and down her arms.

'That's not what I'm saying,' Janice soothed, reaching over, attempting to remove the hand from her friend's mouth. Lisa slapped her hand away and moved out of reach. She nervously ran her hand through her short hair before putting it back to her mouth. 'I'm saying we need another line of investigation. As much as my brother weirds me out, he's not much different from the rest of my family. He's a jerk, you can take that to the bank, yes; but I don't think he's a dangerous one.' She shrugged and shook her head. 'You don't even seem to be on his radar.'

Lisa looked at Janice. Her red eyes were wide, and blotches had recently appeared around her nostrils where a small nest of pimples had begun to sprout. Her skin was pale and moist. 'Then who the fuck could it be? Who hates me enough to goad my *ex*-fucking-boyfriend to rape and beat me to within an inch of my life, in my own fucking house?'

Janice sat back on the bed. She shook her head and sighed. 'I don't know. I wish I did. All I want to do is help you. I really did think it might have been Jamie. Shit, maybe I even wanted it to be him, just so we could just put an end to all this.'

Lisa lifted her head from resting on her knees. She looked at Janice as if she had just said the most profound thing in the whole of the world. 'Do you really mean that?'

'Mean what?'

'Mean that you want to put an end to all this shit?'

'Of course I do. You're my best friend, Lisa. I hate seeing you like this.'

'Then, let's go after Sean!'

'What? Are you fucking crazy?' Janice asked, getting off the bed. 'Are you out of your mind?'

Lisa leaned forward and reached out towards her. 'No, Janice, I'm not. I'm serious. My dad has guns. I could shoot the prick in the face, throw the gun away and—'

'Lisa, stop! Listen to yourself,' Janice almost spat. 'Do you even know how to shoot a gun?'

'No, but—'

'But nothing. You want to take a gun and shoot someone in the face? Do you think you would be able to do that? Do you think, when Sean's in front of you, on his knees, crying, grovelling, tears and snot streaming down his face, pleading with you not to kill him, that you could just pull the trigger and end it all?' She shook her head. 'I don't think that's you, Lisa.'

Lisa didn't say anything in reply, she just sat back on the bed, pulled her knees closer to her chest, and wrapped her well chewed hands around them again. A long, exhausted wind escaped her. 'Maybe it would scare him enough and we could get the identity of Jay from him. At least I'd have closure on some of it.'

Janice tutted. 'I know you're angry. Shit, I think I'd want to kill the prick who did this to me, but you have to think beyond it. No one has seen anything of Sean for over a week, and we go back to school in a couple of months. I need to know you're going to be all right, Lisa. You're the sensible one, remember?'

Lisa never said anything.

Janice took the moment to attempt to give her a hug. At first, Lisa resisted and froze a little, still not comfortable with physical connections. Then, as she realised that Janice didn't mean her any harm, she softened, allowing her friend to wrap her arms around her. It felt nice to have warm human connection. She felt nice against her; her hair smelt nice, like flowers. Lisa closed her eyes and revelled in the hug, finally enjoying the closeness of another human being.

# The Boyfriend

49.

A FEW DAYS of stalking Peter McMahan online, finding out everything about him, Tony found himself parking an unmarked car in the street opposite the laundromat. The lights were on inside, illuminating the sidewalk from the stark glow through the large windows. Six stacks of washers lined both walls of the shop, with a bench down the middle. There were two washers per stack, and another two stacks of dryers along the bottom wall. A small desk area was set up next to the dryers that was currently unmanned. In fact, the whole shop was empty. This information had little bearing on his mission, as he'd already scoped the small alleyway next to the shop, the one that housed the entrance to the apartments above. However, it had Tony's full attention, as anyone inside doing their laundry at this time might cause him to abort.

His destination was on the third floor. Apartment 3B.

After a short wait, he spied a man shuffling down the street. With only the yellow glow from the streetlamps to illuminate him, he looked older, at least mid-sixties, but as taking care of themselves was never really a primary motivation for the residents of these areas, he could have easily been as young as his late twenties. Tony watched him stumble past the laundromat, seemingly in mid-conversation with someone who wasn't present. Tony shook his head and watched as he entered the dark alleyway, disappearing through the grubby door hidden in the shadows.

He watched as the door swung shut behind him and was pleased to see it bounce out of its frame and swing back open. 'Too easy,' he mumbled before checking the little bag next to him.

Everything he needed was inside.

He exited the unremarkable car and crossed the street. With just a casual look to his left and his right, he allowed the depths of the darkness of the alley envelop him. He'd scouted this area for more than an hour. He knew there would be no watchful eyes scrutinising him as he went about his business.

As he entered the lobby, the oppressive, foul stench of urine and vomit assaulted him. He'd smelt it before, and in much worse concentrations than this offered, so it hardly even registered. He almost tripped over a pair of dirty denim-covered legs that were sticking out from below the stairwell. He saw a girl, he guessed she might have been the same age as Lisa, lying underneath. The arm of her jacket had been rolled up, and an elastic band was untied but still around her arm, just above a rather nasty and infected series of scabbed wounds. He observed that she would have been pretty if not for the deathly white pallor of her face and the vacant look in her open, twitching eyes.

He shook his head. 'There but for the Grace of God,' he whispered before moving past her, heading for the stairs. There was a lift, but he didn't want to use that tonight. The stairs would suffice.

He clenched his hands within the thin, black latex gloves he was wearing and continued to climb to the third floor.

He made it unchallenged. There were three doors for him to choose from. One didn't have a number on it. It looked like it had originally been a lime green colour, but age, decay, and any number of boot marks, where it had obviously been kicked through, had long since turned it into a dark grey. Tony surmised this must be Peter's apartment as the other doors, all equally as decrepit as this one, were sporting numbers. 3A and 3C.

He opened his bag and extracted a small kit that would make short, silent work of a flimsy lock like this one.

Within fifteen seconds, he was in.

The apartment was exactly how he expected it to be. Small, dark, and grimy. It smelt of grease, dirty hair, and sweat.

He'd been in worse places!

This was a luxury compared to some of the shit holes he'd frequented during his many years of employment.

He closed the door behind him and looked at his watch. It was ten minutes past twelve. Peter would still be at work for another hour, cleaning up, and then another ten or fifteen minutes to walk home. He decided to make himself comfortable.

Tonight was going to be interesting.

As he got comfortable, he got to thinking about how different his daughter had been since his trip to Europe. Putting the drastic hair cut to one side, she'd been sullen, withdrawn, and—dare he say it?—depressed. A far cry from the bubbly, confident, popular girl they had left behind.

He had also noted that her friends hadn't been around too much either. None of them except for Janice. She had been over every day since they'd gotten back. She was a pleasant enough girl, but there was something going on between them, something he didn't like. He hated secrets. He'd spent his whole life having to keep them and exposing them, only now to find himself on the outside of one happening in his own home. There had been whispers, he'd heard them, in serious tones, only to stop when either he or Flo entered the room or came into earshot.

He had been tempted to break his promise to his wife, to get this flea out of his ear and find out once and for all what was happening.

He had resisted, at least up till now!

Janice had, it seemed, proved to be a good friend to Lisa. She was supporting her through whatever it was she was going through, and Tony was thankful for it.

He had promised Flo he wouldn't pry into their daughter's personal life, and he really had intended to keep that promise, but *something* had happened while they were away, and he needed to know what that something was.

Tonight, one way or another, he would get some answers.

~~~~

He sat in the not so comfortable chair and placed his small black bag at his feet. He opened it and removed an electronic device with an elasticated strap. He slipped his head through the strap, allowing the device to sit just below his Adam's apple. He took his cell phone out of his pocket and activated an app, and a small blue light lit up on the device around his throat.

He sat patiently and waited.

The comings and goings of the apartments around him were interesting in themselves; on more than a few occasions, he thought he'd heard the sound of the door opening, and he'd gotten ready.

These were many false starts, too many for his liking. It was a filthy, annoying apartment, and he wanted nothing more than to get out as soon as he got what he came for.

Before long, the unmistakable sound of a key in the lock of the front door filtered through. Tony scoffed at the distinction between *that* sound and the sounds he'd thought were someone entering.

This one was real.

~~~~

Peter was tired. The shift had taken the best out of him. They had put him on hot drinks duty, and on a Wednesday night, that was the worst. There were always too many angry people demanding their coffee strong, hot, and sweet. All of them ready to fight if you didn't comply with their understanding of the complexities of coffee.

Midnight could not have come quick enough for him.

*I need another job,* he thought miserably as he slammed the door to his apartment behind him. He tossed his keys on a small table and dragged his feet through the small hallway into the messy open-plan kitchenette/living room. He opened the refrigerator and removed a can of beer. He popped the tab, relishing in the light spray that came from it. He loved the smell of a freshly opened beer.

Standing in the kitchen, he chugged the drink, finishing nearly half the can in one swig. Then, after burping loudly, he finished it in his second gulp. He crushed the can, belched, threw the empty towards the bin, missing by a long shot, and got himself another.

As he turned, open drink in hand, he kicked off his shoes and dropped his uniform cap on the floor. Scratching his crotch and yawning, he was looking forward to relaxing on the couch, watching some late night TV, maybe even jerking off. His finger was hovering over the light switch when a bright light shone into his face, blinding him. 'What the fuck?' he cursed, jumping back, lifting his hand to block out the intense illumination, and dropping his freshly opened beer.

'Good morning, Peter,' a voice from somewhere behind the light said. There was a metallic, almost computer sound to it.

*Like that smart guy in the wheelchair,* he thought.

At first, he thought it might be an alien abduction. He'd watched all kinds of shows on TV in the early hours about how aliens took random people and shoved probes up their butts. However, as his eyes became semi-adjusted to the light, he could make out the silhouette of a man sitting on his chair.

'What the—'

'Just relax, Peter. I'm only here for one thing,' the alien said in its robotic tones. This scared him more than the silhouette of the man.

'Wh–wh ...' Peter couldn't get his words out. He was backing up, attempting to distance himself from whoever, or whatever, was causing the light in his face.

'Just relax. I only want information,' the man said. There was no movement from beyond the light or emotion in his voice. 'If you tell me what I want to know, I'll leave you alone and you will never see or hear from me again. If you don't, well ...'

The fact that the man left that sentence hanging scared Peter more than he'd ever been scared before. He could feel his bladder weakening, but he still had the wherewithal to keep the sphincter muscles closed that would have otherwise resulted in him soiling his dark uniform trousers.

'Why don't you sit down, and we'll have a little chat.' the voice said, and the silhouette moved for the first time, indicating a stool that had been placed before him. Peter looked at the stool, then back at the scary man.

'Whothefuckareyou?' It was a question, and it was rushed, all the words merging into one almost unintelligible phrase.

The man leaned forward. Peter thought he could hear creaking, like old leather, as he did, but he didn't know if this was just his overactive and over stimulated imagination. 'Who I am is of no consequence to you. All you need to know is that you could be in some serious trouble if you don't give me the information I require.'

Peter peered into the light. The shadow behind it looked small and well built, but that was all he could tell in the cold light hurting his eyes. He looked over to the corner of the room, where there was a baseball bat leaning against the wall. It was his weapon against

185

intruders, and possible alien abductors. He could feel the build-up of adrenaline within him, and the palms of his hands were moist with sweat as he contemplated the bat. *He's sitting down; I'm standing up and have a few years on him. I can take this prick.* Anger was surging through him, racing through his body and competing with the adrenaline bubbling in his stomach. *Who the fuck does this clown think he is? Breaking into my apartment and demanding I give him information. I'll give him fucking information ...*

In a swift movement, Peter reached for the bat against the wall. With a glance, he noticed the shadow behind the light hadn't foreseen this event and had not even moved. His hand wrapped around the thick, varnished wooden hilt, and he brought it up, ready to strike.

Peter was surprised to see how fast the man was, not only up off the seat but up in his face. He just had time to register one thought before agony tore through his body, making him drop his weapon and rethink any idea of attack.

*Shit, this guy is fast,* was the only thought in his head.

The bat clattered to the floor as the man placed one hand on his shoulder, exerting pressure on the wrist that had held the makeshift weapon with the other. With minimum effort, he exerted more pressure on his wrist, and Peter had no choice but to fall to his knees, agony rolling up and down his arm.

With a sickening, tiny snap, he felt his hand go limp, and then his arm. There was no pain at first, just a dull ache through the numbness. But the understanding of what had just happened made him feel sick.

He couldn't feel his fingers or his thumb. Pain began to creep in, easing through the shock of how easily this man had incapacitated him. His tendons screamed, and where there had been a dull ache a moment ago, there was now searing torture.

'Don't fuck with me, Peter.' The man's electronic voice didn't even sound out of breath. 'I've just broken your wrist, and you're already going to need medical assistance. That's going to mean a cast, a trip to the hospital, time off work. I really hope you have medical insurance.'

The pain was now all consuming. The ache had been replaced by an agonising throb. He could feel the pulsing torment even in his back teeth. 'You goddam maniac,' he spat, his voice octaves higher than usual. 'Why did you do that? Why?'

'You gave me no choice. Now, you've seen what I can do to your hand with minimal effort; if you don't want me to snap your arm in two more places, don't fuck with me. Do you understand?'

'YES ...' he screamed, hoping someone in the adjacent apartments might hear him and call the police. Then he remembered where he lived. There were screams for help every night of the week around here. Crashes, yells, suspiciously loud bangs. Nobody thought anything of them. The realisation he was on his own petrified him.

'Who are you?' he hissed as the man stepped away, back into the light. He was kneeling on the floor, supporting his useless arm with his good hand and couldn't get a look at the man's face. 'What do you want?'

'Good,' the man behind the light replied. 'I think you're now motivated to tell me exactly what I want to know.'

Peter sobbed, and transparent mucus dripped from his nose and down his lip. He looked away from the light, dropping his eyes to look at his swelling hand. Even in the bleaching illumination, he could see it was starting to bruise.

'Now, what I want is really easy.' Even through the metallic voice and his own pain, Peter could tell the man was patronising him. 'Tell me, and tell me the truth, and you'll never have anything to fear from me again. Tell me lies, and well ... to quote a famous movie star, I'll be back!'

'Just fucking ask,' Peter spat, thick, white spittle flying from his mouth.

'You were at a girl's house with your friends a few days ago. Don't bother denying it; there is real evidence you were there.'

'Yeah, so? I go to a lot of girls' houses,' he replied, still looking at his swelling hand. 'I'm going to need to get some ice on this thing. Maybe I need an ambulance.'

'You'll need to go to the hospital. When I've got what I came for, you'll be free to do whatever you need. You can even go to the police if you want, but rest assured, there's not a single scrap of DNA evidence of me being here, and I'm sure your crackhead neighbours never saw a thing. So please, allow me to elaborate on my question!'

Peter snapped his head up; the pain in his neck was momentarily worse than that in his wrist. 'What?' he asked, his eyes closed to the blinding light.

'You were there with Ryan Agatha, Andrew Snow, and Clinton Matthews. It was Saturday night, just over a week ago. An altercation occurred, and you and your friends were ejected from the house.'

Peter thought for a moment; it was hard to do between the throbbing from his wrist and pain in his neck. 'A what occurred?' he gasped.

'An incident … and you were thrown out of the house. Do you remember?'

'Yeah, yeah. I remember. We left early. What's that got to do with anything?'

'You were seen later on, after everyone had gone home. You were seen trying to scale the perimeter of that same house. Do you remember that?'

He did remember. He'd been drunk, and he'd cut his hand pretty bad on the fence. *The same fucking hand that's broken now,* he thought. He looked away from the light. He was ashamed of what he had been trying to do that night and was ashamed of what happened afterwards.

'You were seen talking to someone outside the house. I need to know who that someone was, and I want to know the outcome of the conversation.'

'Jesus, man, you didn't need to break my hand for me to tell you that.'

'You did that to yourself. Now tell me. Who was it you were talking to?'

'It was Sean, Sean Knight. He kicked my ass too. Apparently, his girlfriend, the girl whose house it was, told him I was harassing her. The fucking bitch. She was all over me, then the next thing, I'm smacked across the face and thrown out of the house. The whore was gagging for it, and I think she would have let me if her friends hadn't been there.'

The man in the mask said nothing for a few moments. Peter had never been so scared in his life. He could feel an intense stare from behind the light, reaching into his brain, doing things that no eyes had any right to be doing.

Finally, to his relief, the man spoke. 'Sean Knight? You're one hundred percent sure?'

'Man, how can you not be sure of someone who beats the shit out of you. If I'd have been sober and my hand hadn't been cut, I'd have given him a fight. But, well, you know …'

~~~~

Peter woke up on the floor of his living room. Daylight was streaming in through the dirty window.

As he tried to move, his arm screamed in agony. He looked at it; it was purple and dangerously swollen.

His face hurt too.

He struggled to his feet and stumbled into the bathroom. He looked in the mirror over the sink. His nose was swollen, as were his eyes. There was blood over the front of his grey uniform shirt, and every part of his body hurt.

'Jesus Christ,' he mumbled through swollen lips.

50.

'R U STILL IN TOWN?' the message read. The beeping of his phone had roused him from an ugly dream where he'd been tied down and someone was threatening him with a pool cue. It took a moment for his eyes to adjust to the gloom of the morning sunlight streaming in through the windows of the garage and the windows of the car he was sleeping in.

The message was from Jay.

He hit reply. 'YUP, Y?'

He rested his head back on the jacket he'd been using as a pillow and sighed. His parents had been partying again last night, meaning his room was occupied as a boudoir for who knew how many people.

His phone chimed again. 'I THORT WE TALKED ABOUT THIS. U NEED 2 GET AWAY B4 HEAT COMES FROM LISA'

Sean wasn't the least bit worried about Lisa, her family, or the cops. He didn't care one way or the other. Soon he would be untouchable. He would be part of the society, one of the *made men*. He'd done his deed; he'd proven himself and had the video evidence to back it all up. All he needed now was to sit back and wait for the accolades that would be coming anytime soon.

'I WILL…' he lied in the reply. 'SUM THINGS I NEED 2 DO 1ST. WILL B GON BY NXT WEEK. DID U TALK 2 THE SOCIETY?'

Jay had promised to introduce him to the society. A team of mercenaries around the country who would do *tasks* for money, a lot of money. It had been sold to him like something out of James Bond, but for real. It was his ticket out of this shit-heel town. Away from school, his parents, everything. Living his life from one job to the next, enjoying himself on the way.

He lay back, smiling at his little daydream. He closed his eyes and relaxed, but the vibration from his phone snapped him rudely from his daydream.

'I HAVE. THEY DON'T NEED HEAT FROM A PLEDGE. THEY URGE YOU TO LEAVE TOWN FOR A WHILE AND WILL BE IN TOUCH VIA ME.'

Disappointed, Sean clicked his phone off and sighed. *Maybe I should just fuck off somewhere,* he thought. *But where?*

51.

TONY HADN'T SLEPT a wink since he had gotten back from the stinking apartment. He was in the kitchen drinking his third cup of coffee when his wife entered, tying the belt on her housecoat. 'Have you been up all night?' She yawned, holding the kettle underneath the cold tap.

He nodded. 'I've just picked up a little job.'

She looked at him; he could see the disdain in her eyes. 'Tony, I thought you'd quit for good. We talked about this in Germany.'

'I know, but this came up out of the blue. I won't have to go anywhere this time; I can work it from home, and ...' He came up behind her and slid his hand up the back of the silky housecoat before creeping it around to caress her breast. '... someone has to keep you in your European mood, don't they?'

Playfully pushing him away with her behind, she turned the tap off, chuckling. 'You and your European ways. Are you going to be working on it today?'

He moved away from her and leaned on the island. 'Probably. I have to glue some loose ends together,' he replied, his playful mood short lived. 'This one won't be any more than a few days. I promise.'

'Good, because I don't think I can handle another day hanging around with a moody seventeen-year-old. She's been so ... off since we came back. Don't you think?'

Tony rolled his eyes as he got a cup for her out of the cupboard. 'Totally. And there I was thinking all this shit stopped at her fifteenth birthday,' he quipped, not totally comfortable with the line of conversation.

'I'm going to have a word with her. It's not healthy that she's seeing so much of Janice either. I mean, she's a nice girl and all, but we haven't seen anything of the other three lately.'

'You know how girls are. They probably had a fight over a boy or something. I heard Lisa talking about Ryan, or Clinton, or something like that.'

'You're probably right,' Flo said, turning around and leaning on the island with her arms crossed after flicking the switch on the kettle.

'You know I always am,' he quipped, sidling up and putting his arms around her. He leaned in for a kiss.

'Yes, I know you are …' she replied, lightly tapping him on the chest with her fist before giving in to the kiss.

'I'll be in my study if you need me,' he said, offering a small smile.

'Do I need to use the secret knock to come in?' she asked. There was humour in her voice, but he could tell that she meant it.

'Only if you're feeling all European, what with drinking *tea* in the morning all of a sudden.'

Flo grinned and raised her eyebrows at him.

~~~~

As Tony walked off, blowing into his cup, Lisa walked into the kitchen via the other door.

'Good morning, baby. Did you sleep well?' Flo asked, blowing on her own cup.

Lisa just grunted and walked towards the cupboard at the far end of the room. She took a bowl and returned it to the island.

Flo stopped blowing her cup and looked at her. Her short hair, which Flo didn't really like, was greasy, and the pyjamas she was wearing looked like they should have been in the laundry hamper a week ago. *I haven't seen her wearing anything other than those cover-all pyjamas since we came home,* she thought, squinting to look closer at her daughter. This in itself was strange, as Lisa had favoured shorts and crop-tops no matter the weather.

She put her cup down on the counter and watched her daughter pour cereal into the bowl and then milk. Lisa picked up the bowl, grabbed a spoon, and began to make her way out of the kitchen, towards the stairs.

'Lisa,' Flo offered, hoping the longing and fear she was feeling wasn't too evident in her voice. 'Is there anything you want to talk to me about? Anything bothering you?' she asked.

Lisa just shook her head. 'No, Mom. I'm fine.'

She was smiling, but Flo thought it was a mask. Behind the facade, something dark was lurking. Call it mother's intuition, but it was there. 'Are you, though?' she asked, hoping it wasn't going to start a fight.

'Why do you ask?'

'I don't know, honey. You just seem a little ... different somehow. I see Janice here all the time, but I hardly hear you two laughing anymore. I haven't seen anything of Nichola and Paula, or Kate, for that matter. Have you guys had a falling out or something?'

Lisa, still projecting the same plastic smile, shook her head. 'No, nothing like that. It's just that the other two have hooked up with guys, and they're spending most of the summer with them. It's just me and Janice for the time being. Don't worry, Mom, we're having plenty of fun.'

'So, there's nothing wrong then?'

'Nope!' The false smile was back.

Flo nodded and took a sip of tea. 'OK, baby, but you'd tell me if there was, wouldn't you?'

'Yeah, Mom, you know that. No secrets.' She then surprised Flo by hopping over and kissing her on the head. 'Now, I'm going to eat this and watch some trash TV.'

With that, she was off, leaving Flo in the kitchen alone.

'Enjoy yourself, baby,' Flo shouted, biting her bottom lip, watching her leave. She took a moment, switching to biting the inside of her cheek, before leaving the kitchen and making her way down to the basement, to Tony's study.

She tried the door, knowing it would be locked. She knocked. 'Tony? Tony, can you hear me?' she half whispered through the thick wood.

'Hang on,' his voice replied, and she envisioned him rapidly closing down screens and logging off servers. She would have smiled had her heart not been so heavy right then.

# The Boyfriend

Eventually, the key turned and her husband's smiling face appeared in the doorway. *He's got the exact same smile Lisa had,* she thought. *False.*

Without waiting for an invitation, she walked past him, into the room. 'We need to talk.'

'Come on in then,' he said.

She caught the sarcasm as she sat in his favourite leather seat.

She had never been one to mince words. When something bothered her, she felt it better to get it out in the open and dealt with rather than letting it fester. She had been the same ever since she could remember. 'There's something wrong with Lisa. She's denying it too much for my liking, but I can tell.'

Tony leaned on the wall and folded his arms; he was nodding. 'I was thinking the same thing. She's just so ...'

'Different. Has been since we came back,' she finished for him. 'Listen, I know I told you to stay out of her private life, but I'm worried.' She bit the inside of her cheek. 'I'm scared. She hasn't once even mentioned Sean since we came back. Can you remember before we went? It was Sean this and Sean that. There wasn't a sentence without Sean's name coming up. I know what she said on the phone, but ... I'm scared that something happened while we were away.'

Tony walked over to his wife and put his arms around her. He held her tight.

'I want you to find out. Can you? I know we shouldn't, we said we wouldn't, but can you?' She'd fought hard not to cry, but her defences were crumbling, and soon there would be no stopping the tears.

'I'll try, baby,' he whispered, holding her tight again. As he hugged her closer, she couldn't see his eyes.

She wouldn't have liked what she saw there anyway.

52.

'I'M GETTING A gun,' Lisa announced. 'I'm getting a gun, and I'm going to shoot that prick Sean Knight and whoever the fuck Jay is. I'm going to kill them. Both of them. Stone. Cold. Dead!'

'Lisa, listen to yourself. You don't know the first thing about killing someone,' Janice pleaded.

Lisa was in one of her low moods. They had become more and more frequent over the weeks, and more and more dark.

'I don't care. I want the fuckers dead. No one who can do what he did to me, to another *human*, deserves to live. They're the scum of the earth, Janice, street rats.' Lisa threw herself on her bed, burying her head in a pillow. Her body heaved as she stifled her scream.

Janice leaned in and put her head on her friend's back, wrapping her arms around her. As usual, Lisa's body tightened at her touch, but then it relaxed when she realised the person touching her didn't want to hurt her. 'Come on, Lisa, your physical wounds are healing. You wouldn't even know that you were attacked in such a way.'

Lisa brought her head out of the pillow at such force that Janice was forced back a little. 'I know,' she seethed. 'In my head, Janice,' she almost spat her name, 'I relive it every fucking night, blow by blow. This is what that animal did to me. Look.' She raised her top, exposing her scarred stomach and the sports bra she had to wear because any other fabric rubbing on her breasts stung too much to bear. Most of the bruises that had languished on her stomach were gone, but the cigarette burns would never leave, no matter how much cream they used. Slowly, she lifted her bra, exposing her breasts. Her nipples were still raw, the flesh was red and puffy around the areolas, and the nipples themselves were pink and scabbed. 'If ever I do manage to forget about it for a while, all I need to do is look at this, and I'm right back there, in that fucking kitchen, where I have to eat breakfast and dinner with my parents every single fucking day! Who could do this to another person?' she reiterated, making it a question, her tone softening. 'Whoever it is, they don't deserve to live,' she finished. 'The scars are still in my head, Janice, every single last one of them. No matter how the bruises on my face or my chest might have healed, no matter how much the painful throbbing between my legs has gone away, no matter how infrequent I taste his fucking cum in my mouth, they're all still there. Every last one of them.'

Janice didn't say anything. After a moment, she reached out and touched one of the cigarette burns on Lisa's stomach. The instant she made contact, Lisa inhaled. Janice had touched them before. She'd rubbed ointment and cream into them to take the sting, infections, and, hopefully, the scars away, but this time it was different. This time it felt like there was electricity flowing through her fingers.

Lisa knew that Janice felt it too.

The electricity continued to flow as her fingers passed from one scar to another, moving up her body. Lisa closed her eyes, enjoying the sensation for the first time, allowing the tingle of her friend's touch to sink deep into her flesh. She felt her fingers slow as she moved up another scar, only one away from her breasts.

It was strange. Something was happening. For the first time since … since Sean, she felt happy; aroused!

Janice's hand bypassed the last scar and crept slowly, tentatively, for her left breast. Her fingers lightly circled the areola, and even though they were sore, a small sigh of pleasure escaped Lisa.

There was a small sting as her nipple tightened beneath Janice's fingers, but it wasn't a bad feeling.

It was almost exactly the opposite.

This was all the encouragement Janice needed. She leaned in, invading her personal space. Lisa inhaled the sweet aroma of her friend's skin, of the lotion she'd used and whatever perfume she was wearing. Her eyes flickered open as the soft touch of her friend's lips brushed against hers. There was a moment of surprise when she

197

realised what was happening, but she closed her eyes again, giving her friend the invitation she needed to do what she had so obviously been longing to do.

Janice's lips were soft, moist, and open. Despite everything that was happening in her life, everything she was going through, this was exactly what she needed right then. Softness was something she'd missed. Warmth was also something she'd missed. Yes, she'd had both of these from her parents, but it wasn't the same as someone doing it because they had a desire to do it.

Janice had been there for her through all of this. She had been the one who'd nursed her wounds, both physical and mental. It had been her who had built her up when she'd worried about seeing her parents. Right now, Janice was her world, and right now, that was everything.

She accepted the kiss; hell, she welcomed it. There was nothing else in her heart but thankfulness and gladness that this was happening.

Janice would never beat her with a pool cue. Janice would never put cigarettes out on her breasts.

Her tongue was in her mouth; it was exploring. Lisa sent hers in to chase it, to play with it, to taste it. The simple kiss had become … more. Something was happening inside of her, something she had felt only a few times before when Sean had—

*Don't even think of that name,* she scolded herself.

Suddenly, it stopped, and Janice pulled away, leaving her hand gently on Lisa's cheek. 'What's wrong? Did I … was it too much?' she asked.

Lisa could see the worry on her friend's face. *Are we more than friends now?*

She smiled and touched Janice, coaxing her closer. As she did, she became aware that Janice's hand was still on her breast. She had thought that the next time anyone saw her naked would be awkward, due to the disfigurement of the burns on her sensitive parts, but because Janice had been there for her, helped her, soothed her, this felt like it was the most natural thing in the world.

'There's nothing wrong,' she whispered, closing her eyes again, anticipating another kiss. 'Actually, I think everything is right. Better than it's been for a long time.'

As the two girls fell back onto the bed, Lisa noticed that Janice was careful not to fall on top of her, obviously aware of the tenderness of her wounds. For this, she fell in love with her best friend even more.

53.

TONY DOUBLE CLICKED on an icon on his computer desktop. The image was designed to look like a mechanical insect. As he clicked, it momentarily doubled in size before disappearing down to the bottom of his screen.

A green box appeared with the logo of a government agency in the top corner. More from habit than for any practical purpose, he spared a quick look behind him, making sure no one was loitering back there with malintent.

He was alone, so he continued.

ENTER PIN FOR FLEA SYSTEM, the screen read. He entered a personal identification number and pressed the RETURN key on the keyboard. His cell phone flashed, and a twelve-digit alpha-numeric code appeared. He entered this code, even though he hadn't been prompted by the screen, careful not to get any of the digits wrong.

After a moment, the green box flashed twice, and a new icon appeared at the bottom corner of the screen. This informed him that he was now connecting to the FLEA VPN. A message popped up to remind him that he would need to enter his credentials within the allocated time period at random times within this session. Failure to enter the correct credentials within the time period would result in his disconnection from the FLEA VPN. He clicked the box to agree to these controls and was instantly instructed to enter another password. This one was long and complex, but he knew it from memory. He entered it twice and pressed RETURN again.

He was then confronted with a screen with several options. He selected the image of a cell phone and was prompted with a screen asking him to enter the number of the cell phone he wished to connect to. Carefully, he typed Lisa's number into the box and pressed the RETURN key again.

After a few moments, the words CONNECTION SUCCESSFUL flashed across the screen and a picture of a cell phone, the same model Lisa used, was displayed. It took another moment to replicate Lisa's home screen on his screen. When it was done, he had full covert access to everything on her device.

His hands were sweating.

He'd done this procedure many times on other phones, but this was the first time it had been so close, so ... personal to him.

His hand hovered over the mouse. He wanted to click, to start his investigation, but for the first time in his life, he was genuinely scared. Before he could click, a prompt popped up for him to enter his full credentials within twenty seconds. His fingers danced over his keyboard expertly, and he pressed RETURN with ten seconds to spare.

Once this was done, it somehow gave him the courage to begin the investigation.

He clicked on Lisa's phone, and it connected.

The FLEA system had been launched for agents to gain access to targets' cell phones and devices. Ever since the case against a well-known mobile manufacturer who wouldn't allow access to the locked phone of a terror suspect, the government had been working on ways to bypass this red tape. It was a highly classified application, but it worked, gleaming sensitive information about contacts and their movements. It was a well-known fact that agents used it to keep watchful eyes on their wives, husbands, and children. Technically, that was illegal, but it was something no one was ever going to go get into trouble for, as, officially, the application didn't exist.

He didn't know where to start.

He didn't really *want* to start at all, but something had happened, something bad, and he needed to know what that something was.

He began with her photo album. There were three hundred and twelve images within. Inwardly, he groaned. He knew this was going to be a total invasion of her privacy and he could lose all the trust he had built with his daughter over the years with one click, but still the hunch, the niggling feeling in the back of his mind, like an itch that he couldn't scratch, kept irritating him.

He clicked on the folder, and a number of sub folders opened up. The names of the folders corresponded to dates. He clicked the column and sorted them by the date edited and was relieved to find that the last folder was dated the week before they went away. *Thank God for small mercies,* he thought as he clicked off the folder, glad he didn't have to scroll through all her pics.

Next, he went into the RECENT CALLS list.

Since they had been away, he saw calls from Nichola, Paula, Janice, more from her than from anyone else, and, of course, Sean.

Sean's number stopped reoccurring a couple of days after they had gone on vacation. He made a note of that in his notebook and continued to search. There were a few numbers he didn't recognise. He right clicked on these numbers and searched for them via the FLEA network. After a few moments, the search came back to inform him that they were sales calls originating from Mexico or India.

He dismissed these and closed the recent calls list.

His hands were still moist as the mouse hovered over the MESSAGE icon on the cell phone home screen. He really didn't want to do this, but he had a feeling that whatever he was looking for would probably be in this section.

He took in a deep breath and held it for a few beats before allowing it to exit slowly.

He clicked on the MESSAGE icon and was instantly rewarded with a long list of messages with predominantly one reoccurring name next to them.

Janice.

He skipped through, looking for other names. Paula was there, as was Nichola and a few were labelled Kate. Then he got to Sean's messages. Once again, these stopped on the same date. The second day they were away in Europe.

His hackles were up. Something had happened that first night, the same night Peter tried to get into the house. He needed to know what that something was, but the irony of his situation was that he didn't *want* to know.

Feeding his hunch, he began with Sean's messages.

# The Boyfriend

The correspondence between them appeared normal, the usual flirtations and such, except for the two bottom messages, both within a minute of each other. Tony, with mounting dread, looked at the timestamps and saw they were sent at one-seventeen a.m. The same time the system had gone down.

'TURN CCTV OFF' and 'OPEN THE GATE AND THE FRONT DOOR. HE'S GONE'

He sat for a while, staring at the screen, his hand covering his mouth as he considered the words that had been sent to his daughter.

Anger was building up inside him, a dangerous anger.

He did something then. It was more than illegal; it could land him five to ten years in prison. Even though it was widespread practice, if caught, there would be a real song and dance about it. If he went down for it, he knew it would be soft time, but it wasn't something he needed to worry about, considering his contacts.

He right clicked on Sean Knight's telephone number and selected INITIATE FLEA JUMP. The cursor on his screen turned into a multi-coloured beach ball and began to spin. All he needed to hope for was that Sean's phone wasn't turned off. If it was, the flea wouldn't be able to connect until the next time it pinged onto the network. As it normally took a small while to initiate, Tony took the time to clear his thoughts and calm himself down. He stood, surprised at how badly his legs were shaking from the frustration and anger of what he was doing and, most importantly, why he was doing it. He needed to leave the room, just for a moment, to collect himself. He picked up his cup and returned to the kitchen to make himself another cup of tea.

He returned five minutes later to find his FLEA connection to Sean's cell phone had been successful.

It brought up a graphic of a cell phone that was not dissimilar to Lisa's. The icons were in a different place, but the navigation between the settings and the apps were the same. He decided that this time he would start with the calls. He went straight to the night in question.

Earlier in the day, there had been a large number of interactions between himself and Lisa. He disregarded these but kept a note of the interspersed calls to a contact on his phone called JAY. There were also several calls to someone who was labelled simply as

'T'. He made a note of this number too before continuing on to the text messages.

Once again, there was a large number of interactions between him and Lisa, which abruptly ended at the time he knew about. It seemed that most of his interactions on his phone stopped at that time, except for a few calls and messages to JAY. Tony made a mental note to FLEA jump onto Jay's phone when he was finished with Sean's.

It looked like there had been a few calls from Sean to Lisa after the night in question that had gone unanswered.

He clicked on the last message. 'OPEN THE GATE AND THE FRONT DOOR. HE'S GONE'. He knew what it meant, he knew what the message was instructing her to do, and he knew who 'he' was who had gone. *But what happened after that?*

He pondered on the JAY messages. He wanted to click on them and read them. There were interactions earlier in the evening, but he was more interested in the ones sent about an hour and a half after the last one sent to Lisa. These could hold the key to the questions that had been buzzing around his head for the last few days.

Not quite ready for that knowledge, he decided to click on the PHOTOS icon on the phone's home screen. This app held all the pictures, and videos, that had been taken and saved by this phone.

As he clicked on it, he was confronted with a confusing list of icons with long, complicated names. Sean was not as organised with his folders as his daughter was. The names contained information regarding the dates and times the pictures had been taken. Still not entirely convinced he was doing the right thing, he selected the most recent folder and opened it. With every click, he hoped he didn't see anything he would regret. He hoped they'd brought their daughter up better than that.

He was rewarded with a few nice images of Lisa sending him smiling selfies and a few of her in school looking bored. These piqued his interest, and he continued to click, noticing he was getting closer to the date he was interested in.

As he continued, he became concerned with the continued flicking between nice pictures of his daughter and the increasing filth of porn. This gave him everything he needed to know about the character of the boy.

Then he saw it!

At first, he didn't know what he was looking at. It looked like a torture porn picture, which had become more prevalent as he delved further into the folder. However, there was something about this one that caught his attention.

It was grainy, grainier than the other stock photographs he'd seen. It featured a young girl with dark hair, lying on a floor. Her face was hidden from the lens of the camera. The way she was lying, she looked unconscious. He'd seen enough people lying that very same way in his time, but it wasn't this that piqued his interest. He had been trained to look outside the box at scenes like this, and what he focused on was the wood-panelled flooring she was lying on.

He dragged the picture from the FLEA app to his desktop. It took a moment to download over the VPN. Once it was there, he double clicked on it, and it opened in full high definition. Ignoring the image of the dark-haired girl, he zoomed in on the flooring, more specifically, on the shoe rack he could see next to her body.

He swallowed hard.

A shiver ran through him, and goosebumps rose on every inch of his skin. He felt as though the temperature had dropped by ten degrees. Greasy sweat dripped from every pore, and he absently wiped his brow, hoping upon hope that his eyes were deceiving him.

He knew they weren't, he was too highly trained to be wrong, yet still he prayed.

The shoe rack next to the body was the same shoe rack they had in their hallway.

Not only that, but the walking boots on this rack were the very same walking boots he had, the same boots that were on the rack right now.

He began to shake.

He couldn't stop.

For the first time in his life, that he could remember, he had absolutely no control over his body. He gripped his arms, trying to stop them shaking. He couldn't breathe, his throat was tight, his heart was thrashing, and he was grinding his teeth. A red mist descended over his vision. His insides were churning with horror, revulsion, anger, rage!

He took in a deep breath and held it. He closed his eyes and willed his heart to slow. Eventually, the fit passed, and he had control of his faculties once again.

He looked at the computer screen, his teeth gritted as they ground into one another. He zoomed out of the picture and focused his attention on the young girl lying on the floor.

It was Lisa.

'You're a dead man,' he whispered. 'I'll fucking kill you,' he sobbed as fat tears fell from his eyes. It was the first time this had happened since he saw her sweet little face for the very first time.

He'd cried then, but for a very different reason.

'You piece of shit!'

His hands were sweat-soaked and flexing open and closed.

His throat was dry.

His eyes were stinging, but he couldn't take his eyes off the girl on the screen. 'How did I not see it was Lisa?' he chastised himself as the picture blurred through his tears.

He wiped his face, coughed, and got back to work.

His eyes flicked from the picture back to the phone screen and all the other pictures that were lined up, ready to be opened, the ones that came after this image.

During his career, Tony had been in a number of tight, tense situations. He had been called upon to witness things that would have made lesser people throw up. Things that would have traumatised *civvies*, as they were known to his colleagues.

For the sake of 'National Security,' he had done his duty and he had done it well.

None of that, not one bit of the twenty or so years of intensive, invasive training he'd received, none of the atrocities he'd witnessed in his line of work, nothing had any bearing on what he was looking at now. He knew that he had to click on the next picture, but he also knew that doing so would be the hardest thing he would ever do in his life.

With shaking, sweat-slicked hands, he hovered the cursor over the icon. He closed his wet eyes and swallowed; a dry click issued from his throat.

The picture opened.

# The Boyfriend

This time, the focus of the image was unmistakably Sean. He was smiling into the camera, taking what the kids called a selfie from an angle that enabled the whole body, Lisa's body, to be in the picture.

He was smiling, offering a *thumbs up* to the camera.

Tony clicked on the next one.

Sean had his erect penis in his hand. It was inches away from his daughter's unconscious body. His eyes kept flicking over to the stupid fucking shoe rack in the corner, hoping it would miraculously change, becoming someone else's shoe rack, with someone else's walking boots on it. Someone else who had a daughter who looked strikingly similar to Lisa.

But it didn't.

They were his walking boots resting on his rack.

It was *his* daughter lying on the floor.

He would never, ever be able to wear those boots again.

He didn't want to see where this was going. He already knew what the outcome of this find would mean for Sean, but he had to be sure that it *was* what it looked like.

It wasn't.

It was worse.

The images of his daughter's beautiful, innocent face beaten to a pulp made him want to vomit. The images of his daughter's beautiful skin being burnt with cigarettes caused every fibre of his being to itch as if something nasty was crawling over him.

In a very real sense, the nasty thing was crawling inside him.

All of these photographs paled into insignificance as he clicked on the last picture taken. It was Lisa, lying on the floor, naked. Her poor, ravaged chest looked to be covered in something. On closer inspection, Tony openly sobbed. Spittle flew from his mouth and covered his computer screen. The substance she was covered in was shit. Human shit.

He clenched his fist and banged it onto his desk, causing everything to jump. *Animal,* was his only thought.

He didn't want to continue, didn't think he could continue, but the professional in him took over, and he selected the video footage folder.

He watched through tears of anger, rage, and an overwhelming sadness as his daughter's innocence was forcibly taken from her as she screamed and cried, pleading for him to stop.

He couldn't believe this was playing out before him.

It was too much for him.

His rage was out of control.

He jumped from his seat, sending the leather chair flying across the room, into the door behind him. He clenched his fists, and before he knew what he was doing, he had punched the computer screen that was displaying the vile images. The screen went black, and a hateful, multicoloured circular impact point flashed up. Black seeped from the strands of the spider's web covering the screen.

He didn't care. His rage was all encompassing, but there was a small, distant, voice calling from somewhere deep inside him. It sounded like Flo. It was telling him to calm down, telling him he needed to think rationally about how he was going to deal with this situation. It was telling him he needed to plan. That he couldn't go in half-cocked and angry.

He needed to be meticulous!

He pulled his seat back, sat on it, and breathed a deep, shaking breath. There was no way he was going to get those images out of his head. He knew he would see them every single time he closed his eyes, probably for the rest of his life.

He wanted to cry for his beautiful Lisa, for his poor, innocent daughter, but the snarl on his lips told him there would be plenty of time for that later. Right now, he needed to catch the bastard spider that had spun the web currently adorning his computer monitor.

## 54.

'COME ON, JANICE, you must know someone. Or at least someone who knows someone.'

They were walking through the park together. Out of sight of prying eyes, they dared to walk hand-in-hand, strolling through the park. Even though they had decided their relationship should be kept secret for as long as they could, they just couldn't help but be close to each other at every given opportunity. The section of the park they were in was surrounded by thick trees and bushes, so they dared to be brave.

Lisa needed the closeness, as even though she was fighting it, just being out of her house was terrifying for her. Men, or, more specifically, Sean, was lurking behind every bush, every tree, ready to jump out and finish the job he had started.

'I wish you'd just forget this plan. It's not going to come to any good, for you or for anyone else,' Janice offered.

They continued walking for a few more steps before Lisa broke the awkward silence. 'So that piece of shit gets away with what he did to me with no consequences?'

Janice was shaking her head. 'I'm not saying that at all. I want to see the prick get the justice he deserves, but no one has seen anything of him since that night. It's like he's fallen off the face of the earth. I asked Ryan the other day if anyone had seen him in school. He said no, and that no one was missing him either.'

Lisa didn't care about what her—*is she my girlfriend now?*— was telling her, she was too fuelled, too hyped up with hate to care about much else. 'It's not about getting revenge ... Well, OK, it's not *all* about getting revenge. It's about me. I need to feel safe. I think if I had a gun, then maybe I wouldn't go around jumping at every little noise.'

Janice stopped and tugged on Lisa's hand to stop her. She pulled her back towards her, smiling as she did. 'You've got me to keep you safe.'

Lisa rolled her eyes but allowed herself to be pulled into Janice's embrace. With a quick scan of their immediate environment, just to make sure there was no one around spying on them, the two girls fell into a slow embrace.

After a short but passionate kiss, Lisa pushed away and wiped her mouth. 'No matter how often you do that, it's not going to stop me from wanting that gun.'

'Doesn't your dad have guns?'

'Yeah, but you know how paranoid he is. Could you imagine what he'd be like if he found one missing?' Lisa thought about it rather theatrically for a while before raising her eyebrows and continuing to walk off.

'Yeah, maybe you're right about that,' Janice laughed, catching up.

'So, *do* you know anyone?'

'If I give you a name, will you leave it alone?'

'Once I've got the gun, then yeah. I'll hide it in my room, and we can forget all about it. I'll feel safe, and we can start to move on with the next chapter of our lives.'

Janice shook her head and sighed heavily. 'There's a place you can go where you can get anything you want for a price. One of Jamie's friends used to go there to get drugs. It's not that far away. But you can't even get close without them knowing you're coming. You'll need to be introduced.'

'So, who will introduce me? You?'

Janice shook her head and laughed. 'Me? No. I don't know these people. Who do you think I am, fucking Pablo Escobar? I'll have a word with Jamie and see if his friend can get you introduced. Then, maybe, finally, you'll see how fucking stupid this idea is and let it go.'

'I might.' Lisa smiled and continued walking. The smile was devoid of humour.

55.

IT WAS DARK. The rain had been pouring for at least half an hour, but none of this bothered Tony. He was in the driver's seat of another bland, disposable car. Across the street was the house where Sean Knight lived with his dead-beat parents. He was watching the house through a pair of high-powered, recording binoculars.

He had done his due diligence.

Sean's father, Gregory, was ex-military. He had been deployed to the Gulf during Operation Desert Storm but returned with no medals and without any exemplary commendations. He was a less than average soldier. Since he'd returned and left the army, he'd had a number of low-paying menial jobs until he set up his own small mechanics shop, servicing motorcycles and pickup trucks. He had a police record, mostly for being drunk and disorderly, barroom brawls, and other misdemeanours.

His mother, Annie, had never worked. She was a stay-at-home mom, claiming all kinds of disability allowances from the government. At present, she was a registered addict.

He had watched the house for over an hour. He'd told Flo he had some errands to run and that he might be gone some time. She knew the score; errands usually meant work that she was better off not knowing about and not to expect him home at any reasonable hour. He was grateful for his understanding wife because the way he was feeling, he didn't know if he'd have been able to explain everything to her. The things he'd seen, what their daughter had endured. He didn't want Flo to know anything about that.

He drove to the address that the cell phone had been registered to without a plan. He hadn't had time to develop a feasible one yet, but he thought observing the comings and goings of the residence might help him formulate one.

He hated working off the cuff; it wasn't his style.

He'd fought the urge to storm the house and just take the boy. Every fibre of his being wanted to extinguish the piece of filth from existence, but he knew that would be disastrous.

The house looked like it was being set up for a party, or something resembling one. He'd observed Sean's father coming home with an inordinate haul of booze and his mother running around the house, cleaning and emptying garbage. There had been a lot of shouting, and the music had been cranked up.

The front door opened, and Sean emerged from it, heading towards where the car, the same car that had once pulled up outside his house, was parked on the sidewalk. 'Don't be coming back with just any shit now,' Sean's father shouted from inside the house. 'And I want the fucking change this time, you little thief.'

His heart was beating too fast in his chest as he watched Sean give his father the finger before getting into the car and driving off, down the street. His father shook his head before going back inside, slamming the door behind him.

Tony pulled off slowly and inconspicuously, following the dark blue Chevy.

They drove for maybe ten minutes, out of the run down, formerly nice neighbourhood, into a horrible, ex-industrial area. The buildings here were mostly deserted, but there were still signs of life in one or two of them. With his headlights off, he followed Sean's car as it turned onto a street comprised of old warehouses and crumbled tenements. The boy got out of the car and adjusted the hood on his dark jacket before making his way towards a particularly desolated warehouse. The dirty windows of the three-story building looked like dark holes into the soul of a dying behemoth. They reminded Tony of gunshot wounds.

He watched with interest as Sean was accosted by a youth on a bicycle. The kid—Tony couldn't tell if it was a boy or a girl, he assumed it was a boy—approached Sean, cycled around him a couple of times, then disappeared into the shadows of another dying building on the grey, ugly street. *The lookout,* he mused. He continued watching with interest as Sean made his way towards what looked like a boarded-up alleyway. He dodged beneath a large slab of masonry and disappeared into the darkness beyond.

When he emerged fifteen minutes later, he was cradling his chest, with something obviously stashed beneath his coat. Once he was back in his car, he wasted no time turning the car around and leaving the same way he came.

Tony watched him go. He didn't follow him as he knew he would be followed by one of the lookouts. He knew where the piece of filth was going, and a plan was formulating in his head.

~~~~

When he arrived home, Flo was cooking in the kitchen. 'Honey, could you run out and get some milk and some bread? I think we're all out,' she shouted to him.

'Yeah, no worries. Is Lisa home?'

'No, she's over at Janice's, I think. She said something about all the girls getting together tonight. I think it's a big thing for them.'

'OK ... I think we have some bread in the freezer in the basement.'

'Can you check? I still want that milk, though. Ever since Europe, I'm really craving tea. Are you working tonight?'

Tony took in a deep breath before answering. What he was doing now was more than work. It had crossed a line into his personal life, and the thought of it cut him deep. 'Yeah. I'm sorry, but I'm going to have to. It's an important case.'

Flo tutted and turned back to her cooking. 'Well, go on then, but go get me that milk first.'

Tony moved into the kitchen and wrapped his arms around his wife. He leaned in close and smelled her hair. 'I love you Flo,' he whispered.

'Yeah? Well, you might not if you don't get me that milk,' she laughed.

He went and got the milk, then, with a heavy heart but a desire for vengeance, *or justice,* he went back to his office. He had calls to make. He would be putting his plan it into play very soon.

56.

'That guy is such a prick,' Janice fumed as they sat in the hayloft of an old barn on the edge of town. 'I wasn't asking him to *be* associated with us, fuck that, who wants to be associated with that loser. No, I just wanted the introduction. I know he could do it. But he wanted to know the fucking ins and out of it all. At one point, I thought he was going to want to know the colour of your panties.'

Lisa laughed a little as Janice relayed the conversation she'd had with her brother about helping them get the gun.

The day was warm, and Janice had opted for wearing a light summer dress. However, Lisa had still insisted on dressing in jeans and a light, long-sleeved button-up. Even though most of her wounds were now healing nicely and she was sweltering, she still wasn't comfortable showing off any flesh.

They had both decided that a day away from the rigors of the ugly world would suit them both just fine. They both had a lot on their minds.

'He's a fucking sap in more ways than one,' Janice continued her story.

Lisa laughed, again. Janice always had a way of getting what she wanted, and Lisa had no reason to believe that wouldn't change with her brother.

'So, I told him, either you get me the introduction, or I'll tell the police you've been slipping out of your ankle monitor and going off in the middle of the night.'

'Has he?' Lisa asked, a blossom of panic blooming in her stomach.

'I don't know, and I don't care. He knew that if I told, he'd get more heat than he needed. So he said he'd introduce us.'

Lisa was biting her bottom lip in celebration. 'Thank you, Jamie,' she shouted.

'So, it's tonight, at seven?'

'We need to go tonight?'

'Yeah, and it's going to be a cash deal. Apparently, they are not too hot on using cards, and they definitely don't give credit. Are you good for it? We won't get a second chance at this.'

Lisa nodded. 'I've got seven-hundred dollars in my room; do you think it'll be enough?'

'He mentioned five, with bullets. It'll be unmarked, and the serial numbers will be filed off and the barrels changed. It'll be good for fifteen shots. You'll have to douse it in gas, then throw it into the river once you've used it. That'll remove all traces of DNA. Then, you have to burn the clothes you're wearing and douse your body with the same gas. That gets rid of gunshot residue.'

'He told you all of that?'

Janice grinned and leaned back onto the haystack. 'No, stupid. I watch all the *how to get away with murder* programmes on TV. You don't need to worry about the dousing your body part, though, as I will be more than willing to help out there.'

Lisa laughed and pulled her lover towards her, planting a kiss on her lips before falling back into the hay for a longer, more sensuous embrace.

57.

TONY SPENT MOST of the next day getting things in order. He had a lot to do, so he started early. He'd arranged to collect various *tools* he would need from certain 'safe' locations. As he was well known in these communities, there were no questions asked. All that greeted him was friendly banter and questions centring around the wellbeing of his family. He collected the ordered goods with cheer, informing each and every query that his family were fine, and that everything was fine, and that he was fine, and the whole fucking world was fine.

Tony, despite his cheery exterior, was far from fine.

What he had planned was also far from fine, but he knew deep down in his heart it was needed.

58.

'JAY, I'M LEAVING. I can't sit around waiting for acceptance into this community.'

'I told you to leave days ago,' Jay replied from the other end of the phone. 'They're not going let you in if you put heat on them. These are professional people, not some amateur group of thugs. Professional criminals, and if they get a sniff of weakness, then you're out on a limb, do you hear me? Gone!' The word was spoken with emphasis.

'Yeah, well, I'm out tonight. Mom and Dad are having another fucking sex and drug party. That's one too many for me. I'm going to get their stuff, get some for myself to sell. I'm gonna need to make money, then I'm a ghost. This town has seen the back of Sean Knight.'

'That's the spirit, man. You go; I'll take care of things on this end until you're called, then I'll reach out to you. It could be a few months or so.'

'Are you going to keep the same contact details?'

'I'll keep the email address. I'll burn the mobile once you've gone. Don't message me; I'll message you and let you know when they want to see you. I've already let them know what you did, and believe me, they were impressed. Especially when I sent them the videos. They'll have a need for someone with your … skill set.'

'Really?' Sean was grinning as he lay in the back seat of the car. 'They liked it? Let them know it can be my signature, so to speak. Any work of that nature, I'm their man.'

'I'll let them know. So, it's tonight then? I think you're making the right choice. You never know with these bitches; any given moment she could change her mind and go running to the police.'

'Yeah, well, I enjoyed myself and everything, but I haven't been able to go anywhere since. I've been stuck in this shitty house with my shitty folks, watching them fuck whoever they want, whenever they want. Jesus, they're freaks. There's nothing keeping me here.'

'Good man, that's the kind of shit they want to hear. Someone with no ties, someone who can cut town whenever he needs to. Travel light, and don't let anyone know where you are.'

There was a moment or two of silence as Sean contemplated where he was going to go and how he was going to get there. 'So, I'll be in touch then?' he said, finally breaking the silence.

'No, Sean. I'll be in touch with you. Take it easy. I'll reach out when I need to.'

The phone went dead then, and Sean lay back, looking at the illuminated screen. 'Fuck,' he whispered before clicking it off and putting it in his jacket pocket. He turned onto his side, ready to have a nap before going to do what needed doing. He'd hoped this community would have let him inside as soon as his mission had been completed.

He hadn't factored into the equation going on the lam.

59.

'WHERE THE HELL are we?' Lisa was hanging on to Janice's arm as if her life were dependant on it. In her mind, that's exactly what it was. She had never been to such a desolate place in her entire life and was shocked that it was so close to where she lived. The buildings loomed at them as if they were angry old gods, unhappy that these mere mortals had the audacity to enter their domain. They looked empty, soulless, angry, and hungry.

She knew all of this was folly. Buildings didn't have lives of their own, but she shuddered at the thought of the homeless people, not to mention junkies, that the shadows and husks were sheltering.

Crackheads and hobos with tastes for young girls.

She'd been through enough recently without the added anxiety of being attacked again.

'I think we're close. Rosemont Street should be just around the next corner,' Janice whispered as she consulted her cell phone and the maps app that told her where they needed to go. 'There it is.' She pointed.

Rosemont Street was not as pleasant as it sounded. It was made up of old three-story town houses that looked like they might have been the height of fashion in 1930 but were now ghosts of their former glories. On the opposite side of the street was a warehouse clad in old, dirty bricks that looked like they might have been third hand even before this monstrosity of a building was conceived. The windows were many, and they were dark. A slab of concrete that looked like it had maybe been part of an entrance in a past life had been placed across a dark alleyway. Lisa was dreading Janice telling her that was their destination, but it was exactly what happened.

'I thought we were going to be greeted by a welcoming party,' Janice said, looking around at the growing shadows. 'They said something about a kid on a bike. Have you seen a kid on a bike?'

'Huh?' Lisa grunted; she'd been too busy looking for horny hobo's and drugged up lotharios to listen to Janice's questions.

'A kid on a bike? Have you seen one?'

Lisa shrugged. 'No, I've been too busy worrying for our lives. Why?'

'I don't know; I'm sure there should have been one. That's all.' She scanned their surroundings once again and shrugged. 'Whatever. I think we should just go in anyway. Come on.'

Lisa didn't want to, but she'd come this far, and if it meant getting rid of the bad dreams and the constant menace of *him* hiding behind every bush, in every alleyway, in every shadow, then it was a small price to pay.

She swallowed, grabbed Janice's hand, and followed her around the broken slab and through the wooden board over the entrance, into the darkness beyond.

## 60.

AFTER A FEW stops to get supplies and call in some favours, Tony was back in the ugly neighbourhood where he'd followed Sean the other night. He'd intercepted a call from the boy's mobile to an unknown number while working on the FLEA network. The call had been about merchandise, about tonight, about getting extra, a lot extra, for his own use, and picking it all up at eight-thirty in the usual place.

It seemed that Sean was a creature of habit, as were his parents.

Tony wasn't going to miss this opportunity. He had everything he needed, and he knew where he needed to be. He decided there was no time like the present to put his plan into action. He informed Flo not to wait up for him and left the house, then drove to a remote garage that was owned by his associates. His associates owned everything in the immediate vicinity, so there was little chance of anyone happening upon him, and his activities.

He parked his regular SUV inside and got into another, older vehicle, similar to the bland ones he'd used the last few nights before driving off to do what needed to be done.

~~~~

Tony entered the disused area of the city that Sean had introduced him to and parked the car a few blocks up from Rosemont Street, where the first leg of his mission would take place. He donned his black gloves, black jacket, and black woollen hat, and exited the car. He then disappeared into the shadows of the disused industrial area.

On this journey, he was accosted by one or two panhandlers, hassling him for money or drugs, offering him any number of sexual favours in exchange for fifty bucks. He silenced anyone who saw or talked to him. A quick arm wrapped around their weakened necks put them straight to sleep. They'd wake up tomorrow in the deserted alleyways he dumped them, not knowing where they were or who they'd spoken to.

Keeping to the shadows, he made his way through the run-down neighbourhood until he came to the street he was looking for. He stopped and pressed himself against the wall of a dirty-bricked building. He blended in perfectly with his surroundings. Just around the corner was a youth on a bicycle, obviously the lookout. His head was down, looking at something in his hands. *Cell phone,* Tony thought. He caught the boy in his cell phone screen and zoomed in. It was a boy, probably not even twelve years old. He was wearing wireless earphones, obviously connected to the device in his hands.

He smiled. He was the cat stalking the mouse; he loved this part.

He darted from the shadows, covering the ten, maybe fifteen, yards to where the boy was standing with his bike, in silence. He grabbed his unsuspecting victim from behind, covering his mouth and twisting his head. 'If you move, even so much as to fight me, I swear to God I'll snap your neck like a fucking toothpick,' he whispered in the boy's ear after dragging the earphones out and trampling them under his feet. He then dragged the petrified boy and his bike back into the shadows he had come from.

Still holding his hand over the boy's mouth, he patted him down with his free hand, producing a small gun, a switchblade, and a radio. He dropped them all onto the floor and stamped on the radio. He could feel the boy's heartbeat racing beneath his hand; the little man was terrified. *This is the life you chose, my friend,* he thought before squeezing the boy's airway. There were a few moments of violence as the youth struggled against what was happening before falling to the ground in a heap.

Tony stripped the gun and dispersed the parts into a storm drain. He pocketed the knife and proceeded to drag the boy's unconscious body into a dark doorway behind him. He did the same with the bike, after stamping on the spokes, rendering the vehicle unusable.

He could see the alleyway where he needed to be just ahead of him. He was about to make his way over when two people approached his location from the other end of the street. They were too far away to see who they were, but he recognised at least one of them as female.

He stepped back into the shadows, watching the progress of the newcomers as they headed into the alleyway.

61.

'ARE WE GOING in or what?' Janice asked as Lisa held back.

'I don't know. I've kind of got a bad feeling about all of this now.'

Janice faced Lisa; her eyes were blazing. 'You can't back out now. We're here; they're expecting us.'

Lisa looked towards the alleyway before scanning the rest of the bleak surroundings. She was shaking her head. 'I know. It's just that I've got a feeling ...'

'What feeling?'

'I don't know. Like were being watched.'

Janice sighed. 'That's because we are being watched, you dumb bitch,' she hissed. 'Of course gun runners and drug dealers are going to have people in every one of those windows keeping an eye on who's coming and going.'

This didn't help Lisa at all. 'It's all so fucking ... real.'

'Come on, they're expecting us.' Janice grabbed Lisa's hand and pulled her into the alleyway.

The moment they were inside, they were accosted by three boys, each dressed in what Lisa could only think of as street clothing. Each boy was holding a gun. Lisa thought they couldn't have been any older than she was. Two were black, and one was white. One was chubby, but the other two, including the white guy, were skinny, wiry, ready to take care of business, any business, at the drop of a hat. They all had growths on their faces that couldn't quite be called beards, not for another two years at least.

She was petrified of the wild, abandoned look in their eyes.

# The Boyfriend

All three of them looked the two girls up and down. Lisa noted that there wasn't even a hint of sexuality in their stare. The skinny Black guy stepped forward. Both girls stepped back instinctively.

'What're you two fine bitches doing here?' he asked with a voice that was deeper than his appearance suggested. His accent was what Lisa would have called *street,* and it complimented his dress.

She found herself unable, and unwilling, to talk. She cowered behind Janice, hiding her face from the welcoming committee.

'How did you get past our sentry?' the chubby boy asked, also stepping forward and bringing the gun up to point it at the girls.

Lisa whimpered at the site of it and hid her face again.

'Listen. We're here to buy something. Your boss knows all about it. I was sanctioned. My name is Janice Bowen.'

The first boy turned and looked towards the third one at the back. He took his cell phone out of his back pocket and tapped something into the screen. He then nodded towards the chubby boy, all without saying a word.

'You the bitches who've come looking for artillery?' he asked, as the chubby boy lowered the gun.

'If by that you mean girls looking for a gun, then yeah. That's us,' Janice whispered; her arms were raised as she looked from boy to boy.

The first boy nodded at her. 'Crow ... you up,' he said and stepped back.

The white boy stepped forward. He was the tallest of the three. The handle of a gun was protruding from the waistline of his trousers. He reached in and pulled it out. He then, still without talking, held it out to the two girls. Raising his eyebrows, he offered the handle to Janice.

She turned to Lisa as if asking her what to do. Lisa shrugged, and Janice reached for the offered weapon.

With the speed of someone who had done it before, many times, the boy spun the gun in his hand, flicked the safety off, thrust it to her head, and pulled the trigger five times.

Janice screamed and fell to her knees, as did Lisa.

Both girls were huddled on the floor, holding each other, sobbing.

'You skank-ass motherfucking bitches, get the fuck out of my alley, and don't either of you show your fine asses round here again,' the white boy holding the gun shouted at them. 'The only pieces you need to know anything about is this,' he grabbed his crotch but didn't laugh; in fact, he snarled. 'Bitches like you bring heat around here. Now, fuck off, and don't let me see you around these parts again, or next time, you'll feel my hard dick before the bullets do their work.'

Without any recognition that something drastic had just happened in the two girl's lives, the three boys turned and disappeared down the alleyway, vanishing into the darkness from where they'd come.

~~~~

When they'd stopped crying and shaking uncontrollably, they got up from the floor, dusted off their clothes, and made their way silently out of the alleyway.

As they got to the street, they held hands, pulled the hoods of their jackets over their heads, and walked with urgency back the way they had come.

## 62.

A SCREAM ISSUED from the alleyway where the two girls had entered.

Every instinct in his body and all the training he'd received over the years told him to run towards the sound, to offer help and assistance in any way possible. That was before he remembered where he was. He was on the corner of Rosemont Street, dressed in dark fatigues, with the unconscious body of a twelve-year-old boy stuffed into a dark corner behind him. This was no time for heroics. *Whoever those two girls are,* he thought, *they probably deserve everything they get.*

He took off his backpack and removed a small device and lay it on the floor before him. He removed his phone from his pocket and logged onto it. On the opening of an app, the small device at his feet came to life as four rotary blades unfolded from the top, a flashing blue light confirming the connection with his phone. He pressed another button on the screen, and a barely audible hiss issued from the device as the blades began to whirr. An unseen camera at the front transmitted its feed to the cell phone, and the flashing blue light winked out. The drone lifted from the floor and hovered high above the building he was in. The screen split into two, one was the high-definition feed, and the other was the direction the drone was flying. Expertly, Tony piloted it towards the alleyway.

As it was dark, he activated the night vision, and half of his screen went green. After a second or two, it gave him a clear picture of what he needed to see.

He watched as the two girls hurried past him from the alleyway, their hoods up, hindering any kind of identification.

It didn't matter, he wasn't here for them; he was just glad they were safe and neither had seen him.

He flew the drone into the alley they had come from, hovering it silently over the darkness below. He picked up four heat signals; three looked human, and the fourth looked to be a barrel fire. He lowered the silent drone and zoomed in to see if he could get a decent picture of them. Three youths were sat around a blazing bin, handing a drink container around. He pressed buttons on his phone screen and zoomed into the boy's faces. With three clicks, he took photographs; with another three clicks, he forwarded them to a colleague, who he'd informed about his mission, for identification. He then proceeded to mark out the territory he would be entering.

It was essentially a dead-end alleyway. There was a door behind the three men, and he monitored them as they got up from the burning bin and entered inside. He turned the camera to infrared and watched as the glowing figures walked through a series of different sections. He scanned the rest of the building, satisfied that the camera couldn't pick-up any other heat signatures. He was happy there were only three men to contend with.

After recalling the drone and putting it back into his backpack, he removed a small handgun. There was also a small suppressor in the pack that he screwed onto the barrel. He then slid the encumbering weapon into his nylon shoulder holster and made his way towards the alleyway.

63.

SEAN WAS IN the car. Rock music was blaring from the speakers, and he was singing along with the tune, drumming his hands on the steering wheel in time with the beat.

His cell phone was next to him on the seat, along with a substantial wad of cash.

He turned out of his street, heading towards the wrong end of town.

~~~~

'How the fuck did you get in here?' The youth, who was pointing the gun towards Tony's face, spat the word 'fuck,' and his eyes were wider than eyes were meant to be.

Tony watched as the spray of spittle barely missed him. He held his arms in the air and took a step backwards. 'Whoa, man,' he said nervously towards his aggressor. 'My dog ran down this alleyway. I didn't know ...'

'Didn't know what?' the youth spat again.

'Didn't know there would be anyone back here.'

'Well, there isn't, and there's no dogs here either. So, I suggest you back the fuck away, white boy, and forget you were ever here.'

'It's just a little brown Shih Tzu. It's my wife's, really; she'll kill me if I go home without it.'

'Well, motherfucker, I'll kill you right here if you don't back the fuck aw—'

He never got to finish the sentence as Tony picked that moment to strike. He reached for the pointing gun, grabbing it by the barrel and taking the chubby man holding it completely by surprise.

He twisted the youth's wrist, forcing him drop the weapon into Tony's waiting hand. With deceptive speed, he sidestepped behind the young man's back, wrapped his arm around his neck, and squeezed. The youth put up a fight but not enough of one, and it wasn't long before he was dead weight in Tony's arms. It was just in time, as the other two men appeared, both pointing guns at his head.

'Who the *fuck* are you?' the taller of the two men asked.

Tony was holding the heavy weight of the big man as a shield as he turned towards the newcomers. 'You may want to have a word with your little man's parents, maybe tell them that he won't be coming home tonight.'

'You killed him? You killed Li'l Rider?' the other man shouted. To Tony, it looked like this news hurt him. *Loving father*, he thought.

Still holding the chubby man, Tony began to pace around. 'He's not dead. Let's just say that he won't be going anywhere until at least tomorrow morning. Just like your large friend here.'

'Let go of him, and you might get to walk out of here, old man,' the tall white youth said.

Tony watched as the boy's thumb flicked off the safety. He took that moment to reach into his holster and remove his own gun. As he brought the weapon up, the shot that thudded from the silenced barrel took the loving father in the foot. He buckled onto the floor with a scream that was eerily girlish.

'The next one is in your friend's head before the third one goes into your belly. I'll leave you to die here slowly and agonisingly while I walk away into anonymity. All I want is a favour. It's not going to cost you anything. You aren't going to lose any business or any face. It'll be like I was never here. If you do me this one favour, you'll never see me again. If you don't, or if you renege on the deal, I'll be back, and I'll finish you all with extreme prejudice. Do you hear me?'

The remaining boy looked at his colleague, who was writhing on the floor, gun forgotten as he held his heavily bleeding foot. Tony watched as his eyes moved to the body of the man he was holding before ultimately back to him. With a heavy sigh, he thumbed the safety back in place and let the gun fall limp in his hand, offering it to him.

'I don't want your gun. All I want is the assurance that you'll do this favour. You can try to kill me if you want, but I'll be missed by my friends and your business and lives will be over, in that order. So, do us both a favour and agree to do what I say.'

The tall man nodded solemnly, putting the gun back into the waistband of his trousers. He then bent down slowly to pick up the discarded gun of his friend, who was still moaning with the pain of exploded metatarsals.

The boy glared at Tony. He could sense the hostility towards him for being bettered on his own turf by an old man. 'What do you want?' Even the words sounded begrudged, but he knew he had him exactly where he needed him to be.

'You have a customer coming tonight. Sean Knight.'

The man shrugged, non-committal.

'Don't fuck with me, I have you two recorded arranging the meet. Don't think that because you use burner phones you can't be traced; if you have the right equipment, you can. I have that equipment. Now, he's coming tonight for his stash. All I want from you is to give him *this* stash instead. Charge him the normal rate, act like nothing is wrong, and you'll never hear from or see me again.' Tony shrugged, letting go of the big man he was holding, who dropped to the floor like on old sack. The thud of his head hitting the mottled ground of the alleyway made the other man wince. Tony smiled at this reaction. He removed the backpack and unzipped the front pocket, producing a transparent baggie filled with drug paraphernalia.

He handed it to the dealer, who snatched it like it was dangerous and he didn't want to be seen with it. 'What's so special about this?'

'Nothing that you need to concern yourself with. Just make sure that he gets *this* bag and no other. You good with that?'

'Sure, but what's in it for me?' he asked, looking at the bag closely.

'The pleasure of not being killed tonight or tomorrow. I might even let you take this sack of shit to the hospital,' Tony replied, pointing to the man still writhing on the floor.

'I'm not taking a brother to a hospital with a bullet wound. You fucking trippin'? A street man with a bullet wound?'

Tony gave him a dead-pan stare before shrugging and turning his back on the boy. He exited the alleyway slowly, listening for the sounds indicating guns being raised behind his back.

There were none.

He walked back to where the young boy's body was stashed. As he melded with the shadows, the sound of a car approaching wafted over the otherwise silent street. The deep bass of rock drumming accompanied the over-revving. *Younger driver,* Tony Thought. *Sean Knight. Time to get this plan rolling.* A grin spread across his face.

The car pulled up to the curb, and Tony watched as the cocky bastard who had raped, beaten, and tortured his little girl, the bastard who had bought him an expensive bottle of wine and his wife a bunch of flowers and a box of chocolates. The abomination who had taken his daughter's innocence away from her and walked away with a smile on his face stretched as if he had been on a long journey and looked around the street.

*He's looking for the lookout,* Tony thought. *He won't find him tonight.*

Sean crossed the road and entered the alleyway.

Tony took his tablet out of the backpack and tethered the signal to his cell phone. The connection was fully encrypted. He pressed on the icon that looked like a mechanical flea and waited. After a few moments, he was connected to the FLEA network. Tony rummaged in the pockets of the young boy inside the doorway and found his cell phone. He removed the SIM from the side of the device and entered the IMEA number into the FLEA database. In a few moments, he had the number of the phone.

He connected his FLEA network to Sean's phone and dialled the number.

Instantly, the screen flashed up UNKNOWN NUMBER. He allowed it to ring until it hit voicemail. He waited until the beep and then hit a button on the screen that read INTERFERANCE.

# The Boyfriend

'Li'l Rider, yo! It's Sean, Sean Knight. I've got a hit with the boys tonight. I'm just letting you know I'm outside.'

He disconnected the line and then disconnected his FLEA session. He put the tablet back into his backpack and zipped it up. He put the kid's cell phone back into his pocket, complete with the SIM card.

Removing the drone from the backpack, he re-deployed it over the alleyway. Remotely, he watched the transaction between the tall white man and Sean. He smiled, wondering what he'd told Sean about why he was on his own.

He watched Sean pass a wad of cash and in return receive a bag. Although he couldn't confirm if it was the correct bag, he hoped he'd scared the boy enough to carry out the 'favour' regardless.

He watched as the two exchanged a complex, ritual hand slap before Sean walked out of the shot of the drone, back towards the entrance. He popped his head around the corner and looked towards the alleyway just in time to see Sean emerge, swinging a bag that was obviously drugs. He wanted to jump the little shit now, to kill the asshole right there on the street. The urge was so strong, it took every bit of his will-power to resist it. *There's a better ending for him,* he told himself over and over as the piece of filth got into his dark blue Chevy and drove away.

He recalled the drone, packed up his backpack, and crossed the street, back towards the alleyway. He entered and was instantly accosted by the same man. He came at him with his gun held high as if to pistol whip him, but Tony was ready for it. He ducked low and swiped his leg, taking the man's legs from underneath him. He hit the floor with a sickening thud, dropping the gun as he did. Both men watched it bounce away, clattering into a corner. Both hoped beyond hope that it didn't discharge and send a stray bullet off to kill one of them.

It didn't.

The drug dealer scrambled back against a cement wall and tried to stand. When he was almost upright, he took a swing at Tony, but due to his depleted strength from the winding he had taken upon hitting the hard floor, it was an easy punch to deflect. Tony stepped out of the way of it and kicked the man's legs away from him again. He watched as he slid down the wall. He then kicked the dealer in the face with the flat of his shoe. The kick took all the remaining fight out of him.

The younger man was finished as he fell back to the ground with a wet, gurgling moan. 'Who the fuck are you?' he croaked as he held his collapsed face.

'Never mind who I am. Did you give Sean the correct bag?'

'Yeah …' He swallowed hard, wincing. 'I gave him the bag you wanted. Why you trippin' on Sean?'

Tony leaned in closer, shaking his head. He could smell the boy's fear. 'All these questions. Now, how am I supposed to trust you if you keep asking questions?'

'Man, you can—'

These were the very last words of the ill-fated drug dealer. Tony produced a knife from his trouser pocket, the same knife he had taken from the young kid on the bike. He flicked it open and slid it between the ribs of the younger man.

The youth's eyes went wide, as if in shock, and his head began to shake in short, violent bursts. He tried to speak, but as he opened his mouth, blood poured from it, distorting what he had to say.

As his life ebbed away, Tony removed the knife in one swift action. An ugly hiss escaped the wound, and the death rattle that came from the boy's mouth told Tony everything he needed to know.

The drug dealing piece of filth would soon be dead.

Exactly how he needed it to be.

Without wiping the blade, he made his way inside the door that the three of them had exited earlier. It was pitch dark inside. He withdrew his flashlight from the leg pocket of his trousers, and the narrow beam sliced a shaft through the gloom.

The room was large; it had once been a warehouse but had long ago fallen into disuse and decay. The walls were crumbling, and the windows were mostly smashed.

A small murmur from the corner gave the game away.

'Dice, is that you man? I need to get to the fucking hospital, now. My foot, it's shattered, man! Dice? Dice is that you?'

Tony appeared out of the darkness, the knife still in his hand.

'What the fuck?' was all the white man was able to shout before the knife entered his throat. He threw his hand up to the wound and looked at the blood on it. He looked shocked at what he saw, almost as if it were the last thing he'd been expecting. His wide eyes looked up towards his murderer.

Tony saw the unexpressed questions in his eyes, questions that would never be asked and therefore never answered. He nodded to the dying man and gently pushed him down onto the floor, where he died with a shudder.

He then turned to see the third youth, the chubby one, still unconscious in the corner of the room. He turned the knife on him too, killing him without mercy and without a second thought.

When he was done, he stood back to admire his handiwork. He didn't think it looked frenzied enough for what he wanted, so he repositioned the two men's bodies, making it look like there had been a struggle. It wasn't perfect, but because these were known drug dealers, and well known for violence, there wouldn't be too much scrutiny of the scene. *Besides, they're going to find both knife and gun soon anyway,* he thought with a grin.

He made his way out of the alleyway and back towards the disposable car parked a little further away.

As he climbed into the driver's seat, he removed his bloodied gloves and fished out his cell phone. He dialled three numbers after connecting to the FLEA network again and activating the signal scrambler.

'Nine-one-one, what's your emergency?' the female voice said on the other end of the line.

Tony pressed the INTERFERANCE button again before speaking into the device in an excited fashion. 'I was walking my dog, it's a Shih Tzu, a little brown one! I saw a guy running, he was covered in blood, I think he was holding a gun, but-but I can't be sure.'

'Where did this happen, sir?'

'Rosemont Street, Crystal Lake area.'

'OK, sir, we have officers in the vicinity. I'll alert them, and they will be on the way. Are you in a safe location?'

'I-I think so,' Tony stuttered; he was an accomplished actor.

'Please stay in that location until the officers arrive on the scene.'

'Not a problem, but can you get them to hurry up? I don't want him coming back looking for witnesses; I've seen that happen on TV.'

'No worries, sir, I'll stay on the line with you until they arrive if you prefer,' the woman said.

'No, that's OK. I need to find my dog; she ran off.'

'Sir, can I get your—'

Tony cut off the connection before she had time to ask what his name was. He disconnected from the FLEA network, put the car into drive, checked his mirrors, and drove within the speed limit out of the area.

He could hear police sirens as he pulled onto the main highway.

64.

SEAN ARRIVED HOME to a party in full swing. As he pulled the car into the driveway, he was greeted by the older couple who lived across the street. The man was angry, his wife, anxious. As he got out of the car, the man was attempting to confront him, but his wife was holding him back.

'You there,' he shouted, raising his hand to attract Sean's attention.

Sean turned to see who was yelling at him. He rolled his eyes. *What now?* 'Are you talking to me?' he asked, his voice sounding as angry as his face looked.

'Yes, I am talking to you, young man. This has gone on long enough, and far too often. This used to be a nice neighbourhood until you ... *people* turned up.' The emphasis on the word 'people' was not lost on Sean.

'Us people?' he repeated, walking towards the couple.

The woman was trying to pull her husband back.

'Let me go, Jean. You have to stand up to bullies like these, otherwise, they'll just walk all over you.' He managed to shrug off the attentions of his wife and stood straight, looking Sean in the eye. 'These parties have gone on long enough. There are decent people living in this street, and we don't want to be subjected to this trash every night.'

Sean squared up to the man, invading his personal space. The older man instinctively stepped back just as Sean knew he would. 'If you've got a problem with this, then please, be my guest. Go inside and complain about it. I fucking dare you,' he whispered, the malice in his voice palpable.

The old man, although appearing scared of this youth, stood his ground. Sean respected him for it. His wife was once again attempting to pull him away.

'You got nothing to say? No? I didn't think so. So, why don't you go and take your lovely lady wife back indoors and get the fuck out of my face.' He jerked towards the man in a threatening gesture, and as he stepped back again even further, Sean laughed. 'Stay the fuck away from me. But I want you to know something; these parties will soon be a thing of the past. For me anyway.' Without any further discussion, Sean turned, laughing as he made his way towards the house.

'Well, just to let you know, were sick of this shit. We've threatened it enough in the past, but this time we're going to call the police.'

Turning back to face the couple, Sean sent them his feelings in the form of his middle finger. 'Do what the fuck you have to do, old man,' he shouted as he reached the door and disappeared inside. 'I'm done caring.'

The old man was shaking his head as he wrapped his arm around his wife and shuffled back to their house.

~~~~

'Did you get the shit?' Sean's mom shouted over the thumping music as she fixed her makeup in the hallway mirror.

Without answering, he dropped the bag onto a small table and stomped upstairs.

'Good boy,' she shouted up at him. 'Why don't you join us downstairs for once? There're people here who'd love to meet you.'

'I don't want to fuck your friends, Mom,' he shouted as he made it into his bedroom. He opened the door and scanned the dark for any unwelcomed visitors. Seeing it was vacant, he slammed the door behind him, taking his desk chair and wedging it under the handle to keep it from being opened from the outside. He flopped onto his bed with a sigh. 'No thanks, Mom, you junkie slut,' he mumbled under his breath.

He reached into his jacket and removed the other bag that he had gotten from the dealers. He opened his drawer and took out all his socks, then tapped on the base, removing the false bottom. Inside, there was now quite a stash of baggies filled with white powder, pills, green rocks, and dried green buds. *This should get me by, until I'm called back,* he thought with a smile.

He lay on his bed and closed his eyes, drifting off into sleep, listening to the heavy rock pumping up from downstairs. He would wait until the party was well underway before sneaking off into the night, taking his drugs and as much money he could find in the coats of the party goers with him. He was going to take the car too. He knew he'd have to dump it in a day or so, but by then, he would be out of the state and free of all the bullshit in his life.

As the party grew, it got louder. There was shouting, laughing, screaming, singing, and banging. A few times he heard the rattling of the handle on his door, but he was safe in the knowledge no one could get in. The sanctity of the room and the noises of the party outside it lulled him to sleep.

It would be the last time he ever slept in this house.

~~~~

He awoke to the feeling that something wasn't right.

Something was missing.

At first, his frazzled mind couldn't comprehend where he was, and it took a few moments for him to appreciate the comforts of his bedroom. He remembered the drugs in his drawer, and he reached out in a blind panic to make sure that they were still there.

They were.

With his heartbeat returning to an almost acceptable level, he stretched, and sat up. He listened for the noises of the party and realised that's what it was that was missing.

The silence in the house was deafening.

There was no music, no singing, no one walking up and down the landing outside his room. He spared a glance towards the clock. It was only eleven thirty-five. *Is that a.m. or p.m.?* he thought as he swished the curtains to his window. It was pitch dark outside. *Definitely p.m.,* he thought. *Did the police come?* He was thinking that the old man must have followed up on his threat and called them. 'Good for you, dude,' he laughed.

He moved the chair propped against the door and grasped the handle. He paused again, listening for any sounds, anything that might quell the building anxiety within him. *The party is never ever finished until at least three. Why would the house be silent now?*

Shaking his head to clear the bad thoughts that were building like a storm, he turned the handle and pulled the door open.

Through squinted eyes, he regarded the scene before him.

It shocked him to the core.

He had never seen anything like it before.

The landing and the stairwell were empty!

He turned back to look at the clock again, just in case he'd misread the time. It now displayed eleven thirty-eight. He hadn't got it wrong.

Stepping out onto the carpeted landing, the old cliché he'd heard over the years about how silence could be deafening sprung into his head. There was no noise at all. The peacefulness of the night freaked him out more than anything he'd ever experienced before.

'Mom,' he called. 'Dad. Are you guys here?'

There was no answer. It wasn't just his mother and father who were missing, it was the whole party. There should have been anything from ten to fifty people in the house right then, drinking, snorting, injecting, fucking.

His mind went straight to aliens.

It was an absurd thought, but he'd seen programmes on TV about alien abductions. Little grey men with huge heads and eyes that were black and expressionless. He'd laughed at the shows and the people who'd been interviewed, swearing they'd been taken.

It didn't feel so funny right now.

'Mom! Come on now, this isn't a joke. Where the fuck are you guys?' It felt like there were more stairs than he remembered as he trudged tentatively down them. It wasn't until he got to the bottom that he saw why the house was silent.

His legs buckled, and he fell back onto the stairs. His hand lost its grip of the banister as the corner of the stair dug into his lower back, but his brain wouldn't, or couldn't, process the pain; it already had far too much to deal with.

The view from the stairs obscured some of the horror that was dwelling in the living room. From where he was, all he could see were blood trails. They were bad enough, but he'd glimpsed what was inside the room, waiting for him, and he didn't want to see it again.

He knew that somewhere inside that room were his mother and father. Dead or alive, he didn't know, he didn't want to know. Instead of investigating, he just looked at his hands. They were shaking uncontrollably and were covered in blood. That was when he realised he was sitting in a puddle of the stuff, and it was now all over him.

With an involuntary yell, he jumped up and stumbled down the last two steps. His momentum took him into the living room and into the hell that awaited him there.

He saw everything in a hyper-aware state. There were bodies everywhere. They were either naked or half naked, but they were all dead. The carpet was soaked in coagulating blood. He almost fell into it, into the warmth, the slickness of the drying goo. He knew if he landed in it, it was conceivable that his brain would snap, he would go mad.

He wanted to go mad.

Right then, he would have welcomed madness like an old, lost friend. At least it would erase everything he was seeing from his mind.

Eventually, he hit the floor. The blow was every bit as horrible as he was expecting. The blood was viscous and thick. His impact broke the film, the crust that was settling on the top of it. As the crust cracked, it allowed the stink to escape. It smelt like what he assumed an abattoir would smell like, a mixture of rotten meat with an after-taste of copper. The greasy feel of blood on his skin, up his nose, made him want to vomit, but he knew if he opened his mouth, the foul, thick, fatty substance would enter him. It was a perfect catch twenty-two scenario.

He could feel the vomit churning in his stomach, but he couldn't open his mouth to allow it out; there was too much at stake.

'Do you like how it feels to be scared, Sean?'

He thought the voice was in his head. For all he knew, it might have been. It could even have been the voice of God.

*Or aliens,* he thought.

'I asked if you liked how it feels to be scared,' the voice said. Even though the voice was quiet, monotone, almost emotionless,

241

there was an undercurrent of anger in it. He had no desire, for his own sanity, to irk the speaker any further.

He opened his mouth to reply. As he did, a stream of hot, stinking vomit expelled from him. Blood mixed with the stream; he didn't know if it was his. He didn't care.

'That's right, son. Get that bad blood out of your system. You never know what's in it. I mean, look what it did to this group.'

He lifted himself onto his hands and knees, still retching, spitting, trying to rid himself of the thickening blood and the clumps of vomit from his mouth. His eyes stung, and there was a red haze around the room. He wanted to see where the voice was coming from, but his gaze was drawn to the heap of bodies in the centre of the room.

He couldn't tell how many there were. Their limbs and torsos were intertwined, and blood was seeping from wounds that were still open. He saw a shirt that might have been his father's. It looked like it had once been blue checked plaid. One of his father's favourites.

He tore his stare away from the horror, the atrocities that his brain couldn't comprehend, and scanned the room for the origin of the calm but sinister voice.

There was a man; or at least he thought it was a man, as all he could see was a silhouette. He was dressed from head to toe in black. His hands and head were covered, but his face wasn't.

It was a face he recognised, but in his addled state, his brain refused to allow him access to the parts where that knowledge resided.

'This is fun, isn't it, Sean?' the man asked. 'I do enjoy a good party.'

He saw the man's hand holding a long knife. There was also a handgun with a silencer attached to the barrel on the other arm of the chair he was sat in.

'I–I know you! I know you, don't I?' Sean stuttered. He was in fear of the blood going back into his mouth, he was in fear of vomiting again, he was in fear of the stack of dead bodies lying in his living room, but mostly, he was in fear of this man. 'Are you … from the society?' he croaked.

'You do know me, Sean. Although I'd say you were more acquainted with a close relative of mine. One who I care for dearly.'

The man was motionless, emotionless, as he spoke. 'I would say you know her really well. Her name is Lisa. You might know her as *your little piggy*!'

Sean recognised the voice.

His body deflated as utter dread spread through him. His stomach cramped, and his arms and legs began to shake. 'M-m-mister Quinn?'

'Mister Quinn?' The man nodded, smiling. 'You're correct, boy. Mister Fucking Quinn.'

He watched as the man stood from his seat. In doing so, the silhouette formed in his eyes. It became Lisa's father. Sean's mouth hung low as his eyes flicked between him and the horrific pile of bodies in the centre of the room.

Mr Quinn moved closer. His features all made sense now. *How did I not recognise him?* he thought.

With his face inches from Sean's, he began to speak in the same slow, controlled monotone. 'I saw the horrific things you did to my daughter. I saw them with my own fucking eyes. Now, tell me, Mr Knight, did they teach you Newton's third law in the few days you actually attended school?'

Sean's whole body was quaking. As raw adrenaline coursed through him, he was unable to control even his most basic functions.

'No? Well, let me familiarise you with it. Newton states that for every action, there is an opposite and an equal reaction.' Mr Quinn leaned in closer, his face almost touching Sean's. The stink in the room didn't seem to have any effect on him. 'Now, mostly this law is used in relation to motion, but let us apply it to the situation we have here. Your actions put into motion a string of events. You invaded my house; you violated my daughter. They were the actions. Now it is time for the reaction.' He moved away from him and sighed. 'This is where I differ with Isaac Newton because your actions have caused not an opposite or even an equal reaction but a similar and a whole lot *more than* equal reaction. Your actions have caused the deaths of thirteen people.'

Sean's eyes widened at this news. 'Th-thirteen?' he stuttered, spitting blood-tinged vomit as he did.

'Yes,' Mr Quinn continued, his voice still low and controlled, scaring Sean more than anything. 'Thirteen. These ten here, that include your mother and father, by the way, and your three drug dealing friends.'

Sean could no longer hold himself up on his hands and knees. He sat down in the blood, his body shaking uncontrollably. 'How?' was all he managed to ask.

'I followed you to the drug den. I made a deal with the three scum bags. They took the deal and gave you a bag of drugs that were laced with an untraceable substance that causes a comatose state. After I killed your friends, I came here. I simply walked in and killed everyone. Your father was fucking an old woman in the hallway while your mother had some guy's cock in her mouth as she fell asleep. I simply waltzed in and slit all of their throats. I did it with this.' He presented the knife that had been on the arm of the chair and pushed the hilt into Sean's face.

Sean took a sharp intake of breath, flinching from the weapon.

'It's the very same knife that killed your drug friends. It's the same weapon that the police are going to find here, along with the gun I used to shoot one of the drug dealers in the foot.'

'You're … you're a fucking lunatic!' Sean gasped.

The older man was nodding. 'You're right, Sean. I am. But the difference between me and you is that I'll get away with what I'm doing. You're going to come with me while I freshen up on some of my …' he paused theatrically for a moment before continuing, '…more ingenious interrogation techniques. The police are going to be looking for you for the murder of three drug dealers and the slaughter of your family and their friends. I pinged your phone and put a voicemail message on the phone of a young boy on a bike outside Rosemont Street that will tie you to being there, right about the time they were killed, along with a 911 call from an anonymous caller describing someone who could very well be you. Oh, and, of course, the weapons you used there will be found here.' He shrugged, raised his eyebrows, and grinned. 'It's a bit of an open and shut case, I'm afraid.'

'If you hand me in, they'll put me in prison, and you won't be able to do anything to me.' Sean replied, the emotion in his voice gone as the realisation of the thrilling life as an outlaw he'd been promised, the whole reason he'd done what he did, flittered away.

Mr Quinn smiled.

# The Boyfriend

Sean thought he'd never seen anything more sinister, more scary, in his entire life. He had a flashback to the night in the house, alone with Lisa. *Was that how she saw me?* he thought. A small, involuntary grin broke on his lips. There was no humour, no satisfaction, nothing was in that smile except fear.

'The police won't be catching you anytime soon, my boy,' Mr Quinn said. 'You're about to skip town.'

Sean looked at him. There were questions, big questions, life and death questions, but before he had the chance to ask them, Mr Quinn produced a syringe. Sean's eyes flicked towards it moments before it was thrust into his neck and the world went black.

65.

'GOOD MORNING, PRINCESS,' Tony chirped as Lisa lurched into the kitchen. He noticed she was wincing and was wearing her full-length pyjamas again. The ones that covered every bit of skin on her body except her face, hands, and feet. *She used to wear shorts and crop tops to breakfast,* he thought as she returned his smile. *Now I know why she doesn't, and it breaks my heart.*

'Good morning, Daddy,' she returned, flashing him a big smile and leaning in to plant a kiss on his cheek. 'Where were you till late last night?'

'That's a question I asked this morning,' Flo chirped in as she brought three steaming cups to the table, placing them in front of her family. 'It was nearly four a.m. when he got his sorry ass into bed, and look at him now, full of the joys of summer.'

Tony smiled at his family, raising his eyebrows as he spoke. 'I was out protecting the interests of my family.' He opened his arms, inviting both his girls in for a hug. They obliged, but he noticed Lisa's attempt was half-hearted. Not from the lack of wanting a hug, he guessed, but from being wary of physical embraces from men, any men. His heart broke for the second time that morning, although he did an excellent job of covering it up. *Bastard,* he seethed through his alligator smile.

'So, what's everyone got planned today?' he asked with a chirpiness his soul couldn't replicate.

'I'm meeting your mother for lunch,' Flo replied, sitting down at the island, wrapping her hands around the steaming mug before her.

'And I've got to get ready, I'm meeting Janice,' Lisa said, leaning in to give him another kiss on the cheek. She grabbed her mug and attempted to make her escape from the domesticity of the kitchen at breakfast.

'Where do you think you're going, young lady?' Tony asked.

Lisa stopped half-way out of the kitchen.

'To get ready?' she replied without turning back.

'Not without breakfast, you're not. You know it's the most important meal of the day.'

Lisa harrumphed, and her shoulders slumped as she turned.

He got up and went to the oven. Grabbing the oven gloves, he opened the hatch and removed some fantastic smelling cinnamon rolls.

Lisa's smile broke his heart for the third time. *I don't know how much of this I can take,* he thought as he put the hot tray on the tabletop. 'I wanted us all to sit and eat breakfast together, so I whipped up this batch of cinnamon rolls last night.'

'Hmm,' Flo replied as she spied the rolls. 'Are you sure you whipped these up yourself? They look an awful lot like the ones they sell in the store. What do you think, honey?'

Lisa took in a sniff and smiled. 'I don't think I care.' She grinned, not taking her eyes off the tray. 'They smell divine!'

Tony smiled and reached for the television remote control.

'TV? In the morning?' Flo asked, flashing Tony questioning eyes.

'I know, but there was a big case last night. I wanted to see if there's been any media updates while I've been asleep.'

'What was it, Daddy?' Lisa asked, sitting down at the table.

'Oh, just some boring government thing. Someone has been embezzling funds. Someone up high. I just want to see how its unfolding.'

He turned the TV on and flicked through the channels until he found a local news story. There was a woman standing outside a scruffy looking house, the only scruffy one on the nice street. The house had yellow tape wrapped around it, and there was a large police presence in the background.

'The police are still not sure what the circumstances of the events of last night *are.* All they know is that ten people were massacred in this house, and one person of interest, known to have been inside at one point, is still missing.'

Lisa and Flo watched as the newsfeed at the bottom of the screen scrolled along, informing them of what was being reported. 'Custer Drive, Crystal Lake?' Flo read as she took a sip of her drink. 'That's not far from here. Can you turn that up, honey?' she asked.

Tony obliged, noting that all his family's attention was now on the TV.

'A grisly discovery for local law enforcement late last night, as they were called to this address by neighbours complaining about the noise from *another* loud party.'

An older couple came into view. They were holding each other very tight, and the woman was looking nervously into the camera. The reporter held her microphone tightly as she addressed the couple in sombre tones. 'You're the couple who reported the noise to the police, is that correct?'

The man leaned into the microphone; his eyes were looking into the camera, flicking back and forth between the camera and the interviewer. 'Yes, that's correct. There were parties in that house almost every night, and a lot of the local residents were just getting sick of it.'

'You were telling me earlier about an altercation with a man that the police are calling a person of interest, who they want to eliminate from their enquiries. Can you tell me more about what happened?'

'Yes, well. It was about eight-thirty ...'

*They got the timeline correct,* Tony thought with an inward smile.

'... the youngest member of the family, the son I think, was pulling up to the house. I asked him to have a word with his father, to turn the music down and think about the other residents for once. This used to be a nice neighbourhood until the Knights turned up.'

Tony noticed his daughter's change in body language as the name of the family was mentioned. She stiffened and stopped drinking her coffee almost mid-sip.

'When you asked him, things took a nasty turn, didn't they? Can you tell us what happened?' The reporter offered the microphone back to the man.

248

'Well, when I asked the young man, that was when he turned violent. He threatened me, physically. He looked agitated. I didn't like the look of him at all, so me and my wife, we went back into the house and called the police.'

The reporter turned back to face the camera, a solemn look on her face. 'The youngest son of the family is still missing and has officially been named as a person of interest regarding this massacre. They are asking if anyone has any information on the whereabouts of Sean Knight, eighteen years of age and a resident of Crystal Lake, to contact the police. Do not approach or try to apprehend the individual, as he is now considered dangerous and *could* be armed. We now go over to Rich Davenport, who is live on another side of this same story. Rich, what do we know about the events on Rosemont Street?'

Tony watched from the corner of his eye as Lisa banged her cup down on the counter, splashing the contents onto the table, where it swilled her mother. 'Lisa,' Flo tutted, standing up, wiping the coffee from her arms.

Lisa wasn't taking any notice; she was too involved in the unfolding story on the TV.

'Three young men were found murdered on Rosemont Street in the early evening of last night. The police are treating it as a targeted attack. The victims are all under the age of eighteen and the names have not been released. All the authorities will confirm is that the three victims were known to local law enforcement. It appears that a knife and a gun have been used in these murders, and there is a possibility they are the same weapons that were found in the house on Custer Drive. This is leading law enforcement agencies to conclude that the same perpetrator *may* be responsible for both incidents. A child was in possession of a cell phone with a voice message from someone who the authorities think could be Sean Knight. The young man in question says he was attacked and rendered unconscious during the attack. He is currently being held for questioning about his involvement in these crimes. Law enforcement is working with him to establish a timeline of events.'

Tony muted the TV and turned towards his family. 'Lisa?' he asked, shaking his head. 'What the Hell? Wasn't that the boy you went out with? Sean Knight? Could it have been?'

249

Lisa's face was pale. All colour had drained from it. She stood up without saying a word and ran out of the kitchen. Tony saw the tears in her eyes as she did.

His heart broke for the fourth time that morning.

Flo ran out of the room, chasing her daughter, and he followed closely behind.

'Lisa …' her mother shouted as she ran up the stairs. The door to the bedroom slammed with a bang just as they arrived. 'What the hell is all that about?' Flo whispered towards her husband.

Tony shook his head. 'I don't know. Jesus, Flo, could that be the same boy she went out with?'

'I've got no idea. How many Sean Knights can there be in one area?' She spun her head around to look at him. He knew the look. He knew exactly what she was going to ask.

He shook his head. 'No. You asked me to stay out of it, so that's exactly what I did.'

'No, Tony. I asked you to look into it. That boy, he took our little girl out on dates. He was here, in our house. I need to know if it's the same boy who's killed his whole family. I *need* to know Tony!'

'OK, listen, I'll ask around, see what I can find out. Maybe pull in a few favours. I can't promise anything.'

Flo nodded and moved away from the door into the arms of her husband. She was sobbing as she buried her head in his chest.

66.

'JANICE. HAVE YOU heard?'

On the other end of the line, Janice sounded sleepy, and Lisa heard her yawn. 'What? I only just got up. I'm pissed now; I was dreaming about us,' she replied with a jovial lilt to her voice.

'Sean's on the run. He's murdered his whole family.'

'He what?' Janice sounded one hundred percent awake now.

'He killed those three drug dealers on Rosemont too. The ones we went to get the gun from.' She fell silent. 'Fucking hell, he must have been there; he might have even seen us going in. The way the news is reporting it, it was around the same time we were there.'

'Slow down, Lisa. What's happened?'

'He's murdered his family, ten of them in total. That was *after* he killed the drug dealers. The police found the same knife and a gun they think he used to kill the dealers in his house.'

'Are you sure? You're not screwing with me, are you?'

'Does this sound like something I'd joke about? Janice, he killed them. He cut their fucking throats. He could have done that to me at any time.'

'Calm down, Lisa. Was it definitely him? Have they got evidence?'

'Not yet, nothing concrete; I don't think so anyway. I don't know; they said on the news he's a person of interest and that he shouldn't be approached because he may be armed. He's considered fucking dangerous. If he saw us going into that drug dealer's lair to buy a gun and he's killed them, what the hell is he going to do to me?'

'But you haven't told anyone, have you? About the attack, I mean.'

'No, but if he sees me as a threat, he might come after you too. I mean, you're my best friend, we're always together. He'll know I've told you what happened. Maybe you should come over today. I'm sure Mom'll pick you up. I don't want you out there walking the streets on your own.'

'OK, I'll be ready. I'll see you soon.'

67.

AS TONY CLOSED the shutter-door, the rattle of metal against metal was deafening in the enclosed space of the garage. The moment the door hit the ground and stopped complaining about the inconvenience, the oppressive heat and the darkness of the windowless room hit him. As did the smell.

It was a human smell. It was the distinctive stench of human excrement mixed with sweat, grease, and a healthy dose of fear. *There'll be another smell soon enough,* he thought. *Blood!*

As he made his way further into the darkened room, the stink got worse. Small noises were coming from the back, where a plastic sheet had been raised, effectively making two rooms. There was a light behind the plastic, creating a silhouette of something hideous lurking behind it.

'Do you think you've had enough time to consider what you've done?' he asked aloud. The silhouette jerked, and a murmur of mumblings came from its general location. 'It seems like you've become famous, Sean. The police are combing the city looking for you. There's even an APB out on you. Your name and face are all over the national news. You've gone viral, my friend, a fucking internet sensation.'

The jerking and mumbling became more violent the more Tony spoke.

Eventually, he made his way around the plastic curtain and set his eyes upon his horrible creation. Hanging from a meat-hook attached to the ceiling, strong ropes supporting his uplifted arms, hung a naked Sean Knight. There was a pile of excrement, both solid and liquid, piled beneath him and dripping down his legs.

'Of course, they're not going to find you. This place is so far off the grid that it would take them weeks to get here.' He chuckled as he said this, and Sean's eyes widened as they followed him across the room. Tony made his way to a small chest of drawers in the corner. Whistling a cheery tune, he opened the top drawer and removed a toolbox. He turned his head and winked at the naked man hanging behind him. 'Are you ready for this? Mentally, I mean. Because it's going to hurt. I won't lie to you; it's going to hurt a hell of a lot. Before I begin, I'm going to ask you a question. The answer to the question will have a direct correlation on the amount of pain I inflict. Do you understand me?'

Sean was screaming, shouting, and jerking around on the hook, and the excrement running down his leg dripped faster onto the floor.

'Just a quick FYI: the more you struggle, the tighter those ropes become.' He pointed above him with a pair of stainless-steel plyers that he'd removed from the toolbox. Sean's eyes tried to follow where they were pointing to but failed to reach the destination; his neck wasn't that flexible. 'It's an old trick we used back in the day; it's really quite effective. Now, I'm going to ask you why you did what you did to my daughter. I'm going to ask you once, and then I'm going to hurt you.' He waved the pliers in the air nonchalantly. 'There's no getting away from that. I'm going to do to you some of the things you did to my Lisa, only difference being that I won't be holding back. I know how to do this professionally, plus I don't give two shits if you live or die. Nod if you understand what I'm saying.'

Sean's eyes narrowed angrily, and he grunted something, something Tony didn't think was very nice.

Tony cocked his head to one side and clicked his cheek. 'I don't think I like that attitude.' He stepped forward and took the plyers to Sean's left nipple. There was no hesitation, no pretence of not doing what he was going to do.

He gripped the nipple in the plyers and squeezed.

Sean screamed loudly through the gag in his mouth. Fresh, dark blood ran down his chest as the sensitive skin split between the cold metal. Tony pulled, tearing the ruined flesh from the boy's chest. An inordinate amount of blood poured from the wound. Tony knew it wasn't deep and would heal eventually. People could live without nipples.

He raised the tool with the clump of flesh within its teeth and showed it to the boy. He watched as tears poured down his victim's cheeks.

The screams continued.

With a smile, Tony removed the gag from Sean's mouth.

'HELP ... HELP ME. I'M BEING HELD PRISONER!'

Tony stood back and allowed him to scream and shout. He could imagine Sean's head becoming rather dizzy, what with the pain and the fatigue his body would be experiencing. He pulled his mouth into a comical pout and shook his head slowly. 'Scream and shout all you want, my friend. Not one person is going to hear you. No one's coming to rescue you. Even if they did, they would only be taking you in for multiple murders.'

'What the fuck are you talking about?' Sean pleaded, his voice octaves higher than normal.

Tony could see he was labouring, hanging, and bleeding like he was. He offered him a fake, quizzical look. 'Oh, I thought I mentioned it a moment ago. Maybe it didn't sink in. You're a wanted man. Wanted for the murder of thirteen people.'

Sean's face lost its anger as he stared at his captor. There was a look on his face of total confusion. This made Tony smile again.

'I don't know what you're talking about. You're fucking crazy. Get me down from here. I'll get the fucking cops on you.'

'But, Sean, you killed your mother and father along with eight other guests at your home. You did that after killing your three drug dealing friends on Rosemont Street. There's evidence at both scenes that puts you in the frame for all of it.'

'I haven't killed anyone, you sick fuck.'

Tony rolled his eyes and turned on his cell phone. He pulled up a news website and showed him the lead story.

'LOCAL MAN WANTED FOR MULTIPLE MURDERS IN CRYSTAL LAKE. SUSPECT STILL AT LARGE, THOUGHT TO BE ARMED AND DANGEROUS.'

Tony watched Sean's eyes dance around the screen as he read it at least twice.

'See. Even if you were to get out of here, which isn't likely, where would you go? It's my guess you'd make it maybe two miles towards town before you were picked up. People around here aren't big on familicide. That's the killing of one's own family, by the way.'

Sean's face was blank. There were no expressions on his features whatsoever.

Tony reached into the pocket of his jacket and produced a large knife in a sheath. Slowly, the knife was released from its leather binding, allowing the blade to shine in the light from the lamp.

Sean's eyes fixed on it.

Tony moved towards the boy and brought the knife up to his face. He could see the shudders running through the boy's body. It made him happy to see the bastard squirm and bleed.

The boy's eyes followed the blade as it passed by his face. His eyes closed in what looked like relief as Tony began to saw through the ropes that were suspending him from the ceiling.

As the last shreds were cut, Sean fell the few inches onto the hard cement floor, into the mound of his own blood and excrement. He landed with a thud and a wet slap.

Tony watched the comical scene before him with loathing. The naked boy scrambled and slipped in his own waste, trying to get up off the floor. He guessed Sean wanted to make a charge at him, attempt to overpower him to get away. Eventually, he made it to his feet. He could see Sean's limbs were mostly incapacitated from hanging all night, and his own filth was mixing with the mess that used to be his left nipple.

The boy was no match for him.

He was no match for anyone right now.

He lunged anyway.

Tony saw he had put all his weight into the forward momentum of the run, and it was easy for him to sidestep, leaving his leg trailing for the youth to trip over.

Which he did.

He winced as Sean fell hard onto the concrete. He watched as the boy's nose crunched and split, as blood ran from his ruined face.

'Get up. Even if you were at a hundred percent fitness, you wouldn't be able to take me,' he said as the boy lay on the ground, moaning. 'Now get the fuck up and sit in that chair.' Tony's voice was level and emotionless as he pointed to a wooden chair nestled in the corner of the room.

Sean's eyes glared as he eased himself up.

Tony shook his head. 'Don't even think about it, Sean. I could kill you in so many ways without even breaking a sweat. I don't want to do that. All I want to do is talk. So, sit in the *fucking* chair.'

The aggression in the last command had the desired effect on the boy, and he made his way over to the chair. As he wiped the blood that was pouring from his nose, all he managed to do was wipe a stripe of his own shit across his face. With his other hand, he tried to cover his nakedness. He sat in the chair and glared at Tony. The knife Tony had used to cut the rope was on the small table, next to the bloodied, stainless steel plyers.

'Thank you,' Tony said, his voice again calm and calculated. 'Now, I'm going to ask you one question. I'll repeat this question until I get an answer I'm happy with. If I don't get that answer, I'll take your other nipple before starting on your teeth, your fingers, toes, and eventually, your testicles.' Tony turned back to the small table and picked up the plyers with the tips of his fingers. Gore dripped from the handles. 'Are you ready to talk, Sean?'

Sean didn't say anything.

The screams were pitiful as Tony made good on his promise.

~~~~

Over an hour later, Sean was minus both nipples, the fingernails from his right hand, and was covered in vinegar, which sank into every laceration on his body. Tony was happy with the progress of the interrogation. He looked at his watch and pulled a surprised face. It was later than he thought.

He opened the drawer of the toolbox and removed a glass bottle filled with a yellow/green liquid. In his other hand was a syringe. He held it up for Sean to see.

Two pink, swollen, shit-covered eyes looked at it.

'This is a little concoction my friends and I created,' Tony explained, holding it up to the light. 'It's plant based, believe it or not. I can't remember the exact name of it, but we bring it in from Central America. We considered getting it FDA approved at one point, getting a patent on it, but it turns out that it's not really good for you. In fact, it's almost exactly the opposite. If you were to put this onto tobacco and smoke it, Jesus …' Tony laughed. 'You'd be high as a kite for days. However, if I inject it into your blood stream, even just ten cc's …' Tony looked at the boy and nodded; a small smile crept over his face. 'Then you're going to burn. It disperses through every capillary in your body, turning your blood into pure fire. You'll be in agony for exactly three minutes. That's it, just three minutes. However, I guarantee it'll be the longest, most intense three minutes of your entire sad, miserable life.'

He made a show for his guest of inserting the syringe into the top of the bottle and sucking the liquid into the clear tube. 'I'm going to inject you anyway, just so you can get a taste of it. Then I'm going to leave you for five minutes. I want you take this time to ponder on what you did to my daughter.'

'I don't know what you're—' Sean began his protest through swollen lips, but it ended in a yelp as Tony plunged the needle into the boy's naked shoulder. He pressed the plunger and emptied the whole contents into his body.

Without another word, Tony walked off behind the plastic curtain. He counted exactly ten seconds before the screaming began. With a smile, he walked towards the shutter-door, setting his watch for a five-minute countdown.

## 68.

JANICE WAS PACING Lisa's bedroom. Lisa was sitting at her dresser, watching her. Her routine was to circle around the bed, stop at the chest of drawers, pace to the window, look out through the blinds, then start it all over again.

Lisa was nervous enough without this level of stress adding to it.

'Janice, will you fucking quit?' she shouted. She felt better for roughly three seconds, then the anxiety of the situation forced her fingers back into her mouth, where she continued gnawing away at what was left of her nails.

Janice stopped pacing. She looked like she had been slapped in the face. 'Lisa, I can't. If Sean's going to come after you, then sure as shit he's going to come after me.' She twitched the blinds again and looked out.

'I'm going to call my dad. I need to see if he's heard anything about this. I think he's got some connections or something, so he might know.' Lisa picked up her cell phone and looked at the screen for what felt like the millionth time. She unlocked it and hit call on her father's number.

There was no answer.

Just as it went to voicemail, she pressed the red button and slammed the device onto the dresser behind her.

'I can't stop thinking about those drug dealers,' Janice said as she made another lap of the room. 'I mean, fuck, we must have been there about ten minutes before they were killed. They were assholes, but fuck …'

'Do you think he was watching us as we went into the alley?' Lisa asked through a mouthful of fingernails.

Janice looked at her while running her fingers through her hair. 'Don't! Just don't. OK?'

Lisa's phone began to buzz, and she whipped around to pick it up. 'It's my dad,' she exclaimed, pressing the button perhaps a little too hard. 'Daddy,' she shouted into the device. 'Daddy, have you heard anything yet?'

A small male voice replied something down the phone.

'I'm here with Janice. I thought, what with Sean and everything …'

Her father said something else down the phone.

'No, we're staying here. Mom's downstairs. No, I'll tell her. Why? Does it have something to do with Sean?'

There was another few moments of her father's voice before Lisa shouted, 'What?'

At the ferocity of Lisa's question, Janice broke her routine and looked at her, her eyes pleading for information.

'Has he been caught?' Janice whispered, moving closer, her eyes wide and anxious.

Lisa shook her head. Janice sighed, rolled her eyes, and looked away.

'What's all that shouting in the background? I can hardly hear you. How do you know that if he hasn't been caught?' Lisa continued her one-sided conversation. 'I do trust you. OK, I'll tell Mom. Are you sure everything's OK? That sounds like a lot of shouting. All right, I'll talk to you later. I love you, Daddy.'

'What did he say? Have they got him?'

'Not yet, but apparently, they know where he is. They said it won't be long until he's in custody.'

'So, what did he say about your mom?'

'He wants us to stay here in the house. He said he'll be home soon and tell us what's going on.'

Janice took a series of short, shallow breaths through her nostrils before letting it go out of her mouth. The sound was akin to a helicopter passing by, as she was so on edge. 'What a relief,' she sighed through the hands covering her face. 'I feel better knowing that he's not just going to burst in through the window, waving a knife at us.'

'Yeah. It is kind of a *get out of jail* feeling.'

Janice sat on the bed facing Lisa, and a playful smile crept over her face. 'So, your mom doesn't need to know about this development just yet, does she?'

'Erm, well, no. Not right now,' Lisa replied, the very same playful smile twitching on her lips.

'Well, if she thinks we're up here having fun, then why not ... have fun!' Janice tapped the bed next to her.

Lisa giggled and moved over from her dressing table. She leaned into Janice and kissed her on the mouth. Janice replied in kind and fell back on the bed, taking her girlfriend with her.

69.

TONY ENDED THE CALL and looked back through the plastic sheet at the broken and bloodied body of Sean, who was leaning back in the wooden chair. His naked body was covered in sweat, and his puffed and bruised face had the look of a much older man who had lived a tough life.

The drug Tony had administered had worn off but judging by the way pinkish froth was bubbling from the boy's mouth and the vacant expression on his face, it looked like he was still living the nightmare. 'Now that you've finished ruining my conversation, I'm going to assume you know I'm not fucking around here. Let me reiterate this, I killed your piece of shit parents, I killed their piece of shit friends. I got your piece of shit drug dealers to spike the drugs they sold you. All I had to do was stroll leisurely through your house, killing everyone, one by one, as they slept. I used the same knife I used to kill the dealers. I also shot one of them. Can you guess where that gun is? And the knife?'

Sean's vacant face stared at him; the only movement was from his blinking eyes and the occasional twitch and froth from his mouth.

Tony nodded. 'Yeah, you guessed it. They're in your house. You know what? The lazy police aren't even going to bother looking too deeply, especially after you left a voicemail on their lookout's phone.'

Sean's eyebrows creased, just slightly.

Tony smiled. 'Yeah, you did. You left a voicemail leaving your name and everything. So, you see, Sean Knight ... you're fucked. The only hope you have, the only option really open to you, is to tell me'—he leaned in close, so close he could smell the fear issuing from the youth's skin—'why the fuck you did what you did to my daughter.'

'I–I don't know what you mean. I never did anything to your daughter. She broke up with me. That's all, I promise.' His voice was slow and slurred, but Tony had enough practise listening to people talking after the effects of this drug that he understood.

'I know you're lying, and I'm going to give you one more chance to get the lies off your chest. You lie to me again, just once, and you'll get double the dose of my little concoction. Comprende?' To emphasise his point, he took the bottle and syringe and filled it up again. He held it to Sean's face and squirted a little out of the end of the needle.

Sean's eyes were fixated on the green-yellow fire inside it.

'Tell me now. Why did you put my little girl through everything you did that night? Tell me, Sean.' Tony put the needle to his arm. 'Tell me!'

Even though he wasn't tied to the chair, Tony knew he wouldn't attempt an escape. One reason was that he was in no physical state to get away, the second reason was that he was naked, and the third reason was he was far too scared of the needle and going through what he had gone through earlier again.

'I-I-I didn't touch her, man. I told you; I promise.'

'You are such a disappointment. I'm going to set a projector up; it should take me about ten minutes. During that time ...'

Sean screamed as Tony stuck the needle into his arm and pressed the plunger. He emptied the whole syringe. 'That dose won't kill you, but I think you're going to wish it did. I'll see you in ten.'

~~~~

Sean watched Mr Quinn walk back behind the plastic curtain. His breathing became deep and hurried, and his heart began to thrum, rapidly, as if it were attempting to escape the confines of his chest. The pain began, as it had last time, in his extremities. The tips of his fingers and the tips of his toes began to sting. He had never been bitten by any animal, but he likened the sensation to being bitten by a snake. Or something equally as loathing.

The feeling then spread into his hands and his feet. His very flesh was burning, melting. He looked at his hand and was surprised to see that everything looked perfectly normal. Just a normal looking, everyday hand—but minus the extracted fingernails and with intense, unbelievable agony tearing through it.

His feet were the same.

He felt the scream welling in his chest, fighting with the rapid beating of his heart. He heard it escape, but it sounded so alien that he didn't even know it was him until his mouth ran dry and it stopped.

The agony crept into his arms and legs at the same time, sawing through his bones with rusty metal tools, rendering his limbs useless. He tried to clench his fists, but he had no control over anything past the threshold of the advancing pain.

His muscles cramped and flexed of their own accord, and his back began to spasm as the invisible fire crept up his spine, making the fluid between his vertebrae boil. His body contorted; the torture was unbearable.

Every inch of his body was wet. The damp made his skin itch, and the itch melded with the searing torment. He felt himself getting an erection. The blood that was engorging his cock had come from the infected parts of his body, bringing their corruption with it. His dick pulsed, throbbing so hard it flooded his balls with blistering fire. He wanted to rip his suffering appendage off, to throw it away, discard it to the wind.

But still the pain advanced. It was worse than last time. More intense, slower, taking its merry time to consume him. It was in his balls and his bowels. He felt himself go loose behind, and a stinging trickle of burning defecation leaked from him.

It was in his chest now. The wounds where his nipples used to be pulsated. He felt it in his heart, his liver, his kidneys, his spleen, his stomach. The worst of it focused on his bellybutton. Huge, white-hot needles pierced it; millions of them, deep, sharp pricks, stabbing him again and again.

The torment made it to his neck. It closed his windpipe, making it almost impossible for him to breathe. He clutched his neck as he suffocated, his eyes ready to burst from his skull. He willed them to do it, to end his suffering.

Then, finally, the hot rush settled into his brain.

# The Boyfriend

Once there, it dug its claws into his psyche. The nerve tingling agony in every inch of his body made him writhe and convulse, scream in torment, cry in terror. Foam bubbled from his mouth as he fell to the floor, into his own fresh filth.

In all the time, through the torment of the seven levels of hell the drug gave him, he never once lost consciousness.

He was aware, hyper-aware of everything happening to him. Every single nuance of agony and despair. He was aware of his fingernail-less fingers trying to claw his own eyes out, he was aware of simultaneously losing control of his bladder and his bowels. He was aware of the irregular rhythm of his heart and thinking, hoping, that he would die every time it missed a beat.

Then, as slowly as it had creeped through his body, it began to recede, and the ride was over.

For now!

~~~~

When it was done and his body relaxed, attempting to rebuild its strength, he became aware of Tony. He was sitting in the room with a projector set up next to him. On the white wall behind him was a blank illumination.

'Welcome back, Mr Knight. I hope you had a good trip. Would you like something to clean yourself up with? I'm afraid you've made quite a mess.'

Sean moved his head to look at where he was pointing; the nausea from that small movement turned his stomach, and warm bile streamed from his stomach, projecting from his mouth. It dripped down his chest, merging with the steaming defecation puddled around him. He heard Tony tut, and he looked up at him only to see the hateful man staring down at him with a ridiculous smile on his face. He then grabbed him by his hair, pulling him up from the floor, from his vomit and shit laced resting place, to sit him back in the chair.

'You honestly are a mess, Sean, but if you just tell me why you did what you did, then all of this can just go away.'

'None of this is going away,' he croaked through his ravaged throat. 'I'm going to fucking kill you, then I'm going to kill your daughter and your wife.'

Tony clicked his cheek and pulled a disappointed face. 'I really don't think any of that is going to happen, Sean. If you don't tell me why you did what you did, then you simply won't make it out of this room ever again. Don't worry about me getting caught.' He leaned in, his eyebrows high, nodding. 'I've done this far too many times before. In this very room, to be precise. The only difference here is you've made it personal.'

Sean thought about trying to bite him; he considered bolting his head forward and snapping his nose, maybe even biting it off. But as he moved his neck to attempt the attack, he didn't have the strength. It was that precise moment when he realised that Mr Quinn's threats were not empty.

Tony laughed as he pulled away. He waved a latex gloved hand before his nose and mouth, pulling a disgusted face. 'Jesus, you are one stinky pinky, Sean Knight. You smell like a PIG.'

Sean winced at the word. It was how he'd seen Lisa that night.

Tony sat back down on his new chair next to the projector and rummaged around in the bag at his feet. He took out a tablet computer. 'There's something you need to know about me, Sean. I've got extensive experience with this kind of work. My job was to interrogate ...' He bobbled his head as if admitting something he probably shouldn't. '... suspects, you know, on both sides of the fence. I was so good at it that I still kind of work for these people today, although I'm more freelance than anything else. Doing this gives me access to certain technologies that are not available to regular people like you. One of them is a little something that allows me to hop from one host phone to another without anyone knowing I'm there. I installed it on my daughter's phone. Now, my wife— you've met Flo, haven't you? Yeah, well, she asked me to stay out of things when Lisa had the misfortune of meeting you. So, I gave you the benefit of the doubt. You seemed like a nice kid, not good enough for my daughter, but nice. However, when I got back from Europe and Lisa's beautiful long, dark hair had been cut short and she was acting strange, withdrawn, I got a little suspicious. Something raised my hackles, so to speak. Call it my spider-senses.'

He was talking as if he were sitting at a job interview; his legs were crossed, and he gestured towards the tablet several times. All Sean could think about was how thirsty and cold he was.

# The Boyfriend

'I activated the program on Lisa's phone and accessed a number of messages between you two. When these messages stopped, I dug a little further, into your phone, and that's when I found out you had RAPED HER!'

As Tony shouted the last words, Sean flinched in shock at the man's sudden rage. As rapid as it appeared, it disappeared, and he was once again Mr Quinn taking an interview.

'So, you see, when I got access to your phone, that's when I got ...' He paused and activated the projector. 'These!'

On the wall was a projected picture of Lisa's bare chest with Sean's hand holding a cigarette to her nipple. Then after a click, there was another of in-between Lisa's legs with half a pool cue resting against a bruised and scratched thigh.

Click after click after click, he displayed the degrading photographs taken of Lisa that night. Everything he had sent to Jay.

With every picture, a little slice of hope of getting out of this room ebbed away. It culminated in a video of him ejaculating into Lisa's mouth as the audio track picked up her crying and him laughing.

Sean's eyes flicked to Tony. He wasn't watching the video; he was staring at him.

'I ...'

'Yes, Sean?'

'I-I'm sorry, Mr Quinn.'

Tony stood and grabbed a half pool cue that was on the floor next to him. Sean hadn't even noticed it until just then. The next thing he knew was a sharp pain across his head; dizziness and colours danced in his vision.

'You remember this?' Tony asked as he held the cue towards him.

Sean dared to open one eye and look.

He did remember it.

Tony swung it again; this time, it struck Sean in the arm. The pain in his weakened state hurt more than it should have. He almost fell out of the chair, his feet sliding in his own defecation.

The cue swung again, and again, and again. Each blow was true, and each blow knocked him just a little bit further off the chair. Eventually, he fell to the floor. Blood from his fingernails, his nipples, and his broken nose poured onto the wet, stinking concrete beneath him.

Mr Quinn held the cue over his head as if to strike one last devastating blow to the head. Sean held his hand up in a feeble attempt to stop the cue from crashing down onto him, crushing what little life he had left in him. 'Please stop,' he pleaded.

'WHY DID YOU DO THAT TO MY DAUGHTER?' Tony screamed down at him. The sound was terrifying. It was loud, high-pitched, and empty. Devoid of empathy, devoid of mercy. It was the voice of a man with nothing to lose.

'It wasn't my idea,' he screamed. 'It wasn't me; it was Jay … Jay told me to do everything …' Sean sobbed. His voice was loud but came in laboured moans. He dropped the arm and lay down flat on the floor in his own filth. Shit, piss, and vomit filled his nostrils, but he didn't care. He no longer cared about joining the league, or the club, or whatever it was Jay had promised him. He was filth; he knew that now. His parents were dead; he had no friends, no job, no future.

*I'm better off dead,* he thought. *The world will be a better place with me gone.*

'Jay?' Mr Quinn asked from somewhere above him. 'Now we're getting somewhere. Tell me, Sean, before I ruin your innocence with this cue like you did to my Lisa, tell me who Jay is.'

70.

'IF THEY CATCH him, do you think we'll find out who Jay is and why he wanted him to do those things to me?' Lisa asked as she pulled on the top that had been discarded next to her bed.

Janice was shaking her head as she sat up, fixing her hair. 'I don't know. But at least one menace will be off the streets, and you'll be able to get some closure.' She reached over and began to stroke Lisa's hair. 'I'll help you do that, if you want,' she continued.

'Not if my mom finds you half naked in my bed, you won't,' she scoffed, knocking Janice's hand away with a playful tap.

'Well, why don't we just tell her? Why don't we make it public?' Janice was looking at her, her eyes even more intense than her words. 'We could come out. There's no stigma these days. I bet there's loads of gay people in school.'

Lisa's smile fell at the mention of the word *gay*. It wasn't that she had any issue with gay people, it was just she had never thought of herself that way. Even when her attraction to Janice blossomed. She thought of it as a healing for her soul, something to help her forget what had happened to her at the hands of a real-life monster. 'I don't know, Janice. I mean, I'm not sure if that's a good idea.'

Janice cocked her head. 'What do you mean? Like, you need more time or something?'

Lisa could see the shock on her friend's face, and the hurt. That upset her. 'No. Yes ... I don't know, Janice. My head is completely fucked up with everything that's happened. Shit, I was about to accuse your brother of being Jay.'

'I'm still not convinced he isn't,' Janice interrupted. 'Look, let's forget about all this Jay business. Sean will be in custody soon, and he's never going to get out of prison again, not after everything he's done.' She moved in closer and reached for Lisa's hand. 'Forget the past, just look to the future.'

Lisa got up off the bed and slipped into her shorts. 'What's with the pressure all of a sudden? We're having fun here. You're my special friend; after what we've been doing'—she offered her a coy smile—'you're more than special to me. It's just ...'

'Just what, Lisa? Go on, tell me. Are you too embarrassed by me and my family to call me your girlfriend? You are, aren't you?'

'What are you talking about? I'm talking about me healing after the fucking ordeal I've been through, and you're talking about me being embarrassed about your family? What the fuck, Janice?'

'You think you're better than me, don't you? Go on, admit it. Janice is the kooky one, the strange one. But you know what? Where the fuck were Nichola and Paula after all this happened, huh? Where the fuck was Kate? I'll tell you where they were, living their own lives, banging their own boyfriends. They don't give a shit about you, Lisa. I was the only one there for you. I've been the one rubbing ointment into your wounds, kissing them better.'

Lisa was shocked at the outburst. The very mention of her wounds suddenly brought everything back, and she felt herself on the verge of crying.

Janice got off of the bed. The anger in her face turned Lisa's stomach, but her own anger was simmering away now. 'Is that what this has been? Have you been here to nursemaid me to health, for me to see just how much of a saint you are? For me to what, Janice? Fall in love with you? Just so you could give me fucking head?'

Janice looked like she'd been slapped. 'What? No! How could you even think that?'

'I think you should go. I think you need to go and sort out your head. Your priorities are fucked up!'

Janice stepped back. Lisa had never seen her friend look so hateful in her whole life. A sliver of fear slipped into her at what she might do. What she could be capable of doing to her, in her weakened state.

Without a word, she picked up her shorts and slipped into them before pulling her top over her head. Lisa allowed her to continue, not sure of what she should say or do but relieved that her friend was no longer semi-naked.

Janice continued to dress in silence. When she was done, she picked up her bag and made her way to the bedroom door.

'Janice ...' Lisa said, grabbing her arm.

Janice turned, quick as a flash, and slapped her hard across the bridge of her nose.

The shock and the force of the slap knocked Lisa to the floor. Colours were spinning around her vision, bringing flashbacks of Sean, and for a moment, for one horrible moment, Janice standing over her, her face filled with hate and venom, turned into the face of Sean Knight. She covered her face with her hands.

'You're such a fucking victim,' Janice hissed before the bedroom door slammed shut.

A few moments later, Lisa heard the front door slam too.

71.

SEAN WAS LAUGHING even though he didn't want to. 'All the work you did on my phone, and you didn't even check who I sent the pictures to?'

Tony stepped over to him as he lay on the floor. He reached down and grabbed a handful of the boy's hair, lifting his head off the wet concrete. The stench was unmerciful, but he'd smelt worse in his line of work. 'I know who you sent the pictures to. It was someone called Jay. I can and I will find out who he is, but I thought getting you to give him up would be a whole lot more *fun*. Now I'm going to ask you this once. Who is Jay? What bearing does he have on the atrocities you performed on my daughter?'

Sean laughed again.

This enraged Tony. He balled his hand into a tight fist, ready to smash it into this piece of shit's face, when Sean's expression changed.

He stopped laughing, and a tear welled in the boy's eye, mixing with the shit and the blood. 'Jay told me there was a club. A fucking club! Can you believe that? A group that would be happy to have me.'

As his eyes looked up at him, Tony saw the years of pain and vulnerability within them. Confliction tore through him then. Yes, this boy was a monster, an abomination, something that needed to be put down; but he was also easily manipulated, a follower as opposed to a leader. 'What club?' was all Tony could think of to ask.

'A group of people willing to do whatever it takes to get the job done,' he sobbed. 'Jay told me in order to get in, I had to prove myself.'

'An initiation?' Tony's heartrate was speeding up, and he could feel butterflies battering away in his stomach. He gripped the boy's hair tighter and brought his head closer despite the stink. 'What was the initiation?' he half whispered, half hissed into Sean's face.

'I had to do a task.' Sean tried to look away, but Tony had too tight a hold on him. There was a half-smile on his face.

Tony wanted nothing more than to pummel that half-smile into mush. He wanted, more than anything in this world, more than anything in his life, to just hit and hit and hit, and never stop hitting until all the shitty, worthless life had seeped from the filth he was holding.

'The task was Lisa,' Sean spat.

Tony let go of the boy's hair and listened with interest to the slap of his head hitting the concrete. Despite Sean's obvious fatigue and the agony he'd endured, he managed a laugh. It was more of a giggle, mocking and sad.

The boy's mirth pierced Tony's head. He had to close his eyes to attempt to gain even a modicum of composure. He stood and made it to the chest of drawers. He grasped the bottle and syringe. 'Sean, I'm going to give you a little time to reflect on what you did to my daughter and a little time for you to give up whoever Jay is. But just so you don't get bored, I'm going to give you a little something to fill your time.'

Sean was still on the floor. His giggling stopped abruptly as his eyes fixated on what was in Tony's hands. 'No ... No. Fuck NO!' he shouted as he tried to back away. He was sliding comically in his own waste in his haste to get away.

Tony didn't have a smile in him as he got closer to his subject. He took Sean's arm. There was some resistance, although it was minimal. Normally, he would have taken pride in the fact that his interrogation techniques were working so well and the subject was already weakening, bowing to his will, telling him the things he wanted to know; but now, all he wanted to do was inflict as much pain on this boy as he could. It was difficult to keep a grip on him as his skin was so slimy, but he tightened his hold, and Sean stopped resisting. His head dropped, and Tony guessed he was resigned to his fate.

As the needle slipped into his arm and the liquid emptied into the boy's blood stream, Tony sighed. He let go of Sean, who flopped back onto the cold, wet floor. While his subject began to scream and writhe in untold agony, he removed his latex gloves and activated the FLEA network on his tablet. He connected to Sean's phone and scrolled through the messages. There were several text, picture, and video messages sent from Sean to Jay.

He's seen the name the other day but had dismissed it, putting it aside to investigate later. He'd become so embroiled, so angry at the pictures he'd found, he'd forgotten to check on this Jay character. He clicked on the number and scrolled through the files. They were the same filth he'd seen before. His stomach fell as a sense of dread overcame him. Tony filtered out Sean's screams and shouts by thinking about what his daughter had endured at the hands of this monster.

Lisa had always loved posing for the camera. She had always been the first to run to the front of a crowd when a camera was produced. Funny faces and great poses had ensued. She loved to be videoed either singing or dancing. Both him and Flo had hours of video footage of her goofing around, wearing funny clothes or tutus, always with a huge smile on her face. Now, watching these disgusting, vile, degrading images of his baby, all he could think of was killing Sean, but not before he got an angle on whoever Jay was.

*Who are you, Jay? Why do you hate my little girl so much?*

His hand shook as his cursor hovered over Jay's telephone number. All it took was one click, and his little FLEA would jump onto this phone and reveal to him the identity of the person who had ordered Sean to rape and humiliate his only daughter on a whim.

He swallowed hard, closed his eyes, and clicked.

The FLEA hopped.

72.

'I WILL, DADDY. Yeah, Janice has gone home. Mom's making dinner downstairs. Is everything all right?' Lisa didn't like her father's tone on the other end of the line. There was an edge to it, like he was hiding something. 'The doors and windows? Dad, is everything OK? Are you coming home?'

'I'll be home, honey, there's just a few things I've got to do first. Now, tell me once again, you and Mom are alone? Correct?'

'Jesus, yes, Daddy.'

'Good. Keep it that way. Just the two of you. I'll call you later. We're going to need to sit down and have a conversation tonight, baby. Just me, you, and Mom. Are you OK with that?'

'What's all this about? Am I in danger or something? I thought you were on the verge of catching Sean.'

'No, baby, you're not in any trouble or in any danger, but we need to talk. Let me just tell you this one thing. Sean will no longer be a threat to you, or to anyone else, ever again. But keep the doors and windows locked, don't let *anyone*, and I mean *anyone,* inside the house. I'll be home when I can. Trust me. I love you. Tell your mother I'll call her later.'

The phone went dead, leaving Lisa sitting on the edge of the bed, feeling confused about life, the universe, and everything.

73.

THE FLEA WAS now on Jay's phone, and Tony had everything he needed.

Sean was unconscious, his own filth drying on his skin. Tony had placed the boy back onto the chair and put a blanket over him. The last thing he wanted was for this piece of scum to expire of something as trivial as exposure.

There were better things in store for him.

Over the last five hours, he had injected Sean a total of ten times. The last five times, he introduced an antidote to the pain. He would give him instructions while the nerve agent was working on him. These instructions included cutting himself with a knife, pulling one of his own teeth out with the same stainless-steel plyers Tony had used to ruin his nipples. Each time Sean complied with his request, Tony administered the antidote, killing the pain of the nerve agent and the self-mutilations instantly.

He had successfully broken him.

His work with the boy was almost done.

The emergence of Jay in this sordid scenario had given rise to a further plan. Sean Knight had nasty times ahead of him, for sure, but right now, Tony had bigger, more slippery fish to catch.

After hosing the boy down to rouse him and clean him up a little, Tony flung a pair of black trousers, a black top, and a black cap his way, hitting him in the face. The fact he hadn't even tried to catch them might have been comical, given different circumstances. 'Put them on, were going out.'

'Out?' Sean croaked through swollen lips and bleeding gums.

'Yes, out. And you'll behave yourself. I'll have a few syringes in my pocket ready to use at any given moment. Are we clear on this?'

Sean mumbled a positive response as he slipped on the black clothing. He winced as the material rubbed against his many wounds. 'Where are we going?'

'Were going to pay your friend Jay a visit. I'm going to ask nicely what it was all about.'

'I told you what it was about.'

Tony stared down at him, his face stern as he dropped black shoes onto the floor. 'I want to hear that from Jay, if it's OK with you.'

Sean nodded and put the shoes on, ready to go.

Tony noted there had been little to no eye contact between them since the introduction of the antidote. He was fine with that. He'd seen it a thousand times before. It meant that Sean Knight would now do anything he asked him to do.

~~~~

Twenty minutes later and there was a nondescript car sitting out in the street. Inside were two shadowy figures in the front, both well hidden within the secrets the darkness of the night had to offer. Both were watching the house opposite where they were parked. It was an average house on an average street. The front garden was neat, the picket fence that surrounded it well tended.

There were several lights on inside.

'This is where Jay lives.' Tony wasn't asking a question; he was stating a fact. 'We're going to wait until they've all gone to bed, then we're going inside to have a conversation with your friend.'

'Am I going with you?'

'Yes, Sean, you are. You don't want more injections, do you?'

The boy shook his head. Blood dribbled from his ruined gums. Tony tutted a little and offered him a tissue. 'Clean yourself up. You're a disgrace.'

Sean accepted the tissue and dutifully wiped his mouth.

Tony snatched the tissue off him and put it into his pocket. 'Good, now settle down; this is going to be a long night.'

Sean settled into the seat and closed his eyes.
Tony watched the house.

~~~~

Over the next few hours, the lights began to turn off. Tony watched with interest but made no move to leave the car. Sean was snoring quietly beside him in the passenger seat. On more than one occasion, he woke with a jolt, only to look around and decide that whatever sleeping nightmare he was having was better than the horrific reality he was living.

Tony continued to watch as the house quieted. When there had been no movement for several minutes, he continued to wait.

He looked at his watch. Most people, after putting the lights out, feeling secure in their own houses, reached REM sleep in roughly forty-five minutes. He was going to give it an hour and a half before making his move.

That time was spent listening to the piece of filth next to him sleeping. *Sleep easy, Sean Knight,* he thought. *It's going to be the last peaceful sleep you ever have.* He activated a tracker device on his phone and entered the address of the house that was his target. He entered a code and was gifted with a technical readout of any alarm systems they might have. Within seconds it had detected an electronic alarm. He tapped on the alarm icon, and a series of numbers began to roll onto the screen. Four numbers settled on the screen, and the word DEACTIVATED flashed in red.

The alarm on his watch informed him that the allotted time period had passed; it was time for action. He shook his sleeping partner awake. Sean jumped as if the bogie man was grabbing at him through his sleep.

'Wake up, it's time,' Tony whispered.

'Now?'

'Yes, now. Come on.'

The two men slipped out of the car, closing the doors softly so as not to arouse any of the neighbours or their sleeping dogs. Silently, they made their way to the house they had been observing. Tony removed two small pins from a pocket on his arm. He inserted them into the lock of the side door. Within fifteen seconds, the lock clicked, and he pushed the door open. He turned to Sean and put his finger over his mouth, instructing him to be quiet. He pulled down the mask he'd been wearing as a hat, covering all the important areas of his face, and indicated to Sean to do the same.

'OK, you're going to stay down here until you hear a commotion. Then you're going to make your way upstairs, and you are going to confront Jay. Have you got that?' he whispered to Sean, who was standing behind him. Tony knew he would do as he was told, otherwise he would face another ten-, maybe even twenty-minute exposure to the nerve toxin.

Sean nodded, acknowledging the commands, and Tony brushed past him.

~~~~

As he watched the silhouette of Tony disappear up the stairs, all Sean wanted to do was to get out of this place. He had a feeling something bad was about to happen. He closed his eyes and licked his lips, not enjoying the tastes of his own flesh on his tongue. He tried to think, tried to remember what had happened to him that he would find himself in such a situation, but everything was a blur. He remembered getting the drugs, then falling asleep in his bed, then … waking up in a hell, one of his own making, that was sure enough, but a hell indeed.

He slid the bolt lock from the top of the door and gripped the door handle, it didn't open. He looked around in the gloom, his eyes scared and desperate, trying to locate a key or something he could use to open this door, to escape the madness of his life. He found one on the window ledge. All he needed to do now was insert it, turn it, and he would be away, off into the night, gone. He could be free of the maniac who had drugged him, tortured him, forced him to mutilate himself. The sick fuck who'd injected him with whatever fucking hoodoo was in those syringes. All he needed to do was turn the handle and run down the road. He could run and run, forever, never to be found. He hadn't killed anyone, he hadn't murdered his family or those drug dealers. All he'd done was have a little fun with a pretty girl and send pictures to Jay.

'Fuck Jay,' he mumbled to himself. 'I hope sh—'

The pleading broke his statement.

'Please … please, no. Don't!'

The half-shout, half-cry came from somewhere above. For reasons unknown, he knew it was his cue to go upstairs, to see what was happening. Maybe even to do some of the dirty work. A shudder ran through him as he took his hand off the handle and turned into the darkness of the house.

Almost as if it were a celestial sign, a light came on in one of the rooms, guiding his feet, showing him where he needed to be. Like a fly seduced by the beautiful blue glow of a bug-light, he made his way towards the illuminated room.

'Get out of the house!' The sudden shout made him jump. The last thing he had been expecting was a shout, especially at this time of night. 'Get out and get to the police … *now*!'

Sean cringed as the words echoed through the night. He stopped on the stair, waiting for the house to erupt in response to the obvious urgent alert. After a few moments of inactivity, he continued to climb.

'Wh-wh-why? Why us?'

He heard a sob. It was a man's sob, and it sounded lost. Like it was the last thing he was going to say before he was snuffed from this life and thrown like discarded trash into the next.

Slowly, he made it to the top of the stairs and tentatively crept over to the source of the light. He could hear each and every creak of the floorboards beneath his feet. Each noise was thunderous in his ears and head, and he was amazed that the neighbours hadn't come running in response to the unbelievably loud creeping.

He peeped his head through the door. The first thing he saw, that assaulted his senses, was the bloodbath on the bed. The deep crimson was in shocking contrast to the pale creams of the bedclothes and the wallpaper. The body sprawled on the bed was dead, he could see that, but he could also see she was recently dead. Fresh blood was still gushing from the deep wound across her neck.

Sean felt bile rising in his stomach; it was hot and bitter. His mouth was filled with saliva, and he battled to fight the gag that would surely bring forth the vomit. 'She's dead,' he heard himself say. It was a strange sensation to hear his own words come from somewhere other than where they should come from. They sounded like they came from the dead woman, and also from downstairs, both at the same time.

As his words escaped him, he became aware of the two men on the other side of the room. One was obviously Mr Quinn, stood up and dressed all in black, the other was on the floor looking up at him. His bearded face was pleading. Sean could see tears in his eyes.

At the sound of Sean's voice, the man on his knees turned in his direction. A faint smile of what Sean thought could be recognition, cracked on his lips. 'You,' he heard the man gasp. 'It's you ...'

Mr Quinn turned to look in Sean's direction. Sean thought he saw him shake his head ever so slightly before turning back to the man and sliding the knife he was holding deep within his throat.

The man's eyes bulged.

It was as if he was surprised that what had just happened to him had *actually* happened. The blood pouring from the wound told him it had. Sean watched helplessly as the man put his hands to his throat when the knife slid smoothly out. He looked like he was either trying to keep the blood from pouring out of him or attempting to put the blood that had pooled into his hands back into the wound.

The light in his eyes dimmed, and Sean watched with real horror as he slunk to the ground. It looked like he was deflating.

Mr Quinn grabbed Sean. 'Come with me,' he growled dragging him out of the room, back onto the dimly lit landing.

'You ... you,' Sean was stuttering, sobbing as he allowed himself to be dragged through the house. 'You killed them. You killed Jay's mom and dad!'

Mr Quinn pushed him up against the wall between two of the bedrooms. He held him there with an arm across his chest as he brought his face up close. 'No, Sean,' he hissed. 'I didn't kill them. You did!'

Sean's eyes went wide, and his mouth fell. A million questions flashed through his mind, all of them too fast for him to catch. He couldn't even catch enough breath to speak. A noise distracted them from their impromptu heart-to-heart. A light shone out of the door next to them as it opened, and a figure emerged from inside.

'Jay ...' Sean hissed.

74.

LISA WOKE AS a gentle vibration from her nightstand and a dull illumination roused her. She had been having a horrific dream about a tree that had been tap tapping at her window. As she looked out, the tree had the head of Sean at the top of the trunk. The branches were his fingers, tapping at the window, trying to get in at her.

Shaking off the silly dream, she looked at the phone and then at the window. Another shudder ran through her, covering her in fresh goosebumps. A stinging agony surged through her as what used to be her nipples stiffened in the cool night air. Another constant reminder of her ordeal.

Tearing her eyes away from the window, she picked up her phone and clicked the screen. It was a message from Janice. Her heart began to pound. She'd been feeling awful about their fight and had wanted to call her, to message her and say she was sorry, but she had been just that little bit too stubborn to do it. It seemed that Janice had been having the same idea and had beaten her to it.

She read the message; it was just two words in length:

'I'M SORRY'

Lisa smiled and clicked on reply, but then she saw what time it was. It was a little after three in the morning. *I'll call her tomorrow as soon as I'm up,* she thought. *It'll be a nice start to the day.*

With a smile, she put the phone back on the bedside table, put her head on the pillow, and fell back asleep. This time, her dreams took her to nicer places.

The Boyfriend

75.

'SEAN? WHAT THE fuck's going on here?' the groggy face of Jay asked, looking from Sean to the man holding him against the wall. She ran her hand through her hair, or what was left of it.

Tony turned towards the newcomer and let go of the boy. He removed the ski mask covering his face and grinned.

Jay took a step back and gasped. 'Mr Quinn?'

'Hello, Janice,' Tony said in a level voice, his deep blue eyes glowering in the dim illumination. 'I hope you didn't mind the haircut,' he chuckled. 'I mean, you cut Lisa's, didn't you? I thought I'd return the favour.'

Janice ran her hand through her hair again. The confusion on her face deepened as she realised there wasn't as much as there should be, as there had been before she went to bed. Her eyes moved from Tony's face to the blood on his jacket and then back. They then flicked between the two men. 'What ...?' Without finishing her question, she looked past them, into her parent's room.

As she did, Tony thrust the knife he was holding into Sean's un-gloved hand. 'Keep her in that room,' he hissed. 'If you want to get out of this alive, you keep her in that room.'

Sean nodded and pushed the shocked Janice into her parents' bedroom.

A scream—Tony guessed it was one of anguish—tore through the house, followed by a loud sob. 'Oh my God ... What have you done?'

Ignoring the pleas, Tony entered the last room. The boy in there was still asleep. There was a bottle of pills on the small table next to him. Tony picked them up and looked at the label

DIAMAZOL. *He'll be out for another few hours,* he thought with a nod.

That would suit his needs nicely.

He left the room and re-entered the master bedroom.

Sean was standing by the door while Janice knelt next to the bed, cradling the body of her dead mother. She was covered in blood, almost from head to toe.

'You ... you killed them! You fucking monsters. Why did you have to kill them?' she sobbed as she looked up from her grief to acknowledge Tony's entrance.

'Let's talk about who's the monster here,' he replied, his voice flat, emotionless.

'I stopped her from getting out, Mr Quinn. It was her; it was her all along. She made me do it. You saw the texts. It was her—'

'Shut up, Sean,' Tony said without looking at him.

Sean quit babbling instantly and dropped his head.

'Who are you, Janice?' Tony asked, advancing on her. The young girl in the blood-covered nightgown tried to back away, attempting to put space between her and the man she had known much of her life. 'We welcomed you into our home. We trusted you. *She* trusted you. Why would you do something so despicable to your friend?'

'You stay away from me, Mr Quinn. You stay far away from me, or I'll scream the fucking house down. Me and Sean, we're witnesses to what you've done here. Jamie's in the other room. He'll be on our side too. You found out about your daughter and ... and you couldn't handle it. You snapped, and look what you did.'

Tony shook his head. 'You stupid little bitch,' he whispered. 'Look at what I've done here. Think about what I did to Sean's parents, not to mention the drug dealers.' Tony nodded as Janice's eyes widened at the realisation of who was standing before her. 'I'll get away with this, Janice. This is *not* my first ride on this carousel. Now, if you want *any* chance of getting out of this alive, then explain to me why and how you could do what you did to someone who loved you as her best friend.'

Janice regarded the devastation on the bed and on the floor. Tony watched as the weight of what she had brought about came crashing down on top of her. She physically buckled as it did. Tears were streaming down her cheeks, cutting through the blood on her face; the light of the bedroom made them twinkle.

'I did it because I love her,' she whispered. Her voice was wet and sad.

As she shifted her weight on the mattress, her mother's blood followed her indentation.

Tony watched it roll. 'You did it because you love her?' he asked, shaking his head, not entirely grasping her answer. 'What kind of twisted logic is that? You coerce someone to get close to her, to fucking rape her, almost kill her ... because you *love* her?' The last few words were whispered. He was worried now; he could feel himself shaking, losing control. Self-control had always been his best ally, his main weapon, but now he could feel it slipping away. He edged his way over to the bed and grabbed Janice by her hair. She shrieked as he yanked her head back and held the knife to her throat.

His hand holding her was shaking, and his throat was dry, but the hand with the knife to the young girl's neck was as steady as a rock. He'd held knives to hundreds, maybe even thousands of people's throats before tonight, but it had never, ever, been so ... close. It was almost too personal for comfort.

Her wide eyes moved from Sean, standing in the doorway looking lost and confused, to Tony. She offered no resistance as her hair was pulled tighter.

Tony looked down at her. He fancied he could see his own reflection in the tears that adorned her face. 'Tell me ... the truth,' he growled.

'Because I love her,' she croaked.

'You told me that. Elaborate, you fucking bitch,' he demanded, pulling her head back even further, resting his blade on her exposed throat.

'Because I wanted her. Not as a friend, not *just* as a friend. I wanted to be with her. I wanted her to want me like I needed her. Only she wasn't like that. She was only into guys. All I ever wanted was her to love me back.'

'You were her *best* friend.' The stinging of his eyes from the sweat falling into them was blurring his vision. He could feel the hatred, the anger, the pain swelling inside him. He tightened his sweaty grip on the handle of the knife ... *Just an inch, that's all it will take to snuff this ... this* cunt *out of the world.* He knew it was an ugly word, but she was an ugly human, and the word fit perfectly.

'That wasn't enough for me. I needed her. I wanted to touch her, to taste her. I came up with the plan. More of an idea. If something monumental happened to her, something life-shattering, then she would come running to me as her best friend. I'd offer an ear, a shoulder, then eventually, my lips.'

'Who is Sean in all of this?' Tony whispered; he was fighting hard to combat the shaking of his body.

'I met him through Jamie. He's good looking and as fucking stupid as I needed him to be.'

Tony looked at Sean, or what used to be Sean before he got his hands on him. He was nothing more than a tool now. His head was dropped low, and his hands were by his sides. To Tony, he looked like a robot waiting for someone to press his buttons, to activate him, to tell him what to do.

'You ruined so many lives just to enhance yours? What sort of evil are you?'

Janice laughed; it was a strange sound through her stretched neck. 'Have you seen my family? My junkie mother, my lazy father, my fucked-up brother? I'm a product of my environment, Mr Quinn. Nobody was ever going to give me what I wanted, not like your fucking precious daughter. So I took it. Sean's life wasn't worth shit. He's been destined for jail since the day he was born, and Lisa just needed a nudge in my direction. I knew Sean could provide that.'

Tony's hand clenched in the back of Janice's hair. The tendrils interwound within his gloved fingers, pulling her head back even further.

She continued her scratchy laugh. 'It was a perfect plan. I still have the taste of your daughter on my lips, Mr Quinn. Even though she wasn't quite the virgin when I took her, my plan was perfect.'

A red mist descended over him. A deep, primeval rage shook him as he held the knife to the girl's throat. 'Not quite perfect,' he whispered in her ear. 'You misjudged the love a resourceful father has for his baby girl.'

Tony watched with satisfaction as her smug smile faltered. It fell from her face in an instant to be replaced by a confused frown.

'What?' she whispered as he pulled her hair even tighter, exposing the delicate white flesh of her neck.

'You heard me, you bitch!' he replied as he sliced the knife through the offered flesh. It passed easily across her stretched windpipe. Dark blood flew from the rupture as he moved the blade to divide the walls of her carotid artery.

For Tony, it happened in slow motion. The blood sprayed in an arch, hitting and spattering the already bloody walls of the room, mixing with the blood of her mother on the bed and that of her father on the floor.

He relished her body bucking and thrashing under his grip. He listened with satisfaction to the thick gurgle of blood pumping from her heart and out of the deep gash in her neck. His smile was maniacal as the fresh blood drooled from her mouth and her pink eyes rolled in their sockets.

Those eyes stopped for a moment and looked at him.

He saw surprise, sorrow, and a deep fear in those dying eyes.

Or at least he hoped he did.

76.

'GET YOUR ASS in here and grab this body,' Tony snapped at Sean, who was standing like a dummy in the doorway of the bedroom. His vacant eyes were wide as he stared into the room of horror before him. On Tony's order, he sprang into life and rushed in to help. 'Get them off the bed and onto the floor with that other one.' He indicated towards the bleeding body of Janice and the body of her mother before passing Sean the knife. 'I need to deal with the brother. Don't move from this room.'

The boy didn't question, he just blindly obeyed his orders, exactly as Tony knew he would. As he watched the younger man going to work on the bodies, he stood up and rubbed his back, easing the screaming muscles there before making his way out of the room. Once on the landing, he removed his backpack and took something from it. It was a syringe. The barrel was filled with a yellowish liquid. Tony had filled it himself with a drug that he and others he worked with had used effectively on a number of occasions, probably too many for him to remember. It would knock the recipient out, into a blissful, euphoric sleep, and would remain in their blood stream for up to a week, showing up on toxicology reports as heavy drug use.

He injected the sleeping Jamie, pushing half of the contents into the sleeping man's neck, just below the ear, where any indication of a needle mark would be missed.

Then he re-entered the master bedroom. Sean was just putting the body of Janice's mother on the floor next to her daughter and husband. He stood up on Tony's entrance and looked at him. Tony smiled, looking at the blood covering the boy and the knife. He continued to smile as he plunged the syringe into Sean's neck.

# The Boyfriend

Sean simply slumped into a heap next to the still bleeding body of Janice. After a few moments of rearranging the bodies to make it look like he had been acting alone, he took a spray can from his backpack and sprayed the carpets of the scene, rapidly eliminating any trail he might have left behind. He knew the forensic team would only do the bare minimum, as the perpetrator was about to be caught asleep, covered in the victims' blood, still holding the knife in his hand, with illegal drugs flushing through his system.

When he was satisfied that he'd done everything he could, he made his way calmly downstairs and out into the night.

He drove his nondescript car to the garage. He took everything he'd used, including his clothes, into the lockup next door and burnt them in the installed pit in the back room. He mused on how many times he had used this pit over the course of his job.

He dressed in the spare clothes he kept in the lockup for situations like this and drove to the location of his real car. He smashed the windscreen and the lights of the disposable car, then pulled all the workings out from underneath the dash. He took spray paint from his backpack and sprayed a little graffiti on the chassis before getting into his own SUV and driving off.

He turned the radio up as he drove; he liked the song that was playing. Alice Cooper was singing about not having to go back to school; it was kind of fitting.

77.

IT WAS ALL over the news, both local and national, the very next day.

'Local teenager, Sean Knight, wanted in connection with the deaths of thirteen people, has been apprehended in the home of yet another three victims. A local couple and their teenage daughter were found dead in their home after an apparent break in. The suspect had apparently *fallen asleep* in the bedroom with his victims. He was found when the couple's son awoke to find the grizzly scene with Knight still passed out in the room. What authorities believe to be the murder weapon used on the mother, father, and daughter was still in his hands. Local law enforcement agencies have taken Knight to a secure facility, where he will undergo psychiatric assessment. The survivor, a former psychiatric patient at a facility upstate, has also been admitted for assessment and questioning. The authorities are unsure of the motives behind these killings but are looking into possible ties between the suspect and the brother. We'll have more as the story develops.'

The attractive young woman turned back towards the house behind her, the one where people in white hazmat suits were entering, the one behind the yellow taped cordon, being guarded by police.

78.

LISA DIDN'T TAKE the news of Janice's demise very well.

Tony's heart broke for her yet again, but there was nothing he could do but be there for her as the strong, supportive father she needed.

Flo was a godsend. She knew instinctively what to do. Her daughter needed time, she needed space, but most of all, she needed her friends. She invited Nichola, Paula, and Kate to the house. She gave them all the space they needed to work through their grief as teenage girls do.

She stood at the doorway to Lisa's bedroom with her ear to the closed door, listening to what was happening beyond. There were a few laughs, they were inevitable, but mostly what she heard were sobs.

'Are they all in there?' Tony asked as he came up behind his wife, putting a reassuring hand on her shoulder.

Flo turned, she put one hand on her husband's face, and with the other, she put her finger to her mouth, silencing him. She gestured towards their bedroom, and Tony followed. She closed the door and sat on the bed. There she stayed for a few moments, her hands joined between her knees, her face pensive.

Tony stood by the closed door and looked at her. *She's got something to ask me,* he thought.

He sat next to her on the bed and took one of her hands in his. She looked at him. There was a flash of a smile. *That's a smile of resignation if ever I've seen one,* he thought. He wanted to hold her, he wanted to tell her, share the horrors of what he'd found during his investigation, the investigation she asked him to do.

But he couldn't.

He knew if that particular can of worms was opened, there would be repercussions. Not just for Flo and Lisa but for him too. In his head, he knew he'd done the right thing, done what any father would have dreamed of doing; only he had the resources to go through with it.

*No, I keep this to myself,* he thought as he flashed his wife his own smile of resignation. *She knows anyway. Look at her; she knows who I am and what I'm capable of doing. Can she live with that knowledge? Can she live with me?*

He was worried that it had gotten too personal this time. He knew he'd taken things to an extreme, one that even shocked himself. Not for the first time, he thought about hanging up his boots, giving up the agency for good this time. His family needed him to be strong. *Hell, I need me to be strong,* he thought.

Flo surprised him by leaning into him and nestling her head into his shoulder. He put his arm around her and pulled her close. He held her tight, feeling her tears soaking into his shirt.

'Don't ever tell me,' she whispered between sobs.

Gently, he pushed her away, putting enough distance between them to allow him to look into her face. Her wide, wet eyes reflected him as he looked at her. Thick, clear tears dripped down her cheeks. To him, she had never looked more beautiful.

She was shaking her head. 'Please, don't ever tell me what you had to do or what you found. I can never, ever know.'

Without a word, he pulled her back into him and held her tight.

## 79.

THE FUNERAL WAS a sombre affair. The heavens opened and soaked the mourners who had gathered to pay respects around the three open graves. They had covered themselves with black umbrellas, attempting to keep the teeming rain off them, but other than that, no one seemed to be fazed by the inclement weather.

Tony and Flo were there, both dressed from head to toe in black. They never had much to do with Mr and Mrs Bowen, but with deference to their daughter, who had been their own daughter's best friend, they wanted to pay their respects.

Jamie, the son, brother, and only survivor of the deceased, was there, accompanied by two large men, both dressed in black. They looked like they wanted to be anywhere else but on this damp duty.

Lisa was there, as were Paula, Nichola, and Kate. They all wore identical black dresses and held large umbrellas over their heads.

Tony watched as Lisa stepped forward and placed a single red rose on one of the caskets. He could see the tears of grief and lost love. This time, his heart didn't break for her, as only he knew she was better off this way. As she placed the flower, Flo's arm, currently looped within his, squeezed tighter. It was only for a moment, but it was there. Without taking his eyes off his daughter, he squeezed her back.

Lisa stepped back into the gang of four, and one by one, they placed roses on the casket.

Tony watched his daughter with interest. He supposed he'd *never* take his eyes off her again, for as long as he lived.

Epilogue

Six Months Later

TONY ENTERED THE facility. He signed his name in the register before passing through the metal-detectors leading inside. He removed his car keys, some loose change, and his watch. He put them in the tray provided and passed through.

The buzzer didn't sing for him.

'This way, sir.' A large man in a dark blue uniform ushered him through more security doors as the light of the day behind him disappeared down dark corridors. 'Warden Edwards expressed his sadness at not being able to greet you himself, but he's been called away to a family emergency he couldn't get out of. He sends his regards, sir.'

Tony smiled. 'Tell Warden Edwards there's no need for his regrets. He's done more than enough for me already.'

The big man nodded as they passed through another set of security doors. 'He's all yours,' he said, pointing towards a thick door with a small frosted-glass panel. 'I'll be outside if you need me, sir, and there *is* CCTV in there.'

'Can that be turned off if I want my chat with Mr Knight to be of a ... personal nature?'

'All you need to do is pull the connection from the back of the camera, and you're alone. The system will think the camera needs maintenance and report it to the crew. They'll know to not come running.'

'Thank you,' Tony said, offering the man his hand. The large hand engulfed his, and he thought that it could have easily crushed his to the bone, though he was confident this man would not have done such a thing.

He unlocked the door, and Tony stepped inside.

The room was stark. The only flash of colour in the dark grey was the orange clothing worn by the man currently chained to the table in the centre of it.

As Tony walked in, he turned to the camera behind the door, felt for the connection at the back, and pulled it. The red light at the top of the lens blinked out.

They were now alone.

He took a seat, the only one available, and sat down opposite the old man in the orange.

Slowly, he raised his head. Tony saw that he wasn't old after all. He could see that, in fact, he was rather young, but he knew that already. There was an air about this man that spoke of a knowledge no young man should ever be privy to. His eyes were hollow pits. They were empty, devoid of life; not even a spark could survive in the obsidian of despair that resided in this man's sockets. The boy's soul had been torn, battered, maybe even raped out of him long ago.

He felt no sympathy, no empathy, with this wretch. He was glad he looked like he did.

The ghoul before him opened his thin, stubbled mouth as if he was about to speak. Tony noticed his lack of teeth; the thought of how he lost them didn't move him in the slightest.

He raised a hand to silence him, and the boy closed his mouth and dropped his head.

Tony nodded.

'How've you been, Sean?' he asked.

Sean raised his head, and his prematurely old eyes met his. 'I won't complain,' he croaked. His voice sounded older too, even more broken than he looked.

'Won't, or can't?' Tony asked.

Sean shrugged.

'I'm sure you appreciate the accommodation I arranged for you?'

Sean stared at the tabletop. The only response Tony received was the twitching of the boy's shoulders.

Tony shook his head and made himself as comfortable as he could in the uncomfortable moulded plastic chair. 'When I found out that the wing you were housed in was known as the Rapers' Wing, I thought it was because it was where they housed the men who'd been incarcerated *for* rape. I really didn't know that it was the wing known for notorious rapers *within* the prison. I'm truly sorry, Sean. When I asked Warden Edwards to house you here six months ago, I really thought I was doing you a favour.' The smile across his face felt good.

Sean's head twitched.

'Lisa sends her love, by the way. You'll be glad to know she's doing well. She finished school and has been accepted into college. She's staying local. Her choice. She has a new girlfriend now. Her name is Emily; she's a really nice kid. She opened up to her, you know, all about her ordeal with you, you piece of shit.'

Sean flinched at the name calling. Tony had a good idea why. These prisoners loved pet names for their bitches.

'Anyway, I came here today to do you a favour. As you know, the guilty verdict has earned you up to seven lifetimes in this hellhole. You're never getting out, boy.'

Sean rolled his head, stretching his neck. Tony liked the way his bones and cartilages clicked and popped; it meant his punishment was being dealt accordingly.

'I think it's time you did yourself a favour. I think it's finally time you did the honest tax-paying citizens of this great country a favour. No one wants to be paying to keep scum like you alive. Plus, I don't think you want to live the rest of your worthless life with huge, angry cocks being forced into your every orifice and waking up to cum showers, do you?'

Sean raised his head. His face was still expressionless, but Tony could see desperation seeping into his dead eyes.

He smiled. 'I didn't think so. Well, because I know the warden, he let me bring in a little gift for you.' He reached into the inside pocket of his jacket and produced a tiny, thin package. 'It's made of plastic, but it's as sharp as a razor,' he whispered. He smiled and nodded at the aged youth before him. 'It's more than you're fucking worth,' he added as he slipped the small packet towards the boy.

# The Boyfriend

Sean slipped the present into the waistband of his pants without saying a word.

'Well, I don't believe we'll be seeing each other again. So, all that's required now is for me to wish you happy trails and to encourage you to do what is necessary as soon as possible, for everyone's sake.' He tipped the boy a wink and stood up. With a smile, he turned and banged on the door to be let out.

The same guard opened the door within seconds of him banging and was inside the room in a flash. 'Is everything OK in here, Mr Quinn?' he asked.

Tony nodded. 'Yeah. I've finished my interview with Mr Knight. Although I think the CCTV might be broken. I never noticed the red light on.'

The big man nodded without taking his eyes off the diminutive figure in orange sitting with his head bowed, chained to the table. He closed the door, locking the boy inside.

'Tell the landing men to expect a suicide sometime soon,' Tony said as they walked out through the security doors. 'I slipped him a plastic razorblade. Let them know in case he decides to go the other way. He might try to take a few of the others with him.'

'Wouldn't be no great loss,' the big man replied with a grin.

Tony stopped at the main door, waiting to retrieve his possessions. He turned and smiled at his guide. 'No, I don't suppose it would. Don't forget to thank Warden Edwards for me.'

'I won't. You drive safe now, Mr Quinn.'

'I always do,' he replied before walking towards the parking lot.

~~~~

As he got into the car, he smiled at his passenger in the opposite seat.

'Is it done?' Lisa asked.

Tony nodded. It was just a small nod, but it told his daughter everything she needed to know.

'Good,' she replied, looking out of the window at the other cars in the lot. 'Let's go home then.'

Tony smiled and patted her knee. He frowned a little as she momentarily froze at his touch, but he supposed, or at least hoped, that would pass in time.

~~~~

The news came two days later that a local boy in prison for multiple murders had gone mad with a sharpened plastic knife and killed two inmates. There was a small stand-off with the guards before he turned the blade on himself, mutilating his own wrists and neck. The boy later died in the infirmary as a result of the self-inflicted wounds.

Tony read the small article on page six with a grin, then turned to the back pages to read the sports.

# The Boyfriend

D E McCluskey

## Author's Notes

WELCOME TO MY author's notes.

I'm not even sure if anyone reads these bits, but they are my favourite part, where I get to feel like Stephen King, so they will continue.

Thank you for reading my novel, *The Boyfriend*!

If you are a reader of my books and you do indeed read these notes, you will already know that I have written a lot of my novels based on the rhyming stories or even short comics that I have written in the past and expanded on them. This one is no different. I wrote this to be a short comic story, no longer than ten pages in length. How it came about was my daughter (Grace) had just turned ten, and she informed me that she liked a boy in school. I was infuriated. Grace has blue eyes and long blonde hair and (in my biased opinion) is gorgeous (just like her dad).

Now, anyone who knows me knows that I'm a lover and not a fighter … so I thought to myself, at the time, that I'd best learn how to fight so I could keep back the hordes of potential suitors that would be storming my door, hoping to win the affections and the hand of my daughter in marriage.

That is how it works, isn't it?

Something else you need to know about me is that I am lazy. Yes, I do a bit of running now and then to attempt to stay (?) trim, but learning how to fight seemed like an awful lot of hard work. So, I had to think of another deterrent for the boys, just so they could be intimidated by Grace's mild-mannered, slightly overweight author father.

Then it hit me … I'm an *author*.

# The Boyfriend

I've been known to write a few scary books from time to time. So, I wondered if I could scare them with my words and not my deeds.

The story started life as a tale of a boy who seems to be the perfect fit for the young girl who likes him, until she takes him home to meet her parents. The dad is a little, blading, bespectacled man who looks like he wouldn't say boo to a goose (I have never understood that saying). So, the boy decides to take advantage of her, thinking there would be no repercussions.

What the boy didn't know was that her father was a much-respected ex-CIA agent who finds out about the advantages taken and decides to take a few advantages of his own.

It was a quick revenge story.

The idea was to thrust it into the hands of any and all of Grace's boyfriends the moment they step foot into my house. I would then force them to read it, all the while standing over them, nodding and attempting to look intimidating.

I never got it drawn up; I don't know why, as it was a great little story.

Anyway, on reading it again, I thought it would make a compelling novel, with a few twists and turns here and there.

I wanted to make it with a strong female lead. Someone who survived something terrible happening to her but wasn't afraid to bounce back from her ordeal.

The pages of her attack were the hardest pages to write that I've ever done. As I was writing them, I knew I could take it further, make it more depraved and sicker than I did, but I couldn't remove Grace from Lisa, and I realised the real fear women live with. The misogynist world we live in and the constant berating that women and, by extension, parents endure each and every time they leave the house.

As I was reviewing this manuscript, there was a big case on the news in the UK where a young lady's body was found the day after disappearing while walking home. A few days later, a policeman was charged for her abduction, rape, and subsequent murder. This sparked a huge response on social media, highlighting the plight of women.

So, I wanted to make this character strong, almost as a tribute to that poor woman.

Even though her avenger was a trusted individual, I want to make him as, if not more unhinged than the perpetrator of the heinous crime. Just to highlight that, sometimes, the revenge can be worse than the crime!

I see this book as a creature-feature, only the creatures are human. A monster story with three totally fucked-up monsters, and Lisa like Faye Wray in King Kong's grasp, facing the aeroplanes at the top of the skyscraper.

It's a bit of a fucked-up tale, to be honest.

I also wanted to state that just because the real villain of the piece is homosexual and her motives for her actions were to get someone else to 'turn' gay, this is not an anti-gay message by any stretch of the imagination. The other villains in the piece are heterosexual, which goes to show that you can be fucked up no matter what your sexual persuasion.

~~~~

Anyway, we have now come to the part of the book where I say thank you to the people who have helped me through the ordeal of writing this harrowing book.

So here goes ...

Lisa Lee Tone. Editor extraordinaire. I always get the police uniforms wrong or the wrong Americanism (I am a product of the *A-Team* and *Smokey and The Bandit*; I don't know much about American culture). Her edits are what keep these books together.

Kelly Rickard, she is to beta reading what Lisa is to editing. She picks out stuff I would *never* find.

There are guys out there in the wide horror community who I love for their unending support and cheerful, mostly sarcastic Facebook interactions. The Mothers of Mayhem (you know who you are), Corrina, Crystal, Ryder, Peter Hall ... as I said, too many to mention here.

Lauren, my final proof-reader, who hated the rape scene. Our daughters Grace and Sian. Ted (or Lord Teddington of Netherton, as he is known to the kids in the know). My mum, my sisters, my in-laws, my whole extended and fantastic family.

YOU ... the reader. This is ALL YOUR FAULT!

Stay frosty, kids, and in the words of Billy J: Don't go changin'.

Dave McCluskey
Liverpool
September 2022

Printed in Great Britain
by Amazon

28421318R00167